THE SECRET SERVANT

THE SECRET SERVANT

DANIEL SILVA

G. P. PUTNAM'S SONS   NEW YORK   2007

G. P. PUTNAM'S SONS
Publishers Since 1838
Published by the Penguin Group
Penguin Group (USA) Inc., 375 Hudson Street, New York, New York 10014, USA • Penguin Group
(Canada), 90 Eglinton Avenue East, Suite 700, Toronto, Ontario M4P 2Y3, Canada (a division of Pearson
Penguin Canada Inc.) • Penguin Books Ltd, 80 Strand, London WC2R 0RL, England • Penguin Ireland,
25 St Stephen's Green, Dublin 2, Ireland (a division of Penguin Books Ltd) • Penguin Group
(Australia), 250 Camberwell Road, Camberwell, Victoria 3124, Australia (a division of Pearson
Australia Group Pty Ltd) • Penguin Books India Pvt Ltd, 11 Community Centre, Panchsheel Park, New
Delhi–110 017, India • Penguin Group (NZ), 67 Apollo Drive, Rosedale, North Shore 0745, Auckland,
New Zealand (a division of Pearson New Zealand Ltd.) • Penguin Books (South Africa) (Pty) Ltd, 24
Sturdee Avenue, Rosebank, Johannesburg 2196, South Africa

Penguin Books Ltd, Registered Offices: 80 Strand, London WC2R 0RL, England

Library of Congress Cataloging-in-Publication Data

Silva, Daniel, date.
The secret servant / Daniel Silva.
p.   cm.
Sequel to: The messenger.
ISBN 978-0-399-15422-5
1. Allon, Gabriel (Fictitious character)—Fiction.   2. Intelligence officers—Fiction.   3. Terrorism—
Prevention—Fiction.   4. Israelis—Netherlands—Amsterdam—Fiction.   I. Title.
PS3619.I5443S43   2007b   2007017548
813'.6—dc22

Printed in the United States of America
1   3   5   7   9   10   8   6   4   2

Book design by Stephanie Huntwork

This is a work of fiction. Names, characters, places, and incidents either are the product of the author's
imagination or are used fictitiously, and any resemblance to actual persons, living or dead, businesses,
companies, events, or locales is entirely coincidental.

While the author has made every effort to provide accurate telephone numbers and Internet addresses at
the time of publication, neither the publisher nor the author assumes any responsibility for errors, or for
changes that occur after publication. Further, the publisher does not have any control over and does not
assume any responsibility for author or third-party websites or their content.

For Stacy and Henry Winkler, for their friendship, support, and tireless work on behalf of children. And, as always, for my wife, Jamie, and my children, Lily and Nicholas.

On present demographic trends, by the end of the twenty-first century at the latest, Europe will be Muslim. —BERNARD LEWIS

The threat is serious, is growing and will, I believe, be with us for a generation. It is a sustained campaign, not a series of isolated incidents. It aims to wear down our will to resist.

—DAME ELIZA MANNINGHAM-BULLER,
DIRECTOR GENERAL OF MI5

If you send a prisoner to Jordan, you get a better interrogation. If you send a prisoner, for instance, to Egypt, you will probably never see him again.

—ROBERT BAER, AS QUOTED BY
STEPHEN GREY IN *Ghost Plane*

THE SECRET SERVANT

DEATH OF
A PROPHET

AMSTERDAM

I t was Professor Solomon Rosner who sounded the first alarm, though his name would never be linked to the affair except in the secure rooms of a drab office building in downtown Tel Aviv. Gabriel Allon, the legendary but wayward son of Israeli intelligence, would later observe that Rosner was the first asset in the annals of Office history to have proven more useful to them dead than alive. Those who overheard the remark found it uncharacteristically callous but in keeping with the bleak mood that by then had settled over them all.

The backdrop for Rosner's demise was not Israel, where violent death occurs all too frequently, but the normally tranquil quarter of Amsterdam known as the Old Side. The date was the first Friday in December, and the weather was more suited to early spring than the last days of autumn. It was a day to engage in what the Dutch so fondly refer to as *gezelligheid*, the pursuit of small pleasures: an aimless stroll through the flower stalls of the Bloemenmarkt, a lager or two in a good bar in the Rembrandtplein, or, for those so inclined, a bit of fine cannabis in the brown coffeehouses of the Haarlemmerstraat. Leave the fretting and the fighting to the hated

Americans, stately old Amsterdam murmured that golden late-autumn afternoon. Today we give thanks for having been born blameless and Dutch.

Solomon Rosner did not share the sentiments of his countrymen, but then he seldom did. Though he earned a living as a professor of sociology at the University of Amsterdam, it was Rosner's Center for European Security Studies that occupied the lion's share of his time. His legion of detractors saw evidence of deception in the name, for Rosner served not only as the center's director but was its only scholar in residence. Despite those obvious shortcomings, the center had managed to produce a steady stream of authoritative reports and articles detailing the threat posed to the Netherlands by the rise of militant Islam within its borders. Rosner's last book, *The Islamic Conquest of the West*, had argued that Holland was now under a sustained and systematic assault by jihadist Islam. The goal of this assault, he maintained, was to colonize the Netherlands and turn it into a majority Muslim state, where, in the not-too-distant future, Islamic law, or *sharia*, would reign supreme. The terrorists and the colonizers were two sides of the same coin, he warned, and unless the government took immediate and drastic action, everything the freethinking Dutch held dear would soon be swept away.

The Dutch literary press had been predictably appalled. Hysteria, said one reviewer. Racist claptrap, said another. More than one took pains to note that the views expressed in the book were all the more odious given the fact that Rosner's grandparents had been rounded up with a hundred thousand other Dutch Jews and sent off to the gas chambers at Auschwitz. All agreed that what the situation required was not hateful rhetoric like Rosner's but tolerance and dialogue. Rosner stood steadfast in the face of the withering criticism, adopting what one commentator described as the posture of a man with his finger wedged firmly in the dike. Tolerance and dialogue by all means, Rosner responded, but not capitulation. "We Dutch need to put down our Heinekens and hash pipes and wake up," he snapped during an interview on Dutch television. "Otherwise, we're going to lose our country."

The book and surrounding controversy had made Rosner the most vilified and, in some quarters, celebrated man in the country. It had also placed him squarely in the sights of Holland's home-grown Islamic extremists. Jihadist websites, which Rosner monitored more closely than even the Dutch police, burned with sacred rage over the book, and more than one forecast his imminent execution. An imam in the neighborhood known as the Oud West instructed his flock that "Rosner the Jew must be dealt with harshly" and pleaded for a martyr to step forward and do the job. The feckless Dutch interior minister responded by proposing that Rosner go into hiding, an idea Rosner vigorously refused. He then supplied the minister with a list of ten radicals he regarded as potential assassins. The minister accepted the list without question, for he knew that Rosner's sources inside Holland's extremist fringe were in most cases far better than those of the Dutch security services.

At noon on that Friday in December, Rosner was hunched over his computer in the second-floor office of his canal house at Groenburgwal 2A. The house, like Rosner himself, was stubby and wide, and tilted forward at a precarious angle, which some of the neighbors saw as fitting, given the political views of its occupant. If it had one serious drawback it was its location, for it stood not fifty yards from the bell tower of the Zuiderkirk church. The bells tolled mercilessly each day, beginning at the stroke of noon and ending forty-five minutes later. Rosner, sensitive to interruptions and unwanted noise, had been waging a personal jihad against them for years. Classical music, white-noise machines, soundproof headphones—all had proven useless in the face of the onslaught. Sometimes he wondered why they were rung at all. The old church had long ago been turned into a government housing office, a fact that Rosner, a man of considerable faith, saw as a fitting symbol of the Dutch morass. Confronted by an enemy of infinite religious zeal, the secular Dutch had turned their churches into bureaus of the welfare state. *A church without faithful*, thought Rosner, *in a city without God.*

At ten minutes past twelve he heard a faint knock and looked up to find Sophie Vanderhaus leaning against the doorjamb with a batch of files clutched to her breast. A former student of Rosner's, she had come to work for him after completing a graduate degree on the impact of the Holocaust on postwar Dutch society. She was part secretary and research assistant, part nursemaid and surrogate daughter. She kept his office in order and typed the final drafts of all his reports and articles. She was the minder of his impossible schedule and tended to his appalling personal finances. She even saw to his laundry and made certain he remembered to eat. Earlier that morning she had informed him that she was planning to spend a week in Saint-Maarten over the New Year. Rosner, upon hearing the news, had fallen into a profound depression.

"You have an interview with *De Telegraaf* in an hour," she said. "Maybe you should have something to eat and focus your thoughts."

"Are you suggesting my thoughts lack focus, Sophie?"

"I'm suggesting nothing of the sort. It's just that you've been working on that article since five-thirty this morning. You need something more than coffee in your stomach."

"It's not that dreadful reporter who called me a Nazi last year?"

"Do you really think I'd let her near you again?" She entered the office and started straightening his desk. "After the interview with *De Telegraaf*, you go to the NOS studios for an appearance on Radio One. It's a call-in program, so it's sure to be lively. Do try not to make any more enemies, Professor Rosner. It's getting harder and harder to keep track of them all."

"I'll try to behave myself, but I'm afraid my forbearance is now gone forever."

She peered into his coffee cup and pulled a sour face. "Why do you insist on putting out your cigarettes in your coffee?"

"My ashtray was full."

"Try emptying it from time to time." She poured the contents of the ashtray into his rubbish bin and removed the plastic liner. "And don't forget you have the forum this evening at the university."

Rosner frowned. He was not looking forward to the forum. One of the other panelists was the leader of the European Muslim Association, a group that campaigned openly for the imposition of *sharia* in Europe and the destruction of the State of Israel. It promised to be a deeply unpleasant evening.

"I'm afraid I'm coming down with a sudden case of leprosy," he said.

"They'll insist that you come anyway. You're the star of the show."

He stood and stretched his back. "I think I'll go to Café de Doelen for a coffee and something to eat. Why don't you have the reporter from *De Telegraaf* meet me there?"

"Do you really think that's wise, Professor?"

It was common knowledge in Amsterdam that the famous café on the Staalstraat was his favorite haunt. And Rosner was hardly inconspicuous. Indeed, with his shock of white hair and rumpled tweed wardrobe, he was one of the most recognizable figures in Holland. The geniuses in the Dutch police had once suggested he utilize some crude disguise while in public, an idea Rosner had likened to putting a hat and a false mustache on a hippopotamus and calling it a Dutchman.

"I haven't been to the Doelen in months."

"That doesn't mean it's any safer."

"I can't live my life as a prisoner forever, Sophie." He gestured toward the window. "Especially on a day like today. Wait until the last possible minute before you tell the reporter from *De Telegraaf* where I am. That will give me a jump on the jihadists."

"That isn't funny, Professor." She could see there was no talking him out of it. She handed him his mobile phone. "At least take this so you can call me in an emergency."

Rosner slipped the phone into his pocket and headed downstairs. In the entry hall he pulled on his coat and trademark silk scarf and stepped outside. To his left rose the spire of the Zuiderkirk; to his right, fifty yards along a narrow canal lined with small craft, stood a wooden double drawbridge. The Groenburgwal was a quiet street for the Old Side: no bars or cafés, only a single small hotel that never seemed to have more than a handful of guests. Directly opposite Rosner's house was the street's only eyesore, a modern tenement block with a lavender-and-lime pastel exterior. A trio of house-painters dressed in smudged white coveralls was squatting outside the building in a patch of sunlight.

Rosner glanced at the three faces, committing each to memory, before setting off in the direction of the drawbridge. When a sudden gust of wind stirred the bare tree limbs along the embankment, he paused for a moment to bind his scarf more tightly around his neck and watch a plump Vermeer cloud drift slowly overhead. It was then that he noticed one of the painters walking parallel to him along the opposite side of the canal. Short dark hair, a high flat forehead, a heavy brow over small eyes: Rosner, connoisseur of immigrant faces, judged him to be a Moroccan from the Rif Mountains. They arrived at the drawbridge simultaneously. Rosner paused again, this time to light a cigarette he did not want, and watched with relief as the man turned to the left. When he disappeared round the next corner, Rosner headed in the opposite direction toward the Doelen.

He took his time making his way down the Staalstraat, now dawdling in the window of his favorite pastry shop to gaze at that day's offerings, now sidestepping to avoid being run down by a pretty girl on a bicycle, now pausing to accept a few words of encouragement from a ruddy-faced admirer. He was about to step through the entrance of the café when he felt a tug at his coat sleeve. In the few remaining seconds he had left to live, he would be tormented by the absurd thought that he might have prevented his own murder had he resisted the impulse to turn around. But he did turn around, because that is what one does on a glorious December afternoon in Amsterdam when one is summoned in the street by a stranger.

He saw the gun only in the abstract. In the narrow street the shots reverberated like cannon fire. He collapsed onto the cobblestones and watched helplessly as his killer drew a long knife from the inside of his coveralls. The slaughter was ritual, just as the imams had decreed it should be. No one intervened—hardly surprising, thought Rosner, for intervention would have been intolerant—and no one thought to comfort him as he lay dying. Only the bells spoke to him. *A church without faithful*, they seemed to be saying, *in a city without God*.

2

BEN-GURION
AIRPORT, ISRAEL

W hat are you doing here, Uzi?" Gabriel asked. "You're the boss now. Bosses don't make midnight airport runs. They leave that sort of work to the flunkies in Transport."

"I had nothing better to do."

"Nothing better to do than hang around the airport waiting for me to come off a plane from Rome? What's wrong? You didn't think I'd really come back this time?"

Uzi Navot didn't respond. He was now peering through the one-way glass window of the VIP reception room into the arrivals hall, where the other passengers from the Rome flight were queuing up at passport control. Gabriel looked around: the same faux-limestone walls, the same tired-looking leather couches, the same smell of male tension and burnt coffee. He had been coming to this room, or versions of it, for more than thirty years. He had entered it in triumph and staggered into it in failure. He had been fêted in this room and consoled by a prime minister; and once, he had been wheeled into it with a bullet wound in his chest. But it never changed.

"Bella needed an evening to herself," Navot said, still facing the glass. He looked at Gabriel. "Last week she confessed that she liked it better when I was in the field. We saw each other once a month, if we were lucky. Now . . ." He frowned. "I think Bella's starting to have buyer's remorse. Besides, I miss hanging around in airport lounges. By my calculation I've spent two-thirds of my career waiting in airport terminals, train stations, restaurants, and hotel rooms. They promise you glamour and excitement, but it's mostly mind-numbing boredom with brief interludes of sheer terror."

"I like the boring parts better. Wouldn't it be nice to live in a boring country?"

"But then it wouldn't be Israel."

Navot relieved Gabriel of his leather garment bag and led him out into a long, harshly lit corridor. They were roughly equal in height and walked with the same purposeful gait, but the similarities ended there. Where Gabriel was angular and narrow, Navot was squat and powerfully built, with a round, turretlike head mounted atop wrestler's shoulders and a thick waist that attested to an affinity for heavy food. For years Navot had roamed western Europe as a *katsa*, an undercover case officer. He was now chief of Special Operations. In the words of the celebrated Israeli spymaster Ari Shamron, Special Ops was "the dark side of a dark service." They were the ones who did the jobs no one else wanted, or dared, to do. They were executioners and kidnappers, buggers and blackmailers; men of intellect and ingenuity with a criminal streak wider than the criminals themselves; multilinguists and chameleons who were at home in the finest hotels and salons in Europe or the worst back alleys of Beirut and Baghdad. Navot was new to the job and had been granted the promotion only because Gabriel had turned it down. There was no animosity between them. Navot was the first to admit he was a mere field hand. Gabriel Allon was a legend.

The corridor led to a secure door, and the door to a restricted area just off the main traffic circle outside the terminal. A dented Renault sedan stood in the reserved parking place. Navot opened the trunk and tossed Gabriel's bag inside. "I gave my driver the night off," he said. "I wanted a word in private. You know how the drivers can be. They sit around down there in the motor pool all day with nothing to do but gossip. They're worse than a sewing circle."

Gabriel got into the passenger seat and closed the door. He looked into the backseat. It was stacked with Bella's books and files. Bella was an academic who specialized in Syria and drifted in and out of government service. She was far more intelligent than Navot, an openly acknowledged fact that had been a source of considerable tension in their long and turbulent relationship. Navot started her car with a hostile twist of the key and drove it too hard toward the airport exit ramp.

"How did the painting turn out?" he asked.

"It turned out just fine, Uzi."

"It was a Botticelli, wasn't it?"

"Bellini," Gabriel corrected him. "*Lament over the Dead Christ.*" He might have added that the sublime panel had once formed the cyma of Bellini's remarkable altarpiece in the Church of San Francesco in Pesaro, but he didn't. The fact that Gabriel was one of the world's finest art restorers had always made him the target of professional envy among his colleagues. He rarely discussed his work with them, even with Navot, who had become a close friend.

"Botticelli, Bellini—it's all the same to me." Navot shook his head. "Imagine, a nice Jewish boy like you restoring a Bellini masterpiece for the pope. I hope he paid you well."

"He paid me the standard fee—and then a little more."

"It's only fair," Navot said. "After all, you did save his life."

"You had a hand in it, too, Uzi."

"But I wasn't the one who got his picture in the paper doing it."

They came to the end of the ramp. Overhead was a blue-and-white traffic sign. To the left was Tel Aviv, to the right, Jerusalem. Navot turned to the right and headed toward the Judean Hills.

"How's the mood at King Saul Boulevard?" Gabriel asked.

King Saul Boulevard was the longtime address of Israel's foreign intelligence service. The service had a long name that had very little to do with the true nature of its work. Men like Gabriel and Uzi Navot referred to it as "the Office" and nothing else.

"Consider yourself fortunate you've been away."

"That bad?"

"It's the night of the long knives. Our adventure in Lebanon was an unmitigated disaster. None of our institutions came out of it with their reputations intact, including the Office. You know how these things work. When mistakes of this magnitude are made, heads must roll, the more the better. No one is safe, especially Amos. The Commission of Inquiry wants to know why the Office didn't realize Hezbollah was so well armed and why our vast network of well-paid collaborators couldn't seem to find Hezbollah's leadership once the fighting started."

"The last thing the Office needs now is another power struggle and battle for succession—not with Hezbollah gearing up for another war. Not with Iran on the verge of a nuclear weapon. And not with the territories about to explode."

"The decision has already been made by Shamron and the rest of the wise men that Amos must die. The only question is, will it be an execution, or will Amos be allowed to do the deed himself after a decent interval?"

"How do you know where Shamron stands on all this?"

Navot, by his edgy silence, made clear that his source was Shamron himself. It had been years now since Shamron had done his last tour as chief, yet the Office was still very much his private fiefdom. It was filled with officers like Gabriel and Navot, men who had been recruited and groomed by Shamron, men who operated by a creed, even spoke a language, written by him. Shamron was known in Israel as the *Memuneh*, the one in charge, and he would remain so until the day he finally decided the country was safe enough for him to die.

"You're playing a dangerous game, Uzi. Shamron is getting on. That bomb attack on his motorcade took a lot out of him. He's not the man he used to be. There's no guarantee he'll prevail in a showdown with Amos, and I don't need to remind you that the door to

King Saul Boulevard for men like you is one way. If you and Shamron lose, *you'll* be the one who ends up on the street hawking your
services to the highest bidder, just like the rest of the Office's washed-
up field men."

Navot nodded his head in agreement. "And I won't have a pope
to throw me a little work on the side."

They started the ascent into the Bab al-Wad, the staircaselike
gorge that leads from the Coastal Plain to Jerusalem. Gabriel felt his
ears pop from the altitude change.

"Does Shamron have a successor in mind?"

"He wants the Office to be run by someone other than a soldier."

It was one of the many peculiarities about the Office that made
little sense to outsiders. Like the Americans, the Israelis nearly always chose men with no intelligence experience to be their chief
spies. The Americans preferred politicians and party apparatchiks,
while in Israel the job usually went to an army general like Amos.
Shamron was the last man to ascend to the throne from the ranks of
Operations, and he had been manipulating every occupant since.

"So that's why you're conspiring with Shamron? You're angling
for Amos's job? You and Shamron are using the debacle in Lebanon
as grounds for a coup d'état. You'll seize the palace, and Shamron
will pull the strings from his villa in Tiberias."

"I'm flattered you think Shamron would trust me with the keys
to his beloved Office, but that's not the case. The *Memuneh* has someone else in mind for the job."

"Me?" Gabriel shook his head slowly. "I'm an assassin, Uzi, and
they don't make assassins the director."

"You're more than just an assassin."

Gabriel looked silently out the window at the orderly yellow
streetlights of a Jewish settlement spreading down the hillside toward the flatlands of the West Bank. In the distance a crescent moon
hung over Ramallah. "What makes Shamron think I'd want to be the
chief?" he asked. "I wriggled off the hook when he wanted to make
me chief of Special Ops."

"Are you trying to drop a not-so-subtle reminder that I got the job only because you didn't want it?"

"What I'm trying to say, Uzi, is that I'm not fit for Headquarters—and I certainly don't want to spend my life in endless Security Cabinet meetings in the Prime Minister's Office. I don't play well with others, and I won't be a party to your little conspiracy against Amos."

"So what do you intend to do? Sit around and wait for the pope to give you more work?"

"You're starting to sound like Shamron."

Navot ignored the remark. "Sit around while the missiles rain down on Haifa? While the mullahs in Tehran build their nuclear bomb? Is that your plan? To leave the fighting to others?" Navot took a long look into the rearview mirror. "But why should you be any different? At the moment it's a national affliction. Fortress Israel is cracking under the strain of this war without end. The founding fathers are dying off, and the people aren't sure they trust the new generation of leaders with their future. Those with the resources are creating escape hatches for themselves. It's the Jewish instinct, isn't it? It's in our DNA because of the Holocaust. One hears things now that one didn't hear even ten years ago. People wonder openly whether the entire enterprise was a mistake. They delude themselves into thinking that the Jewish national home is not in Palestine but in America."

"America?"

Navot fixed his eyes back on the road. "My sister lives in Bethesda, Maryland. It's very nice there. You can eat your lunch in an outdoor café without fear that the next person who walks by your table is a *shaheed* who's going to blow you to bits." He glanced at Gabriel. "Maybe that's why you like Italy so much. You want to make a new life for yourself away from Israel. You want to leave the blood and tears to mere mortals."

Gabriel's dark look made clear he had shed more blood and tears for his country than most. "I'm an art restorer who specializes in Italian Old Masters. The paintings are in Italy, Uzi, not here."

"Art restoration was your cover job, Gabriel. You are not an art restorer. You are a secret servant of the State of Israel, and you have no right to leave the fighting to others. And if you think you're going to find a quiet life for yourself in Europe, forget it. The Europeans condemned us for Lebanon, but what they don't understand is that Lebanon is merely a preview of coming attractions. The movie will soon be showing in theaters all across Europe. It's the next battleground."

The *next* battleground? No, thought Gabriel, it had been his battleground for more than thirty years. He looked up at the looming shadow of Mount Herzl, where his former wife resided in a psychiatric hospital, locked in a prison of memory and in a body destroyed by Gabriel's enemies. His son was on the other side of Jerusalem, in a hero's grave on the Mount of Olives. Between them lay the Valley of Hinnom, an ancient burning ground believed by both Jews and Muslims to be the fiery place where the wicked are punished after death. Gabriel had spent the better part of his life traversing the valley. It was clear that Uzi Navot wanted him to return again.

"What's on your mind, Uzi? Surely you didn't come all the way to the airport just to ask me to join your plot against Amos."

"We have an errand we'd like you to run for us," Navot said.

"I'm not an errand boy."

"No offense, Gabriel."

"None taken. Where's the errand?"

"Amsterdam."

"Why Amsterdam?"

"Because we've had a death in the family there."

"Who?"

"Solomon Rosner."

"Rosner? I never knew Rosner was ours."

"He wasn't *ours*," said Navot. "He was Shamron's."

3

JERUSALEM

They drove to Narkiss Street, a quiet, leafy lane in the heart of Jerusalem, and parked outside the limestone apartment house at Number 16. It was three floors in height and largely concealed by a towering eucalyptus tree growing in the front garden. Gabriel led Navot through the small foyer and mounted the stairs. Despite his long absence he didn't bother to check the postbox. He never received mail, and the name on the box was false. As far as the bureaucracy of the State of Israel was concerned, Gabriel Allon did not exist. He lived only in the Office, and even there he was a part-time resident.

His flat was on the top floor. As always he hesitated before opening the door. The room that greeted him was not the same one he had walked out of six months earlier. It had been a small but fully functioning art studio; now it was meticulously decorated in the subtle beiges and soft whites that Chiara Zolli, his Venetian-born fiancée, so adored. She'd been busy while he was away. Somehow she'd neglected to mention the redecoration during her last visit to Italy.

"Where are my things?"

"Housekeeping has them in storage until you can find some

proper studio space." Navot smiled at Gabriel's discomfort. "You didn't expect your wife to live in an apartment without furniture, did you?"

"She's not my wife yet." He laid his bag on the new couch. It looked expensive. "Where is she?"

"She didn't tell you where we were sending her?"

"She takes rules of compartmentalization and need to know very seriously."

"So do I."

"Where is she, Uzi?"

Navot opened his mouth to reply, but a voice from the kitchen answered for him. It was familiar to Gabriel, as was the elderly figure who emerged a moment later, dressed in khaki trousers and a leather bomber jacket with a tear in the left breast. His head was shaped like a bullet and bald, except for a monkish fringe of cropped white hair. His face was more gaunt than Gabriel remembered, and his ugly wire-framed spectacles magnified pale blue eyes that were no longer clear. He was leaning heavily on a handsome olive-wood cane. The hand that held it seemed to have been borrowed from a man twice his size.

"Argentina," said Ari Shamron for a second time. "Your wife-to-be is in Argentina."

"What type of job is it?"

"Surveillance of a known terrorist operative."

Gabriel didn't have to ask the affiliation of the operative. The answer lay in the location of the operation. Argentina, like the rest of South America, was a hotbed of Hezbollah activity.

"We think it's only a matter of time before Hezbollah tries to take its revenge for the damage we inflicted on them in Lebanon. A terror attack that leaves no fingerprints is the most likely scenario. The only question in our mind is the target. Will it be us or our supporters in America?"

"When will she be finished?"

Shamron shrugged noncommittally. "This is a war without end, Gabriel. It is forever. But then you know that better than any of us, don't you?" He touched Gabriel's face. "See if you can find us some coffee. We need to talk."

.   .   .

Gabriel found a tin of coffee in the pantry. The seal had been broken and a single sniff of the grinds confirmed his suspicions that it was long past its prime. He poured some into the French press and set a kettle of water to boil, then returned to the sitting room. Navot was pondering a ceramic dish on the end table; Shamron had settled himself into an armchair and was in the process of lighting one of his vile-smelling Turkish cigarettes. Gabriel had been gone six months, but in his absence it seemed nothing had changed but the furniture.

"No coffee?" Shamron asked.

"It takes more than a minute to make coffee, Ari."

Shamron glared at his big stainless-steel wristwatch. Time had always been his enemy, but now more so than ever. It was the bombing, Gabriel thought. It had finally forced Shamron to confront the possibility of his own mortality.

"Solomon Rosner was an Office asset?" Gabriel asked.

"A very valuable one, actually."

"How long?"

Shamron tilted his head back and blew a stream of smoke toward the ceiling before answering. "Back in the mid-nineties, during my second tour as chief, we began to realize the Netherlands was going to be a problem for us down the road. The demographics of the country were changing rapidly. Amsterdam was well on its way to becoming a Muslim city. The young men were unemployed and angry, and they were being fed a steady diet of hate by their imams, most of whom were imported and funded by our friends in Saudi Arabia. There were a number of attacks against the local community. Small stuff, mostly—a broken window, a bloody nose, the odd Molotov cocktail. We wanted to make sure those small incidents didn't turn into something more serious. We also wanted to know whether any of our more determined enemies were using Amsterdam as a base of operations for major attacks against Israeli targets in Europe. We needed eyes and ears on the ground, but we didn't have the resources to mount any sort of operation on our own."

Gabriel opened the doors leading onto his small balcony. The smell of the eucalyptus tree in the front garden filled the apartment. "So you turned to Rosner?"

"Not right away. We tried the traditional route first, a liaison relationship with the AIVD, the Dutch security service. We courted them for months, but the Dutch at that time weren't interested in dancing with us. After the last rejection, I authorized an attempt to get into the AIVD through the back door. Our local chief of station made a rather clumsy pass at the AIVD deputy in charge of monitoring the Muslim community and it blew up in our faces. You remember the scandal, don't you, Gabriel?"

He did. The affair had been splashed all over the pages of the Dutch and Israeli newspapers. There had been heated exchanges between the foreign ministries of both countries and angry threats of expulsions.

"When the storm died down, I decided to try again. This time, though, I chose a different target."

"Rosner," Gabriel put in, and Shamron nodded his head in agreement.

"He monitored what was being said in the mosques when no one else in Amsterdam was listening, and read the filth running through the sewers of the Internet when everyone else averted their eyes. On more than one occasion, he supplied information to the police that prevented violence. He also happened to be Jewish. As far as the Office was concerned, Rosner was the answer to our prayers."

"Who handled the recruitment?"

"I did," Shamron said. "After the AIVD scandal, I wasn't about to entrust the job to anyone else."

"And besides," said Gabriel, "there's nothing you love better than a good recruitment."

Shamron responded with a seductive smile, the same smile he had used on a searing afternoon in September 1972, when he had come to see Gabriel at the Bezalel Academy of Art in Jerusalem. Gabriel had been a promising young painter; Shamron was a brash operations man who had just been ordered by Prime Minister Golda Meir to hunt down and kill the members of Black September, perpetrators of the Munich Massacre. The operation was code-named Wrath of God, but in reality it was the Wrath of Gabriel. Of the twelve members of Black September killed by the Office, six were dispatched by Gabriel at close range with a .22 caliber Beretta.

"I flew to Amsterdam and took Rosner to dinner in a quiet restaurant overlooking the Amstel. I told stories about the old days—the War of Independence, the Eichmann capture. You know the ones, Gabriel, the stories you and Uzi have heard a thousand times before. At the end of the evening, I laid a contract on the table. He signed without reservation."

Shamron was interrupted by the sudden scream of the teakettle. Gabriel went into the kitchen and prepared the coffee. When he returned, he placed the French press on the coffee table, along with three mugs and a sugar bowl. Navot gave him a disapproving look. "You'd better put something under that," he said. "If you leave a ring, Chiara will kill you."

"I'll take my chances, Uzi." Gabriel looked at Shamron. "Who serviced him? You, I suppose."

"Rosner was my creation," Shamron said somewhat defensively. "Naturally I was reluctant to turn over the reins to anyone else. I gave him a bit of money to hire an assistant, and when Rosner had something to report I was the one who went to see him."

"In Amsterdam?"

"Never," said Shamron. "Usually we met across the border, in Antwerp."

"And when they ran you out of the Office for the second time?"

"I hung onto a few bits and pieces to keep me occupied in my dotage. Rosner was one of those bits. Another was *you*, of course. I didn't trust you with anyone else." He spooned sugar into his coffee and gave it a melancholy stir. "When I went to work for the prime minister as his senior security adviser, I had to surrender control of Rosner." He glanced at Navot. "I entrusted him to Uzi. After all, he was our western European *katsa*."

"And your protégé," Gabriel added.

"It wasn't exactly heavy lifting," Navot conceded. "Ari had already done all that. I just had to handle Rosner's reports. Eighteen months ago, he gave me a nugget of pure gold. According to one of Rosner's sources inside the Muslim community, an al-Qaeda-affiliated cell operating in west Amsterdam had got their hands on a missile and was planning to shoot down an El Al jetliner on approach at Schiphol Airport. That evening we diverted the flight to Brussels and tipped off the Dutch. They arrested four men sitting in a parked car at the end of the runway. In the trunk was an antiaircraft missile that had been smuggled into Amsterdam from Iraq."

"How did Rosner know about the plot?"

"He had sources," said Shamron. "Very *good* sources. I tried on a number of occasions to convince him to turn them over to us, but he always refused. He said his sources talked to him because he wasn't a professional. Well, not quite a professional, but no one else in Holland knew that."

"And you're sure about that?" asked Gabriel. "You're certain Rosner didn't die because of his links to us?"

"Unfortunately, there was no shortage of people in Amsterdam who wanted Solomon dead. Some of the city's most prominent jihadist imams had been openly calling for a volunteer to step forward. They finally found their man in Muhammad Hamza, a housepainter from north Amsterdam who just happened to be working on a project across the street from Rosner's home. The Amsterdam police found a videotape inside Hamza's apartment after his arrest. It was shot the morning of Rosner's murder. On it Hamza calmly says that today would be the day he killed his Jew."

"So what type of errand do you want me to run in Amsterdam?"

Navot and Shamron looked at each other, as if trying to get their story straight. Shamron let Navot answer. He was, after all, chief of Special Ops.

"We'd like you to go to Amsterdam and clean out his files. We want the names of all those golden sources, of course, but we also want to make sure there's nothing there that might link him to us."

"It would be deeply embarrassing if our ties to Solomon were ever exposed," Shamron added. "And it would also make it more difficult for us to recruit *sayanim* from the Jewish communities around the world. We're a small service. We can't function without them."

The *sayanim* were a worldwide network of volunteer Jewish helpers. They were the bankers who supplied Office agents with cash in emergencies; the doctors who treated them in secret when they were wounded; the hoteliers who gave them rooms under false names, and the rental-car agents who supplied them with untraceable vehicles. The vast majority of the *sayanim* had been recruited and nurtured by Shamron himself. He devotedly referred to them as the secret fruit of the Diaspora.

"It also has the potential to make a volatile situation in the Netherlands much worse," Gabriel said. "Solomon Rosner was one of the most well-known critics of militant Islam in Europe. If it ever came out that he was our paid mouthpiece, the Jewish community in Holland might find itself at risk."

"I disagree with your characterization," said Shamron, "but your point is duly noted."

"How am I supposed to get into Rosner's office?"

It was Navot who answered. "About a year ago, when the threats against Rosner started coming fast and furious, we knew we had to make plans for just such a contingency. Rosner told his assistant, a young woman named Sophie Vanderhaus, that, in the event of his death, she would be contacted by a gentleman named Rudolf Heller and given a set of instructions she was to follow to the letter."

Herr Rudolf Heller, venture capitalist for Zurich, was one of Shamron's many false identities.

"I contacted Sophie last night," Shamron said. "I told her that a colleague of mine would be arriving in Amsterdam tomorrow afternoon and that he was to be given complete access to all of Professor Rosner's files."

"Tomorrow afternoon?"

"There's an El Al flight that leaves Ben-Gurion at six forty-five and arrives in Amsterdam at two. Sophie will meet you in front of the Café de Doelen at four."

"It could take me days to go through all of Rosner's files."

"Yes," Shamron said, as though he were glad the task had not been inflicted on him. "That's why we've decided to send along some help. He's already in Europe on a personal matter. He'll be there when you arrive."

Gabriel raised his coffee cup to his lips and eyed Shamron over the rim. "And what about the promises we made to the European security services? The covenant we signed in blood in exchange for getting them to drop all the charges and lawsuits against me?"

"You mean the covenant that forbids you from operating on European soil without first obtaining permission from the security service of the country involved?"

"Yes, that one."

They all three shared a conspiratorial silence. Making promises they had no intention of keeping was what they did best. They abused the passports of other nations, recruited agents from allied security and intelligence services, and routinely ran operations on foreign soil forbidden by long-standing accords. They did this, they told themselves, because they had no choice; because they were surrounded by enemies who would stop at nothing to ensure their destruction; and because the rest of the world, blinded by their hatred of Zionism and the Jews, would not allow them to fight back with the full force of their military might. They lied to everyone but each other and were truly at ease only in each other's company.

"You're not going behind the Iron Curtain," Shamron said. "With proper cover and a bit of work on that now-famous face of yours, you'll have no problems getting into the country. The new realities of European travel have made life much easier for Office agents—and, unfortunately, for the terrorists as well. Osama bin Laden could be living quietly in a cottage by the North Sea and the Dutch would never know it."

Navot reached into his attaché case. The envelope he removed was an old-fashioned model, with a string instead of an aluminum clasp. The Office was one of the most technologically advanced services in the world, but it still used envelopes from the days when Israel had no television.

"It's an in-and-out job," Shamron said. "You'll be home by the weekend. Who knows? Perhaps your wife will be, too."

"She's not my wife yet."

Gabriel took the envelope from Navot's grasp. *An in-and-out job*, he thought. It sounded nice, but somehow it never turned out that way.

4

AMSTERDAM

Name, please?" asked the front-desk clerk at the Hotel Europa.

"Kiever," Gabriel replied in German-accented English. "Heinrich Kiever."

"Ah, yes, here it is. Your room is ready." There was genuine surprise in her voice. "You have a message, Herr Kiever."

Gabriel, playing the role of the travel-weary businessman, accepted the small slip of paper with a frown. It stated that his colleague from Heller Enterprises in Zurich had already checked into the hotel and was awaiting his call. Gabriel squeezed the message into a ball and shoved it into the pocket of his overcoat. It was cashmere. The girls in Identity had spared no expense on his wardrobe.

"Your room is on the sixth floor. It's one of our premier suites." She handed him an electronic card key and recited a long list of luxurious hotel amenities Gabriel had no intention of using. "Do you require assistance with your bag?"

Gabriel glanced at the bellman, an emaciated youth who looked like he had spent his lunch hour in one of Amsterdam's notorious brown cafés. "I think I can manage, thank you."

He boarded a waiting elevator and rode it up to the sixth floor. The door to Suite 612 was located at the end of a corridor, in a small, private alcove. Gabriel ran his fingertips around the jamb, searching for any sign of a foreign object such as a fragment of loose wiring, and held his breath as he inserted the card key into the electronic lock. There was little "premier" about the room he entered, though the view of the canal houses along the Amstel River was one of the finest in the city. A bottle of mediocre champagne was sweating in an ice bucket on the coffee table. The handwritten note said: *Welcome back to the Europa, Herr Kiever.* Strange, because, to the best of Gabriel's recollection, Herr Kiever had never stayed there before.

He removed a Nokia mobile phone from his coat pocket. It was indeed a telephone, but it contained several features unavailable on ordinary commercial models, such as a device capable of detecting the signals and electrical impulses of concealed transmitters. He held the phone in front of his face and spent the next five minutes padding slowly round the rooms of the suite, watching the power meter for subtle fluctuations. Satisfied the room had not been bugged, he conducted a second search, this one for evidence of a bomb or any other lethal device. Only then did he pick up the phone on the bedside table and dial Room 611. "I'm here," he said in German, and immediately set down the receiver.

A moment later there was a gentle knock at the door. The man who entered was several years older than Gabriel, small and bookish, with wispy, unkempt gray hair and quick brown eyes. As usual he seemed to be wearing all his clothing at once: a button-down shirt with ascot, a cardigan sweater, a rumpled tweed jacket. "Lovely accommodations," said Eli Lavon. "Better than that *pensione* where we stayed in Rome the night before the Zwaiter hit in seventy-two. Do you remember it, Gabriel? My God, what a dump."

"We were posing as university students," Gabriel reminded him. "We can't pose as students anymore. I suppose that's one of the few fringe benefits of growing old."

Lavon gave Gabriel an elusive smile and lowered himself wearily
into an armchair. Even Gabriel, who had known Lavon more than
thirty years, sometimes found it hard to imagine that this fussy
hypochondriacal little man was without question the finest street
surveillance artist the Office had ever produced. They had worked
together for the first time during the Wrath of God operation. Lavon,
an archaeologist by training, had been an *ayin*, a tracker. When the
unit disbanded, he had settled in Vienna and opened a small inves-
tigative bureau called Wartime Claims and Inquiries. Operating on
a shoestring budget, he had managed to track down millions of dollars in looted Jewish assets and had played a significant role in pry-
ing a multibillion-dollar settlement from the banks of Switzerland.
He had recently returned to Israel and was teaching biblical archae-
ology at Hebrew University. In his spare time he lectured on the fine
art of physical surveillance at the Academy. No Office recruit ever
made it into the field without first spending a few days with the
great Eli Lavon.

"Your disguise is quite effective," Lavon said with professional
admiration. "For an instant even I didn't recognize you."

Gabriel looked at his reflection in the mirror over the dressing
table. He wore a pair of black-framed eyeglasses, contact lenses that
turned his green eyes to brown, and a false goatee that accentuated
his already-narrow features.

"I would have added a bit more gray to your hair," Lavon said.

"I have enough already," Gabriel said. "How did you get roped
into this affair?"

"Proximity, I suppose. I was at a conference in Prague delivering
a lecture on our dig at Tel Megiddo. As I came off the stage my mobile phone was ringing. You'll never guess who it was."

"Trust me, Eli—I can guess."

"I hear that voice, the voice of God with a murderous Polish
accent, telling me to leave Prague for Amsterdam at once." Lavon
shook his head slowly. "Does Shamron really have nothing better
to do at his age than worry about a dead *sayan*? He's lucky to be

alive. He should be enjoying his last few years on this earth, but instead he clings to the Office like a drowning man grasping at a life ring."

"Rosner was his *sayan*," Gabriel said. "And I'm sure he feels partly responsible for his death."

"He could have let Uzi handle it. But he doesn't fully trust Uzi, does he, Gabriel? The old man wanted *you* in Special Ops, not Uzi, and he's never going to rest until you're running the place." Lavon pushed up the sleeve of his tweed jacket and looked at his watch. "Sophie Vanderhaus awaits us. Have you given much thought to how you're going to play it with her?"

"She's an intelligent woman. I suspect she already has a good idea about Herr Heller's true affiliation—and why Rosner always met with him outside the country."

Lavon frowned. "I must confess I'm not really looking forward to this. I suppose there's a ritual to these things. When agents die, their secrets have to go with them to the grave. It's like *tahara*, the washing of the dead. Next time it could be one of us."

"Promise me something, Eli."

"Anything."

"Promise me that if anything happens to me, you'll be the one who buries all my secrets."

"It would be my honor." Lavon patted the pocket of his jacket. "Oh, I nearly forgot this. A *bodel* gave this to me at the airport this morning after I arrived."

The *bodelim* were Office couriers. The item Lavon had been given was a Beretta 9mm pistol. Gabriel took it from his grasp and slipped it into the waistband of his trousers at the small of his back.

"You're not really going to bring that, are you?"

"I have enemies, Eli—lots of enemies."

"Obviously, so did Solomon Rosner."

"And one of them might still be hanging around his house."

"Just try not to kill anyone while we're in Amsterdam, Gabriel. Dead bodies have a way of spoiling an otherwise uneventful trip."

. . .

It was beginning to get dark when Gabriel stepped out of the hotel. He turned to the right and, with Lavon trailing several paces behind, walked the length of the narrow street until he came to an iron bridge. On the opposite side stood Café de Doelen. It was open for business again, and the spot where Solomon Rosner had been standing at the time of his murder was piled high with tulips. There were no mourners or protesters condemning the ritual slaughter of their fellow countryman, only a single banner, hung from the façade of the café, that read ONE AMSTERDAM, ONE PEOPLE.

"I've been staring at it for two days now and I still don't quite know what it means."

Gabriel turned around. The words had been spoken by a woman in her late twenties with sandstone-colored hair and pale blue eyes that shone with a calm intelligence.

"I'm Sophie Vanderhaus." She extended her hand and added primly: "Professor Rosner's assistant." She released his hand and gazed at the makeshift memorial. "Quite moving, don't you think? Even the Dutch press are treating him like a hero now. Too bad they weren't so glowing in their praise when he was alive. For years they attacked him, all because he had the courage to say the things they chose to ignore. In my judgment they are complicit in his murder. They are as guilty as the extremist imams who filled Muhammad Hamza's head with hate." She turned and looked at Gabriel. "Come," she said. "The house is this way."

They set off down the Staalstraat together. Gabriel glanced over his shoulder and saw Lavon start after them. Sophie Vanderhaus gazed down at the cobbles, as if organizing her thoughts.

"It's been five days since his murder," she said, "and not a single Muslim leader has bothered to condemn it. In fact, given a chance to do so by the Dutch media, they have chosen to blame it on *him*. Where are these so-called moderate Muslims one always hears about in the press? Do they exist or are they merely figments of our imagination? If one insults the Prophet Muhammad, our Muslim countrymen pour into the streets in a sacred rage and threaten us with beheading. But when one of them commits murder in the Prophet's name . . ."

Her voice trailed off. Gabriel completed the thought for her.

"The silence is deafening."

"Well put," she said. "But you didn't come to Amsterdam to listen to a lecture by me. You have a job to do." She scrutinized him carefully for a moment while they walked side by side in the narrow street. "Do you know, Herr Kiever, it was exactly a year ago that Professor Rosner first told me about his relationship with a man named Rudolf Heller and what I was to do in the event anything ever happened to him. Needless to say, I hoped this day would never come."

"I understand you and Professor Rosner were very close."

"He was like a father to me. I had a dozen other job offers when I completed my degree—jobs that paid much more than the Center for European Security Studies—but I chose to work for Professor Rosner for a pittance instead."

"You're a historian?"

She nodded. "While I was researching my thesis, I learned that we Dutch have a habit of trying to reach accommodation with murderous ideologies, be it National Socialism or Islamic fascism. I wanted to help break that cycle. Working for Professor Rosner gave me that chance." She pushed a stray lock of hair from her forehead and looked at Gabriel. "I was at Professor Rosner's side for five years, Herr Kiever. I had to endure the taunts and threats as well. And I believe that entitles me to ask a few questions before we start."

"I'm afraid asking too many questions about who I am and why I'm here will make your life more complicated and dangerous than it already is."

"Will you permit me to posit a hypothesis?"

"If you insist."

"I don't believe Herr Rudolf Heller is Swiss. And I certainly don't believe he's a venture capitalist who had an interest in supporting the work of a terrorism analyst in Amsterdam."

"Really?"

"Professor Rosner didn't talk much about his feelings toward Israel. He knew it would only make him more radioactive in Amsterdam than he already was. But he was a Zionist. He believed in Israel and the right of the Jewish people to a homeland. And I suspect that if a clever Israeli intelligence officer came along and made him the right sort of offer, he would have done almost anything to help."

She stopped walking and looked at Gabriel for a moment with one eyebrow raised, as if giving him a chance to respond.

"My name is Heinrich Kiever," he said. "I'm a colleague of Herr Rudolf Heller from Zurich, and I've come to Amsterdam to review the private papers of Professor Solomon Rosner."

She capitulated, though judging from her expression she remained deeply skeptical of his cover story. Gabriel didn't blame her. It was hardly airtight.

"I hope you're not planning on leaving Amsterdam any time soon," she said. "At last estimate, we had more than a hundred thousand pages of documents in our archives."

"I brought help."

"Where?"

Gabriel nodded toward Lavon, who was gazing into a shopwindow twenty yards behind them.

"Since when do Zurich venture capitalists employ professional surveillance men?" She set off down the Groenburgwal. "Come on, Herr *Kiever*. You have a long night ahead of you."

. . .

Her original estimate of Rosner's archives proved wildly optimistic. Gabriel, after conducting a brief tour of the canal house, reckoned the true number of pages ran closer to a quarter million. There were files in Rosner's office and files in Sophie's. Files lined the hallway, and there was a dank chamber filled with files in the cellar. And then, of course, there was all the material contained on the hard drive of Rosner's computer. So much for Shamron's prediction that they would be back in Jerusalem by the weekend.

They started in Rosner's office and worked as a threesome. Gabriel and Lavon, the restorer and the archaeologist, sat side by side at Rosner's desk, while Sophie placed the files before them one by one, providing a bit of background where appropriate, translating the odd passage when necessary. Files of interest or of a sensitive nature were separated out and packed into cardboard boxes for shipment to King Saul Boulevard. By nine o'clock they had filled four boxes and found not a single reference to Ari Shamron, Herr Rudolf Heller, or the Office. Rosner, it seemed, had been a careful asset. He also had been a meticulous researcher and collector of intelligence. Contained in the rooms of the old canal house on the Groenburgwal was a remarkably detailed and frightening portrait of the radical Islamic networks operating in Amsterdam and beyond.

By ten o'clock they were all famished. Unwilling to suspend work, they decided on takeaway. Gabriel voted for kebabs, Sophie for Indonesian, and Lavon for Thai. After ten minutes of spirited debate, they resorted to drawing a name from one of Rosner's old felt hats. Sophie did the honors. "Thai," she said, smiling at Lavon. "Shall we draw again to see who has to go pick it up?"

"I'll go," said Gabriel. "There's someone I need to have a word with."

. . .

A gentle snow was falling when Gabriel stepped outside five minutes later. He stood for a moment atop Rosner's iron steps, buttoning his overcoat against the cold, while scanning the street for signs of surveillance. It was deserted except for a single bundled soul, perched on a public bench on the opposite bank of the canal. He wore a threadbare woolen overcoat and a black-and-white checkered kaffiyeh for a scarf. His gray beard was unkempt and atop his head was the white *kufi* skullcap of a devout Muslim. Gabriel descended the steps and walked to the drawbridge at the end of the street. As he turned into the Staalstraat, he could hear footfalls on the cobblestones behind him. He swiveled his head deliberately and took a long, highly unprofessional look over his shoulder. The Muslim man who had been seated on the bench was now thirty yards behind and walking in the same direction. Two minutes later, as Gabriel passed Rosner's memorial outside Café de Doelen, he looked over his shoulder a second time and saw that the man with the *kufi* and the kaffiyeh had cut the distance between them in half. He thought of the words Lavon had spoken to him earlier that afternoon at the Hotel Europa. *Just try not to kill anyone while we're in Amsterdam*, Lavon had said. Gabriel had no intention of killing the man. He just wanted answers to two simple questions. Why had a devout Muslim spent the better part of the evening sitting outside Solomon Rosner's house? And why was he now following Gabriel through the dark streets of Amsterdam?

· · ·

The restaurant where Sophie Vanderhaus had placed the takeaway order was in the Leidsestraat, not far from the Koningsplein. Gabriel, after crossing the Amstel, should have gone to the right. He went left instead, into a narrow pedestrian lane lined with sex shops, American fast-food restaurants, and tiny Middle Eastern cafés. It was crowded in spite of the hour; even so, Gabriel had no trouble keeping track of his pursuer in the garish neon light.

The street emptied into the Rembrandtplein, but twenty yards before the busy square Gabriel turned into a darkened shoulder-width alley that led back to the river. The man with the kaffiyeh and the *kufi* paused at the mouth of the alley, as though reluctant to enter, then followed after him.

Gabriel removed the Beretta from its resting place at the small of his back and chambered a round. As he did so, he could almost hear Shamron's voice echoing in his head: *We do not wave our guns around in public like gangsters and make idle threats. When we take out our*

*weapons we do so for one reason and one reason only. We start shooting.
And we keep shooting until the target is dead.* He slipped the gun into
the pocket of his overcoat and walked on.

At the midpoint of the alley, the darkness was nearly impenetrable. Gabriel turned into a bisecting passageway and waited there
with his hand wrapped around the butt of the Beretta. As the
bearded man came past, Gabriel stepped from the alley and delivered a knifelike blow to his left kidney. The man's legs buckled instantly, but before he could crumple to the ground, Gabriel seized
hold of the kaffiyeh and hurled him hard against a graffiti-spattered
brick wall. The look in the man's eyes was one of genuine terror.
Gabriel struck him again, this time in the solar plexus. As the man
doubled over, Gabriel quickly searched him for weapons but found
only a billfold and a small copy of the Quran.

"What do you want with me?" Gabriel asked in rapid Arabic.

The man managed only a single, wet cough.

"Answer me," Gabriel said, "or I'll keep hitting you until
you do."

The man lifted his hand and pleaded with Gabriel not to strike
him again. Gabriel let go of him and took a step back. The man
leaned against the wall and fought for breath.

"Who are you?" Gabriel asked. "And why are you following me?"

"I'm the person you're looking for in Solomon Rosner's files," he
said. "And I've come to help you."

5

AMSTERDAM

M y name is Ibrahim."
        "Ibrahim what?"
"Ibrahim Fawaz."

"You were a fool to follow me like that, Ibrahim Fawaz."

"Obviously."

They were walking along the darkened embankment of the Amstel River. Ibrahim had one hand pressed to his kidney and the other wrapped around Gabriel's arm for support. A gritty snow had begun to fall and the air was suddenly brittle with the cold. Gabriel pointed to an open café and suggested they talk there.

"Men like me don't have coffee in places like that, especially in the company of men like you. This is not America. This is Amsterdam." He swiveled his head a few degrees and glanced at Gabriel out of the corner of his eye. "You speak Arabic like a Palestinian. I suppose the rumors about Professor Rosner were true."

"What rumors?"

"That he was a pawn of the Zionists and their Jewish supporters in America. That he was an Israeli spy."

"Who said things like that?"

"The angry boys," said Ibrahim. "And the imams, too. They're worse than the young hotheads. They come from the Middle East. From Saudi Arabia. They preach Wahhabi Islam. The imam in our mosque told us that Professor Rosner deserved to die for what he had written about Muslims and the Prophet. I warned him to go into hiding, but he refused. He was very stubborn."

Ibrahim stopped and leaned against the balustrade overlooking the sluggish black river. Gabriel looked at the Arab's right hand and saw it was missing the last two fingers.

"Are you going to be sick?"

"I don't think so."

"Can you walk, Ibrahim? It's better if we walk."

The Arab nodded and they set off slowly along the riverbank. "I suppose you were the professor's handler? That's why you and your friend are digging frantically through his files."

"What I'm doing inside his house is no business of yours."

"Just do me a favor," the Arab said. "If you come across my name, please do me the courtesy of dropping the document in question into the nearest shredder. I respected Professor Rosner very much, but I don't want to end up like him. There are men in Amsterdam who will slit my throat if they knew I was helping him."

"How long did you work for him?"

"A long time," said Ibrahim. "But it wasn't *work*. We were partners, Professor Rosner and I. We shared the same beliefs. We both believed the jihadists were destroying my religion. We both knew that if they weren't stopped, they would destroy Holland, too."

"Why work for Rosner? Why not the police?"

"Perhaps you can tell from my accent that I am Egyptian by birth. When one comes from Egypt, one has a natural fear of the police, secret or otherwise. I've lived in Holland for twenty-five years now. I am a citizen of this country, as are my wife and son. But to the Dutch police, and the rest of my countrymen, I will always be an *allochtoon*. An alien."

"But you must have guessed Rosner was passing along some of your information to the police and the Dutch security service."

"And to the Israeli secret service as well—or so it appears." He looked at Gabriel and managed a sage smile. "I must confess that Israelis are not terribly popular in my home. My wife is a Palestinian. She fled to Egypt with her family in 1948 after *al-Nakba* and settled in Cairo. I've heard about the suffering of the Palestinian people every night at my dinner table for thirty-five years now. My son drank it with his mother's milk. He is Egyptian and Palestinian, a volatile mix."

"Is this the reason you followed me tonight, Ibrahim—to engage in a debate about the Palestinian Diaspora and the crimes of Israel's founders?"

"Perhaps another time," the Egyptian said. "Forgive me, my friend. Now that you are no longer striking me, I was just trying to make polite conversation. I was a professor in Egypt before I immigrated to Holland. My wife and son accuse me of being a professor still. They've spent their lives listening to me lecture. I'm afraid they no longer tolerate me. When I get a chance to teach, I take it."

"You were a teacher in Holland, too?"

"In Holland?" He shook his head. "No, in Holland I was a tool. We decided to leave Egypt in 1982 because we thought our son would have more opportunities here in the West. I was an educated man, but my education was an Egyptian education and so it was worthless here. I built roads until I ruined my back, then I got a job sweeping the streets of Rotterdam. Eventually, when I could no longer even push a broom, I went to work in a furniture factory in west Amsterdam. The plant supervisor made us work fourteen hours a day. Late one night, when I was falling asleep on my feet, I made a mistake with the circular saw." He lifted his ruined hand for Gabriel to see. "During my recuperation I decided to put my time to good use by learning to speak proper Dutch. When the factory manager heard what I was doing, he told me not to waste my time, because one day soon all the *allochtoonen* would be going home. He was wrong, of course."

A gust of wind blew pellets of snow into their faces. Gabriel turned up his coat collar. Ibrahim slipped his hand back into the pocket of his overcoat.

"Our children heard all the insults that were hurled at us by our Dutch hosts, too. They spoke better Dutch than we did. They were more attuned to the subtleties of Dutch culture. They saw the way the Dutch treated us and they were humiliated. They became angry and resentful, not only at the Dutch but at us, their parents. Our children are trapped between two worlds, not fully Arab, not quite Dutch. They inhabit the *ghurba*, the land of strangers, and so they seek shelter in a safe place."

"Islam," said Gabriel.

Ibrahim nodded his head and repeated, "Islam."

"You still make furniture for a living, Ibrahim?"

He shook his head. "I retired several years ago. The Dutch state pays me a generous pension and even a bit of disability because of my two missing fingers. I manage to do a little work on the side. It's good for my self-respect. It keeps me from growing old."

"Where do you work now?"

"Three years ago the state gave us funding to open an Islamic community center in the Oud West section of the city. I took a part-time job there as counselor. I help new arrivals find their footing. I help our people learn to speak proper Dutch. And I keep an eye on our angry young men. That's where I first heard the rumor about a plot to shoot down a Jewish airplane." He glanced at Gabriel to see his reaction. "When I looked into the matter further, I found out it was more than just a rumor, and so I told Professor Rosner. You have me to thank for the fact that two hundred and fifty Jews weren't blown to pieces over Schiphol Airport."

A pair of middle-aged homosexual men came toward them along the embankment. Ibrahim slowed his pace and lowered his gaze reflexively toward the paving stones.

"I have another job as well," he said when the men were gone. "I work for a friend in the Ten Kate Market selling pots and pans. He pays me a share of what I take in and lets me leave the stall to pray. There's a small mosque around the corner on the Jan Hazenstraat. It's called the al-Hijrah Mosque. It has a well-deserved reputation for the extremism of its imam. There are many young men at the al-Hijrah. Young men whose minds are filled with images of jihad and terror. Young men who speak of martyrdom and blood. Young men who look to Osama bin Laden as a true Muslim. These young men believe in *takfir*. You know this term? *Takfir?*"

Gabriel nodded. *Takfir* was a concept developed by Islamists in Egypt in the nineteen seventies, a theological sleight of hand designed to give the terrorists a sacred license to kill almost anyone they pleased in order to achieve their goals of imposing *sharia* and restoring the Caliphate. Its primary target was other Muslims. A secular Muslim leader who did not rule by *sharia* could be killed under *takfir* for having turned away from Islam. So could a citizen of a secular Islamic state or a Muslim residing in a Western democracy. To the *takfiri*, democracy was a heresy, for it supplanted the laws of God with the laws of man; therefore, Muslim citizens of a democracy were apostates and could be put to the sword. It was the concept of *takfir* that gave Osama bin Laden the right to fly airplanes into buildings or blow up embassies in Africa, even if many of his victims were Muslims. It gave the Sunni terrorists of Iraq the right to kill anyone they wanted in order to prevent democracy from taking root in Baghdad. And it gave Muslim boys born in Britain the right to blow themselves up on London subways and buses, even if some of the people they were taking to Paradise with them happened to be other Muslims who wished to remain on earth a little longer.

"There is a leader of these young men," Ibrahim resumed. "He has not been in Amsterdam long—eighteen months, maybe a bit more. He is an Egyptian. He works in an Internet shop and phone center in the Oud West, but he likes to think of himself as an Islamist theoretician and a journalist. He claims to be a writer for Islamist magazines and websites."

"His name?"

"Samir al-Masri—at least that's what he calls himself. He claims to have connections to the mujahideen in Iraq. He tells our boys it is their sacred duty to go there and kill the infidels who have defiled Muslim lands. He lectures them about *takfir* and jihad. At night they gather in his apartment and read Sayyid Qutb and Ibn Taymiyyah. They download videos from the Internet and watch infidels being beheaded. They have taken trips together. A few of them went to Egypt with him. There is talk about Samir in the al-Hijrah. There usually is talk in the mosque, but this is different. Samir al-Masri is a dangerous man. If he is not al-Qaeda, then he is a close relative."

"Where does he live?"

"On the Hudsonstraat. Number thirty-seven. Apartment D."

"Alone?"

Ibrahim tugged thoughtfully at his beard and nodded his head.

"You told Solomon about Samir?"

"Yes, many months ago."

"So why follow me tonight?"

"Because two days ago Samir and four other young men from the al-Hijrah Mosque disappeared."

Gabriel stopped walking and looked at the Egyptian. "Where did they go?"

"I've been asking around, but no one seems to know."

"Do you have the names of the other four men?"

The Egyptian handed Gabriel a slip of paper. "Find them," he said. "Otherwise, I'm afraid buildings are going to fall."

6

OUD WEST, AMSTERDAM

I was really looking forward to that Thai food," said Eli Lavon.

"I'll get you Thai food after we break into Samir's apartment."

"Please tell me where you're going to get me Thai food at three in the morning."

"I'm very resourceful."

Gabriel rubbed a porthole in the fogged windshield and peered out toward the entrance of the Hudsonstraat. Lavon looked down and tugged at the buttons of his overcoat.

"We're not supposed to use rental cars in operational situations unless they're procured from clean sources."

"I know, Eli."

"We're also not supposed to conduct break-ins and crash searches without proper backup or approval from King Saul Boulevard."

"Yes, I've heard that."

"You're bending too many rules. That's how mistakes happen. I was looking forward to spending the night at the Hotel Europa, not a Dutch holding cell."

"Please tell me where I'm supposed to get a clean car and proper backup at three o'clock in the morning in Amsterdam."

"So much for your resourcefulness." Lavon stared gloomily out the window. "Look around, Gabriel. Have you ever seen so many satellite dishes?" He shook his head slowly. "They're monuments to European naïveté. The Europeans thought they could take in millions of immigrants from the poorest regions of the Muslim world and turn them into good little social democrats in a single generation. And look at the results. For the most part the Muslims of Europe are ghettoized and seething with anger."

Trapped between two worlds, thought Gabriel. Not fully Arab. Not quite Dutch. Lost in the land of strangers.

"This place has always been an incubator for violent ideologies," Gabriel said. "Islamic extremism is just the latest virus to thrive in Europe's nurturing environment."

Lavon nodded thoughtfully and blew into his hands. "You know, for a long time after I came back to Israel, I missed Vienna. I missed my coffeehouses. I missed walking down my favorite streets. But I've come to realize that this continent is dying a slow death. Europe is receding quietly into history. It's old and tired, and its young are so pessimistic about the prospects of the future they refuse to have enough children to ensure their own survival. They believe in nothing but their thirty-five-hour workweek and their August vacation."

"And their anti-Semitism," said Gabriel.

"That's the one thing about Vienna I never miss," Lavon said. "The virus of modern anti-Semitism started here in Europe, but after the war it spread to the Arab world, where it mutated and grew stronger. Now Europe and the radical Muslims are passing it back and forth, infecting one another." He looked at Gabriel. "And so here we are again, two nice Jewish boys sitting on a European street corner at three o'clock in the morning. My God, when will it end?"

"It's never going to end, Eli. This is forever."

Lavon pondered this notion in silence for a moment. "Have you given any thought to how you're going to get into the apartment?" he asked.

Gabriel reached into his coat pocket and produced a small metal tool.

"I could never use one of those things," Lavon said.

"I have better hands than you do."

"Best hands in the business—that's what Shamron always said. But I still don't know what you think you're going to find inside. If Samir and his cell are truly operational, the apartment will be sanitized."

"You'd be surprised, Eli. Their masterminds are brilliant, but some of their foot soldiers aren't exactly brain surgeons. They're sloppy. They leave things laying around. They make little mistakes."

"So do intelligence officers," Lavon said. "Have you at least considered the possibility that we're about to walk straight into a trap?"

"That's what Berettas are for."

Gabriel opened the door before Lavon could object again and climbed out of the car. They crossed the boulevard at an angle, pausing once to allow an empty streetcar to rattle past, and rounded the corner into the Hudsonstraat. It was a narrow side street lined with terraces of small tenement buildings. They were two levels in height and Orwellian in their uniformity and ugliness. At the front of each building was a small semicircular alcove with four separate doors, two leading to the apartments on the first floor and two leading to the apartments upstairs.

Gabriel stepped immediately into the alcove of Number 37 and, with Lavon at his back, went to work on the standard five-pin lock on the door for Apartment D. It surrendered ten seconds later. He slipped the lockpick into his pocket and removed the Beretta, then turned the latch and stepped inside. He stood motionless for a moment in the darkness, gun leveled in his outstretched hands, listening for the faintest sound or slightest suggestion of movement. Hearing nothing, he motioned for Lavon to come inside.

Lavon switched on a small Maglite and led the way into the sitting room. The furnishings were of flea market quality, the floor was cracked linoleum, and the walls were bare except for a single travel poster depicting the Dome of the Rock in Jerusalem. Gabriel walked over to the long trestle table that served as Samir's desk. It was empty except for a single yellow legal pad and a cheap desk lamp.

He switched on the lamp and examined the pad. Two-thirds of it had been used and the top page was blank. He moved his fingers over the surface and felt impressions. An amateur's mistake. He handed the pad to Lavon, then took hold of the flashlight and shone it at an angle over the surface of the table. It was covered in a fine layer of dust except for a precise square in the center—the spot, Gabriel reckoned, where Samir's computer had been before his flight from Amsterdam.

"Search the furniture cushions," Gabriel said. "I'll have a look around the rest of the flat."

He went through a doorway into the kitchen. The debris of Samir's final gathering with his acolytes from the al-Hijrah Mosque lay strewn across the linoleum countertops: empty takeaway containers, greasy paper plates, discarded plastic utensils, squashed teabags. Gabriel opened the refrigerator, a favorite terrorist storage space for explosives, and saw that it was empty. The same was true of all the cabinets. He looked in the cupboard beneath the sink and found nothing but an unopened container of kitchen cleaner. Samir, Islamic theoretician and spokesman for the jihadi cause, was a typical bachelor slob.

Gabriel paused for a moment in the sitting room to check on Lavon's progress, then headed down a short hallway toward the back of the apartment. Samir's bathroom was as appalling as the kitchen. Gabriel gave it a rapid search, then entered the bedroom. A stripped mattress lay slightly askew on the metal frame and the three drawers of the dresser were all partially open. Samir, it seemed, had packed in a hurry.

Gabriel removed the top drawer and dumped the remaining contents onto the bed. Threadbare underwear, mismatched socks, a book of matches from a discotheque in London's Leicester Square, an envelope from a photo-processing shop around the corner. Gabriel slipped the matches into his pocket, then opened the envelope and leafed through the prints. He saw Samir in Trafalgar Square and Samir with a member of the Queen's Life Guard outside Buckingham Palace; Samir riding the Millennium Wheel and Samir outside the Houses of Parliament. The last photograph, Samir posing with four friends in front of the American embassy in Grosvenor Square, caused Gabriel's heart to skip a beat.

Five minutes later he was walking calmly along the empty pavements of the Hudsonstraat, with the photographs in his pocket and Lavon at his side. "If the dates on the pictures are correct, it means Samir and his friends were in London four months ago," he said. "Someone should probably go to London to have a word with our friends at MI5."

"I can see where this is heading," Lavon said. "You get to go to ride into London like a knight on a white horse and I get to go blind reading the rest of Solomon Rosner's files."

"At least you get to have your Thai food."

"Why did you have to mention the Thai food?"

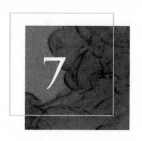

HEATHROW AIRPORT, LONDON

Gabriel had spent much of his life eluding the police forces and security services of Europe, and so it was with considerable reluctance that he agreed to be met at Heathrow Airport the following afternoon by MI5.

He spotted the three-man reception team as he came into the arrivals hall. It was not difficult; they were wearing matching mackintosh raincoats, and one was holding Gabriel's photograph. He had been instructed to let the MI5 men make the approach, so he went to the information kiosk and spent several minutes pretending to scrutinize a list of London hotels. Finally, anxious to deliver his briefing *before* the terrorists struck, he walked over and introduced himself. The officer with the photograph took him by the arm and led him outside to a waiting Jaguar limousine. Gabriel smiled. He had always harbored a secret envy of British spies and their cars.

The rear window slid down a few inches and a long, boney hand beckoned him over. The hand was attached to none other than Graham Seymour, MI5's long-serving and highly regarded deputy director general. He was in his late fifties now and had aged like fine wine. His Savile Row pin-striped suit fit him to perfection, and his

full head of blond hair had a silvery cast to it that gave him the look
of those male models one sees in advertisements for costly but needless trinkets. As Gabriel climbed into the car, Seymour appraised
him silently for a moment with a pair of granite-colored eyes. He did
not look pleased, but then few men in his position would. The
Netherlands, France, Germany, and Spain all had their fair share of
Muslim radicals, but among intelligence professionals there was little disagreement over which country was the epicenter of European
Islamic extremism. It was the country Graham Seymour was sworn
to protect: the United Kingdom.

Gabriel knew that the crisis now facing Britain was many years
in the making and, to a large degree, self-inflicted. For two decades,
beginning in the 1980s and continuing even after the attacks of 9/11,
British governments both Labour and Tory had thrown open their
doors to the world's most hardened holy warriors. Cast out by countries such as Egypt, Saudi Arabia, Jordan, and Syria, they had come
to London, where they were free to publish, preach, organize, con-
spire, and raise money. As a result, Great Britain, the land of John
Locke, William Shakespeare, and Winston Churchill, had unwittingly allowed itself to become the primary incubator of a violent ide-
ology that sought to destroy everything for which it had once stood.
The British security and intelligence services, confronted by a gathering storm, had responded by choosing the path of accommodation
rather than resistance. Extremism was tolerated so long as it was directed *outward*, toward the secular Arab regimes, America, and, of
course, Israel. The failure of this policy of appeasement had been
held up for all the world to see on July 7, 2005, when three bombs
exploded inside the London Underground and a fourth tore a London city bus to shreds in Russell Square. Fifty-two people were killed
and seven hundred more wounded. The perpetrators of this bloodbath were not destitute Muslims from abroad but middle-class
British boys who had turned on the country of their birth. And all
evidence suggested it was only their opening salvo. Her Majesty's security services estimated the number of terrorists residing in Britain

at sixteen thousand—three thousand of whom had actually trained in al-Qaeda camps—and recent intelligence suggested that the United Kingdom had eclipsed America and Israel as al-Qaeda's primary target.

"It's funny," said Seymour, "but when we checked the manifest for the flight from Amsterdam we didn't see anyone on the list named Gabriel Allon."

"Obviously you didn't look hard enough."

The MI5 man held out his hand.

"Let's not do this, Graham. Haven't we more pressing matters to deal with than the name on my passport?"

"Give it to me."

Gabriel surrendered his passport and stared out the window at the traffic rushing along the A4. It was 3:30 in the afternoon and already dark. No wonder the Arabs turned to radicals when they moved here, he thought. Perhaps it was light deprivation that drove them to jihad and terror.

Graham Seymour opened the passport and recited the particulars. "Heinrich Kiever. Place of birth, Berlin." He looked up at Gabriel. "East or West?"

"Herr Kiever is definitely a man of the West."

"We had an agreement, Allon."

"Yes, I know."

"It stated that we would grant you absolution for your multitude of sins in exchange for a simple commitment on your part—that you would inform us when you were coming to our fair shores and that you would refrain from conducting operations on our soil without obtaining our permission and cooperation beforehand."

"I'm sitting in the back of an MI5 limousine. How much more cooperation and notification do you require?"

"What about the passport?"

"It's nice, isn't it?"

"Do the Germans know you're abusing their travel documents?"

"We abuse yours, too, Graham. It's what we do."

"*We* don't do it. SIS makes a point of traveling only on British or Commonwealth passports."

"How sporting of them," Gabriel said. "But it's far easier to travel the world on a British passport than it is on an Israeli one. Safer, too. Take a trip to Syria or Lebanon some time on an Israeli passport. It's an experience you'll never forget."

"Smart-ass." Seymour handed the passport to Gabriel. "What were you doing in Amsterdam?"

"Some personal business."

"Elaborate, please."

"I'm afraid I can't."

"Did the Dutch know you were there?"

"Not exactly."

"I'll take that as a no."

"I always heard you were good, Graham."

Seymour pulled his face into a fatigued frown, a sign that he'd had enough of the verbal sparring match. The inhospitality of his reception came as little surprise to Gabriel. The British services did not care much for the Office. They were Arabists by education, anti-Semites by breeding, and still resented the Jews for driving the Empire out of Palestine.

"What have you got for me, Gabriel?"

"I think an al-Qaeda cell from Amsterdam might have entered Britain in the last forty-eight hours with the intention of carrying out a major attack."

"Just one cell?" Seymour quipped. "I'm sure they'll feel right at home."

"That bad, Graham?"

Seymour nodded his gray head. "At last count we were monitoring more than two hundred networks and separate groupings of known terrorists. Half our Muslim youth profess admiration for Osama bin Laden, and we estimate that more than one hundred thousand supported the attacks on the London transport system, which means they have a very large pool of potential recruits from which to draw in the future. So you'll excuse me if I don't sound the alarm just because another cell of Muslim fanatics has decided to put ashore."

"Maybe it isn't *just* another cell, Graham. Maybe they're the real thing."

"They're all the real thing," Seymour said. "You said you *think* they're here. Does that mean you're not sure?"

"I'm afraid so."

"So let me make sure I understand correctly. I have sixteen thousand *known* Islamic terrorists residing in my country, but I'm supposed to divert manpower and resources into finding a cell that you *think* might be in Britain?" Greeted by silence, Graham Seymour answered his own question. "If it were anyone but you, I'd pull over and let him out. But you do have something of a track record, don't you? What makes you think they might be here?"

Gabriel handed him the envelope of photographs.

"This is all you have? Some snapshots of Ahmed's holiday in London? No train tickets? No rental car receipts? No e-mail intercepts? No visual or audio surveillance?"

"They were here on a surveillance mission four months ago. And his name isn't Ahmed. It's Samir."

"Samir what?"

"Samir al-Masri, Hudsonstraat 37, Oud West, Amsterdam."

Seymour looked at the photo of Samir standing in front of the Houses of Parliament. "Is he Dutch?"

"Egyptian, as far we know."

"As far as you know? What about the other members of this phantom cell? You have any names?"

Gabriel handed him a slip of paper with the other names Ibrahim Fawaz had given him in Amsterdam. "Based on what we know, the cell was operating out of the al-Hijrah Mosque on the Jan Hazenstraat in west Amsterdam."

"And you're sure he's Egyptian?"

"That's the flag he was flying in Amsterdam. Why?"

"Because we've been picking up some chatter recently among some of our more radical Egyptian countrymen."

"What sort of chatter?"

"Blowing up buildings, bringing down bridges and airplanes, killing a few thousand people on the Underground—you know, the usual things people discuss over tea and biscuits."

"Where's it coming from?"

Seymour hesitated, then said, "Finsbury Park."

"But of course."

There was perhaps no more appropriate symbol of Britain's current predicament than the North London Central Mosque, known commonly as the Finsbury Park mosque. Built in 1990 with money donated by the king of Saudi Arabia, it was among the most radical in Europe. Richard Reid, the infamous shoe-bomber, had passed through its doors; so had Zacarias Moussaoui, the so-called twentieth hijacker, and Ahmed Ressam, the Algerian terrorist who was arrested shortly before the millennium for plotting to blow up Los Angeles International Airport. British police raided the mosque in January 2003—inside they discovered such sacred items as forged passports, chemical-protective suits, and a stun gun—and eventually it was turned over to new leadership. It was later revealed that one member of the new board of trustees was a former Hamas terror mastermind from the West Bank. When the former terrorist gave the British government assurances that he was now a man of peace, he was permitted to remain in his post.

"So you think Samir is the cell leader?"

"That's what my source tells me."

"Has your source ever been right in the past?"

"Do you remember that plot to shoot down an El Al jetliner at Schiphol last year?"

"The one that the Dutch broke up?"

"The *Dutch* didn't break it up, Graham. *We* broke it up, with the help of this same source."

Seymour looked down at the photographs. "It's not much to go on," he said, "but I'm afraid it does fit the profile of a major attack scenario we've developed."

"What sort of scenario?"

"An action cell based abroad, working with surveillance and support cells buried within the local community here. The action cell members train and prepare in a place where we can't monitor them, then come ashore at the last minute, so we have no time to find them and disrupt their plans. Obviously it would take complex planning and a skilled mastermind to pull it off." He held up the snapshots. "Can I keep these?"

"They're yours."

"I'll have Immigration run the names and see if your boys have actually entered the country, and I'll give copies of the pictures to our colleagues in the Anti-Terrorist Branch of Scotland Yard. If the Metropolitan Police deem the threat credible, they might put a few more men at some of the sites al-Masri visited."

"What about raising the overall threat level?" Gabriel asked. "What about stepping up the surveillance of your local Egyptian radicals in Finsbury Park?"

"We're not like our American brethren. We don't like to move the needle on the threat meter each time we get nervous. We find it only serves to make the British public more cynical. As for our local Egyptians, we're watching them closely enough already."

"I hope so."

"How long are you planning to stay in London?"

"Just tonight."

Seymour handed him a business card. It had nothing on it but a telephone number. "It's for my mobile. Call me if you pick up anything else in Amsterdam. Can I drop you at your hotel?"

"No thanks, Graham."

"How about your safe flat?"

"Our embassy would be fine. I'm going to have a quiet word with our local chief of station and the head of embassy security to make sure *we* take appropriate measures."

"Give my best to your station chief. And tell him to behave himself."

"Is it your intention to follow me after I leave the embassy?"

"I don't have the spare manpower or I would."

He was lying, of course. Honor among spies went only so far.

. . .

Gabriel's meetings at the embassy ran longer than expected. The chief of security had turned what should have been a five-minute briefing into an hour-long question-and-answer period, while the Office's chief of station had used a routine courtesy call as an opportunity to try to impress the man he clearly assumed would one day be his boss. The debacle was made complete at six, when the ambassador appeared without warning and insisted Gabriel accompany him to dinner in Knightsbridge. Gabriel had no excuse at the ready and was forced to endure a painfully boring evening discussing the intricacies of Israel's ties to the United Kingdom. Throughout the meal he thought often of Eli Lavon quietly reading files in snowy Amsterdam and wished that he was still there with him.

It was after ten o'clock by the time he finally entered the Office safe flat on the Bayswater Road overlooking Hyde Park. He left his bag in the entrance hall and quickly took stock of his surroundings. It was simply furnished, as most safe flats were, and rather large by London standards. Housekeeping had left food in the fridge and a 9mm Beretta in the pantry, along with a spare magazine and two boxes of ammunition.

Gabriel loaded the gun and carried it with him into the bedroom. It had been three days since he'd had a proper night's sleep and it had taken all his training and substantial powers of concentration to get through dinner with the ambassador without falling asleep over his coq au vin. He undressed quickly and climbed into bed, then switched on the television and turned the volume down very low so that if there was an attack in the night he would be awakened by the news bulletins. He wondered whether the Metropolitan Police had acted yet on the information he'd brought from Amsterdam. *Two hundred active terror networks, sixteen thousand known terrorists, three thousand men who had been through the training camps of al-Qaeda . . .* MI5 and the Met had more to worry about than five boys from Amsterdam. He'd sensed something in Graham Seymour's demeanor that afternoon, a resignation that it was only a matter of time before London was hit again.

Gabriel was reaching for the light when he noticed Samir's yellow legal pad poking from the side flap of his overnight bag. *Probably nothing there,* he thought, but he knew himself well enough to realize that he would never be able to sleep unless he made certain. He found a pencil in the top drawer of the bedside table and spent the next ten minutes rubbing it gently over the surface of the pad. Samir's secrets came slowly to life before his eyes. Pine trees on a mountaintop, sand dunes in a desert, a spider web of bisecting lines. Samir al-Masri, jihadist and bachelor slob, was a doodler.

8

BAYSWATER, LONDON:
7:02 A.M., FRIDAY

The telephone woke him. Like all phones in Office safe flats, it had a flashing light to indicate incoming calls. This one was luminous blue. It was as if a squad car had driven into his bedroom on silent approach.

"Are you awake?" asked Ari Shamron.

"I am now."

"Sleeping in?"

Gabriel squinted at his wristwatch. "It's seven in the morning."

"It's nine here."

The vagaries of international time zones had always meant little to Shamron. He assumed every Office employee, no matter his location on the planet, rose and slept in harmony with him. Inside the Office the phenomenon was known as "Shamron Central Time."

"How did your meeting with Graham Seymour go?"

"Remind me never to use my Heinrich Kiever passport to enter Britain again."

"Did he act on the information you gave him?"

"He seems to have bigger headaches than a few boys from west Amsterdam."

"He does."

"We're going to have to bring the Dutch into the picture at some point."

"As soon as Eli is finished purging Rosner's archives, we'll summon the Dutch liaison officer in Tel Aviv and have a quiet word with him."

"Just make sure we protect our source. He's someone we need to slip in our back pocket for a rainy day."

"Don't worry—it will be a *very* quiet word."

"My plane arrives in Amsterdam in the early afternoon. If Eli and I work through the night, we should be finished by morning."

"I'm afraid Eli will have to finish the job without you. You're not going back to Amsterdam."

"Where am I going?"

"Home," said Shamron. "A *bodel* will collect you in an hour and take you to Heathrow. And don't get off the plane looking like something the cat dragged in, the way you usually do. We're having dinner together tonight at Kaplan Street."

Kaplan Street was the address of the Prime Minister's Office.

"Why are we having dinner there?"

"If it's all the same with you, I'd rather not discuss our highest affairs of state and intelligence while the eavesdroppers of MI5 and GCHQ are trying to listen in."

"It's a secure phone."

"There's no such thing," Shamron said. "Just make sure you're on that plane. If you get stuck in traffic, call me from the car. I'll have El Al hold the plane for you."

"You wouldn't."

The line went dead. Gabriel placed the receiver back in the cradle. *We're having dinner together tonight at Kaplan Street . . .* He supposed he knew what the topic of conversation would be. Apparently Amos didn't have long to live. He looked at the television screen. Three telegenic young people were engaged in a deeply serious discussion about the sexual antics of Britain's most famous footballer.

Gabriel groped for the remote control and instead found Samir's legal pad. Then he remembered waking in the middle of the night and gazing at the image—not the pine trees and the sand dunes but the pattern of crisscrossing lines.

He looked at it again now. Gabriel had been blessed with near-perfect visual recall, a skill enhanced by his study of art history and his work as a restorer. He had hundreds of thousands of paintings stored in the file rooms of his memory and could authenticate a work simply by examining a few brushstrokes. He was convinced the lines were not random but part of a pattern—and he was certain he had seen the pattern somewhere before.

He went into the kitchen and made coffee, then carried his cup over to the window. It was beginning to get light, and the London morning rush was in full force. A woman who looked too much like his former wife was standing on the corner, waiting for the light to change. When it did, she crossed the Bayswater Road and disappeared into Hyde Park.

Hyde Park . . .

He looked at the notepad, then looked out the window again.

Was it possible?

He walked over to the desk and opened the top drawer. Inside was a *London A–Z* street atlas. He took it out and opened it to map number 82. It showed the northeast corner of Hyde Park and the surrounding streets of Mayfair, Marylebone, Bayswater, and St. John's Wood. The footpaths of the park were represented with dotted lines. Gabriel compared the pattern to Samir's markings on the legal pad.

They matched perfectly.

Hyde Park . . .

But why would a terrorist want to attack a park?

He thought of the pictures he'd found in Samir's flat: Samir in Trafalgar Square. Samir with a member of the Queen's Life Guard outside Buckingham Palace. Samir riding the Millennium Wheel. Samir outside the Houses of Parliament. Samir with four friends posing in front of the American embassy in Grosvenor Square . . .

He looked at the map in the *London A–Z* again.

Grosvenor Square was two blocks east of the park in Mayfair.

He picked up the telephone and dialed.

.   .   .

"Graham Seymour."

"I want you to warn the Americans about the Amsterdam cell."

"What Amsterdam cell?"

"Come on, Graham—there isn't time."

"Immigration spent the night looking for them. So far they've come up with no evidence to suggest any of the men whose names you gave me are even in the country."

"That doesn't mean they're not here."

"Why do you think they're going to go after the Americans?"

Gabriel told him.

"You want me to sound the alarm at Grosvenor Square because of some lines on a legal pad?"

"Yes."

"I'm not going to do that. There's not enough evidence to support making a call like that. Besides, have you been to Grosvenor Square lately? It's an American fortress now. A terrorist can't get close to that building."

"Call them, Graham. If you don't, I will."

"Listen to me, Allon, and listen very carefully. If you make a mess of my town, so help me God, I'll—"

Gabriel severed the connection and dialed another number.

9

GROSVENOR SQUARE,
LONDON: 7:13 A.M., FRIDAY

The streets at the northern end of posh Mayfair
have a distinctly American flavor. Tucked
amid the stately Georgian buildings one can find the headquarters
of the American Chamber of Commerce, the American Club, the
American Church, the American Society, and the Society of American Women. Along the northern side of Grosvenor Square is the U.S.
Navy building, and on the western side stands the American embassy. Nine stories in height and adorned by a monstrous gilded
eagle, it is one of the largest American diplomatic missions in the
world and the only one to reside on land not owned by the federal
government. The Duke of Westminster, who owns most of Mayfair,
leases the property to the American government for the very reasonable sum of a single peppercorn a year. There is little danger the
Americans will be evicted from their patch of Mayfair any time soon,
since the lease on the property does not expire until Christmas Day
in the year 2953.

Fifty-eight men and a single woman have served as the American
ambassador to the Court of St. James's—including five who would

become president—but only one has ever come from the ranks of the career Foreign Service. The rest have been political appointees and diplomatic debutants, known more for their money and connections than their foreign policy expertise. Their names read like an honor roll of American high society and wealth: Mellon, Kennedy, Harriman, Aldrich, Bruce, Whitney, and Annenberg.

The current American ambassador to the Court of St. James's, Robert Carlyle Halton, was not born to wealth, and few Americans knew his name, though he was by far the richest man to ever occupy the post and his political connections were second to none. The president and CEO of the Denver-based Red Mountain Energy, Halton's personal fortune exceeded five billion dollars at last estimate. He also happened to be a lifelong friend of the president of the United States and his largest political donor. The *Washington Post*, in a rather unflattering profile of Halton published shortly after his nomination, declared that he "had pulled off the extraordinary political feat of putting his best friend in the White House." When asked about the accuracy of the report during his confirmation hearings, Halton said he only wished he had been able to give the president more money, a remark that had cost him several Democratic votes.

Despite the fact Robert Halton was no longer responsible for a global energy empire, he remained an early riser and kept a rigorous daily schedule that was far more punishing than those of his predecessors. As usual that morning, he had left Winfield House, his official residence in Regent's Park, at the thoroughly undiplomatic hour of 6:45, and by seven he was leafing through the London papers at his desk overlooking Grosvenor Square. The pages were filled with dire news from Iraq. Halton was convinced the British, who had already made drastic cuts to their troop levels in Iraq, would soon be looking for the exits entirely, an assessment he had given directly to the president during their last meeting at Halton's sprawling Owl Creek estate in Aspen. Halton hadn't minced words during the meeting. He rarely did.

At 7:10, a tall young woman dressed in a cold-weather tracksuit and fleece headband appeared in his doorway. She had long dark hair, pale green eyes set in an attractive face, and a trim athletic figure. Without waiting for permission to enter, she crossed the room and sat on the arm of Halton's chair. It was a gesture of obvious intimacy, one that might have raised eyebrows among the embassy staff were it not for the fact that the attractive woman's name was Elizabeth Halton. She kissed the ambassador's cheek and smoothed his head of thick gray hair.

"Good morning, Daddy," she said. "Anything interesting in the papers?"

Robert Halton held up the *Times*. "The mayor of London is angry at me again."

"What's eating Red Ken now?"

Halton's relations with London's infamously left-wing mayor were frosty at best—hardly surprising, given the fact that the mayor had expressed compassion for the suicide bombers of Hamas and had once publicly embraced a Muslim Brotherhood leader who had called for the murder of Jews and other infidels.

"He says our security is causing major disruptions to the flow of traffic throughout Mayfair," Robert Halton said. "He wants us to pay a congestion tax. He's suggesting I pay for it out of my personal funds. He's quite sure I won't miss the money."

"You won't."

"That's not the point."

"Shall I have a word with him?"

"I wouldn't inflict that on my worst enemy."

"I can be a charmer."

"He doesn't deserve you, darling."

Robert Halton smiled and stroked his daughter's cheek. The two had been nearly inseparable since the death of Halton's wife five years earlier in a private-plane crash in northern Alaska—so inseparable, in fact, that Halton had refused to accept the president's offer to become his envoy to London until first making certain Elizabeth would accompany him. While most young women would have leaped at the chance to live in London as the daughter of the American ambassador, Elizabeth had been reluctant to leave Colorado. She was one of the most highly regarded emergency-room surgeons in Denver and was discussing marriage with a successful real estate developer. She had wavered for several weeks, until one evening, while on duty at Denver's Rose Medical Center, she had received a call from the White House on her mobile phone. "I need your father in London," the president had said. "What do I have to say to you to make that happen?"

Few people were better positioned to turn down a request from the commander in chief than Elizabeth Halton. She had known the president her entire life. She had skied with him in Aspen and hunted deer with him in Montana. She had been toasted by him on the day she graduated from medical school and comforted by him on the day her mother was buried. But she had not turned him down, of course, and upon her arrival in London had thrown herself into the assignment with the same determination and skill with which she approached every other challenge in life. She ruled Winfield House with an iron hand and was nearly always on her father's arm at official events and important social affairs. She did volunteer work in London hospitals—especially those that served the poor immigrant communities—and was a skillful public advocate for American policy in Iraq and the broader war on terror. She was as popular with the London press as her father was loathed, despite the fact that the *Guardian* had published a little-known fact that Elizabeth, for reasons of security, had tried to keep secret. The president of the United States was her godfather.

"Why don't you skip the newspapers this morning and come out for a run with us?" She patted his midsection. "You're starting to put on weight again."

"I'm having coffee with the foreign secretary at nine. And don't forget we're having drinks at Downing Street tonight."

"I won't forget."

Robert Halton folded his newspaper and looked at his daughter seriously.

"I want you and your friends to be careful out there. NCTC raised the threat level in Europe yesterday."

NCTC was the National Counterterrorism Center.

"Anything specific?"

"It was vague. Heightened activity among known al-Qaeda cells. The usual crap. But that doesn't mean we should ignore it. Take a couple Marines with you for good measure."

"The Marines are only supposed to guard the embassy itself. If they start leaving the premises, Scotland Yard will throw a fit. And I'll be back on the treadmill in the gym."

"There's no law against American Marines running in Hyde Park—at least, not yet. I suppose if Red Ken has his way there will be soon." He tossed the newspaper onto his desk. "What's on your calendar for today?"

"A conference on African health care issues and afternoon tea at the Houses of Parliament."

"Still glad we came to London?"

"I wouldn't have traded it for the world." She stood up and headed toward the door. "Give my best to the foreign secretary."

"Don't forget drinks at Downing Street."

"I won't forget."

Elizabeth left her father's office and rode the elevator down to the atrium. Four other people, attired as she was in cold-weather athletic suits, were already there: Jack Hammond, the embassy's public affairs officer; Alex Baker, an FBI special agent who served as legal affairs liaison, Paul Foreman from Consular, and Chris Petty from the State Department's Bureau of Diplomatic Security. Petty served as London's Regional Security Officer, which meant he was responsible for the safety of the embassy and its staff. Two of Petty's assistant RSOs arrived a moment later. Their matching blue tracksuits did little to conceal the fact that they were powerfully built and well armed.

"Where's Kevin?" Elizabeth asked.

Kevin Barnett, the CIA's deputy chief of station, rarely missed the morning run when he was in town.

"Stuck in his office," said Chris Petty.

"Anything to do with that NCTC alert?"

Petty smiled. "How did you know about that?"

"I'm the ambassador's daughter, Chris."

Alex Baker looked at his watch. "Let's get rolling. I have a nine o'clock at New Scotland Yard."

They headed outside and slipped through a gate in the north fence reserved for embassy personnel. A moment later they were jogging west along Upper Brook Street, heading for Hyde Park.

.   .   .

The Ford Transit panel van was painted forest green and bore a stencil on the side that read: ADDISON & HODGE LTD. ROYAL PARKS CONTRACTORS. The van did not belong to Addison & Hodge but was a meticulously produced forgery, just like a second one already inside Hyde Park. As the group of Americans came trotting along Upper Brook Street, the man behind the wheel watched them calmly, then pressed a button on his mobile phone and brought it to his ear. The conversation he conducted was coded and brief. When it was over he slipped the phone into the pocket of his coverall—also a forgery— and started the engine. He entered the park through a restricted access point and made his way to a stand of trees north of the Serpentine lake. A sign read AUTHORIZED VEHICLES ONLY, and warned of heavy fines for violators. The man behind the wheel climbed out and started collecting rubbish, praying softly to himself while he worked. *In the name of Allah, the beneficent, the merciful . . . master of the day of judgment . . . show us the straight path . . .*

CIA HEADQUARTERS: 2:32 A.M., FRIDAY

Later, during the inevitable Congressional inquiry, much emphasis would be placed on determining precisely when and how the intelligence services of the United States first became aware of the calamity about to befall London. The answer was 2:32 A.M. local time, when a telephone call from an individual identified only as an FIS, or "foreign intelligence source," arrived on an emergency line in the seventh-floor executive suite of CIA Headquarters in Langley, Virginia. The foreign intelligence source, though never identified, was Gabriel, and the emergency line he dialed belonged to none other than Adrian Carter, the CIA's deputy director of operations. In normal times, the call would have been automatically transferred to Carter's home in nearby McLean. But these were hardly normal times, and, in spite of the appalling hour, Carter was standing in the window of his office anxiously awaiting word on the outcome of a sensitive operation under way in the mountains of Pakistan.

Aside from the grand view toward the Potomac, there was little about Carter's lair to suggest it belonged to one of the most powerful members of Washington's vast intelligence establishment. Nor would one have guessed as much from Carter's rather churchy appearance. Only a handful of people in Washington knew that Adrian Carter spoke seven languages fluently and could understand at least seven more. Or that Carter, before his ascension to the rarified atmosphere of Langley's seventh floor, had been one of his nation's most faithful clandestine warriors. His fingerprints were on every major American covert operation of the last generation. He'd tinkered with the odd election, toppled the odd government, and turned a blind eye to more executions and murders than he could count. Morality had rarely entered into Carter's calculus. Carter was Operations. Carter didn't make policy, he simply carried it out. How else to explain that, within the span of a single year, he'd done the Lord's work in Poland and propped up the Devil's regime in Salvador? Or that he'd showered dollars and Stingers on the Muslim holy warriors in Afghanistan, even though he knew one day they would rain fire and death on him.

These days, longevity was Carter's most notable achievement. The sages of Langley liked to joke that the war on terror had claimed more lives in the Operations Directorate than in the top ranks of al-Qaeda. Not Carter's, though. He had survived the blood purges and the nights of long knives and even the horrors of reorganization. The secret to his endurance lay in the fact that he had been right far more often than he had been wrong. In the summer of 2001, he had warned that al-Qaeda was planning a major attack on American soil. In the winter of 2003, he had cautioned that some of the sources regarding Iraq's weapons program were suspect, only to be overruled by his director. And as war loomed in Mesopotamia, he had written a secret memorandum forecasting that Iraq would become another Afghanistan, a proving ground for the next generation of jihadists, a generation that would ultimately be more violent and unpredictable than the last. Carter laid claim to no special powers of analysis, only a clarity of thinking when it came to the intentions of his enemy. Fifteen years earlier, in a mud hut outside Peshawar, a man with a turban and a beard had told him that one day the forces of Islam would turn America to ashes. Carter had believed him.

And so it was this Carter—Carter the secret warrior, Carter the survivor, Carter the pessimist—who, in the early morning of that ill-fated Friday in December, wearily brought his telephone to his ear expecting news from a distant land. Instead he heard the voice of Gabriel, warning that there was about to be an attack in London. And Carter believed him.

. . .

Carter jotted down Gabriel's number, then severed the connection and immediately dialed the operations desk at the National Coun-terterrorism Center.

"How credible is the information?" the duty officer asked.

"Credible enough for me to be calling you at two thirty-four in the morning." Carter tried to keep his temper in check. "Get the RSO at the embassy on the phone immediately and tell him to put the en-tire compound and staff on lockdown until we get a better handle on the situation."

Carter hung up before the duty officer could pose another inane question and sat there for a moment, feeling utterly helpless. *To hell with the NCTC*, he thought. He would take matters into his own hands. He dialed the CIA station at the London embassy and a mo-ment later was talking directly to Kevin Barnett, the deputy COS. Barnett, when he spoke for the first time, sounded deeply shaken.

"There's a group of embassy personnel that does a run in Hyde Park every morning."

"You're sure?"

"I'm usually one of them."

"Who else goes?"

"The chief press officer, the FBI liaison, the Regional Security Officer . . ."

"Jesus Christ," Carter snapped.

"It gets worse."

"How much worse?"

"Elizabeth Halton."

"The ambassador's daughter?"

"I'm afraid so."

"What time do they leave?"

"Seven-fifteen sharp."

Carter looked at his watch. It was 7:36 in London.

"Get them back inside the embassy, Kevin. Run over to Hyde Park and do it yourself if you have to."

The next sound Carter heard was the sound of the deputy COS in London slamming down the phone. Carter hung up, waited ten seconds, and called Gabriel back.

"I think I may have a group of diplomats running in Hyde Park at the moment," he said. "How quickly can you get down there?"

Carter heard another click.

.   .   .

They had entered the park through Brook Gate, headed south along Broad Walk to Hyde Park Corner, then westward along Rotten Row, past the Rose Garden and the Dell. Elizabeth Halton moved to the front of the pack when they reached the Albert Memorial; then, with a DS agent at her side, she steadily increased the pace as they headed north up Lancaster Walk to Bayswater Road. Jack Hammond, the embassy spokesman, slipped past Elizabeth and pushed the pace hard to Victoria Gate, then down the West Carriage Drive to the shore of the Serpentine. As they approached the boathouses, a mobile phone began to ring. It belonged to Chris Petty, the RSO.

.   .   .

They looked like ordinary rolling suitcases. They were not. The sides and wheels had been reinforced to accommodate the weight of the explosives, and the buttons on the collapsible handles had been wired to the detonators. The bags were now in the possession of

four men who, at that moment, were approaching four separate targets: the Underground stations at Piccadilly Circus, Leicester Square,
Charing Cross, and Marble Arch. The men knew nothing of each
other but had much in common. All four were Egyptian. All four
were *takfiri* Muslims who embraced death as much as the infidels
loved life. And all four were wearing Seiko digital watches that
would sound an alarm at precisely 7:40 A.M.

· · ·

It took two minutes for Gabriel to dress and get the Beretta and another minute to make his way downstairs to the street. The traffic signal along the Bayswater Road was blinking red when he arrived. He
ignored it and sprinted through the oncoming traffic into the park.
Just then he heard the rumble of an explosion deep underground and
felt the earth shift suddenly beneath his feet. He stopped for a moment, uncertain of what he had just heard and felt, then turned and
raced toward the center of the park.

· · ·

Chris Petty slowed to a stop and pulled the phone out of the clip attached to the waist of his sweatpants.

"You guys go ahead," he called out. "Take the usual route. I'll
catch up if I can."

The rest of the group turned away from the shore of the Serpentine and headed into the stand of trees north of the lake. Petty looked
at the caller ID screen. It was his office inside the embassy. He opened
the phone and brought it quickly to his ear.

"Petty."

Static . . .

"This is Chris Petty. Can you hear me?"

Silence . . .

"Shit."

He killed the connection and set off after the others. Twenty seconds later the phone rang again. This time, when he raised it to his ear, the connection was perfect.

.   .   .

The man in the Addison & Hodge uniform collecting rubbish along the pathway looked up as the group of runners turned onto the foot-path leading from the Old Police House to the Reformers' Tree. The second false Addison & Hodge van was parked on the opposite side of the path, and another uniformed man was scratching at the earth with a rake. They had been preparing for this moment for over a year. *Thirty seconds*, the operational planner had said. *If it lasts more than thirty seconds, you'll never make it out of the park alive.* The man reached into the plastic rubbish bag he was holding in his hand and felt something metallic and cold: a Heckler & Koch MP7 machine pistol, loaded with forty armor-piercing rounds. He blindly thumbed the fire-selector switch to the proper setting and counted slowly to ten.

.   .   .

Whether it was by design or accident, Chris Petty failed to terminate the telephone call from the embassy before setting off in pursuit of his colleagues. He saw them almost immediately after making the turn at the Old Police House. They had covered about half the dis-tance to the Reformers' Tree and were approaching a pair of forest green Ford Transit vans parked along the edge of the path. It was not unusual to see workmen in the park early in the morning—Hyde Park was 350 acres in size and required near-constant care and maintenance—but their true purpose was revealed a few seconds later when the rear cargo doors swung open and eight well-armed men in black jumpsuits and balaclava hoods poured out. Petty's fu-tile warning shouts were heard and recorded inside the RSO ops center, as was the sound of gunfire and screaming that followed. Petty was hit ten seconds after the initial burst and his death agonies were captured on the center's digital recorders. He managed to say only one word before succumbing to his wounds, though it would be several minutes before his stricken colleagues inside the embassy understood its meaning. *Gardeners* . . .

. . .

Gabriel heard the first shots while he was still in the open ground at the northern edge of the park. He drew his Beretta as he sprinted into the trees, then stopped on the footpath and looked in the direction of the Reformers' Tree. Fifty yards away was a scene from his nightmares: bodies on the ground, men in black jumpsuits pulling a struggling woman toward the back of a waiting van. He raised the gun but stopped himself. Was this truly the attack or had he stumbled into a police drill or the set of an action film? Were the men in black really terrorists or were they police officers or actors? The closest body lay thirty yards away. On the ground next to the man were a mobile phone and a SIG-Sauer P226 9mm pistol. Gabriel crept quickly to the fallen man's side and knelt beside him. The blood and bullet wounds were real, as was the look of death in the man's frozen eyes. He knew then that this was not a drill or a film set. It was the attack he had feared, and it was unfolding before his eyes.

The terrorists had not noticed him. Gabriel, still on one knee, leveled the Beretta in both hands and took aim at one of the black-suited men pulling the woman toward the van. It was thirty yards, a shot he had made countless times before. He squeezed his trigger twice in quick succession, *tap-tap*, just as he had been trained to do. An instant later there was a flash of pink and the man spiraled lifelessly to the ground, like a toy released by the hand of a child. Gabriel moved his aim a degree to the right and fired again. Another flash of blood and brain tissue. Another attacker gone.

This time there was answering fire. Gabriel rolled off the footpath and took cover behind the trunk of a tree as a hailstorm of gunfire tore the bark to shreds. When the firing stopped, he pivoted from behind the tree and saw that the terrorists had succeeded in getting the woman into the back of the van. One was closing the rear cargo door; the others were scurrying toward the second van. Gabriel took aim at the one closing the door and fired. The first shot hit the terrorist in the left shoulder blade, spinning him around. The second struck in the center of the chest.

The vans shot forward and started across the broad green, toward Marble Arch and the busy intersection at the northeast corner of the park. Gabriel rose to his feet and sprinted after them, then stopped and fired several shots into the back of the van that he knew contained only terrorists. The vans continued toward the perimeter of the park. Gabriel gave chase for a few more seconds; then, realizing he could not possibly close the gap, he turned and ran back to the site of the assault.

Nine bodies lay scattered over the blood-soaked footpath. The six Americans were all dead, as were the two terrorists that Gabriel had taken down with head shots. The one who a moment ago had been forcing the woman into the back of the van now lay gasping for breath, blood pouring from the mouth of his balaclava. Gabriel kicked the machine pistol from his grasp and tore the hood from his head. The face staring up at him was vaguely familiar. Then he realized it was Samir al-Masri, the Egyptian from west Amsterdam.

The Egyptian's eyes were beginning to lose focus. Gabriel wanted something from him before he died. He lifted the Egyptian by the front of his jumpsuit and slapped him hard across the face.

"Where are they taking her, Samir? Tell me what you're going to do with the girl!"

The eyes focused for a moment.

"How do you know my name?"

"I know everything, Samir. Where are they taking the girl?"

He managed a mocking smile. "If you know everything, then why are you asking me?"

Gabriel hit him again, harder this time, and shook him so violently he feared he may have broken his neck. It didn't matter. Samir was dying. Gabriel pointed the gun into his face and screamed, "Where are they taking her, you motherfucker! Tell me before I blow your head off!"

But Samir only smiled again, not a mocking smile but the sublime grin of a man who had achieved his desire to die. Gabriel had brought him to death's doorway and was only too happy to see him through to the other side. He placed the barrel of the Beretta to the terrorist's face and was about to pull the trigger when he heard a voice behind him shouting: "Drop the gun and put your hands in the air."

Gabriel released the Egyptian, then laid the Beretta on the ground and slowly raised his hands. His memory of what transpired next would be vague at best. He remembered being driven forward into the ground and could recall the sight of Samir's dead eyes staring into this own. Then someone hit him in the back of the head, a heavy blow that seemed to split his skull in two. He felt a burst of excruciating pain and saw a flash of brilliant light. Then he saw a woman, a woman in a dark blue tracksuit, being led into a valley of ashes by murderers in black hoods.

.   .   .

The telephone call arrived in the Family Quarters on the second floor of the White House at 3:14 A.M. The president snatched the receiver from the cradle after the first ring and brought it quickly to his ear. He immediately recognized the voice at the other end of the line: Cyrus Mansfield, his national security advisor.

"I'm afraid there's been another attack in London, Mr. President."

"How bad?"

Mansfield answered the question to the best of his ability. The president closed his eyes and whispered, "My God."

"The British are doing everything they can to seal off London and prevent them from escaping," Mansfield said. "But as you might expect, the situation is extremely chaotic."

"Activate the Situation Room. I'll be downstairs in five minutes."

"Yes, sir."

The president hung up the phone and sat up in bed. When he switched on the bedside lamp, his wife stirred and looked at his face. She had seen the expression before.

"How bad?" she asked.

"London has been hit again." He hesitated. "And Elizabeth Halton has been taken hostage."

PART
TWO

THE LAND OF
STRANGERS

New Scotland Yard:
12:26 a.m., Saturday

I wouldn't complain too much about a nasty bump on the head."

Graham Seymour's limousine lurched out of the forecourt of New Scotland Yard, headquarters of the Metropolitan Police, and turned into Broadway. The MI5 man looked very tired. He had a right to. Bombs had exploded in the Underground at Marble Arch, Piccadilly Circus, Leicester Square, and Charing Cross. Six American diplomats and security men had been slaughtered in Hyde Park and the daughter of the American ambassador, Elizabeth Halton, was missing and presumed kidnapped. And thus far the only person to be arrested was Gabriel Allon.

"They asked me to put my hands in the air and drop the gun," said Gabriel. "I complied with their order."

"Do try to see it from their point of view. You were about to shoot a man in the head and were surrounded by eight other bodies. You're damned lucky they even gave you a *chance* to surrender. They would have been well within their rights to use lethal force. That's what they're trained to do when confronted by a man they believe might be a suicide bomber."

"Wouldn't that have been perfect. The one person who tried to prevent the attacks, shot dead by London police." Greeted by Graham Seymour's angry silence, Gabriel pressed his case. "You should have listened to me, Graham. You should have raised the threat level and rousted a few of your known terrorists. Maybe Elizabeth Halton and the rest of the Americans would have stayed in their embassy instead of going for a morning jog in Hyde Park."

"And I told you to stay out of it."

"Is that why you left me sitting in that holding cell for sixteen hours, Graham? Is that why you let them file charges against me? Is that why you let them take my fingerprints and my photograph?"

"Forgive me for not coming to your rescue sooner, Gabriel. I've been a little busy."

Gabriel looked out at the wet streets of Westminster. They were abandoned, except for the uniformed Met officers standing watch at every other corner. Graham Seymour did have a point. London had just experienced its bloodiest single day since the Second World War. Gabriel could hardly complain about spending most of it inside New Scotland Yard.

"How many dead, Graham?"

"The toll is much higher than the attacks of July 2005," Seymour said. "So far we're at three hundred dead, with more than two thousand injured. But these bombings obviously had a second purpose—to create an atmosphere of chaos in the capital that allowed the kidnappers to slip away undetected. Unfortunately, it worked to perfection. Whoever planned this attack was bloody diabolical—and damned good."

"What have you picked up about the identity and affiliation of the bombers?"

"They're all second-generation British boys from Finsbury Park and Walthamstow in East London. All four are of Egyptian heritage, and all four were members of a small storefront mosque in Walthamstow called the al-Salaam Mosque."

"The Mosque of Peace," Gabriel said. "How appropriate."

"The imam has disappeared and so have several other members of the flock. Based on what we know now, it appears local boys handled the bombing operation, while your boy Samir and his associates saw to the kidnapping."

"Have you been able to trace the vans?"

"They were all purchased by companies owned or controlled by a man called Farouk al-Shahaki. He's a London-born entrepreneur of Egyptian heritage with business interests across Britain and in the Middle East."

"Where is he?"

"He boarded a flight for Pakistan last night. We've asked the Pakistani ISI to find him."

"Good luck," said Gabriel. "Were you able to follow them on street surveillance cameras as they left Hyde Park?"

"For a time," Seymour said. "Then they turned into an alley with no camera coverage and we lost them. We found the vans in a garage in Maida Vale that had been rented by one of the suicide bombers."

"Any claim of responsibility?"

"Too many to keep track of at the moment. Clearly it has all the hallmarks of an al-Qaeda attack. I suppose we'll learn more when the kidnappers make their demands."

"It would be better for everyone if you found Elizabeth Halton *before* her captors start making demands."

"We're operating under the assumption she's still somewhere inside the British mainland. We've got men at every airport, train station, and ferry terminal in the country. The Coastguard is attempting to seal our shoreline, no easy undertaking since it measures nearly eight thousand miles in length. SO13 are questioning informants and those suspected of terrorist sympathies, along with known associates of the suicide bombers. They're also conducting house-to-house searches in predominantly Muslim districts of the city. Our Muslim countrymen are already getting angry. If we're not careful, things could get out of hand very quickly." Seymour looked at Gabriel. "Too bad you didn't manage to wound one or two of those terrorists you killed in Hyde Park. We need information badly."

"I may have," Gabriel said.

"What are you talking about?"

"I fired several shots into the back of one of those vans. Keep an eye out for Arabs coming into hospital trauma centers with unexplained bullet wounds."

The limousine turned into Millbank and headed along the Thames toward Lambeth Bridge. Seymour's mobile phone chirped. He brought it to his ear, murmured a few words, then rang off. "The Americans," he said by way of explanation. "As you might expect, they're on war footing. They've put the embassy and all its personnel and dependents on lockdown status. They've also issued a terrorist travel alert for the United Kingdom, which hasn't exactly gone over well with Downing Street or the Foreign Office, since it puts us on a par with Pakistan, Afghanistan, and Lebanon. Two hundred investigators from CIA, FBI, and the departments of State and Justice touched down at Heathrow earlier this evening and set up shop at Grosvenor Square. They have an open line to the State Department Task Force in Washington and another one to COBRA, the special committee chaired by the Home Secretary that oversees the British government response to a national emergency such as this."

"Are they behaving themselves?"

Seymour exhaled heavily. "As well as can be expected, given the circumstances. For now, this is essentially a matter for the British police, which means there's little for them to do except sit on the sidelines and pressure us to look harder and faster. They've made it clear that despite the appalling loss of British life, our first priority must be finding Elizabeth Halton. They've *also* made clear that they have no intention of negotiating for her release."

"If they do negotiate, no American diplomat anywhere in the

world will ever be safe again," Gabriel said. "It's a difficult lesson we learned a long time ago."

"We prefer a more subtle interpretation of that principle. If a good-faith negotiation can bring that woman back alive, then I don't see the harm in it."

"I suppose that depends entirely on what you have to give up to get her back."

Gabriel looked out the window at the Thames. *Eight thousand miles of coastline, countless marinas and private airfields . . .* He knew from personal experience that a terrorist with enough intelligence and money could move a hostage almost at will. A year earlier, his wife had been kidnapped from her bedroom in an exclusive British psychiatric hospital. She was on a boat bound for France before anyone even knew she was missing.

"It seems you and the Americans have everything in hand," he said. "Which means there's nothing left for me to do but leave London and pretend I was never here."

"I'm afraid that's not going to be possible, Gabriel."

"Which part?"

"Both."

Seymour removed a copy of that morning's *Times* from his briefcase and handed it to Gabriel. The banner headline read: TERROR AND KIDNAPPING IN LONDON. But it was the headline at the bottom of the page that seized Gabriel's attention: ISRAEL INTELLIGENCE OFFICER INVOLVED IN AMBUSH IN HYDE PARK. Beneath the headline was a grainy image of Gabriel pointing his Beretta into the face of Samir al-Masri. Inside was a second photograph: the mug shot taken of him in New Scotland Yard in the hours after the attack.

"The photograph of you in the park was taken by a passerby with a mobile phone camera. Poor quality, but quite dramatic. Congratulations, Gabriel. I suppose you now have another group of terrorists that would like your head on a platter."

Gabriel switched on his reading lamp and scanned the article. It contained his real name, along with a largely accurate depiction of his professional exploits.

"Is your service responsible for this?"

"Trust me, Gabriel, I have enough headaches at the moment. I don't need one more. The sourcing is vague, but obviously the leak must have come from someone at the Met. If I had to guess, I'd say it was a senior officer attempting to curry favor with an important newspaper. Regardless of how it happened, it does mean that you're not going to be allowed to leave the country until all the questions of your involvement in this affair are sorted out and aired in a proper forum."

"The details of my involvement in this affair are quite clear, Graham. I came to London to warn you that a cell of terrorists from Amsterdam was probably in England preparing for a major attack. You chose to ignore that warning. Would you like me to air that in front of a proper forum?"

Seymour appeared to give the question serious thought before responding. "You are charged with several serious offenses, including entering Britain on a false passport, illegal possession of a firearm, and the unlawful discharge of that firearm in a public place."

"I discharged my illegal firearm into three terrorist murderers."

"It doesn't matter. You have to remain in Britain until we get this sorted out. To release you now would be to invite wailing and gnashing of teeth from all quarters." Seymour gave a weak smile. "Don't worry, Gabriel. We've arranged comfortable quarters for you. You're lucky. You get to leave London. The rest of us have to stay here and live with the aftermath of this attack."

"Does my service know I'm in custody?"

"They will shortly. We've just notified the legal liaison officer at your embassy, as well as your declared chief of station."

The car turned into the driveway of Thames House, MI5's imposing riverfront headquarters. Vauxhall Cross, the headquarters of MI6, the foreign intelligence service, stood on the opposite side of the river overlooking the Albert Embankment.

"My driver will run you out to one of our safe houses," Seymour said. "Don't even consider attempting to escape. He's well armed and an excellent shot."

"Where would I go, Graham? I don't have a passport."

"I'm sure you could come up with one."

Seymour reached for the door but stopped himself. "Is there anything else you can tell us, Gabriel? Anything that might help us locate Elizabeth Halton?"

"I've told you everything I know."

"Everything except the name of your source in Amsterdam."

"I promised to protect him, Graham. You remember what it means to protect a source."

"At times like these, sources aren't for protecting. They're to be used and burned."

"I'd rather not torch this one, Graham. He risked his life by coming to us."

"Have you at least considered the possibility that he's somehow linked to this affair?"

"He's not."

"I hope you're right," Seymour said. "It's been my experience that sources rarely tell the whole truth. In fact, more times than not, they lie. That's what sources do. That's why they're sources in the first place."

.   .   .

Gabriel's temporary home turned out to be a charming limestone cottage, surrounded by two hundred acres of private land, in the rolling hills of the Cotswolds. The manager of the facility, a bluff, ginger-haired MI5 veteran called Spencer, briefed Gabriel on the rules of his stay the following morning over a leisurely meal in the light-filled breakfast room. Gabriel would be granted access to television, radio, and the London papers, though, of course, no telephones. All the rooms of the main cottage were available for his use, though he was to keep interaction with the household staff to a bare minimum. He could walk the grounds alone, but if he wished to go into the village, it would be necessary to arrange an escort. All his movements would be monitored and recorded. Any attempt to escape would end in failure and result in the revocation of all privileges.

Gabriel occupied his time by carefully monitoring the progress of the British investigation. He rose early each morning and read the stack of London newspapers that awaited him in the breakfast room with his tea and toast. Then he would retire to the library and search the British and American television news channels for reliable information about the identity of the perpetrators and the fate of Elizabeth Halton. Seventy-two hours after her abduction there was still no authenticated claim of responsibility and no demands from her captors. Ambassador Halton made a stoic appeal for his daughter's release, as did the American president and the British prime minister. As the days ground slowly on, the television experts began to speculate that the ambassador's daughter had already been murdered by her captors or was somehow killed in the initial attack. Gabriel regarded the speculation as premature and almost certainly incorrect. He had seen the elaborate operation in action. Eventually, he knew, the kidnappers would surface and make their demands.

On the afternoon of his fourth day in captivity, he arranged for a ride into the village and spent an hour roaming the shops of the high street. He bought a wool sweater for Chiara and a handsome oak walking stick for Shamron. When he returned to the cottage, he found Spencer waiting for him in the gravel forecourt, waving a single sheet of paper as though it held news of great import from a distant corner of the realm. It did. The British had agreed to drop all charges against Gabriel in exchange for his testimony at the official inquiry into the attacks. A seat was being held for him on that evening's flight to Tel Aviv and arrangements had been made for private and expedited boarding. A car would collect him in an hour. The car, however, turned out to be a convoy. The vehicles were of American manufacture, as was the distinguished-looking man, clothed in diplomatic gray, seated in the back of the limousine. "Good afternoon, Mr. Allon," said Ambassador Robert Halton. "Let me give you a lift to the airport. I'd like a word."

.   .   .

"You have me to thank for your release," the ambassador said. "When I found out you were still in custody, I telephoned the prime minister and told him to free you at once."

"I knew the Americans wielded considerable influence at Downing Street, but I never knew you had the power to free prisoners."

"The last thing the prime minister wanted was to see me make my demand in public. The polls show that I am now the most popular man in Britain. Please tell me why the press bother to even take such a poll."

"I've given up trying to understand the press, Ambassador Halton."

"That same poll found a majority of Britons believe I brought this calamity upon myself because of my friendship with the president and my outspoken support for the war in Iraq. The war is now being used by our enemies to justify all manner of sins. So is our support for the State of Israel."

"I'm afraid it will be for a long time to come."

The ambassador removed his glasses and massaged the bridge of his nose. He looked as though he had not slept in many days. "I only wish I could free my daughter with a phone call. It's not easy to be a powerful man made powerless. I've had everything in life I wanted, but they took from me the one thing I cannot afford to lose."

"I just wish I'd arrived a few seconds earlier," Gabriel said. "If I had, I might have been able to stop them from taking your daughter."

"Don't blame yourself for what happened. If there's anyone to blame, it's me. I was the one who took this job. I was the one who asked Elizabeth to put her life on hold and come here with me. And I was the one who let her go running in Hyde Park three mornings a week even though I feared something like this could happen."

The American ambassador put his glasses back on and gazed at Gabriel thoughtfully for a moment. "But imagine my surprise when I heard that the mysterious man who killed three of the terrorists in Hyde Park was *you*. The president is my closest friend, Mr. Allon. If it weren't for you, he might have been killed at the Vatican earlier this year."

Actually, it was the pope's private secretary, Monsignor Luigi Donati, who had saved the president's life. Gabriel had only killed the assassin, a convert to radical Islam who had managed to penetrate the ranks of the Swiss Guard.

"What are the British telling you about the prospects of finding your daughter?" he asked.

"Maddeningly little, I'm afraid. They conducted raids at three locations today where they thought she might be being held. The intelligence turned out to be incorrect. What I don't understand is why the terrorists haven't made any demands yet."

"Because they know the uncertainty is causing you a great deal of pain. They want you to be grateful when they finally come forward and make their demands."

"You're sure they want something in return?"

"Yes, Mr. Ambassador. But you have to be prepared for the fact that it's almost certainly something you can't give them."

"I'm trying to remind myself that there are larger principles and issues of policy involved than the fate of my daughter," the ambassador said. "I'm preparing myself for the possibility that my daughter might have to die to keep diplomats safe around the world. But it hardly seems a fair tradeoff, Mr. Allon. And I'm not at all sure it's a price I'm prepared to pay. In fact, I'm quite certain I'd give them anything they wanted to get my daughter back alive."

"That's what they want, Mr. Ambassador. That's why they're waiting to make their demands."

"Your government has experience in these kinds of matters. What do you think they want?"

"Prisoners," Gabriel said. "That's almost always what they want. It might be several prisoners. Or it might be just one important prisoner."

"Like one of the 9/11 masterminds that we're holding?"

"It depends on who's taken her."

"I'm considering offering a sizeable reward for information."

"How sizeable?"

"Fifty million dollars."

"A reward like that will almost certainly bring out the charlatans and the con artists. And then the British will find themselves buried beneath a blizzard of false tips and leads. It will get in the way of the investigation rather than help it. For the time being, I would recommend keeping your wallet closed, Mr. Ambassador."

"That's probably sound advice." He looked at Gabriel for a moment without speaking. "I don't suppose there's any way I can convince you to stay in London for a few days and help find my daughter?"

"I'm afraid I have to go home and face the music for getting my picture in the newspaper. Besides, this is a matter for you and the British. Obviously, if we happen to pick up any intelligence, we'll pass it along right away."

The telephone rang. The ambassador lifted the receiver out of the console and brought it to his ear. He listened for a moment, face tense, then murmured, "Thank you, Prime Minister." He hung up the phone and looked at Gabriel. "The Metropolitan Police just raided a house in Walthamstow in East London. Nothing." He lapsed into a contemplative silence. "It just occurred to me that *you* were the last person to see my daughter—the last *decent* person, I should say."

"Yes, Mr. Ambassador, I suppose I was."

"Did you see her face?"

Gabriel nodded. "Yes, sir, I saw her face."

"Did they harm her?"

"It didn't look as though she was injured."

"Was she frightened?"

Gabriel answered truthfully. "I'm sure she was very frightened, sir, but she didn't go willingly. She fought them."

The ambassador's eyes shone suddenly with tears.

"I'm glad she fought them," Robert Halton said. "I hope she's fighting them right now."

12

She *had* fought them. Indeed she had fought them with more rage, and for much longer, than they had anticipated. She had fought them as they raced up the Edgware Road from Hyde Park, and she had fought them in the mews garage in Maida Vale, where they had transferred her to a second van. She had clawed and kicked. She had spit in their faces and called them murderous cowards. In the end, they had been forced to use the needle on her. She didn't like the needle. She didn't fight them anymore.

Her room was small and square, with cinder-block walls painted bone white and a cement floor. It contained nothing except for a folding army cot with a bricklike pillow and a scratchy woolen blanket that smelled of mothballs and disinfectant. Her hands were cuffed and her legs shackled, and they left the light on always so that she had no idea whether it was day or night. There was a spy hole in the metal door through which a malevolent brown eye watched her constantly. She dreamed of ramming a scalpel into it. When she slept, which was seldom, her dreams were filled with violence.

Interaction with her captors was kept to an absolute minimum and strictly regulated. The ground rules were established early on the first day, after she had awakened from the drugs. All communication was conducted in writing, with notes slipped beneath the door of her cell. Upon receipt of such a note, she was to reply yes or no in a low voice. Any deviation from the procedures, they warned, would result in a loss of food and water. Thus far they had asked her only two questions. One was: *Do you want food?* The other was: *Do you wish to use the toilet?* Each time a question appeared beneath her door, she replied yes, regardless of whether she was hungry or needed to relieve herself. Saying yes to them meant a break from the tedium of staring at the featureless white walls. Saying yes meant a moment of contact with her kidnappers, which, no matter how much she loathed them, she found strangely comforting.

Her food never varied: a bit of bread and cheese, a bottle of water, a few pieces of chocolate if she had been behaving herself. Her toilet was a yellow plastic bucket. Only two of the kidnappers ever entered her cell. They wore balaclava hoods in her presence to conceal their faces, but she learned to recognize them by their eyes. One had brown eyes; the other had green eyes that she found perversely beautiful. She nicknamed "brown eyes" Cain and "green eyes" Abel. Cain always brought her food, but poor Abel was the one who had to collect her bucket. He was kind enough to avert his green eyes when he did so.

She played mind games with herself to fill the long empty hours. She floated down endless ski runs through perfect crystalline air. She performed difficult surgeries and reread all her dreary medical school textbooks. She spoke often to her mother. But it was the moment of her capture she thought of most. It played ceaselessly in her memory, like a loop of videotape over which she had no control: the men in black jumpsuits pouring out of the vans, the shredded bodies of her friends lying in Hyde Park, the man who had tried to save her. She had glimpsed him briefly as they were forcing her into the back of the van, an angular figure with gray temples, crouched on one knee with a gun in his outstretched hands. She wondered often who he was. She hoped that one day, if she were ever rescued, she would have an opportunity to thank him.

If she were ever rescued . . . For some reason she found it easier to contemplate her own death than to picture the moment of her liberation. She knew that she was almost certainly the target of a massive search, but her hope of ever being found faded as the days ground slowly past—and as the notes came with a mind-deadening regularity. *Do you want food? . . . Do you wish to use the toilet? . . .* But on the fifth day, as the man with gray temples was boarding a jetliner at Heathrow Airport, a different note appeared. It said: *One of my men needs a doctor. Will you help us?* "Yes," she replied in a low voice, and a moment later Cain and Abel entered her cell and lifted her gently to her feet.

.   .   .

They led her wordlessly up a flight of steep narrow stairs, slowly, so that she did not trip over the shackles. At the top of the stairs they passed through a creaking metal door and entered a small warehouse. It was abandoned and dark, except for a single utility lamp burning above a cluster of cots in the far corner. On one of the cots lay a man whose face was not covered by a balaclava. It was twisted into a grimace of pain and damp with sweat. Cain lifted the blanket, exposing his right leg.

"Jesus Christ," Elizabeth said softly.

The bullet had entered below the knee and had shattered the crown of the tibia. The entrance wound was about two centimeters in diameter and was imbedded with bits of debris from the clothing he had been wearing the morning of the attack. The surrounding skin was now reddish brown and badly swollen, and red streaks had begun to radiate up the thigh. It was obvious he was suffering from a severe local infection and was on the verge of sepsis. She reached toward his wrist, but one of the terrorists seized her arm. It was the one with brown eyes: Cain.

"I have to take his pulse."

She pulled away from Cain's grasp and placed her fingertips on the inside of his wrist. The pulse was rapid and weak. Next she placed her hand upon his forehead and found it was damp and burning with fever.

"He needs to go to a trauma center right away. A good one."

Cain shook his head.

"If he doesn't, he'll die."

The terrorist lifted a gloved hand and pointed his finger at Elizabeth's face like a loaded gun.

"*Me*? I can't do anything for him here. He needs to be in a sterile environment. He needs to go to a hospital *now*."

Once again the terrorist shook his head.

"If I help him, will you let me go?"

This time he didn't bother to respond. Elizabeth looked down at the wounded man. He was no more than twenty-five, she guessed, and if she didn't intervene immediately he would die a very painful death within thirty-six hours. It was a death he deserved, but that didn't matter now. He was a human being in great pain, and Elizabeth was oath bound to treat him. She looked at the brown-eyed terrorist.

"I'll need some things. We *are* still in Britain, aren't we?"

The terrorist hesitated, then nodded.

"Then your friend is in luck. It's still possible to get some very strong over-the-counter antibiotics here. Get me a piece of paper and something to write with. I'll make you a list. Get me everything I ask for. If you don't, your friend is going to die."

13

BEN-GURION AIRPORT:
10:47 P.M., THURSDAY

The VIP reception room was empty when Gabriel arrived at Ben-Gurion Airport later that same evening. He walked the long white corridor alone and stepped into the frigid night air. Shamron's armored limousine was idling in the traffic circle, cigarette smoke wafting through the half-open rear window. Parked behind it was a second car filled with absurdly young security men, a new addition to his detail since the attempt on his life. Shamron had spent his old age surrounded by children with guns. Gabriel feared it would be his fate, too.

He climbed into the back of the limousine and closed the door. Shamron regarded him silently, then lifted a liver-spotted hand and gestured to his driver to move. A moment later, as they were speeding into the Judean Hills toward Jerusalem, he placed a stack of Israeli newspapers in Gabriel's lap: *Haaretz, Maariv, Yediot Aharonot*, the *Jerusalem Post*. Gabriel's photograph appeared on the front page of each.

"I send you to Amsterdam for a few days of quiet reading and this is what you bring me? You know, Gabriel, there *are* easier ways of getting out of dinner with the prime minister."

"I was actually looking forward to it."

Shamron gave him a dubious look. "At least the tone of the articles is positive—not like the drubbing we usually endure when our agents are exposed in the field. Once again you're a national hero. *Haaretz* has dubbed you 'Israel's not-so-secret super-agent.' That's my favorite."

"I'm glad you find this all so entertaining."

"I don't find it the least bit entertaining," Shamron said. "We took the extraordinary step of sending you to London to make certain that the British understood the seriousness of our warning. They chose to ignore it, and the result was a holocaust in the Underground and the daughter of the American ambassador in the hands of Islamic terrorists."

"Not to mention six dead American diplomats and security men."

"Yes, everyone seems to have forgotten them." Shamron ignited another cigarette. "How did you know they were going to hit in Hyde Park?"

"I didn't *know*. It was just a theory that unfortunately turned out to be correct."

"And what led you to this theory?"

Gabriel told him about the image on the legal pad he'd taken from Samir al-Masri's apartment in Amsterdam. Shamron smiled. He regarded Gabriel's flawless memory as one of his finest achievements. Gabriel had come to him with the mechanism in place, but it was Shamron who taught him how to use it.

"So you warned them not once but *twice*," Shamron pointed out. "It's no wonder the British were behaving like such jackasses during the negotiations for your release. I got the distinct impression that they were using your arrest and incarceration as a means of bringing pressure to bear against us."

"For what purpose?"

"So that your testimony at the inevitable public inquiry into the attacks doesn't reflect the true nature of your two conversations with Graham Seymour."

"Seymour's covering his ass?"

"He's entered the final lap of a long and distinguished career. He can almost see his country house and his knighthood and comfortable seat on the board of a respectable financial house in the City. He doesn't want some gunslinging Israeli to trip him up as he nears the finish line."

"The last thing I'm going to do is fall on my sword to protect Graham Seymour's reputation and retirement."

"No, but you're not going to go out of your way to embarrass him either. We'll need to concoct some subtle variation on the truth that protects both your reputation and his." Shamron smiled; concocting subtle variations on the truth was one of his favorite pastimes. "Burning Graham Seymour serves no useful purpose. You're going to need him, and his friends, in your next life."

"And what life is that?"

Shamron scrutinized Gabriel through a cloud of cigarette smoke. "Being deliberately obtuse serves no useful purpose either, Gabriel. You know very well what we have in store for you. The time has come for you to lead. The keys to the throne room are within your grasp."

"Perhaps, Ari, but there's only one problem. I don't want them. I have other things I want to do with the rest of my life."

"I'm afraid it's time for you to put away childish things."

"You're referring to restoration?"

"I am."

"You didn't consider it a childish thing when you were using it as cover to conceal an assassin."

"Restoration served both our needs for a long time," Shamron said, "but its season has faded."

They passed the charred hulk of an armored personnel carrier, a remnant of the fierce fighting that took place in the Bab al-Wad during Israel's War of Independence.

"I've been in the Cabinet Room in times of crisis," Gabriel said. "I've seen our leaders tear each other to shreds. It's not the way I want to spend the next ten years. Besides, when all those former generals look at me, they're just going to see a boy with a gun."

"You're not a boy any longer. You are approaching the age when men in government reach the summit of their careers. You'll just reach yours a little sooner than most. You were always a bit of a wunderkind."

Gabriel held up the copy of *Haaretz*. "And what about this?"

"The scandals?" Shamron shrugged. "A career free of scandal is not a proper career at all. For the most part, your scandals have earned you valuable allies in Washington and the Vatican."

"They've earned me enemies, too."

"They would be your enemies regardless of your actions. And they'll be your enemies long after your body is placed next to Dani's on the Mount of Olives." Shamron crushed out his cigarette. "Don't worry, Gabriel, this is not something that's going to happen overnight. Amos's death will be a slow one, and only a handful of people will even know the patient is terminal."

"How long?"

"A year," Shamron said. "Perhaps eighteen months at the most. Plenty of time for you to repair a few more paintings for your friend in Rome."

"There's no way you'll be able to keep it a secret for a year, Ari. You always said that the worst place to try to keep a secret is inside an intelligence service."

"At the moment only three people are privy to it—you, me, and the prime minister."

"And Uzi."

"I needed to bring Uzi into the picture," Shamron said. "Uzi serves as my eyes inside the Office."

"Maybe that's why you want me there."

Shamron smiled. "No, Gabriel, I want you there so I can *close* my eyes."

"You're not thinking of dying, are you, Ari?"

"I'd just like to take a short nap."

Gabriel turned and peered out the rear window of the limousine. The chase car was following closely behind them. He looked at Shamron and asked whether there had been any news from London about Elizabeth Halton.

"Still nothing from her captors," Shamron said. "And nothing from the British, at least nothing they're willing to say in public. But it is possible that we might be coming into some useful intelligence."

"From where?"

"Egypt," said Shamron. "Our most important asset inside the SSI sent us a signal early this morning that he had something for us."

The full name of the SSI was the General Directorate of State Security Investigations, a polite way of saying the Egyptian secret police.

"Who is he?" Gabriel asked.

"Wazir al-Zayyat, chief of the Department for Combatting Religious Activity. Wazir has one of the toughest jobs in the Middle East: making certain Egypt's homegrown Islamic extremists don't bring down the regime. Egypt is the spiritual heartland of Islamic fundamentalism, and of course the Egyptian Islamists are a major component of al-Qaeda. Wazir knows more about the state of the global jihadist movement than anyone in the world. He keeps us apprised of the stability of the Mubarak regime and passes along any intelligence that suggests Egyptian terrorists are targeting us."

"What does he have for us?"

"We won't know until we sit down with him," Shamron said. "We meet with him outside the country."

"Where?"

"Cyprus."

"Who's his case officer?"

"Shimon Pazner."

Pazner was the chief of station in Rome, which doubled as the headquarters for Office operations throughout the Mediterranean.

"When is Pazner going to Cyprus?"

"He leaves in the morning."

"Tell him to stay put in Rome."

"Why would I do that?"

"Because I'm going to Cyprus to meet with the Egyptian."

Shamron greeted Gabriel's declaration with an obstinate silence. "Your involvement in this affair is officially over," he said finally. "This is an American and British problem now. We have enough of our own to worry about."

Gabriel pushed back. "I was there when it happened, Ari. I want us to do anything we can to find her."

"And we will. Shimon Pazner has been handling Wazir for three years now. He's more than capable of going to Cyprus and conducting a crash debriefing."

"I'm sure he is, but I'm going to go to Cyprus for him."

Shamron's old stainless steel lighter flared in the darkness. "You're not the *Memuneh* yet, my son. Besides, have you forgotten that your picture is in all the newspapers?"

"I'm not going behind the Iron Curtain, Ari."

Shamron touched his cigarette to the flame and extinguished it with a flick of his sturdy wrist. "You use my own words against me," he said. "Go ahead, Gabriel, go to Cyprus tomorrow. Just make sure Identity does something about that face of yours. You made yourself another enemy with your actions in Hyde Park."

"Graham Seymour said the same thing."

"Well," Shamron said reflectively, "at least he was right about something."

. . .

When Gabriel entered his apartment twenty minutes later, he found lights burning in the sitting room and a faint trace of vanilla on the air. He tossed his bag onto the new couch and walked into the bedroom. Chiara was perched at the end of the bed, scrutinizing her toes with considerable interest. Her body was wrapped in bath towels, and her skin was very dark from the sun. She looked up at

Gabriel and smiled. It was as if it had been several minutes since they had seen each other last and not several weeks.

"You're here," she said in mock surprise.

"Shamron didn't mention that I was coming home tonight?"

"He may have."

Gabriel walked over and removed the towel from her hair. Heavy and wet, it tumbled riotously onto her dark shoulders. She lifted her face to be kissed and loosened the towel around her body. Maybe Shamron was right, Gabriel thought as she pulled him onto the bed. Maybe he would let Pazner go to Cyprus to meet with the Egyptian after all.

. . .

They were both famished after making love. Gabriel sat at the small table in the kitchen, watching the news on television, while Chiara made fettuccine and mushrooms. She was wearing one of Gabriel's dress shirts, unbuttoned to her abdomen, and nothing else.

"How did you find out that I'd been arrested?"

"I read it in the newspapers like everyone else." She poured him a glass of red wine. "You were all the rage in Buenos Aires."

"What kind of work were you doing there?"

"You know I can't tell you that."

"I know you were watching members of a Hezbollah cell. I just want to know whether you were part of the actual surveillance team or just an escort officer?"

"I was part of the team," she said. "I don't do much escort work anymore."

"Why did they pull you out?"

"Overexposure to the targets." Elizabeth Halton's face appeared suddenly on the television screen. "Pretty girl," Chiara said. "Why did they take her?"

"I may find out tomorrow." He told her about his trip to Cyprus.

"What about your dinner with the prime minister?"

Gabriel looked up from the television. "How did you know about that?"

"Shamron told me."

"So much for operational security," he said. "What exactly did he say to you?"

She placed the fettuccine in the water to boil and sat down next to him. "He said that you had agreed to succeed Amos as director."

"I've agreed to no such thing."

"That's not what Shamron says."

"Shamron has a long history of hearing exactly what he wants to hear. What else did he say?"

"He wants us to get our personal life in order as soon as possible. He doesn't think it's proper for the director to be living with a woman out of wedlock, especially one who happens to be an employee of the Office. He thinks we should accelerate our wedding plans." She placed a finger beneath his chin and turned his face toward hers. "You agree, don't you?"

"Oh, yes, of course," said Gabriel hastily. He had learned that any hesitation to engage in a discussion of wedding plans was always wrongly interpreted by Chiara as a reluctance to marry. "We should get married as soon as possible."

"When?"

"What do you mean?"

"It's a very simple question, Gabriel. When do you think we should get married?"

"Late spring," he said. "Before it gets too hot."

"May?"

"May would be perfect."

Chiara removed her fingertip from beneath Gabriel's chin and nibbled nervously at her nail. "How am I going to plan a wedding in six months?"

"Hire a professional planner to help you."

"A wedding isn't an operation, Gabriel. It's supposed to be planned by family, not a professional."

"What about Gilah Shamron? She's the closest thing to a mother I have."

"Gilah has enough on her plate at the moment looking after her husband."

"All the more reason to ask her to help with the wedding. Trust me, she'll jump at the chance."

"It's not a bad idea, actually. No wonder Shamron wants you to be the chief. The first thing we have to do is settle on a guest list."

"That's easy," Gabriel said. "Just invite everyone from the Office, Shabak, AMAN, most of the Cabinet, and half of the Knesset. Oh, and don't forget the prime minister."

"I'm not sure I want the prime minister to attend my wedding."

"You're afraid of being overshadowed by a chubby octogenarian?"

"Yes."

"The prime minister has three daughters of his own. He'll make certain not to steal the limelight on your big day."

"*Our* big day, Gabriel." The water began to boil over. She stood up and walked back over to the stove. "Are you sure you have to go to Cyprus tomorrow?"

"I want to hear what the Egyptian has to say with my own ears."

"But you've only just come home."

"It's just for a day or two. Why don't you come with me? You can work on that suntan of yours."

"It's cold in Cyprus this time of year."

"So you want me to go alone?"

"I'll come," she said. "You didn't say anything about the way I decorated the apartment. Do you like it?"

"Oh, yes," he said hastily. "It's lovely."

"I found a ring on the coffee table. Did you put a hot drink on it without a coaster?"

"It was Uzi," Gabriel said.

Chiara poured the fettuccine into a colander and frowned. "He's such a slob," she said. "I don't know how Bella can live with him."

T he items she had requested lay arranged on an adjacent cot: isopropyl alcohol, cotton swabs, rubber gloves, tweezers, needle-nose pliers, a straight razor, codeine and cephalin tablets, four-by-four sterile pads, medical tape, two eighteen-inch strips of wood, two rolls of bandaging, and two liters of bottled water. She held out her cuffed hands to the one she thought of as Cain. He shook his head.

"I can't do this with my hands cuffed."

He hesitated, then removed them.

"The drugs you gave me after you kidnapped me—you have more, I assume."

Another hesitation, then a reluctant nod.

"I need them. Otherwise, your friend is going to suffer terribly."

He walked over to the van and returned a moment later with a syringe wrapped in plastic and a vial of clear liquid. Elizabeth looked at the label: KETAMINE. No wonder she'd suffered such terrible hallucinations while the drug was in her system. Anesthesiologists almost never used ketamine without a secondary sedative such as

Valium. These idiots had given her several injections of the drug with nothing to blunt its side effects.

She loaded an appropriate dosage, two hundred and fifty milligrams, and injected it into the wounded man's upper arm. As he slipped slowly into unconsciousness, she broke the needle off the syringe and placed it in the plastic sack from the chemist shop where Cain had purchased the medical supplies. The name and address of the shop were written on the bag in blue lettering. Elizabeth recognized the village. It was located on the Norfolk coastline, northeast of London.

She lifted the blanket and adjusted the lamp, so that the light shone directly into the wound. The round was lodged within the fracture fragments. She opened the bottle of rubbing alcohol and poured a generous amount directly into the wound, then wiped away the puss and other infectious material with a cotton swab. When the wound was sufficiently clean, she sterilized the straight razor and used it to debride the ragged necrotic material along the edges. Then she sterilized the tweezers and spent the next twenty minutes carefully removing fragments of shattered bone and filaments of embedded fabric. Finally, she sterilized the needle-nose pliers and slipped them carefully into the wound. The round was out a moment later, deformed from its impact with the terrorist's tibia but intact.

She gave the bullet to Cain as a souvenir and prepared for the final stage of the procedure: the dressing and the splint. First she flushed the wound thoroughly with the sterile water, then covered it with a four-by-four sterile pad. Last, she laid the two strips of wood along each side of his lower leg from the knee to the ankle and bound the splint tightly with the rolls of bandaging. When she was finished, she propped the leg on a pillow and looked at Cain.

"When he wakes up, give him two of the cephalin tablets. Then give him one tablet every four hours. Keep the leg elevated. I'd like to see him every two hours, if that's possible. If not, I've given you seventy-two hours at the most. After that he's going to need to go into a hospital."

She held out her hands. Cain applied the cuffs and led her downstairs to her cell. As she lay down on her cot, she felt an almost drunken sense of elation. The crude surgery, the brisk commands: she had been in control, if only for a few moments. And she had managed to uncover a single piece of valuable information. She was still in England, still within reach of the British police and intelligence services.

She closed her eyes and tried to sleep, but an hour later she was jolted by a knock at the door. *We have a present for you*, the note said. *Lay down on your cot*. She did as she was told and watched as Cain and Abel entered her cell. They put packing tape across her mouth and a hood over her head. She fought them. She fought them even after they gave her the needle.

15

CYPRUS: 10:15 A.M.,
FRIDAY

Much can be gleaned about the value of a source by the accommodations that are made to handle him. For the debriefings of Wazir al-Zayyat, the Office had purchased a lovely whitewashed villa on the southern coast of Cyprus with a small swimming pool and a shaded terrace overlooking the Mediterranean Sea. Gabriel and Chiara arrived several hours before the Egyptian was due. Gabriel had hoped to spend the time relaxing, but Chiara, alone with him for the first time in weeks, wanted to use the opportunity to discuss wedding plans. Place settings and flowers, guest lists and music—this is how Israel's legendary secret agent passed the time before the arrival of the Egyptian spy. He wondered what *Haaretz* and the rest of the Israeli newspapers would write about him if they knew the truth.

Shortly after two in the afternoon, Gabriel glimpsed a Volkswagen sedan speeding along the coast road. It passed by the villa and disappeared around a bend, then, five minutes later, approached from the opposite direction. This time it slowed and turned into the drive. Gabriel looked at Chiara. "You'd better wait upstairs in the bedroom," he said. "From what I've read about Wazir, your presence will only be a distraction."

Chiara gathered up her papers and bridal magazines and vanished. Gabriel went into the kitchen and opened one of the cabinets. Inside was the control panel for the built-in recording system. He put in a fresh set of tapes and pressed the RECORD button, then went into the entrance hall and opened the front door as al-Zayyat was coming up the steps. The Egyptian froze and regarded Gabriel suspiciously for a moment through the lenses of his mirrored sunglasses. Then a trace of a smile appeared beneath his dense mustache and he extended a clublike hand in Gabriel's direction.

"To what do I owe the honor, Mr. Allon?"

"Something came up in Rome," Gabriel said. "Shimon asked me to fill in."

The Egyptian pushed his sunglasses onto his forehead and studied Gabriel again, this time with obvious skepticism. His eyes were dark and bottomless. They were not a pair of eyes Gabriel would ever want to see on the other side of an interrogation table.

"Or maybe you volunteered to come here to see me," the Egyptian said.

"Now, why would I do that, Wazir?"

"Because if what I read in the newspapers is true, you now have something of a personal stake in the outcome of this case."

"You shouldn't believe everything you read in the newspapers."

"At least not the Egyptian papers."

Al-Zayyat followed Gabriel into the villa, then walked over to the drinks cabinet with a proprietary air and loosened the cap on a new bottle of single-malt Scotch. "You'll join me?" he asked, waving the bottle at Gabriel.

"I'm driving," Gabriel replied.

"What is it with you Jews and alcohol?"

"It makes us do silly things with lampshades."

"What kind of agent-runner doesn't have a drink with a source?" Al-Zayyat poured himself a very large glass and put the cap back on the bottle without tightening it. "But then you're not an agent-runner, are you, Allon?" He drank half the whisky in a single swallow. "How's the old man? Back on his feet?"

"Shamron is fine," Gabriel said. "He sends his regards."

"I hope he sent more than regards."

Gabriel looked at the leather briefcase laying in a rectangle of sunlight on the sailcloth couch. Al-Zayyat sat next to it and popped the latches. Satisfied by the contents, he closed the briefcase and looked at Gabriel.

"I know who kidnapped the ambassador's daughter," he said. "And I know why they did it. Where would you like me to start?"

"The beginning," said Gabriel. "It tends to put things in proper perspective."

"You're just like Shamron."

"Yes, I've heard that."

The Egyptian's gaze wandered over the bag again. "There's fifty thousand, right?"

"You can count it if you like."

"That won't be necessary. Do you want me to sign a receipt?"

"You sign the receipt when you get your money," Gabriel said. "And you get your money after I hear the information."

"Shimon always gave me the money first."

"I'm not Shimon."

The Egyptian swallowed the rest of his whisky. Gabriel refilled his glass and told him to start talking.

• • •

The beginning, the Egyptian said, was the day in September 1970 when Nasser died and his vice president, Anwar Sadat, came to power in Egypt. Nasser had regarded Egypt's Islamic radicals, especially the Muslim Brotherhood, as a grave threat to his regime and had used mass arrests, executions, and torture to keep them in their place. Sadat had tried a different approach.

"Sadat had none of Nasser's charisma and no popular base of

support," al-Zayyat said. "He was also a rather religious man. He was more afraid of the Communists and the Nasserites than the Brothers, and so he made what would turn out to be a fatal reversal of Egypt's approach to Islamic extremism. He branded the Communists and the Nasserites as enemies of his new regime and let the Brothers out of jail."

And then he compounded the mistake, al-Zayyat explained. He allowed the Muslim Brotherhood to operate openly and encouraged them to spread their fiery brand of Islam abroad, especially into the newly occupied West Bank and Gaza Strip. He also encouraged and funded the creation of groups that were even more radical than the Brotherhood. One was al-Gama'a al-Islamiyya, or the Islamic Group. Another was al-Jihad. In October 1981, al-Jihad turned on the man who had helped bring it into existence, assassinating Sadat as he stood on a military reviewing stand outside Cairo. In the eyes of the Islamists, Sadat's sins were many, but none so egregious as his peace treaty with Israel. Before opening fire, Sadat's assassin, Lieutenant Khaled Islambouli, screamed: "I have killed Pharaoh, and I do not fear death."

"The Gama'a and al-Jihad, of course, are with us still," al-Zayyat said. "Their goal is to destroy the Mubarak regime, replace it with an Islamic republic, and then use Egypt as a base of operations to wage a global jihad against the West and Israel. Both groups are signatories of al-Qaeda's declaration of war against the Crusaders and the Jews, and both are formally under the umbrella of Osama bin Laden's command structure. Egyptians make up more than half of al-Qaeda's core personnel, and they hold five of the nine positions in the ruling Shura Council. And, of course, Osama's right-hand man is Ayman al-Zawahiri, the leader of al-Jihad."

"So Egypt is no different than the Saudis," Gabriel said. "You thought you could reach accommodation with the Islamic terrorists by giving them money and encouragement and deflecting their rage outward. And now they're threatening to destroy you."

"You did the same thing, my friend. Don't forget that the Office and Shabak gave money and support to Hamas in the early days because you thought the Islamists were a good counterweight to the secular leftists of the PLO."

"Point taken," Gabriel said. "But please don't tell me I'm supposed to pay you fifty thousand dollars to tell me that al-Qaeda is responsible for kidnapping the daughter of the American ambassador to London. I could have saved my money and just turned on CNN instead. They have lots of experts saying the same thing."

"It's not just al-Qaeda," al-Zayyat said. "It's a joint operation, a merging of assets, if you will."

"Who's the other partner?"

The Egyptian walked over to the drinks cabinet and refilled his glass. "There were other groups besides the Gama'a and al-Jihad that formed in the seventies. More than fifty in all. Some were just cells of university students that couldn't organize a bucket brigade. Others were good. *Very* good." He took a drink of the whisky. "Unfortunately, a group that sprang up at the University of Minya was one of the good ones. They called themselves the Sword of Allah."

The Sword of Allah . . . Gabriel knew the name, of course. Anyone who worked in the field of Islamic terrorism did. In the late 1970s, after Sadat's historic visit to Jerusalem, a group of university students, professors, and civil servants from the Upper Egyptian town of Minya had coalesced around a fiery Islamist cleric named Sheikh Tayyib Abdul-Razzaq. Sheikh Tayyib adopted a simple program for seizing power in Egypt: inflict as much terror and bloodshed on Egyptian society as possible and the regime would collapse under its own weight. In the early 1990s, he nearly succeeded. Flushed with the prospects of success, the sheikh decided to take his campaign global, long before there was such a thing known as al-Qaeda. He sent emissaries to Europe to open branch offices of the Sword among the burgeoning Muslim communities there and dispatched his older brother and closest advisor, Sheikh Abdullah Abdul-Razzaq, to suburban Washington to wage jihad against the most important patron of the Egyptian regime: the government of the United States. In 1998, Sheikh Abdullah was found guilty on charges of conspiring to bomb the State Department, the Capitol, and the headquarters of the FBI and was sentenced to life in prison. He had recently been diagnosed with cancer. Freeing the sheikh before his death was now one of the Sword's top priorities.

"Al-Qaeda has been itching to hit London again for a long time," al-Zayyat said. "And, of course, Sheikh Tayyib wants to get his brother back from the Americans. They decided to merge the two priorities into a single terror spectacular. Al-Qaeda handled the bombings, while the Sword and its European networks saw to the hostage-taking side of the operation."

"What evidence do you have of Sword involvement?"

"You had the proof in your own hands for a few seconds in Hyde Park," the Egyptian said. "Samir al-Masri, former student of engineering at the University of Minya, is a member of the Sword of Allah and one of its more talented terrorist operatives."

"It would have been helpful, Wazir, if you'd told the Dutch he was living quietly in west Amsterdam."

"We didn't know he was in Holland or we would have." The Egyptian sat down on the couch next to his bag of money. "Samir left Egypt a few months after the Americans went into Iraq. When the insurgency started up, he joined forces with Abu Musab al-Zarqawi and perfected his craft. Apparently he slipped out of Iraq shortly before Zarqawi's death and made his way to Europe via Damascus. If you want to blame anyone for the fact that Samir was living quietly in west Amsterdam, blame the Syrians. And the Dutch, of course. Christ, they'll let anyone into their country."

"What else do you have besides Samir's connection?"

"The al-Hijrah Mosque."

"What about it?"

"The imam there is a graduate of al-Azhar in Cairo and a member of the Sword of Allah."

"That's still not enough."

"This discussion is academic," al-Zayyat said. "In twenty-four hours you'll have proof the Sword of Allah is behind this. That's when they'll offer to trade Elizabeth Halton for Sheikh Abdullah."

"How can you be so sure about the timing?"

"The Sword has carried out a number of kidnappings inside Egypt. Most of the time the outside world doesn't even hear about them. Their method of operation is always the same. They wait one week before making demands. And if they set a deadline for killing the girl, they'll do it when the second hand reaches twelve. And there won't be any extensions or delays."

"The Americans will never release Sheikh Abdullah."

"If they don't, the Sword of Allah and al-Qaeda are going to send the American president's goddaughter home in a bag—or what's left of her, I should say. They'll kill her the same way they took her. With a great deal of bloodshed."

"Have you told the Americans about any of this?"

Al-Zayyat shook his head.

"Why not?"

"Orders from on high," said al-Zayyat. "Our fearless leader is afraid his patrons in Washington will be angry when they find out the plot to kidnap the ambassador's daughter originated in Egypt. He's trying to delay the day of reckoning as long as possible. In the meantime, he's directed the SSI and the other security services to gather as much intelligence as possible."

"Who's the mastermind?"

"If I had to guess, it goes all the way to the top."

"Zawahiri?"

The Egyptian nodded.

"But surely there's someone between him and the operatives," Gabriel said. "Someone like Khaled Sheikh Mohammad. Someone who made the trains run on time."

"There is." Al-Zayyat held his tumbler of whisky up to the sunlight and contemplated its color for a moment without speaking. "And if I had to venture a guess as to his identity, I'd say it's almost certainly the work of the Sphinx."

"Who's the Sphinx?"

"We're not sure who he is, but we know his handiwork all too well. All told, he's killed more than a thousand people inside Egypt—tourists, government ministers, wealthy friends of the regime. We assume he's highly educated and very well connected. We believe he has agents of influence and spies at the highest level of Egyptian society and government, including inside my service. He operates through cutouts like Samir. We've never been able to get close to him."

"Could he have planned something like this from Egypt?"

"Highly unlikely," al-Zayyat said. "He's probably in Europe. In fact, I'd be willing to wager a fair amount of money that he is. The Sword has been very quiet in Egypt for the last year. Now we know why."

"Where's Sheikh Tayyib?"

"The same place he's been for the last fifteen years: underground. He moves between a string of hideouts in Upper Egypt and the oasis towns of the Western Desert. We also think he moves in and out of Libya and the Sudan."

"Find him," Gabriel said.

"Elizabeth Halton will be dead long before we ever find the sheikh."

"Start rounding up Sword operatives and bringing them in for quiet chats. That's your specialty, isn't it, Wazir? Quiet chats with Islamic extremists?"

"Let he who is without sin cast the first stone," al-Zayyat replied. "Trust me, Allon, we're kicking down doors as we speak, but the Sphinx knew we would. No one in Egypt knows where the girl is. I doubt even Sheikh Tayyib knows the operational details. Your best chance at finding her alive died with Samir al-Masri. The Sword is good at hiding people."

"Someone knows," Gabriel said. "Someone has to know."

"The Sphinx knows. Find the Sphinx and you'll find the girl."
The Egyptian put his hand on the grip of the briefcase. "So have I
earned my fifty thousand yet?"

"I want everything you have on the Sword of Allah," Gabriel
said. "Case files, membership rolls, known front organizations in
Europe. Names, addresses, telephone numbers."

"It's in a suitcase in the trunk of my car," the Egyptian said. "But
it's going to cost you."

Gabriel sighed. "How much, Wazir?"

"Another fifty thousand."

"I don't happen to have another fifty thousand on me."

The Egyptian smiled. "I'll take an IOU," he said. "I know you're
good for it."

.   .   .

The Samsonite suitcase that Wazir al-Zayyat produced from the
trunk of his rented Volkswagen contained the lifeblood of one of the
world's most violent terror organizations and was therefore a steal
at fifty thousand. When the Egyptian was gone, Gabriel opened a di-
rectory of known Sword members and started reading. Five minutes
later he came across a name that was familiar to him. He located a
photocopy of the corresponding file and examined the photograph.
It was dated and of poor quality; even so, Gabriel could tell it was
the same man he had encountered a week earlier in Amsterdam. *I'm
the person you're looking for in Solomon Rosner's files*, the man had said
to him that night. *And I've come to help you.*

16

PARIS: 3:45 A.M., FRIDAY

The knock was cautious and contrite. Dr. Yusuf Ramadan, professor of Near Eastern history at American University in Cairo, looked up from his work and saw a woman standing in the doorway of his office. Like all female employees of the Institute of Islamic Studies, she was veiled. Even so, the professor averted his eyes slightly as she spoke.

"I'm sorry to interrupt, Professor, but if it's all right with you, I'll be leaving now."

"Of course, Atifah."

"Can I get you anything before I go? More tea, perhaps?"

"I've had too much already." He glanced at his wristwatch. "In fact, I'm going to be leaving soon myself. I'm meeting a colleague from the Sorbonne for coffee at four-thirty."

"Don't forget your umbrella. It's still raining."

"It's been raining for five days."

"Welcome to Paris. Peace be upon you, Professor Ramadan."

"And you, Atifah."

The woman slipped out of the office and quietly closed the door. Ramadan spent another ten minutes tapping away at the keyboard of his laptop computer, then placed the computer and his research files into his briefcase and stood up. He was slender and bearded, with receding curly hair, soft brown eyes, and the fine aquiline features often associated with Egyptian aristocracy. He was not of aristocratic birth; indeed, the man now regarded as one of Egypt's most influential intellectuals and writers was born the son of a postal clerk in a poor village at the edge of the Fayoum Oasis. Brilliant, charismatic, and a self-professed political moderate, he had taken a leave of absence from the university eighteen months earlier and signed on as a visiting scholar in residence with the institute. The ostensible purpose of his stay in Paris was to complete his masterwork, a critical reexamination of the Crusades that promised to be the standard against which all future books on the subject would be measured. When he was not writing, Professor Ramadan could often be seen in the lecture halls of the Sorbonne, or on French television, or even in the corridors of government power. Embraced wholeheartedly by the intelligentsia and media of Paris, his opinions were much in demand on matters ranging from the Israeli-Palestinian conflict to the American occupation of Iraq and, of course, the scourge of Islamic terror, a topic with which he was intimately familiar.

He walked over to his narrow window and looked down into the boulevard de la Chapelle. Dark and raw, a halfhearted drizzle: Paris in winter. It had been many days since the sun had made its last appearance, and even then it was only a furtive peak from behind the blanket of cloud. Ramadan longed to be back in Cairo: the thunder of the traffic, the smells both putrid and magical, the music of a thousand muezzins, the kiss of the desert wind at night . . . It had been six months since his last visit. *Soon,* he thought. Soon it would be over and he would go home again. And if things went according to plan, the country to which he would return would be very different from the one he had left behind. Strange to think that it had all been set in motion here, in dreary Paris, from his tiny office in the eighteenth arrondissement.

He pulled on his overcoat and hat, then snatched up his briefcase and umbrella and stepped into the corridor. As he passed by the staff lounge he saw several colleagues gathered around the television, watching a briefing by the commissioner of London's Metropolitan Police. Mahmoud Aburish, the tubby, owl-like director of the institute, motioned for Ramadan to join him. Ramadan walked over and looked up at the screen.

"What's he saying?"

"No word yet from the kidnappers," said Aburish. "And no clues about the woman's whereabouts."

"Do you believe him?"

"The British are very good, but judging from the expression on that man's face, he's not holding any cards up his sleeve." Aburish regarded Ramadan through his smudged eyeglasses. "You're the resident expert on matters like these, Yusuf. Who do you think has kidnapped this woman? And what on earth do they want?"

"I suppose we'll know soon enough," Ramadan said.

"How goes the writing?"

"It goes, Mahmoud, just not as quickly as I had hoped. In fact, I'm having drinks with my French publisher in a few minutes to tell him I won't be able to deliver the manuscript on time. He's not going to be pleased. Neither are my British and American publishers."

"Is there anything the institute can do?"

"You've done more than you'll ever know, Mahmoud."

Aburish gazed toward the television as Dame Eleanor McKenzie, the director general of MI5, stepped before the television cameras. Yusuf Ramadan, the man known to the Egyptian security services only as the Sphinx, slipped silently from the lounge and headed downstairs.

. . .

Though Yusuf Ramadan had been far from forthright during his brief encounter with Mahmoud Aburish, he had been truthful about one thing. He was indeed having drinks with his French publisher that evening—at Fouquet's on the Champs-Elysées, to be precise—but not until five o'clock. He had one appointment before then, however, on the Quai de Montebello directly across the Seine from Notre-Dame. The man waiting for him there was tall and heavily built, dressed in a dark cashmere overcoat with a silk scarf knotted rakishly at his throat. His real name was Nidal Mutawalli, though Ramadan referred to him only as Abu Musa. Like Ramadan, he was from the Fayoum Oasis. They had grown up together, attended school together, and then gone their separate ways—Ramadan into the world of books and writing, Abu Musa into the world of finance and money. The jihad and their shared hatred of the Egyptian regime and its American backers had reunited them. It was Abu Musa, Yusuf Ramadan's childhood friend, who allowed him to keep his identity a secret from the Egyptian security services. They were, quite literally, two of the most dangerous men on earth.

A light drizzle was drifting through the lamplight along the Seine embankments and beading like teardrops on the plastic sheets covering the stalls of the *bouquinistes*. Ramadan wandered over to a trestle table stacked with books and thumbed a worn volume of Chekhov. Abu Musa joined him a moment later and picked up a copy of *L'Etranger* by Camus.

"Have you read him?" Abu Musa asked.

"Of course," said Ramadan. "I'm sure you'll find it to your liking."

Ramadan moved on to the next table of books. Abu Musa joined him again a moment later, and again they exchanged a few harmless-sounding words. On it went like this for the next ten minutes as they moved slowly together down the row of booksellers, Ramadan leading, Abu Musa trailing after him. *I've always enjoyed the poetry of Dryden. . . . I saw this play the last time I was in London. . . . The DVD has been shot and is ready to be handed over. . . . We're ready to make the phone call on your orders. . . .*

Ramadan picked up a copy of Hemingway and held it up for Abu Musa to see. "This has always been one of my favorites," he said. "Allow me to give it to you as a gift."

He handed the bookseller a five-euro note, then, after jotting a brief inscription on the title page of the volume, presented it formally to Abu Musa with his hand over his heart. They parted a moment later as Emmanuel, the thirteen-ton bell in Notre-Dame's south tower, tolled five o'clock. Abu Musa disappeared into the streets of the Latin Quarter; Yusuf Ramadan crossed to the other side of the river and walked in the Tuileries gardens, thinking about the question Mahmoud Aburish had posed to him earlier that afternoon. *Who do you think has kidnapped this woman? And what on earth do they want?* Because of the meeting that had just transpired in plain sight along the banks of the Seine, the Americans soon would be told the answers to those questions. Whether they chose to inform the rest of the world was none of Professor Ramadan's concern—at least not yet.

He walked for several minutes more in the gardens, checking his tail for signs of surveillance and thinking about his pending meeting with his French publisher on the Champs-Elysées. He supposed he had to come up with some suitable explanation as to why his book was now hopelessly behind schedule. He would think of something. The Sphinx was an extremely good liar.

U.S. Embassy, London:
5:19 p.m., Friday

There was one telephone in the makeshift operations center that was never used for outgoing calls. It was attached to a sophisticated digital recording device and linked to the call-tracing network of the Metropolitan Police. The receiver itself was red, and the ringer volume was set to foghorn level. Only one person was allowed to touch it: Supervisory Special Agent John O'Donnell, head of the FBI's Critical Incident Response Group and the Bureau's chief hostage negotiator.

The telephone had rung forty-seven times since the disappearance of Elizabeth Halton. Thus far none of the calls had been deemed credible by O'Donnell or his counterparts at the Met, though the demands of some of the callers had managed to provide a few brief interludes of comedy in what were otherwise very dark days. One caller said he would release Elizabeth Halton in exchange for the sum of one hundred thousand British pounds. O'Donnell agreed to the deal, and the man was arrested later that evening in the parking lot of a pub in West Sussex. One demanded a date with a famous American actress of questionable talent. One said he would free his American captive in exchange for tickets to that weekend's Arsenal–Chelsea football match. One called because he was depressed and needed someone to talk to. O'Donnell chatted with him for five minutes to make sure Scotland Yard had a good trace and bade the man good evening as officers moved in for the arrest.

The call that arrived at the embassy's main switchboard shortly after six that evening was different from the start. The voice was male and electronically disguised, the first caller to employ such a device. "I have information about Elizabeth Halton," he calmly told the switchboard operator. "Transfer me to the appropriate individual. If more than five seconds elapse, I will hang up and she will die. Do you understand me?"

The operator made it clear that she did indeed understand and politely asked the caller to stand by. Two seconds later, O'Donnell's phone sounded in the ops center. He snatched the red receiver from the cradle and brought it quickly to his ear. "This is John O'Donnell of the Federal Bureau of Investigation," he said crisply. "How can I help you?"

"The beach at Beacon Point," the electronically altered voice said. "Look beneath the overturned rowboat. This will be our first and only contact."

The line went dead.

O'Donnell hung up the phone and listened to the call again on his recorder, then picked up the receiver of a separate dedicated line that rang automatically at Scotland Yard.

"That sounded legit to me," O'Donnell said.

"I concur," said the Met officer at the other end of the line.

"Did you get a trace?"

"It was placed with a mobile phone. Something tells me we're not going to catch this one. He sounded like a real pro."

"Where's Beacon Point?"

"The south coast, about ten miles east of Plymouth."

"How far from central London?"

"About a hundred and fifty miles."

"I want to be on site for the retrieval—whatever it is."

"The Royal Navy has been kind enough to leave a Sea King at the London Heliport for just this kind of scenario."

"Where's the heliport?"

"South bank of the Thames between the Battersea and Wandsworth bridges."

"Tell them to warm up the engines. Can you give me a lift through town?"

"I'll have a pair of patrol cars outside the embassy in two minutes."

"Send them to Upper Brook Street," O'Donnell said. "There are no reporters back there."

"Right."

.   .   .

The flight to the south coast was ninety minutes in duration and thoroughly unpleasant because of high winds swirling ahead of a strong Atlantic storm front. As the Sea King swooped down toward Beacon Point, O'Donnell looked out his window and saw arc lamps blazing away on the little sand beach and blue police lights flashing along roads linking the surrounding villages of Kingston, Houghton, and Ringmore. The landing zone was a small patch of moorland behind the beach. O'Donnell was met there by the officer in charge, a stubby deputy chief constable from the Devon and Cornwall Constabulary aptly named Blunt. He briefed the FBI man as they walked down a sandy pathway to the beach.

"We've determined that the beach and surrounding grounds are free of bombs or any other weaponry," he said. "About twenty minutes ago we used a remote-control robotic device to have a look under the overturned boat."

"Anything there?" O'Donnell asked.

"Nothing that we could see with the camera, but it's possible something could be buried beneath it. We decided to wait until you arrived before moving the boat."

They clambered out of the dunes and stopped about twenty yards from the boat. An eight-foot dinghy with peeling gray and white paint, it was surrounded by a half-dozen policemen in blast-protection suits and visors. With a terse nod, Blunt spurred them into action, and the boat was soon resting on its hull. Taped to the seat in the stern was a DVD in a clear plastic case. Blunt retrieved it and immediately handed it to O'Donnell, who carried it back to the helicopter and inserted it into a laptop computer. As the image flickered to life on the screen, O'Donnell swore beneath his breath and looked at the British police official.

"I need a favor from you."

"Anything," said Blunt, his tone grave.

"Tell your men it was just a hoax. Apologize to them for the inconvenience, and thank them on behalf of the American people and Ambassador Halton for their fine work tonight."

"I'm afraid I don't understand, Mr. O'Donnell."

O'Donnell glanced at the screen. "This DVD does not exist. Now do you understand?"

Blunt nodded. He understood perfectly.

18

ANDREWS AIR FORCE BASE:
7:12 A.M., SATURDAY

The Gulfstream V executive jet touched down at Andrews Air Force Base outside Washington and taxied to a secure hangar with floors as smooth as polished marble. Gabriel descended the airstair, Samsonite bag in hand, and headed toward a waiting Suburban with Virginia license plates. The two CIA security men inside did not speak as he tossed the suitcase into the backseat and climbed in after it. Gabriel was used to this sort of behavior by the Americans. They were trained by their counter-intelligence people to believe that Office agents viewed every encounter with Agency personnel, no matter how mundane, as an opportunity for intelligence gathering. He was tempted to pose an inappropriate question or two, just to keep the myth alive. Instead he asked only where they were taking him.

"Headquarters," said the man in the passenger seat.

"I don't want to go to Headquarters."

"You'll go into the building black. No one will know you're there."

"Why can't we meet in a safe house, the way we usually do?"

"Your contact doesn't have time to leave the building today. I'm sure you can understand that."

Gabriel was about to object again but stopped himself. Twice in the past year his photograph had appeared in the world's newspapers, once for his actions inside the Vatican, and again for his attempt to prevent the kidnapping of Elizabeth Halton. Making his first appearance at Langley didn't seem to matter much in comparison. Besides, if Shamron and the prime minister had their way, it wouldn't be his last.

There was little traffic on the road at that hour on a Saturday, and it took them just thirty minutes to make the drive from Andrews to the woods of Langley. After a brief pause at the heavily fortified gatehouse for a credential check, they headed up the long immaculate drive toward the OHB, the Original Headquarters Building. Because Gabriel was entering the building "black," they sped past the main entrance and turned into an underground parking garage. One of the security men helped Gabriel with the Samsonite bag; the other led the way into a secure elevator. A card key was inserted, buttons were pushed, and a moment later they were ascending rapidly toward the seventh floor. When the doors opened, two more security men were waiting in the foyer, guns visible beneath their blazers. Gabriel was escorted along a carpeted corridor to a secure door, beyond which lay a suite of spacious offices occupied by the most powerful intelligence officers in the world. The man standing in the anteroom, dressed in gray flannel trousers and a wrinkled oxford cloth shirt, looked as though he had wandered in by mistake.

"How was the flight?" asked Adrian Carter.

"You have a very nice plane."

He shook Gabriel's hand warmly and looked at the bag.

"Planning to stay long, or just a day or two?"

"Only as long as I'm welcome," Gabriel said.

"I hope you brought more than clean shirts and underwear."

"I did."

Carter gave a fatigued smile and led Gabriel wordlessly into his office.

. . .

Gabriel accepted a cup of black coffee and lowered himself onto Carter's couch. Carter picked up a remote control from the edge of his tidy desk and fired it at a bank of television monitors. Elizabeth Halton's image immediately appeared on one of the screens. She was seated on the floor of a featureless room, dressed in the same cold-weather running suit she had been wearing in Hyde Park the morning of her kidnapping. In her hands was a copy of the *Times*, headlined with her own abduction. Four men were standing behind her: black jumpsuits, black balaclavas, green headbands with crossed swords and crescent moons. The one directly behind Elizabeth had a large knife in one hand and a sheet of paper in the other. He was reading a statement in Egyptian-accented Arabic.

"I take it you don't require translation," Carter said.

Gabriel, listening intently, shook his head. "He says he's from the Sword of Allah. He says they want you to release Sheikh Abdullah Abdul-Razzaq from prison and return him to Egypt by six P.M. London time next Friday. He says that if you don't comply with their demands, the ambassador's daughter will die. There will be no extensions, no negotiations, and no more contact. If there is any attempt at a rescue, Elizabeth Halton will be killed immediately."

The image turned to hash. Carter killed it with a flick of his remote and looked at Gabriel.

"You don't seem surprised."

"I learned about the Sword of Allah connection yesterday. It's why I'm here."

"How did you find out?"

"Sources and methods, Adrian. Sources and methods."

"Come now," Carter said mildly. "A woman's life is at stake. Now is not the time to be territorial."

"Just because we are technically at peace with Egypt doesn't mean we don't spy on them. We need to know whether the regime is going to stand or fall. We need to know whether we are about to be facing a hostile Islamic republic armed with advanced American weaponry. And we don't always get the information we need from our friends here at Langley."

"Your spy is SSI, I take it?"

Gabriel gave a sigh of resignation. "Our spy is in the business of keeping Mubarak and his regime alive."

Carter took that as confirmation of his suspicions. "Why is it that we've spent upward of fifty billion dollars propping up that regime, but you found out about the Sword connection before we did?"

"Because we're better than you, Adrian, especially in the Middle East. We've always been better and we always will be. You have your unquestioned military might and the power of your economy, but we have a nagging fear that we might not survive. Fear is a far more powerful motivation than money."

Carter placed the remote thoughtfully on his desk and sat down in his executive swivel chair.

"When did you get the video?" Gabriel asked.

Carter told him.

"Has word gotten out to the British media?"

"Not yet," Carter said. "It's our wish that it doesn't—at least not right away. We'd like to preserve the luxury of planning our response without the media screaming at us at every turn."

"I wouldn't count on MI5 and Scotland Yard safeguarding your secret for long. Someone will leak it, just the way they leaked my involvement and arrest."

"Don't be too hard on Graham Seymour," Carter said. "We need him and so do you. We brethren of the secret world don't burn each other at the stake at times like these. We band together and bind our wounds. We have to. The barbarians are at the gates."

"The barbarians broke down the gates a long time ago, Adrian.

They're living among us now and devouring our children." Gabriel sipped his coffee. "What is the position of the president?"

"It's not one I'd wish on my worst enemy," Carter replied. "As you know, he is a deeply religious man, and he takes his responsibilities as Elizabeth's godfather very seriously. That said, he knows that if he complies with the demands of the kidnappers, no American diplomat anywhere in the world will ever be safe again. He also knows that if Sheikh Abdullah Abdul-Razzaq is allowed to return to Egypt, the Mubarak government will find itself in a very precarious state. For all its problems, Egypt is still the most important country in the Arab world. If Egypt goes Islamic it will have a disastrous ripple effect across the entire region—disastrous for my country *and* yours. That means Elizabeth Halton is going to die one week from now, unless we can somehow find her and free her first."

Carter walked over to the window and peered out toward the leafless trees along the river. "You've been in a position like this, Gabriel. What would you do if you were the president?"

"I'd tell my biggest, meanest sons of bitches to do whatever it takes to find her."

"And if we can't? Do we make a deal and save our child from the barbarians?"

Gabriel left the question unanswered. Carter gazed silently out the window for a moment. "My doctor says the stress of this job is bad for my heart. He says I need to get more exercise. Take a walk with me, Gabriel. It will do us both good."

"It's twenty degrees outside."

"The cold air is good for you," Carter said. "It lends clarity to one's thoughts. It steels one's resolve for the travails that lay ahead."

. . .

They slipped from the OHB through a side exit and set out along a paved jogging trail through the trees overlooking the river. Carter was bundled in a thick toggle coat and wool hat. Gabriel had only the leather jacket he'd taken with him the previous morning to Cyprus and within a few moments he was numb with cold.

"All right," Carter said. "No one's listening now. How did you know they were going to strike in London?"

"No one's *listening*?" Gabriel looked around at the trees. "This place is littered with cameras, motion sensors, and hidden microphones."

"That's true," said Carter. "But answer the question anyway."

Gabriel told him about the tip he had received from Ibrahim Fawaz, the photographs he discovered during his hasty search of Samir al-Masri's apartment, and the lines on the legal pad he had correctly identified as a sketch of Hyde Park.

"Amazing," said Carter with genuine admiration in his voice. "And what was the great Gabriel Allon doing in Amsterdam?"

"I'm afraid you don't get to know that part of the story."

Carter, a consummate professional, moved on without objection. "Ibrahim Fawaz sounds like exactly the sort of Muslim we've been looking for—a man who's willing to expose the extremists and terrorists residing within his community and his mosque."

"That's what I thought, too. Unfortunately, there's a catch. Inside that suitcase I brought with me is a substantial portion of the SSI's dossier on the Sword of Allah. Guess whose file I found in there?"

"Your source is Sword of Allah?"

Gabriel nodded. "Before leaving Egypt, Dr. Ibrahim Fawaz served as a professor of economics at the University of Minya. According to his file, he was one of the group's earliest organizers. He was arrested after Sadat's assassination. The file is a bit vague on the reasons why, along with the duration of his detainment."

"They usually are," Carter said. "Why did he leave Egypt and come to Europe? And why did he tell you there was a plot being organized from within the al-Hijrah Mosque in west Amsterdam?"

"Obviously someone needs to put those very questions to him— and sooner rather than later. He lied to me or didn't tell me the whole story. Either way, he was being deceptive. He's hiding something, Adrian."

They came to the intersection of two pathways. Carter guided Gabriel to the left, and together they set out through a stand of leafless trees. Carter dug a pipe and a pouch of tobacco from the pocket of his overcoat and slowly loaded the bowl. "They don't let us smoke in the building anymore," he said, pausing to ignite the tobacco with an elegant silver lighter.

"I wish we'd pass a similar rule."

"Can you imagine Shamron without his Turkish cigarettes?" Carter started walking again, trailing a plume of maple-scented smoke behind him like a steam engine. "I suppose we have two options. Option one, we pass along your information about Fawaz to the Dutch police and allow them to bring him in for questioning, with the FBI in close attendance, of course."

"Option number two?"

"We pick him up for an off-the-record chat, in a place where the usual rules of interrogation don't apply."

"You know which option I would vote for."

"I'm glad you feel that way," Carter said. "I think you should go to Amsterdam and personally supervise the operation."

"Me?" Gabriel shook his head. "I'm afraid my role in this affair is officially over. Besides, it's not as if the CIA doesn't have experience in these kinds of operations."

"We do indeed," Carter said. "But, unfortunately, we've screwed up quite a few of them—under my watch, I'm ashamed to say. The Europeans are no longer willing to turn a blind eye to our extralegal activities on their soil, and our own covert operatives are so afraid of prosecution at home and abroad that they no longer undertake sensitive missions without first consulting a lawyer. Our intrepid director has his finger firmly in the air and has detected that, for the moment, the wind is no longer at our backs. The days when we roamed Europe and the Middle East, breaking laws and limbs as we saw fit, are now over. The doors of the secret prisons are now closed, and we no longer deliver our enemies into the hands of men who dream up novel uses for rubber hoses and cattle prods. We've put away our brass knuckles. We're a club fit for gentlemen from Princeton and Yale again, but that's as it should be."

"We like to keep our gentlemen from Princeton and Yale confined to King Saul Boulevard, where they can't get into trouble."

Carter walked in silence for a moment with his eyes on the pavement. "We've been preparing for something like this to happen for a long time. Our brethren at the FBI have overall responsibility for hostage recovery efforts under a scenario like this. We are gathering intelligence, of course, and liaising with allied services in Europe and the Middle East. We would regard you and your team as a black element of our larger multinational effort. You would, in effect, be a subcontractor of the Agency. It's unconventional, but, given our past association, I think we can make it work."

"I would need the approval of the prime minister." Gabriel hesitated. "And, of course, Shamron would have to sign off on it."

"I'll set up a secure link to Jerusalem from my office. I promise no one will listen in."

"I'll call from our embassy, if you don't mind."

"Suit yourself." Carter paused and knocked his pipe against the trunk of a tree. "Did your source happen to tell you who he thinks is behind this?"

Gabriel answered the question. Carter nodded and stuffed more tobacco into his pipe. "We know all about the Sphinx," he said. "We think he's the one who planned the attack on the tourists at the Pyramids three years ago that left seventeen Americans dead. We also think he's responsible for the murder of two of our diplomats in Cairo. One of them was CIA, by the way. There's a star for him on the wall in the main lobby. I'm afraid the Sphinx has something of a reputation when it comes to dealing with those who arrest or kill Sword personnel. Thanks to your efforts in London, you can be sure you're at the top of his hit list. You'll need to watch your step when you're back in the field."

"I assume you've told the Egyptians about the video and the demands?"

"We felt we had no choice," Carter said. "They've pledged their full support, and they've also made it clear to us that caving in to the Sword's demands would be a very bad idea. The Egyptian foreign minister is traveling to Washington secretly later today to reinforce that point with the secretary of state and the president. He's bringing along a team from the Interior Ministry and representatives of all the Egyptian security and intelligence services. We're adding Egyptian components to our task force here and in London."

"Just make sure no one mentions our little *black* operation in front of them. The Islamists have penetrated every level of Egyptian society and government, including the security services. You can be sure the Sphinx has contacts inside the SSI."

"Your operation does not exist, and no one will know about it but me." Carter looked at his watch. "How long will it take you to deploy in Amsterdam?"

"I have a man there already who can begin surveillance of the target immediately."

"One man? I hope's he's good."

"He is."

"And the rest of your team?"

"Forty-eight hours."

"That leaves only five days before the deadline." Carter said. "Take my plane back to Ben-Gurion. That will save you several critical hours. We'll need someone from the Agency on your team in order to coordinate your activities with the larger effort. Otherwise we run the risk of tripping over each other in the field."

"I don't want anyone from the CIA on my team. He'll just get in the way. And besides, I fully anticipate we'll be doing things that violate American law. I can't have him stopping every five minutes to consult with his Washington lawyer."

"I'm afraid I have to insist."

"All right, Adrian, we'll let you come along."

"Nothing would make me happier, but leaving Headquarters is not an option, at least not at the moment. I do have another candidate in mind, someone who's experienced in the field and has been forged by fire. And the best part is you trained her."

Gabriel stopped walking. "You can't be serious."

"I'm quite serious."

"Where is she?"

"The Saudi desk at the Counterterrorism Center."

"How soon can she be ready to leave?"

"I'll make one phone call and she's yours."

19

OFF LE HAVRE, FRANCE:
4:49 P.M., SATURDAY

The lights of the French coastline pricked the darkness off the prow of the Portsmouth–to–Le Havre ferry. The man seated near the observation windows in the upper lounge glanced at his wristwatch. Thirty minutes remained of the five-hour crossing. He signaled the waitress and, with a small gesture of his hand, ordered another Carlsberg, his fourth of the journey. She brought it a moment later and placed it suggestively on his table. She had bleached-blond hair and a jeweled stud in her lower lip. Her name tag said CHRISTINE. The man stared directly at her, the way infidel men always stared at their women, and allowed his eyes to wander over her breasts.

"You have a name?" she asked.

"Thomas," he said.

It wasn't his real name. It was borrowed, like his borrowed driver's license and borrowed British passport. His Yorkshire accent was the real thing. He was a Yorkshire lad, born and bred.

"I could be wrong, Thomas, but I think you have an admirer."

"Oh, really? Who?"

The waitress glanced toward the other side of the lounge. Seated alone at a table near the opposite window was a small woman in her mid-twenties with short dark hair and stormy black eyes. She was dressed in tight jeans and a snug-fitting pullover embroidered with the word OUI.

"She's been looking at you ever since we left Portsmouth," the waitress said. "Can't keep her eyes off you, actually."

"Not my type."

"What is your type?"

He remembered the words his controller had spoken during the final briefing. *Whatever you do, don't sit by yourself looking as though you are a terrorist. Strike up a conversation. Buy someone a drink. Flirt with a girl if there's a girl to flirt with.*

"I like girls named Christine who serve drinks on Channel ferries."

"You don't say."

She smiled at him. He felt his stomach churn with rage.

"When are you going back to England?" she asked.

"Tomorrow, midday."

"What a coincidence. I'm going back on the same boat. I'll see you then, I hope."

"Cheers to that."

The waitress walked back to the bar. The man with the Yorkshire accent raised his beer to his lips and, before taking a swallow, begged Allah for forgiveness. He had done other things during the past few days for which he had sought Allah's pardon. He had shaved his beard for the first time since he was a teenager and had dyed his dark hair platinum blond to look more like a native European. He had eaten pork sausage in a roadside café in Britain and had spoken to many women with unveiled faces. He had sought no absolution, however, for his role in the kidnapping of the American woman. Her father served the Crusader regime—a regime that oppressed Muslims around the world, a regime that supported Israel while the Palestinians suffered, a regime that supported an apostate thug like Hosni Mubarak who grew rich while the Egyptian people slipped deeper into poverty and despair with each passing day. The American woman was nothing more than a tool to be used to secure the release of Sheikh Abdullah from the Crusader jail, an infidel cow that could be taken to market and, if necessary, slaughtered without mercy and without fear of Allah's retribution.

A voice crackled over the ship's loudspeaker. It was the captain informing the passengers that the ferry would soon make landfall. The man in the bar finished the rest of his beer, then headed down a flight of stairs to the vehicle-loading deck. The silver LDV Maxus panel van was parked in the center column, three rows from the stern. He opened the rear doors and peered into the darkened cargo area. Inside were several dozen large crates that bore the markings of a fine bone china from a manufacturer in Yorkshire. The shipment, which was fully documented, was bound for an exclusive shop in the French city of Strasbourg—a shop that happened to be owned by an Egyptian with close links to the Sword of Allah. Several of the crates had been opened by British police at the Portsmouth ferry terminal, presumably in an effort to locate the missing American woman. Their search had uncovered nothing besides fine bone china from Yorkshire.

The man closed the rear doors, then walked around to the driver's side and climbed behind the wheel. The dark-haired girl from the lounge bar was now seated in the passenger seat, her snug-fitting pullover concealed by a heavy leather jacket.

"It looked to me like you actually enjoyed flirting with that infidel cow," the girl said.

"I wanted to slap her face the entire time."

"She's definitely going to remember you," the girl said. "In fact, she's going to remember us both."

He smiled. That was exactly the point.

Five minutes later the ferry eased into the landing at Le Havre. The man with platinum blond hair and a Yorkshire accent guided the van onto French soil and headed for Rennes.

20

ANDREWS AIR FORCE BASE:
2 : 1 7 P . M . , SATURDAY

S o whose bright idea was this anyway?" asked
Sarah Bancroft. "Yours or Adrian's?"

Gabriel looked at the woman seated opposite him in the passenger cabin of the CIA Gulfstream V. She had shoulder-length
blond hair, skin the color of alabaster, and eyes like a cloudless
summer sky. Dressed as she was now, in a cashmere pullover,
trim faded jeans, and shapely leather boots, she was dangerously attractive.

"It was definitely Adrian's."

"You, of course, balked at the suggestion."

"Absolutely."

"Why did you cave?"

"It was either a knuckle dragger from the Clandestine Service or
you. Naturally I chose you."

"It's good to know one is wanted."

"I didn't *want* anyone. Adrian insisted we include someone from
the Agency and you seemed like the least harmful option. After all,
we trained you. You know some of our personnel and you know
how we operate. You know the difference between a *bodel* and a

neviot officer. You speak our language." He frowned. "Well, almost. I suppose the fact you don't speak Hebrew is an advantage. It means we can still talk about you behind your back."

"I can only imagine the things you all said about me."

"Rest assured it was all complimentary, Sarah. You were the quickest study any of us had ever seen. But then we always knew you would be. That's why we chose you in the first place."

Actually, it was Adrian Carter who had chosen her. *You find the painting,* Carter had said. *I'll get you the girl.* The painting Gabriel had found was a lost masterpiece by van Gogh called *Marguerite Gachet at Her Dressing Table,* which had vanished after Vincent's death into the private collection of a Paris lawyer. Carter had managed to find a lost masterpiece of his own, a European-educated, multilingual art historian who was working as a curator at the Phillips Collection museum in Washington, D.C. Gabriel had used her to penetrate the business entourage of a Saudi billionaire terrorist financier named Zizi al-Bakari, and her life had never been the same since.

"You know, Gabriel, if I'm not mistaken, that might well have been the first compliment you ever paid me. During my preparation for the al-Bakari operation you barely said a word to me. You left me in the hands of your instructors and the other members of your team. Why was that?" Greeted by silence, she answered her own question. "Maybe you had to keep your distance. Otherwise, you wouldn't have been able to send me into Zizi's camp. Who knows? Maybe you liked me a little too much."

"My feelings for you were strictly professional, Sarah."

"I wasn't suggesting otherwise." She was silent for a moment. "You know, after the operation ended, I missed you all terribly. You were the first real family I ever had." She hesitated, then added: "I even missed *you,* Gabriel."

"I almost got you killed."

"Oh, that." She looked down and made a church steeple of her ringless fingers. "It wasn't your fault. It was mine. It was a beautiful operation. I'll let you in on a little secret. The Agency isn't as good as the Office. Our operations are like bricks and mortar. Yours are like . . ." She paused, searching for the right word. "Like art," she said. "They're like one of your grandfather's paintings."

"My grandfather was a German Expressionist," Gabriel said. "Some of his paintings were rather chaotic and violent."

"And so are your operations."

Sarah reclined her seat and propped one boot on the armrest of Gabriel's chair. An image flashed in Gabriel's memory: Sarah, in a black veil, chained to a torturer's table in a chalet in the mountains of Switzerland.

"You're looking at me that way again," she said.

"Which way is that?"

"The way you used to look at that van Gogh we sold Zizi. You used to look at me and Marguerite Gachet the same way. You're assessing me. You're looking for losses and abrasions. You're wondering whether the canvas can be brought back to life or whether it's beyond repair."

"What's the answer?"

"The canvas is fine, Gabriel. It doesn't need any work at all. In fact, it's quite suitable for hanging just as it is."

"No more nightmares? No more sessions with the Agency psychologists?"

"I wouldn't go that far." She looked down again, and a shadow seemed to pass over her eyes. "No one at Langley knows what Elizabeth Halton is going through better than I do. Maybe that's why Adrian chose me for this assignment. He's a former case officer. He knows how to push buttons."

"I've noticed that."

She looked up at him as the Gulfstream swept down the runway. "So where are we going?"

"First we're going to make a brief stop in Tel Aviv to assemble my team. Then we're going to Amsterdam to have a quiet word with a man who's going to help us find Elizabeth Halton."

"Anyone I know?"

"Probably not."

"Tell me about him," she said.

Gabriel waited until the plane was airborne. Then he told her everything.

. . .

It was shortly after dawn the next morning when they arrived at King Saul Boulevard in Tel Aviv. Gabriel stopped briefly at the Operations Desk to collect Eli Lavon's first surveillance photographs and watch reports from Amsterdam, then led Sarah along a subterranean corridor to a doorway marked 456C. For many years the room was nothing but a dumping ground for obsolete computers and worn-out office furniture, often used by the night staff as a place for romantic trysts. Now it was known throughout King Saul Boulevard as Gabriel's Lair. Affixed to the door was a faded paper sign, written in his own stylish Hebrew hand, that read: TEMPORARY COMMITTEE FOR THE STUDY OF TERROR THREATS IN WESTERN EUROPE. The sign had served him well through two tumultuous operations. Gabriel decided to leave it for now.

He opened the combination lock, then switched on the fluorescent lights and stepped inside. The room was precisely as he had left it a year earlier. One wall was covered by surveillance photographs, another by a diagram of a global business empire, and a third by a collection of Impressionist prints. Gabriel's chalkboard stood forlornly in the corner, its surface bare except for a single name: SARAH BANCROFT. She followed him inside tentatively, as though entering a forgotten room from her childhood, and stared at the photographs: Zizi al-Bakari with his spoiled daughter, Nadia, at his side; Abdul and Abdul, his American-educated lawyers; Herr Wehrli, his Swiss banker; Mr. bin Talal, his chief of security; Jean-Michel, his French personal trainer and Sarah's main tormentor. She turned around and looked at Gabriel.

"You planned it all from here?"

He nodded his head slowly. She looked around the room with her eyes narrowed in disbelief.

"Somehow I expected something more . . ." Her voice trailed off, then she added: "Something more impressive."

"This is the Office, Sarah, not Langley. We like to do things the old-fashioned way."

"Obviously." She looked at his chalkboard. "I haven't seen one of those since I was in grade school."

Gabriel smiled, then began removing the debris of the al-Bakari operation from the walls of the room as the other members of his team trickled slowly through the door. No introductions were necessary, for Sarah knew and adored them all. The first to arrive was Yossi, a tall, balding intellectual from the Office's Research division who had read classics at Oxford and still spoke Hebrew with a pronounced British accent. Next came Dina Sarid, a veritable encyclopedia of terrorism from the History division who could recite the time, place, and casualty count of every act of violence ever committed against the State of Israel. Ten minutes later came Yaakov, a battle-hardened case officer from the Arab Affairs Department of Shabak, followed by Rimona, an IDF major who served as an analyst for AMAN, Israel's military intelligence service. Oded, a brooding, all-purpose field operative who specialized in snatches, arrived at eight with breakfast for everyone, and Mordecai, a wispy figure who dealt in all things electronic, stumbled in fifteen minutes later looking as though he had not slept the night before. The last to arrive was Mikhail, a gray-eyed gunman of Russian birth, who had single-handedly killed half of the terrorist infrastructure of Hamas and Palestinian Islamic Jihad. It was because of Mikhail and his proficiency with a handgun that Sarah was alive. She kissed his cheek as Gabriel walked to the front of the room and pinned Lavon's surveillance photographs to the bulletin board.

"Now that we're all reacquainted," he said, "it's time to get to work. This is the man who's going to lead us to Elizabeth Halton. He is a founding member of Sword of Allah, currently living in Amsterdam. We're going to make him vanish into thin air, then we're going to squeeze him dry. We have to work quickly, and we're not going to make any mistakes."

.   .   .

The Office prided itself on its ability to improvise in times of crisis, but even the vaunted Office chafed under the pressure of Gabriel's demands. Safe accommodations were his biggest concern, and Housekeeping, the division that maintained and acquired Office properties, was his most stubborn opponent. Unlike cities such as Paris, London, and Rome, where the Office maintained dozens of safe flats, Amsterdam had no standing inventory of secure lodging. That meant accommodations had to be acquired quickly and on the open market, something the notoriously deliberate Housekeeping never liked to do. By ten o'clock they had taken a six-month lease on a two-bedroom apartment on the Herengracht canal, and by eleven they had secured a luxury houseboat on the Prinsengracht called the *Heleen*. That left only a site for the interrogation. Gabriel needed something large enough for his entire team and remote enough so that their presence would go undetected. He had a property in mind—a tumbledown country house outside Oldenburg that they had used during the Wrath of God operation—and eventually he was able to pry it from Housekeeping's grasp.

Once Housekeeping capitulated, the rest fell like dominoes. By noon Travel had lined up a string of untraceable rental cars, and by one Identity had coughed up enough clean passports to allow every member of the team to travel as a European. Banking section initially balked at Gabriel's request for a briefcase filled with petty cash, but at one-thirty he staged what amounted to an armed stickup and left Banking ten minutes later carrying a handsome attaché case filled with fifty thousand dollars and another fifty thousand in well-circulated euros.

By the middle of the afternoon the first members of his team were slipping quietly from King Saul Boulevard and heading off to Ben-Gurion. Oded, Mordecai, and Rimona left at three-thirty and boarded a flight to Brussels. Yossi, Yaakov, and Dina left an hour later on a Lufthansa flight to Frankfurt. Gabriel and Sarah left last and, shortly after eight o'clock, they were taking their seats in the first-class section of El Al's evening flight to Paris. As the rest of the passengers filed on board, Gabriel telephoned Chiara to tell her he had been in the country and was leaving again. She didn't ask where he was going. She didn't need to know.

21

IMBABA, CAIRO:
8:23 A.M., SUNDAY

The Cairo slum known as Imbaba is one of the most desperately poor places on earth. Located just across the Nile from the fashionable island district of Zamalek, Imbaba is so crowded its rickety tenement buildings often collapse beneath the weight of their occupants. The alleys are unpaved, without names, and in perpetual darkness. They run with raw sewage and are choked with mounds of uncollected garbage. At night they are ruled by packs of wild dogs. The children of Imbaba wear rags, drink from cesspools, and live in fear of being eaten alive by the rats. There is little running water, only brief interludes of electricity, and even less hope. Only Islam. Radical Islam. It is written on the crumbling walls in green spray paint: *ISLAM IS THE ANSWER . . . ONLY THE SWORD CAN SAVE US . . .*

The mood in Imbaba that morning was more tense than usual. Riot police were roaming the alleyways and SSI men in plain clothes were surveying their surroundings from coffee shops and falafel stands. Hussein Mandali, a fourth-grade teacher at the Imbaba middle school, had seen it like this before. The security forces were about to move in for a sweep. Any man with a beard and a galabiya—or any woman in a *niqab*—would be arrested and thrown into the Scorpion, the dreaded facility inside Cairo's Torah Prison complex reserved for Islamists. Everyone, regardless of sex, would spend at least a few minutes on the torture table. Pharaoh's secret police did not concern themselves much with laws or rules of evidence. Their task was to instill fear, and they did so with ruthless efficiency.

Hussein Mandali did not wear a beard, though he did dress in the galabiya, the only garment he could afford on his pittance of a salary. Egypt's education system, like nearly everything else in the country, was crumbling. Teachers earned nothing and students learned little. For many years the country's twenty-five thousand public schools had been under the control of Islamists. As a result they were little more than factories that each year churned out thousands of young men and women committed to the destruction of the regime and its supporters in the West. Hussein Mandali knew this phenomenon all too well. He lectured his students daily on the rewards of jihad and martyrdom, and told them it was their sacred duty to kill Americans and Jews and topple their puppet, Hosni Mubarak. The children of Imbaba were always willing recruits. The proof of Pharaoh's indifference to their plight was all around them.

A group of police officers was standing guard at the end of the street. They eyed Mandali suspiciously as he slipped past without a word and set out along the cacophonous boulevard overlooking the western bank of the Nile. Two minutes later he turned left onto a bridge and crossed over onto Zamalek. How different it was here, he thought. Zamalek was an island of privilege surrounded by a sea of misery, a place where the vast majority of Egypt's population could not afford to buy a pastry or a cup of coffee. Zamalek would soon feel the wrath of Egypt's legions of downtrodden Muslims, Mandali thought. So would the entire world.

He followed July 26 Street across the island, then wandered for a time through the quiet side streets north of the Gezira Sporting Club to make certain he wasn't being followed. Thirty minutes after leaving Imbaba, he approached a luxury high-rise apartment house called the Ramses Towers. The tall Sudanese standing guard over the entrance was a member of the Sword of Allah. He guided Mandali into the marble lobby and instructed him to use the back staircase so that none of the other tenants would see a poor man in their gilded elevator. As a result, Mandali was heavily winded when he presented himself at the door of Apartment 2408 and knocked in the prescribed fashion: two knocks, followed by a brief pause, then three more knocks.

The door was opened a few seconds later by a man dressed in a pale gray galabiya. He admitted Mandali into a formal entrance hall, then showed him into a magnificent sitting room overlooking the Nile. Seated cross-legged on the floor, dressed in a white galabiya and a crocheted white skullcap, was an elderly man with a long gray beard. Hussein Mandali kissed the old man's leathery cheeks and sat before him.

"You have news from the street?" asked Sheikh Tayyib Abdul-Razzaq.

"Mubarak's forces have surrounded Imbaba and have started to infiltrate the district. In other parts of the country, the army and the police are hitting us very hard. Fayoum, Minya, Asyut, and Luxor have all seen heavy raids. The situation is tense. One spark and it could explode."

The sheikh fingered his prayer beads and looked at the other man. "Bring me a tape recorder," he said, "and I'll give you a spark."

The man laid the recorder at the feet of the sheikh and switched it on. One hour later Hussein Mandali was once again picking his way through the alleys of Imbaba, this time with a cassette tape concealed inside his sock. By nightfall the sermon would be circulating through a network of popular mosques and underground jihadists cells. After that it would be in the hands of Allah. Hussein Mandali was sure of only one thing. The open sewers of Imbaba would soon be flowing red with the blood of Pharaoh's soldiers.

22

AMSTERDAM:
9:30 A.M., MONDAY

eleen was squat and boxy, painted chocolate brown and trimmed in red. Flower boxes lined her gunwales, and a skiff with an outboard motor bobbed at her stern. Her interior had been recently renovated; stainless-steel appliances shone in the small but sophisticated kitchen, and Scandinavian-style furniture adorned the comfortable sitting room. Three modern paintings of questionable taste had been removed from the walls and in their place hung a large-scale map of Amsterdam and several dozen surveillance photographs of a Muslim man of late middle age. A notebook computer with secure communications software stood on the glass dining-room table, and before it sat a small figure who seemed to be wearing all of his clothing at once. Gabriel pleaded with him to extinguish his cigarette. The overnight drive from Paris had left him with a splitting headache.

"If Ibrahim Fawaz is a terrorist, he certainly doesn't act like one," Eli Lavon said. "He doesn't engage in anything that might be construed as a rudimentary countersurveillance, and his movements are predictable and direct."

Gabriel looked up at the map of Amsterdam on the wall, where Ibrahim's daily routine was represented by a thick red line. It ran from his apartment in the August Allebéplein to the West Amsterdam Islamic Community Center, then to the Ten Kate Market, and finally to the al-Hijrah Mosque. Times of arrival and departure were meticulously noted and supported by photographic evidence.

"Where?" Gabriel asked. "Where should we take him?"

Lavon stood and walked over to the map. "In my learned opinion, there's only one spot that's suitable. Here"—he stabbed the map twice with his stubby forefinger—"at the end of the Jan Hazenstraat. He walks by there on the way home from evening prayers at the mosque. It's reasonably quiet for Amsterdam, and if we can take out the streetlamps he'll never see us coming." He turned and looked at Gabriel. "When are you thinking about doing it?"

The answer came from the kitchen, where Sarah was making a fresh pot of coffee. "Tonight," she said. "We have no choice but to take him tonight and start the interrogation."

"Tonight?" Lavon looked at Gabriel and gave him an incredulous smile. "A year ago I was teaching this child how to walk the street like a professional. Now she is telling me that I have to kidnap a man from a densely populated European city after watching him for less than forty-eight hours."

"Unfortunately, the child is right, Eli. We have to do it tonight and get started."

Lavon sat down again and folded his arms. "Do you remember how long I watched Zwaiter in Rome before we even began talking about how to kill him? Three weeks. And that was for an assassination, not a kidnapping. And you know what Shamron always says about kidnap operations."

"He says it's much easier to leave a dead man on a sidewalk than it is to get a live one into a getaway car." Gabriel smiled. "Shamron *does* have a way with words, doesn't he?"

Sarah brought the pot of coffee to the table and sat down next to

Gabriel. Lavon lit a cigarette and blew a stream of smoke toward the ceiling in frustration.

"The police in this city are on high alert because of the links between the Amsterdam cell and the attack in London," he said. "We need to watch Ibrahim for at least another week. We have to plan a primary escape route, a backup escape route, and a backup to the backup escape route. We have to put the snatch zone under twenty-four-hour surveillance, so we know there won't be any surprises on the night of the operation. Have I forgotten anything?"

"The dry runs," said Gabriel. "We should make at least three dry runs. And in a perfect world we would do all those things. But in the real world, Elizabeth Halton has less than five days to live. We prepare as much as we can, but we take him tonight."

"And we pray to God we all don't end up in jail, which is what's going to happen if we make a mistake." Lavon gazed despondently at his wristwatch. "Let's take a walk over to the Oud West. Who knows? It might be our last opportunity for a very long time."

.   .   .

The bustling outdoor market that ran for several blocks along the Ten Kate Straat reflected the altered demographics of Amsterdam's Oud West neighborhood. There were dates and lentils, barrels filled with olives and chickpeas, shwarma stands and falafel vendors, and three different halal butchers. Gabriel paused briefly in the open-air shoe store and picked through a pile of counterfeit American basketball shoes, the ultimate status symbol of the young, even among the street toughs of west Amsterdam. At the stall on the opposite side of the street, Sarah was scrutinizing a canvas book bag emblazoned with the face of Che Guevara, while Lavon was feigning interest in a hooded sweatshirt that proclaimed FREE PALESTINE NOW!

Lavon looked at Gabriel and gave an almost imperceptible nod of his head, the signal that he had detected no surveillance. A moment later they were all three walking side by side toward the far end of the market. The stall where Ibrahim Fawaz worked in the afternoon was occupied by an elderly Moroccan man in a white djellaba. Sarah paused to examine an electric teakettle while Gabriel and Lavon walked on to the end of the market. On the opposite side of the street, in a drab, postwar building, was the al-Hijrah Mosque. Two bearded men were conversing outside on the pavement, under the watchful gaze of two uniformed Amsterdam policemen. Twenty yards away was a dark van with blacked out windows.

"It hasn't moved in forty-eight hours," Lavon said.

"Dutch security?"

Lavon nodded. "If I had to guess, I'd say they have a static post in the building across the street as well."

Gabriel looked back toward the kitchen supplies stall and motioned for Sarah to join them. Then they turned to the left and walked along the Jan Hazenstraat. It was a quiet street lined with squat, mismatched tenement buildings and small storefronts. At the far end, overlooking a broad canal, was a tiny park with a few benches, a swing set, and a pair of rusted hobbyhorses on steel springs. Gabriel rounded the corner to the left and paused: more apartment blocks, but no storefronts or cafés, nothing that would be open after dark.

"Evening prayers begin tonight at six thirty-seven," Lavon said. "Which means that Ibrahim will be passing by this spot at approximately seven o'clock. Once he comes around the corner, no one in the van or the static post will be able to see him. We just have to make sure we get him without making any noise. I recommend we put the getaway vehicle on this corner where the Dutch agents can't see it. Then we have to do something that makes Ibrahim slow down long enough so that we can get him cleanly."

Gabriel thought of the night he and Ibrahim had walked along the Amstel River together and a single image flashed in his memory— Ibrahim Fawaz lowering his gaze in disgust as two men strolled toward them arm in arm.

"He doesn't like homosexuals," Gabriel said.

"Few Islamists do," Lavon replied. "What do you have in mind?"
Gabriel told him. Lavon smiled.

"To whom do you intend to give this assignment?"

"Mikhail and Yaakov," Gabriel said without hesitation.

"Perfect," said Eli Lavon. "But you tell them. Those boys make me nervous."

THE WHITE HOUSE:
12:45 P.M., MONDAY

There was no mistaking the perpetrator of the assault on the door of Nicholas Scanlon's office. Two knocks, sharp as a tack hammer. The White House press secretary allowed ten uncomfortable seconds to elapse before looking up from his work. Melissa Stewart, NBC's chief White House correspondent, was leaning against the doorjamb, her arms folded defiantly, her newly tinted hair tousled from her last live shot on the North Lawn.

"What's on your mind, Melissa?"

"We need to talk."

"No paper in the ladies' room again?"

Stewart stepped inside the office and closed the door.

"Please come in, Melissa," Scanlon said sarcastically. "Have a seat."

"I'd love to, Nick, but I'm in a bit of a rush."

"What can I do for you?"

"Confirm a story."

Scanlon shuffled the papers on his desk and played for time. "What have you got?"

"I know who's holding Elizabeth Halton hostage."

"Do tell, Melissa. We'd all like to know."

"It's the Sword of Allah, Nick. A few days ago a DVD of Elizabeth was left in the countryside of southern England. They want Sheikh Abdullah back, and if we don't have him on a plane bound for Egypt by Friday night, they're going to kill her."

"What's your source?"

"That doesn't sound like a denial."

"Answer the question, please."

"You don't really expect me to divulge my source, do you?"

"At least characterize the nature of the source for me."

"Law enforcement," she said. "But that's as far as I go."

Scanlon swiveled his chair around and gazed through his bullet-proof window toward the North Lawn. *A fucking leak . . .* It was a miracle they had managed to keep a lid on it this long. It had been just six months since Scanlon had left his lucrative job as a lobbyist and public relations executive to come to work for the president, but in that time he had been given ample evidence of Washington's proclivity to leak. And the worse the news, the faster it gushed out. He wondered what would possibly motivate a federal law enforcement official to slip a piece of news like this to a reporter. He rotated his chair around and looked into Melissa Stewart's large blue eyes. *But of course,* he thought.

"You still sleeping with that guy from the Bureau?"

"Stay out of my personal life, Nick."

"I'm going to give you a piece of advice, and I hope you take it in the spirit it is offered. This is not a story you want to be first on."

"That doesn't sound like a denial either."

"As you can imagine, we are in the middle of some very delicate operations around the globe right now—operations that will be placed in jeopardy if this news is revealed before we're ready."

"I'm sorry, Nick, but this is just too big to sit on. If it's true, we have to go with it. The American people deserve to know who's holding Ambassador Halton's daughter."

"Even if it gets her killed?"

"You've sunk into the depths before, but that's the lowest."

"I can go much lower, Melissa. I'll deny it's true, and then I'll denounce you from the podium."

She turned and reached for the doorknob.

"Wait," Scanlon said, his tone suddenly conciliatory. "Perhaps we can reach an accommodation."

"What do you have in mind?"

"How long can you give me?"

"Ten minutes."

"Twenty," Scanlon countered.

"Fifteen."

Scanlon nodded in agreement. Stewart looked at her watch.

"If the phone in my booth doesn't ring in fifteen fucking minutes," she said, "I'm going to march out to the lawn and tell the world who's holding Elizabeth Halton."

. . .

The president was seated at his desk when Nicholas Scanlon entered the Oval Office three minutes later, accompanied by White House Chief of Staff William Burns and National Security Advisor Cyrus Mansfield.

"Why the long faces, gentlemen?" the president asked.

"There's been a leak, Mr. President," Scanlon said. "NBC knows who's holding Elizabeth."

The president closed his eyes in frustration. For more than a week now, he had been walking a fine line, attempting to show appropriate concern in public for the fate of his friend's daughter while at the same time making it clear to the terrorists that they had not managed to incapacitate the most powerful man on the planet. Only those closest to the president knew the physical and emotional toll the kidnapping had taken on him.

"What do you suggest, Nick?"

"Taking the bull by the horns, sir. I think it would be better for the country and the rest of the world to hear the news from your mouth than Melissa Stewart's."

"How long do we have before she goes on the air with it?"

Scanlon looked at his watch. "Nine minutes, sir."

The president looked from his press secretary to his national se-curity advisor. "I need to know whether I'm going to be placing any sensitive operations in jeopardy if I go public now. Get the director of the CIA on the line. The secretary of state, too."

"Yes, sir."

The president looked at Scanlon again. "Assuming no one has any objections, where would you like to do this?"

"The Briefing Room feels appropriate to me."

"No questions, though."

"I'll make that clear to the reporters beforehand."

"How are you going to handle Melissa Stewart?"

"We'll have to promise her something," Scanlon said. "Some-thing big."

"Couldn't we just appeal to her sense of decency and patriotism?"

"We're talking about Melissa Stewart, Mr. President. I'm not sure she has a pulse, let alone a sense of patriotism."

The president exhaled heavily. "You can tell her the first interview I do after this is over will be with NBC News. That should make her happy."

"That's going to cause me problems elsewhere in the press room, sir."

"I'm afraid that those are *your* problems, Nick, not mine."

"Would you like me to draft a statement for you, sir?"

The president shook his head. "This is one I can handle on my own."

· · ·

Melissa Stewart was pulling on her overcoat and preparing to head for the North Lawn when the telephone in her booth rang.

"Cutting it close, don't you think?"

"I'm sorry, Melissa. For a moment I forgot that you're the center of the universe."

"I'm late for an important live shot, Nick."

"Cancel it."

"What have you got for me?"

"The president is going into the Briefing Room in twenty minutes to tell the world that the Sword of Allah is holding Elizabeth Halton hostage and is demanding the release of Sheikh Abdullah. Before his appearance, you may report that NBC News has learned that Elizabeth Halton is being held by Egyptian militants and that the president is expected to say more on the situation. If you stick to the script, your network will get the first exclusive with the president when this affair is over. If you don't, I'll devote the rest of my time at the White House to making your life miserable. Do we have a deal?"

"I believe we do."

"See you in the Briefing Room in ten minutes. And don't try to slip one past me, Melissa. I'll be listening carefully."

· · ·

The president of the United States stepped to the podium in the White House Briefing Room at precisely 1:30 P.M. Eastern time and informed the world that his goddaughter had been taken hostage by the Egyptian terror group known as the Sword of Allah. In exchange for Elizabeth's release, said the president, the terrorists had demanded that the United States free Sheik Abdullah Abdul-Razzaq. It was a demand, the president made clear, that would never be met. He called on the terrorists to release Elizabeth immediately, warned them and their sponsors that they would be brought to justice, and thanked the American people for their prayers and support.

At 1:32, the president stepped away from the podium and left Nicholas Scanlon, his press secretary, to face the stunned press corps alone. Adrian Carter pressed the MUTE button on his remote control and looked toward the door of his office, where Shepard Cantwell, the deputy director for intelligence, was standing in his shirtsleeves and suspenders.

"What did you think?" Cantwell asked.

Carter hesitated before answering. Shepard Cantwell only asked questions of others when he wanted to venture an opinion of his own. Cantwell couldn't help it. He was Analysis.

"I thought he did as well as expected under the circumstances," Carter said. "He made it clear to the Sword that we won't be held hostage and that we won't negotiate."

"You're assuming that's what the Sword really wants: to negotiate. I'm not so sure about that." Cantwell came into Carter's office and sat down. "Our analysts have been poring over every word Sheikh Tayyib Abdul-Razzaq has ever written or said publicly: sermons, fatwas, transcripts of interviews, anything we can lay our hands on. A couple of years ago he gave an interview to an Arabic-language newspaper from London under conditions of extreme secrecy somewhere inside Egypt. During the interview the sheikh was asked to name the most likely scenario under which the Islamists might seize power in Egypt—an election, a coup, or a popular uprising. The sheikh was very clear in his response. He said the *only* way the Islamists will ever seize power in Egypt is by inciting the masses to rise up against their oppressors. Demonstrations, rioting, clashes in the street with the army: an intifada of sorts, from the Nile Delta to Upper Egypt."

"What's your point, Shep?"

"Sheikh Tayyib is a religious fanatic and mass murderer who also happens to be a very shrewd and clever character. The fact that he is still alive after all these years is proof of that. He had to know we would never bow to his demands to release his brother in exchange for Elizabeth Halton. But maybe he doesn't really want his brother. Maybe what he really wants is his uprising."

"And he gets his uprising by provoking a confrontation with us?"

"At this moment the Egyptian security services are tearing the country to pieces in order to help the infidel Americans find the daughter of a billionaire ambassador," Cantwell said. "Think how that must look to an Egyptian Islamist who lives in desperate poverty, who's lost a brother or a father to Mubarak's torture chambers. Those torture chambers are filling up as we speak, and they're filling because the regime is looking for *one* American woman."

"How bad is the situation in Egypt right now?"

"The reports we're getting from Cairo Station say it's extremely bad. In fact, it's worse than anyone there has ever seen it. If this goes on much longer, Sheikh Tayyib is going to get his uprising. And history is going to remember our president as the man who lost Egypt."

Cantwell stood and started to leave, then stopped and turned suddenly. "One more thing," he said. "The president just sent our friend the Sphinx a very clear message. I wouldn't be surprised if the Sphinx sent one in return. If I were you, I'd get on the phone to Homeland Security and raise the National Threat Advisory immediately."

"How high?"

"Red," said Cantwell as he slipped from the room. "*Blood* red."

Carter looked at his watch. It was 1:37 P.M. The Muslim evening prayer had just begun in Amsterdam. He stared at his telephone and waited for it to ring.

24

OUD WEST, AMSTERDAM:
7:09 P.M., MONDAY

Agust of cold wind froze Ibrahim Fawaz in
his tracks as he pulled open the door of the
al-Hijrah Mosque. This was his twenty-fifth winter in Holland and
still he was not accustomed to the cold. Providence and fate had
brought him here, to this garden of cinder block and cement in
northern Europe, but in his heart he was still an *ibn balad* from Upper
Egypt—a son of the soil and a child of the river. He stood in the
vestibule for a moment, turning up his coat collar and tightening his
scarf, then stepped tentatively into the street under the watchful
gaze of two rosy-cheeked Amsterdam policemen. He exchanged
pleasantries with them in fluent Dutch, then turned and set out along
the Jan Hazenstraat.

The two police officers were now a permanent fixture outside the
mosque. The al-Hijrah had been searched twice by Dutch investigators in the wake of the attack in London. Files and computers had
been seized, and the imam and several of his associates had been
questioned about their knowledge of Samir al-Masri and the other
members of his cell. Tonight the imam had accused the infidels of
using the attacks in London and the murder of Solomon Rosner as

justification for a crackdown against Islam in the Netherlands. Ibrahim Fawaz had lived through a crackdown against Muslims before, one that had been conducted with a ruthlessness and a savagery that the Europeans, even in their worst nightmares, could scarcely imagine. The imam was only using the police investigation as a pretext to stir up trouble. But then that was what the imam did best. That was why the imam had been sent to Amsterdam in the first place.

A car overtook him. Ibrahim saw his shadow stretch on the pavement in front of him, then disappear as the car slid past. When it was gone, he found that he was in pitch-darkness. It seemed that three lamps near the end of the street were no longer burning. In the small park on the embankment of the canal, a man was seated alone on one of the benches. He had a pinched face, haunted dark eyes, and was as thin as Nile reed grass. *A heroin addict,* he thought. They were all over Amsterdam. They came from Europe and America to take advantage of Holland's permissive drug laws, and the generous welfare benefits, and, once hooked, many never found the power or the will to leave again.

Ibrahim lowered his gaze to the pavement and rounded the corner. The sight that greeted him next was far more offensive to his Islamic sensibilities than that of a heroin addict sitting alone in a freezing park. It was also a sight he saw all too often in Amsterdam: two men in leather groping each other in the darkness against the side of a Volkswagen van. Ibrahim stopped suddenly, outraged by the shamelessness of the act he was witnessing, unsure of whether he should hurry past with his gaze averted or flee in the opposite direction.

He decided on the second course of action, but before he could move, the side door of the van slid open and a small troll-like figure reached out and seized him by the throat. Then the two men in leather suddenly lost all interest in each other and turned their passion on him. Someone clamped a hand over his mouth. Someone else squeezed the side of his neck in a way that made his entire body go limp. He heard the door slam shut and felt the van lurch forward. A voice in Arabic ordered him not to move or make a sound. After that, no one spoke. Ibrahim did not know who had taken him or where he was going. He was certain of only one thing: If he did not do exactly what his captors wanted, he would never see Amsterdam or his wife again.

He closed his eyes and began to pray. An image rose from the deepest well of his memory, the image of a bloody child suspended from the ceiling of a torture chamber. *Not again,* he prayed. *Dear Allah, please don't let it happen again.*

THE SACRIFICE

OF ISAAC

NORTHERN GERMANY:
10:18 P.M., MONDAY

The landlords of Housekeeping referred to it as Site 22XB, but among the old hands it was known simply as Château Shamron. It stood one hundred yards from an isolated farm road, at the end of a rutted drive lined with bare plane trees. The roof was steeply pitched and, on that evening, was covered by a dusting of brittle snow. The shutters were missing several slats and drooped at a vaguely drunken angle. In the woodwork of the front doorjamb were four tiny perforations, evidence of a mezuzah removed a long time ago.

The party that arrived at the house that evening entered not by the front door but through the old servants' entrance off the rear courtyard. They came in four vehicles—a Volkswagen van, two matching Renault sedans, and a rather flashy Audi A8—and had anyone inquired about the purpose of their visit, they would have spoken of a long-planned reunion of old friends. A cursory inspection of the house would have supported their story. The kitchen had been well stocked with food and liquor, and the hearth in the drawing room had been laid with seasoned firewood. A more careful check of the premises, however, would have revealed that the once formal dining room had been made ready for an interrogation and that the house contained several pieces of sophisticated communications equipment unavailable on any commercial market. Such an examination might also have revealed that the small limestone chamber in the basement had been turned into a holding cell—and that the cell was now occupied by an Egyptian man of late middle age who was blindfolded, shackled, and stripped to his underwear. Gabriel regarded him silently for a moment, then climbed the stairs to the pantry, where Yaakov was standing with Sarah at his side.

"How long has he been in there?" Gabriel asked.

"A little over an hour," replied Yaakov.

"Any problems?"

Yaakov shook his head. "We got out of Amsterdam cleanly, and he behaved himself nicely during the ride."

"Did you have to use drugs on him?"

"It wasn't necessary."

"What about force?"

"I may have given him a couple love taps, but nothing he'll ever remember."

"Did anyone speak in front of him?"

"Just a few words in Arabic. Ibrahim did a bit of talking, though. He's convinced he's in the hands of the Americans."

Good, thought Gabriel. That was exactly what he wanted Ibrahim to think. He led Sarah into the drawing room, where Dina and Rimona were reading the Sword of Allah dossiers before a crackling fire, then slipped through a pair of double doors into the dining room. It was empty, except for the rectangular table and two high-backed chairs. Mordecai was balanced on one of the chairs, fitting a miniature transmitter into the cobwebbed chandelier.

"This one's the backup." He leaped down off the chair and wiped his dusty hands against the legs of his trousers. "The primary microphone is down here." He tapped the tabletop. "Put Ibrahim in this chair. That way the mic won't miss a thing he says."

"What about the secure link?"

"It's up and running," Mordecai said. "I'll feed the signal live to King Saul Boulevard and they'll bounce it to Langley. Based on what we're picking up from the Americans, you're the hottest ticket in town tonight."

Mordecai walked out of the room and closed the doors behind him. Sarah looked around at the blank walls. "Surely there's a good story behind this place," she said.

"Before the war, it was owned by a prominent Jewish family named Rosenthal," Gabriel said.

"And when the war broke out?"

"It was confiscated by an SS officer, and the Rosenthal family was deported to Auschwitz. A daughter managed to survive and reclaim the property, but in the fifties she gave up on trying to stay here and emigrated to Israel. The German people weren't terribly kind to their fellow countrymen who managed to survive the Holocaust."

"And the house?"

"She never sold it. When Shamron found out she still owned it, he convinced her to let us have use of it. Shamron always had a way of tucking things away for a rainy day. Houses, passports, people. We used it as a safe house and staging point during the Wrath of God operation. Eli and I spent many long nights here—some good, some not so good."

Sarah lowered herself into the chair that would soon be occupied by Ibrahim Fawaz and folded her hands on the table. "What's going to happen here tonight?" she asked.

"That depends entirely on Ibrahim. If he cooperates and tells me the truth, then things will go very smoothly. If he doesn't . . ." Gabriel shrugged. "Yaakov is one of Shabak's most skilled interrogators. He knows how to talk to men who aren't afraid of death. It's possible things might get unpleasant."

"How unpleasant?"

"Are you asking me whether we will torture him?"

"That's exactly what I'm asking."

"My goal tonight is to create an ally, Sarah, and one doesn't create an ally with clubs and fists."

"What if Ibrahim doesn't want to be your ally?"

"Then he might soon find himself in a place where men aren't shy about using extremely violent methods to extract information. But let us hope it doesn't come to that—for all our sakes."

"You don't approve of torture?"

"I wish I could say it doesn't work, but that's not the case. Done properly, by trained professionals, placing physical and emotional stress on captured terrorists very often produces actionable intelligence that saves lives. But at what cost to the societies and security services that engage in it? A very high cost, unfortunately. It puts us in the same league as the Egyptians and the Jordanians and Saudis and every other brutal Arab secret police force that tortures its opponents. And ultimately it does harm to our cause because it turns believers into fanatics."

"You condemn torture but have no qualms about killing?"

"No qualms?" He shook his head slowly. "Killing takes its toll, too, but I'm afraid killing is our only recourse. We have to kill the monsters before they kill us. And not with boots on the ground, as you Americans like to say, because that only gives the terrorists another moral victory when we invade their territory. The killing has to take place in the shadows, where no one can see it. We have to hunt them down ruthlessly. We have to terrorize *them*." He looked at her again. "Welcome to our war, Sarah. You are now a true citizen of the night."

"Thanks to you, I've been a citizen of the night for several months now."

There was a knock at the door. It was Yaakov.

"I think he's ready to talk."

"You're sure?"

Yaakov nodded.

"Give him ten more minutes," Gabriel said. "Then bring him to me."

. . .

They bore him carefully up the stairs and deposited him, still blind-folded and with his hands bound behind his back, in his designated seat. He made no protest, requested nothing, and revealed no sign of any fear. Indeed, he seemed to Gabriel like a martyr heroically waiting for the executioner's ax to fall. It had been dark in the cel-lar; now, in the proper light, Gabriel could see his skin was covered in dark blotches. After allowing several minutes to elapse, he reached across the table and removed the blindfold. The Egyptian squinted in the sudden light, then opened his eyes slowly and glared malev-olently at Gabriel across the divide.

"Where am I?"

"You are in a great deal of trouble."

"Why have you kidnapped me?"

"No one has *kidnapped* you. You have been taken into custody."

"By whom? For what reason?"

"By the Americans. And we both know the reason."

"If I am in the hands of the Americans, then why are *you* here?"

"Because, obviously, I was the one who told them about you."

"So much for your assurances about protecting me."

"Those assurances were nullified the moment it became clear that you lied to me."

"I did no such thing."

"Really?"

"I told you everything I knew about the plot. If you and your British friends had acted more quickly, you might have been able to prevent it." The Egyptian appraised him silently for a moment. "I en-joyed reading about your checkered past in the newspapers, Mr. Allon. I had no idea I was dealing with such an important man that night in Amsterdam."

Gabriel placed a file on the table and slid it across the divide so that it came to rest in front of Ibrahim. The Egyptian looked down at it for a long moment, then lifted his gaze once more to Gabriel.

"Where did you get this?"

"Where do you think?"

He managed a superior smile. "The Americans, the Jews, and the Egyptian secret police: the unholy trinity. And you wonder why you are loathed by the Arabs."

"Our time together is limited, Ibrahim. You can waste it delivering another one of your lectures, or you can use it wisely by telling me everything you know about the kidnapping of the American woman."

"I don't know anything."

"You're lying, Ibrahim."

"I am telling you the *truth!*"

"You are a member of the Sword of Allah."

"No, I *was* a member. I left the Sword when I left Egypt."

"Yes, I remember. You came to Europe for a better life—isn't that what you told me? But it isn't true, is it? You were dispatched to Europe by your friend Sheikh Tayyib to establish an operational cell in Amsterdam. The al-Hijrah Mosque, the West Amsterdam Islamic Community Center: they're both Sword of Allah fronts, aren't they, Ibrahim?"

"If I am an active member of the Sword of Allah, then why was I working with your spy, Solomon Rosner? Why did I tell him about the plot to shoot down your jetliner? And why did I warn you about Samir al-Masri and his friends from the al-Hijrah Mosque?"

"All valid questions. And you have exactly thirty minutes to answer them to my satisfaction. Thirty minutes to tell me everything you know about the operation to kidnap Elizabeth Halton. Otherwise, I'll be asked to leave and the Americans will take over. They're angry right now, Ibrahim. And you know what happens when Americans get angry. They resort to methods that go against their nature."

"You Israelis do far worse."

Gabriel cast a desultory glance at his wristwatch. "You're wasting time. But then, maybe that's your plan. You think you can hold out until the deadline expires. Four days is a very long time to hold out, Ibrahim. It cannot be done. Start talking, Ibrahim. Confess."

"I have nothing to confess."

His words were spoken with little conviction. Gabriel pressed his advantage. "Tell me everything you know, Ibrahim, or the Americans will take over. And if the Americans don't get the information they want from you using their methods, they're going to put you on a plane to Egypt and let the SSI take over the questioning." He looked at the burn marks on the Egyptian's arms. "You know all about their methods, don't you, Ibrahim?"

"The cigarettes were the kindest thing they did to me. Rest assured that nothing you say frightens me. I don't believe there are any Americans—and I don't believe anyone's going to send me to Egypt to be interrogated. I am a citizen of the Netherlands. I have my rights."

Gabriel leaned back in his chair and thumped the side of his fist twice against the double doors. A moment later Sarah was standing at his side and staring unabashedly at Ibrahim, who averted his gaze in shame and squirmed anxiously in his chair.

"Good evening, Mr. Fawaz. My name is Catherine Blanchard, and I am an employee of the Central Intelligence Agency. One mile from here, there is a plane fueled and waiting to take you to Cairo. If you have any further questions, I'll be right outside the door."

Sarah left the room and closed the doors behind her. Ibrahim glared at Gabriel in anger.

"How dare you let that woman see me like this?"

"Next time you won't doubt my word."

The Egyptian looked down at the file. "What does it say about me?"

"It says you were one of the original members of the first Sword of Allah cell in Minya. It says you were a close associate of Sheikh Tayyib Abdul-Razzaq and his brother, Sheikh Abdullah. It says you organized a terrorist cell at the University of Minya and recruited a number of young students to the radical Islamist cause. It says you wanted to bring down the regime and replace it with an Islamic state."

"Guilty on all counts," said Ibrahim. "All but one very important count. There was indeed a Sword cell at the university, but it had nothing to do with terrorism. The Sword of Allah turned to terror only *after* Sadat's assassination, not before." He looked down at the file again. "What else does it say?"

"It says you were arrested the night of Sadat's murder."

"And?"

"That's the last entry."

"That's hardly surprising. What happened after my arrest is not something they would want to put down on paper." Ibrahim looked up from the file. "Would you like to know what happened to me that night? Would you like me to fill in the missing pages of that file you wave in front of me as though it were proof of my guilt?"

"You have thirty minutes to tell me the truth, Ibrahim. You may use them any way you wish."

"I wish to tell you a story, my friend—the story of a man who lost everything because of his beliefs."

"I'm listening."

"May I have some coffee?"

"No."

"Will you at least remove the handcuffs?"

"No."

"My arms hurt terribly."

"Too bad."

. . .

He had been a professor once and spoke like one now. He started his account not with the story of a man but with the struggle of a generation, a generation that had been raised to believe in secular isms—Nasserism, Baathism, Communism, Pan-Arabism, Arab

Socialism—only to learn, in June 1967, that all the isms were merely a mask for Arab weakness and decay.

"You were the ones who unleashed the storm," he said. "The Palestinians had their Catastrophe in forty-eight. For us, it was sixty-seven—six days in June that shook the Arab world to its core. We had been told by Nasser and the secularists that we were mighty. Then you Jews proved in a matter of hours that we were nothing. We went in search of answers. Our search led us home again. Back to Islam."

"You were in the army in sixty-seven?"

He shook his head. "I'd done my army service already. I was at Cairo University in sixty-seven. Within weeks of the war ending, we organized an illegal Islamist cell there. I was one of its leaders until 1969, when I completed my doctorate in economics. Upon graduation, I had two choices: go to work as a bureaucrat in Pharaoh's bureaucracy or take a job teaching in Pharaoh's schools. I chose the latter and accepted a position at the University of Minya in Middle Egypt. Six months later Nasser was dead."

"And everything changed," said Gabriel.

"Almost overnight," Ibrahim said in agreement. "Sadat encouraged us. He granted us freedom and money to organize. We grew our beards. We established youth organizations and charities to help the poor. We did paramilitary training at desert camps funded by the government and Sadat's wealthy patrons. We lived our lives according to God's law and we wanted God's laws to be the laws of Egypt. Sadat promised us that he would institute *sharia*. He broke his promise, and then he compounded his sins by signing a peace treaty with the Devil, and for that he paid with his life."

"You approved of Sadat's assassination?"

"I fell to my knees and thanked God for striking him down."

"And then the roundups began."

"Almost immediately," Ibrahim said. "The state feared that Sadat's death was only the opening shot of an Islamic revolution that was about to sweep the country. They were wrong, of course, but that didn't stop them from using the mailed fist against anyone whom they believed was part of the conspiracy or conspiracies to come."

"They came for you at the university?"

He shook his head. "I left the university at sundown and went home to my apartment. When I arrived no one was there. I asked the neighbors if they had seen my wife and children. They told me they'd been taken into custody. I went to the police station, but they weren't there, and the police said there was no record of their arrest. Then I went to the Minya headquarters of the SSI." His voice trailed off, and he looked down at the file in front of him. "Do you know about the bridge over Jahannam, my friend? It is the bridge all Muslims must cross in order to reach Paradise."

"Narrower than a spider web and sharper than a sword," Gabriel said. "The good cross swiftly and are rewarded, but the wicked lose their footing and are plunged into the fires of Hell."

Ibrahim looked up from the file, clearly impressed by Gabriel's knowledge of Islam. "I'm one of the unfortunate few who's actually seen the bridge over Jahannam," he said. "I was made to walk it that night in October 1981 and I'm afraid I lost my footing."

Gabriel removed Ibrahim's handcuffs and told him to keep talking.

. . .

He was taken to a cell and beaten mercilessly for twelve hours. When the beatings finally ceased, he was brought to an interrogation room and placed before a senior SSI man, who ordered him to reveal everything he knew about planned Islamist terror operations in the Minya region. He answered the question truthfully—that he knew of no plans for any attacks—and was immediately returned to the cell, where he was beaten on and off for several days. Again he was brought before the senior officer and again he denied knowledge of future attacks. This time the SSI man led him to a different cell, where an adolescent girl, naked and unconscious, hung by her hands from a hook in the ceiling. She had been flogged and slashed to ribbons with a razor and her face was distorted by swelling and bleeding. It took Ibrahim a moment to realize that the young girl was his daughter, Jihan.

"They revived her with several buckets of cold water," he said. "She looked at me and for a moment didn't recognize me either. The senior man whipped her savagely for several minutes, then the others took her down from the hook and raped her in front of me. My daughter looked at me while she was being mauled by these animals. She pleaded with me to help her. 'Please, Papa,' she said. 'Tell them what they want to know. Make them stop.' But I couldn't make them stop. I didn't have anything to tell them."

He began to shiver violently. "May I have my clothing now?"

"Keep talking, Ibrahim."

He lapsed into a long silence. For a moment Gabriel feared he had lost him, but eventually, after another spasm of trembling, he began to speak again.

"They placed me in the cell next door, so that I was forced to endure the screams of my daughter all through that long night. When I was brought before the senior officer for a third time, I told him anything I could think of to ease her suffering. I gave him crumbs from my table, but then crumbs were all I had to give. I gave him the names of other Sword members. I gave him the addresses of apartments where we had met. I gave him the names of students at the university who I believed might be involved in radical activities. I told him what he wanted to hear, even though I knew I was condemning innocent friends and colleagues to the same suffering I had endured. He seemed satisfied with my confession. Even so, I was given one more beating that night. When it was over, I was tossed into a cell and left for dead. For the first time, I was not alone. There was another prisoner there."

"You recognized him?" Gabriel asked.

"Eventually."

"Who was it?"

"It was Sheikh Abdullah. He recited the words of the Prophet to me. 'Rely on God. Don't be defeated.' He soothed my wounds and prayed over me for the next two days. I am alive because of him."

"And your daughter?"

Ibrahim glanced at Gabriel's wristwatch. "How much time do I have left before I am handed over to the Americans?"

Gabriel removed the watch and slipped it into his jacket pocket.

"May I have my clothing now?"

Gabriel leaned back in his chair and hammered twice on the double doors.

26

NORFOLK, ENGLAND:
10:34 P.M., MONDAY

The same bright moon that hung over the plains of northern Germany was visible in the skies above the Norfolk coast that evening as Marcia Cromwell, an unmarried woman of thirty-six, headed down the sandy pathway to the beach at Walcott with Ginger, her Welsh springer spaniel, following closely at her heels. Questions about the morality of torture or even the fate of the missing American woman were of no concern to her at that moment. She had just been informed by her latest lover that, after much deliberation, he had decided not to leave his wife and children for her after all. Marcia Cromwell, a lifelong resident of Norfolk, had decided to deal with the pain the same way she had dealt with every other setback, by taking a late-night walk along the North Sea.

At the end of the pathway the beach opened suddenly before her, flat and seemingly limitless in the darkness, with wind-driven waves breaking in a phosphorous arc along the crest of hard dark sand. Ginger was behaving oddly. Usually he was straining at his leash at this point, anxious to be let loose on the beach so he could torment the gulls and sandpipers. Now he was sitting warily at her feet, peering intently into the grove of pine trees at the base of the dunes. Marcia Cromwell removed his leash and encouraged him to head down to the water's edge. Instead, he immediately trotted off into the trees.

Marcia Cromwell hesitated before going after him. The police had recently uncovered an encampment of vagrant travelers there, and the trees were always strewn with empty beer cans and litter. She called out to Ginger several times, then removed a flashlight from her coat pocket and went in search of him. She spotted him a moment later, pawing at something on the ground at the base of one of the trees. Marcia Cromwell walked over to investigate. Then she began to scream.

.   .   .

The discovery of a corpse on the beach at Walcott immediately triggered activation of the Norfolk Constabulary's Major Investigation Team. Established in September 2004 to conduct probes into crimes such as homicide, manslaughter, and rape, each team consists of a senior investigating officer, his deputy, an exhibits officer who processes crime-scene evidence, and an inquiry officer who interviews witnesses and suspects. Within thirty minutes of receiving Marcia Cromwell's call, all four officers were on scene. Only two, the SIO and the exhibits officer, entered the trees at the base of the dunes. They wore yellow protective shoe covers in order to preserve any forensic evidence and examined the corpse by flashlight.

"How long has he been here?" asked the SIO.

"Between forty-eight and seventy-two hours, I'd say."

"Preliminary cause of death?"

"Single gunshot wound to the back of the head. Execution-style, by the looks of it. But here's the interesting thing."

The crime-scene analyst shone a small Maglite at the lower right leg of the corpse.

"A splint?"

"Quite a good one, actually. But look at the wound. The coroner will have to make the final determination, but I'd be willing to wager it was caused by a bullet."

"Caliber?"

"Looks like a nine-millimeter to me, but that's not the interesting part. It's several days older than the head wound, and whoever treated it knew exactly what she was doing?"

"*She?*"

"Elizabeth Halton is an emergency-room surgeon from Denver, Colorado. I could be wrong, but I think this corpse could well be one of the terrorists from Hyde Park. Didn't COBRA and the Home Office tell us to be on the lookout for unexplained bullet wounds?"

"Yes, they did," the SIO said.

"The wound and surrounding tissue exhibit signs of severe infection. I'd say our man was wounded by that Israeli chap during the actual kidnapping. His comrades tried to keep him alive, but apparently they finally gave up and put him out of his misery with a neat bullet in the back of the head. He probably suffered terribly. I suppose there is some justice in the world after all."

SIO crouched next to the body and examined the lower leg of the corpse, then began searching the corpse itself for evidence. The coat pockets were empty, as were the front pockets of his trousers, but in the back right pocket he found a single sheet of paper, folded in quarters and flattened by many days of pressure. The SIO unfolded it carefully and read it by the beam of his flashlight.

"Draw me up a list of supplies one would need to treat a bullet wound in the field—things that can be purchased over the counter at an ordinary chemist's shop. And put a very wide cordon around this scene. If your theory about this chap is correct, this beach is going to be invaded soon by several hundred men from the Anti-Terrorist Branch, MI5, the FBI, and the CIA."

"Done."

The SIO turned and walked quickly out of the trees. Two minutes later he was behind the wheel of his car, speaking by radio to the duty officer in the Operations and Communications Center. "It looks like the body might be linked to the missing American woman," he said. "Get the chief constable on the phone immediately and bring him into the picture."

"Anything else, sir?"

"I found a receipt in his pocket for the Portsmouth–to–Le Havre ferry. If this chap is really one of the terrorists, it could mean that the American girl is now in France."

. . .

The series of events that occurred next unfolded with precision and remarkable swiftness. The Operations and Communications Center immediately located the Norfolk chief constable, who was dining with friends and family in Norwich, and told him of the discovery. The chief constable stepped away from the table and quietly relayed the information to his superiors at the Home Office, who in turn informed the COBRA committee and the Police Nationale of France. Fifteen minutes after the SIO's initial dispatch from the beach, news of the discoveries reached the American team at Grosvenor Square. A secure cable was sent priority status from the embassy to all federal agencies involved in the search for Elizabeth Halton, including the CIA.

At 6:18 P.M. Eastern time, a copy reached the hands of Adrian Carter, who at that moment was seated in his regular chair in the CIA's Global Ops Center, monitoring a highly illegal clandestine interrogation now taking place at a derelict farmhouse in the plains of northern Germany. He read the note quickly and for the first time in more than a week felt a fleeting sense of hope. Then he set the cable aside and stared at his monitor. The feed had been silent for five minutes. Gabriel, it seemed, had taken a break for dinner.

NORTHERN GERMANY:
12:36 A.M., TUESDAY

They brought his clothing, then they brought him food: rice and beans, hard-boiled eggs and feta cheese, flatbread and sweet tea. He took a single bite, then pushed the plate a few inches toward Gabriel. Gabriel refused at first, but Ibrahim insisted, and so they sat there for several moments, prisoner and interrogator, sharing a simple meal in silence.

"We Muslims have a tradition called Eid," Ibrahim said. "If a sheep is to be slaughtered, it is given one final meal." He looked up from his food at Gabriel. "Is that what you are doing now, my friend? Giving your sacrificial lamb one final taste of life?"

"How long did they hold you?" Gabriel asked.

"Six months," said Ibrahim. "And my release was as undignified as my arrest and incarceration. They turned me onto the streets of Minya in rags and ordered me to go home. When I entered my apartment, my wife screamed. She thought I was an intruder. She didn't recognize me."

"I take it your daughter wasn't there when you arrived."

Ibrahim tore off a piece of the flatbread and pushed it around the rice for a moment. "She died that night in the torture chambers of

Minya. She was raped to death by Mubarak's secret policemen. They buried her body in a criminal's grave on the edge of the desert and refused to let me even see it. For them it was just another form of torture."

He sipped at his tea contemplatively. "My wife blamed me for Jihan's death. It was her right, of course. If I hadn't joined the Sword of Allah, Jihan never would have been taken. For many days, my wife refused even to look at me. A week later I was informed by the university that my services were no longer needed. I was a broken man. I'd lost everything. My job. My daughter. My dignity."

"And so you decided to leave Egypt?"

"I had no choice. To remain would have meant living underground. I wanted to sever my ties with the Sword. I wanted no part of jihadist politics. I wanted a new life, in a place where men did not murder little girls in torture chambers."

"Why Amsterdam?"

"My wife had family living in the Oud West. They told us that the Muslim community in Holland was growing and that for the most part the Dutch were welcoming and tolerant. I applied for a visa at the Dutch embassy and was granted one straightaway."

"I take it you neglected to inform the Dutch of your connection to the Sword of Allah."

"It might have slipped my mind."

"And the rest of the story you told me that night in Amsterdam?"

"It was all true. I built roads, then I swept them. I made furniture." He held up his ruined hand. "Even after I lost my fingers."

"And you had no contact with other Sword members?"

"Most of those who fled Egypt settled in America or London. Occasionally one would blow through Amsterdam with the wind."

"And when they did?"

"They tried to draw me back into the fight, of course. I told them I was no longer interested in Islamic politics. I told them I wanted to live an Islamic life on my own and leave matters of governance and state to others."

"And the Sword abided by your wishes?"

"Eventually," Ibrahim said. "My son wasn't so accommodating, however."

"It is because of your son that we're here tonight."

Ibrahim nodded.

"A son who is half Egyptian and half Palestinian—a volatile mix."

"Very volatile."

"Tell me his name."

"Ishaq," the Egyptian said. "My son's name is Ishaq."

. . .

"It began with harmless questions, the kind of questions any curious adolescent boy might ask of his father. Why did we leave our home in Egypt to come to Europe? Why, if you were once a university professor, do you sweep streets? Why do we live in the land of strangers instead of the House of Islam? For many years, I told him only lies. But when he was fifteen, I told him the truth."

"You told him you were a member of the Sword of Allah?"

"I did."

"You told him about your arrest and torture? And about the death of Jihan?"

Ibrahim nodded. "I hoped that by telling Ishaq the truth, I would snuff out any jihadist embers that might be smoldering inside him. But my story had precisely the opposite effect. Ishaq became *more* interested in Islamic politics, not less. It also turned him into an extremely angry young man. He began to hate. He hated the Egyptian regime and the Americans who supported it."

"And he wanted revenge."

"It is something you and the Americans never seem to fully comprehend about us," Ibrahim said. "When we are wronged, we *must* seek revenge. It is in our culture, our bloodstream. Each time you kill or torture one of us, you are creating an extended family of enemies that is honor bound to take retribution."

Gabriel knew of this phenomenon better than most. He scooped up a bit of rice and beans with the bread and motioned Ibrahim to keep talking.

"Ishaq began to withdraw from Dutch society," he said. "He no longer maintained friendships with Dutch boys and started routinely referring to Dutch girls as temptresses and whores. He wore a *kufi* and galabiya. He listened only to Arabic music and stopped drinking beer. When he was eighteen, he was arrested for assaulting a homosexual man outside a bar in the Leidseplein. The charges were dropped after I went to the injured man and offered to make restitution."

"Did he go to university?"

Ibrahim nodded. "At nineteen he was accepted into the school of information and computer sciences at Erasmus University in Rotterdam. I hoped that the demands of his studies would temper his Islamic fervor, but once he settled in Rotterdam he became *more* Islamic in his outlook, not less. He fell in with a group of like-minded young jihadists. He traveled constantly to various marches and meetings. He grew his beard. It was as if my youth were being played out in front of me all over again." He ate in silence for a moment. "I came to Europe to get away from Islamic politics. I wanted a new life, for myself and for my son. But by the mid-nineties radical Islamist politics had come to the West. And in many ways it was more radical and toxic than the Islam of the Orient. It had been tainted by Saudi money and Saudi imams. It was Wahhabi and Salafist in its outlook. It was toxic and violent."

"Was he involved in terrorist activities then?"

Ibrahim shook his head. "He was too confused to make a commitment to any one group or idea. He wasn't sure if he was an Egyptian or a Palestinian. One day he was with the friends of Hamas, the next he was singing the praises of the mujahideen in Afghanistan."

"So what happened?"

"Osama bin Laden flew airplanes into buildings in New York and Washington," Ibrahim said. "And everything changed."

. . .

Gabriel was not ready to relinquish the illusion of a waiting American airplane just yet, and so he summoned Sarah with two firm raps on the dining-room door and murmured a few barely intelligible words into her ear about delaying its departure for a few minutes. Then he looked at Ibrahim and said, "You were telling me about 9/11. Please, continue."

"It was an earthquake, a tear in the fabric of history—not only for the West but for us."

"Muslims?"

"*Islamists*," he said, correcting Gabriel. "The Americans made a terrible miscalculation after 9/11. They saw Muslims dancing in the streets across the Arab world and in Europe and therefore assumed that all Muslims and Islamists supported Osama. They lumped us all together with the global jihadists like bin Laden and Zawahiri. They didn't realize that for someone like me, a moderate Islamist, the attacks of 9/11 were just as unconscionable and barbaric as they were to the civilized world. We moderate Islamists believed that Osama and al-Qaeda made a terrible tactical blunder by attacking the United States and by picking a fight it could not possibly win. We believed that Osama was an Islamic charlatan who had done more to hurt the cause of Islamism than all the secular apostate regimes combined. What's more, we believed that the massacre of thousands of innocent people was a decidedly un-Islamic act that violated Islamic law and custom. The nineteen hijackers were invited *guests* in America and, as such, they were honor bound to behave accordingly. Instead, they slaughtered their hosts. Regardless of how you feel about us and our religion, we Muslims are hospitable people. We do not slaughter our hosts."

He pushed his plate toward Gabriel again. Gabriel took half of a hard-boiled egg and a lump of feta.

"I take it Ishaq didn't see it that way."

"No, he didn't," Ibrahim said. "Nine-eleven pushed him to the edge of the precipice."

"What pushed him over the edge?"

"Iraq."

"Where was he recruited?"

"He was living in Amsterdam at the time with his wife, an Egyptian girl named Hanifah, and their son, Ahmed. Within days of the American invasion, he traveled to Egypt, where he made contact with the Sword of Allah. The Sword gave him elementary training in their clandestine schools and desert camps, then helped him to travel to Iraq, where he trained and practiced his craft with al-Qaeda in Mesopotamia. He left Iraq after six months and returned to Amsterdam, where he was in close contact with this man Samir al-Masri. A month later, he moved his family to Copenhagen, where he took a job at something called the Islamic Affairs Council of Denmark. The Council, I'm afraid, is nothing more than a front for jihadist activities."

"Your son organized a second cell from Copenhagen?"

"So it would appear."

"And so when Samir and his cell vanished from Amsterdam a few days before the attack, you decided to approach me. You gave me just enough information in hopes of derailing the operation, so that your son might not be caught up in it."

Ibrahim gave a stoic nod of his head.

"You lied to me," Gabriel said. "You deceived me in order to save your son's life."

"Any decent father would have done the same."

"No, Ibrahim, not when innocent human lives are at stake. More than three hundred people are dead because of you and your son. If you had told me the truth—the entire truth—we could have stopped the attack together. Instead you gave me crumbs, the same bread crumbs you gave the SSI twenty-five years ago when you tried to save your daughter's life."

"And if I'd told you more that night? Where would I have ended up? The Americans would have assumed I was a terrorist. They would have placed me on a plane and shipped me back to Egypt to be tortured again."

"Did you know London was the target? Did you know they were planning to kidnap Elizabeth Halton and ransom her for your friend, Sheikh Abdullah?"

"I knew nothing of their plans. These boys are extremely well trained. Someone highly skilled is pulling the strings."

"Someone is." Gabriel hesitated. "Maybe that someone is *you*, Ibrahim. Maybe you're the one who masterminded the entire operation. Maybe you're the one they call the Sphinx."

"The willingness to believe outlandish things is an Arab disease, Mr. Allon, not a Zionist one. The more time you waste pursuing silly notions like that, the less time we have to find the ambassador's daughter and bring her home alive."

Gabriel seized on a single word of Ibrahim's last answer, the word *we*.

"And how are *we* going to do that?"

"I believe Ishaq is one of the terrorists holding the American woman hostage."

Gabriel leaned forward in his chair. "Why would you think that?"

"Ishaq left Copenhagen two weeks ago. He told Hanifah that he was going to the Middle East for a research trip on behalf of the Islamic Affairs Council. In order to maintain that fiction, he telephones the apartment every evening at Ahmed's bedtime."

"How do you know?"

"Because Hanifah has told me so."

"Have you spoken to him yourself?"

"I've left messages for him, but he never calls me."

Gabriel placed a notepad and pen on the table and slid them toward Ibrahim.

"I need the address of the apartment in Copenhagen. And I need the telephone number."

"Hanifah and Ahmed have nothing to do with this."

"Then they have nothing to fear."

"I want you to promise me that no harm will come to them."

"You're in no position to ask for anything, Ibrahim."

"Promise me, Mr. Allon. Promise me you won't harm them."

Gabriel nodded once. Ibrahim wrote down the information, then pushed the pad toward Gabriel and recited two lines from the twenty-second chapter of Genesis:

" 'So early the next morning, Abraham saddled his ass and took with him two of his servants and his son Isaac. He split the wood for the burnt offering, and he set out for the place of which God had told him.' "

"You know your Hebrew scripture," said Gabriel. "But he's no longer your son, Ibrahim. He's infected with the virus of jihad. He's a monster."

"Perhaps, but he'll always be my son." He looked down at the notepad in shame. "If I remember correctly, the Jews believe that Abraham went to Beersheba after passing God's test. But what will happen to me? Will I be shipped to Egypt for further questioning or do I remain here?" He looked around the room. "Wherever *here* is."

"I suppose that depends on the Americans."

The disdainful look in Ibrahim's eyes made it clear how he felt about Americans. "I suggest leaving the Americans out of this," he said. "It would be better for you and I to cross the bridge over Jahannam alone. Whatever you decide, do it quickly. The ambassador's daughter is in the hands of a young man whose sister was murdered by Pharaoh's henchman. If he is ordered to kill her, he will not hesitate."

28

PARIS: 9:25 A.M.,
TUESDAY

The interviewer from France 2 was shuffling his note cards, a sign that time was rapidly dwindling. Yusuf Ramadan, professor of Near Eastern history from the American University in Cairo, resident scholar at the Institute of Islamic Studies in Paris, and terror mastermind from the Sword of Allah, knew he would have to make his final point quickly.

". . . And so I think the greatest danger of this crisis is not here in Europe but in Egypt itself," he said in his faultless French. "It is my understanding that the security services of the Egyptian regime have responded with a rather heavy hand, and if this behavior continues, it is likely to provoke a backlash that might very well threaten the stability of the regime itself."

The interviewer, intrigued by Ramadan's comment, ignored the instructions of the floor director to conclude the segment. "Are you accusing the government of Egypt of torture, Professor Ramadan?"

"The methods of the Egyptian police and security services are well known," Ramadan said. "You can be sure they are using torture and other unsavory methods in order to help the Americans find the ambassador's daughter."

"Thought-provoking as always, Professor Ramadan. I hope you'll join us again to help us analyze this ongoing crisis."

"It would be my pleasure," said Ramadan, smiling warmly for the camera.

The interviewer informed the audience that France 2's coverage of the crisis would continue after a commercial break, then he extended his hand toward Ramadan and thanked him privately for agreeing to appear on the program. Ramadan rose from his seat and was escorted off the set by a youthful female production assistant. Five minutes later, he was climbing into a Citroën car waiting outside in the esplanade Henri de France. He looked at his wristwatch. It was 9:25. The men and women of France 2 did not know it but their morning was about to get a good deal more hectic.

· · ·

At that same moment in Zurich, a black Mercedes-Benz S600 sedan pulled sedately to the curb on the arrivals level of Kloten Airport. The man who emerged from the backseat looked a great deal like the vehicle itself, narrow at the head and a bit wide in the midsection for added stability. His suit was Italian, his overcoat cashmere, his leather suitcase large and expensive-looking. A Swiss policeman was standing watch at the entrance to the terminal with an automatic weapon across his chest. The well-dressed man nodded politely to him, then brushed past and went inside.

He paused for a moment and gazed up at the departure board. The ticket in his breast pocket was for that morning's United Airlines flight to Dulles Airport. He had purchased the ticket despite the fact that he had no valid visa. It didn't matter—he wasn't planning to go to America, let alone board the airplane. He was a *shaheed*, a martyr, and the journey he was about to take had nothing to do with air travel.

After determining the check-in counters for the flight, the *shaheed* set out across the glistening modern terminal, towing his suitcase behind him. It had undergone several modifications to suit his specific needs. The sides and wheels had been reinforced to accommodate a larger payload, and the button on the collapsible handle was a detonator. *Twelve pounds of pressure,* the engineer had said. Just a little push—that's all it would take to start his journey.

A civilian security agent was standing a few yards from the United Airlines check-in area examining tickets and passports. Behind him, several dozen travelers, mostly Americans, were waiting in line. Because the *shaheed* had no valid visa, he would be able to get no closer to his victims then the security agent. Their lives would not be spared, however. Along with a hundred pounds of high explosive, the suitcase was packed with thousands of ball bearings and nails. The infidels standing in line would soon be reduced to ribbons of blood-soaked flesh. It would be a beautiful sight, thought the *shaheed.* He only hoped that his soul might linger in the terminal for a moment after his death so that he might see it.

The security agent finished examining the travel documents of an American woman traveling with two young children, then motioned the *shaheed* forward. He did as he was instructed and handed the security man his ticket and passport.

"Egyptian?" the security agent asked with barely concealed suspicion.

"Yes, that's correct."

"You have a valid visa for travel to the United States today?"

"I was told I didn't need a visa."

"By whom?"

"By Allah," he said.

The security agent reached for his radio.

The *shaheed* put his thumb on the detonator button. Twelve pounds of pressure. *Paradise . . .*

. . .

Though he did not know it, the *shaheed* at Kloten Airport was not alone. Two other suicide bombers had been dispatched to European airports that morning—one to Madrid's Barajas Airport and another to Schwechat in Vienna—and all had been instructed to hit their detonators at the same instant. The martyr in Madrid was one minute late, but his comrade in Vienna did not explode his weapon until 9:35 Central European time. Investigators in Austria would later determine that the martyr, for reasons known only to himself, had stopped in an airport café for one last Viennese coffee before blasting himself to Paradise.

Yusuf Ramadan was made aware of the bombings at 9:38 while stuck in the midmorning traffic along the Seine. It was not Abu Musa who broke the news to him but the production assistant from France 2 who a few moments earlier had escorted him from the building. It seemed that the station was planning extensive coverage of the terrorist attacks and was wondering whether Ramadan would consider spending the day as a paid consultant and commentator. He immediately agreed without bothering to ask the fee and, ten minutes later, was taking his seat once more on the set.

"Welcome back, Professor Ramadan. What do you think these latest attacks mean?"

"They mean that the United States had better open a channel of communication to the Sword of Allah soon," Ramadan said. "Otherwise I'm afraid a good deal more blood will be shed here in Europe."

29

C O P E N H A G E N :
3 : 0 3   P . M . ,   T U E S D A Y

They decided a crash meeting was in order
and settled on Copenhagen's airport Hilton
Hotel as a suitable site. Adrian Carter arrived first and was sitting
in the lounge bar as Gabriel and Sarah strode into the lobby. He directed them toward the elevators with a weary glance, and a moment
later they were huddled around the television in Carter's junior executive suite. Carter turned up the volume very loud. The room had
been swept by CIA security, but Carter was a traditionalist when it
came to matters of tradecraft and, like Gabriel, regarded electronic
gadgetry as a necessary but unfortunate corruption of a once-
noble art.

"Zurich, Paris, Vienna: three airport attacks, identical in design
and perfectly coordinated." Carter, staring at the images of carnage
and destruction on the screen, shook his head slowly. "One hundred
and twenty-nine people confirmed dead, five hundred injured, and
Europe's air transport system in tatters."

"And what about Europe's politicians?" asked Gabriel.

"Publicly, they're saying all the right things: deplorable, barbaric, outrageous. Privately, they're pleading with us to make a deal with the devil. They're telling us to end this thing before more blood is shed on *their* soil. Even our close friend at Downing Street is beginning to wonder whether we should find some way of negotiating our way out of this. The Sphinx, whoever he might be, is a mass murderer and a ruthless bastard, but his timing is impeccable."

"Any chance that the president is going to bend?"

"Not after this. In fact, he's more determined than ever that this affair end without a negotiated settlement. That means we have no option but to find Elizabeth Halton *before* the deadline." Carter's gaze moved from the screen to Gabriel. "And as of this moment, your Joe appears to be our best and only hope."

"He's not my Joe, Adrian."

"He is now, at least as far as official Washington is concerned." Carter lowered the volume a decibel or two. "You caused quite a storm in Washington last night, Gabriel. Your interrogation with Ibrahim Fawaz is now required listening from Langley to the J. Edgar Hoover Building to the National Security Council."

"How were the reviews?"

"Mixed," said Carter. "Expert opinion is divided over whether Ibrahim was being truthful or whether he was having you on for a second time. Expert opinion thinks you may have hitched your star to him too quickly. Expert opinion also fears you may have treated him far too gingerly."

"What does *expert opinion* have in mind?"

"A second interrogation," said Carter.

"Conducted by whom?"

"By Agency men with proper Christian names instead of an Israeli assassin."

"So you're telling me that I'm being fired?"

"That's exactly what I'm telling you."

"You didn't have to come all the way to Copenhagen to fire me, Adrian. A secure phone call would have sufficed."

"I felt I owed it to you. After all, I was the one who roped you into this."

"How decent of you. But tell me something, Adrian. Tell me exactly what your Agency interrogators think they're going to get from Ibrahim that I didn't get from him."

"Full and forthright answers, for starters. Expert opinion believes he was being highly deceptive and evasive in his answers."

"Oh, really? Did they come up with this on their own, or did the computers do it for them?"

"It was a combination of the two, actually."

"How much more forthright would you like Ibrahim to be? He's agreed to help us find Elizabeth Halton, and he's given us the number of a telephone in Copenhagen that his son is calling every evening."

"No, he's given us a number he *says* his son is calling."

"And tonight we'll find out whether he's telling the truth."

"Higher authority isn't willing to wait that long. They want Ibrahim chained to a wall *now*."

"Where do they think they're going to conduct this interrogation?"

"They were wondering whether they could borrow your facility in Germany."

"That's not going to happen."

"I was afraid you were going to say that. In that case, we have two other options. We could take him to one of our facilities in eastern Europe, or we could put him on a plane to Egypt."

Gabriel shook his head slowly. "Ibrahim's not going to eastern Europe, Adrian, and he's not going back to Cairo. No one's strapping him to any water boards and no one's chaining him to any more walls."

"Now you're being unreasonable." Carter looked at Sarah, as though she might be able to talk some sense into him. "Where exactly is Ibrahim at the moment?"

Gabriel made no response. When Carter repeated the question, there was an edge to his voice that Gabriel had never heard before.

"He's back in Amsterdam," Gabriel said. "In his apartment in the August Allebéplein."

"Why on earth did you send him back?"

"We had no choice *but* to put him back," Gabriel said. "If Ibrahim had vanished from the face of the earth, his wife would have called the Dutch police, and we both would have been faced with a force-ten scandal in Holland."

"Avoiding a scandal in Holland is not high on our list of priorities at the moment," Carter said. "We want him, and we want him now. I assume he's under watch."

"No, Adrian, that slipped our mind."

"Do try to control your fatalistic Israeli sense of humor for a few moments."

"Of course he's under watch."

"Then I assume you would have no trouble delivering him into our hands."

"No trouble at all," Gabriel said. "But you can't have him."

"Be reasonable, Gabriel."

"I'm the only one who *is* being reasonable, Adrian. And if your goons go anywhere near him, they're going to get hurt."

Carter exhaled heavily. "It appears we have reached an impasse."

"Yes, we have."

"I suppose you have an alternative plan," Carter said. "I also suppose I have no choice but to listen to it."

"My advice to you is be patient, Adrian."

"Elizabeth Halton dies at six o'clock Friday night. We don't have time to be patient."

"I've given you the location and number of a telephone that one of her captors is calling on a regular basis. You have in your arsenal the National Security Agency, the largest and most sophisticated electronic intelligence service in the world, a service that is capable of vacuuming up every fax, phone call, and Internet communication in the world, every second of the day. Give Ishaq's number in Copenhagen to NSA, and tonight, when Ishaq calls, tell NSA to bring all their considerable resources to bear on answering a single question: Where is he?"

Carter stood up and ambled over to the minibar. He selected a soft drink, then, after consulting the price list, thought better of it. "To do this job right, you need to put a bug on the telephone in that apartment and a full-time surveillance team on Ishaq's wife and son."

"What do you think we've been doing all day, Adrian? Watching movies in our hotel room?" Gabriel looked at Sarah. "You're the liaison officer, Sarah. Please give your superior an update on our activities today."

"Hanifah and Ahmed Fawaz live in a section of Copenhagen called Nørrebro," Sarah said. "Their apartment is located in a large turn-of-the-century block, almost a city within a city. Each apartment can be accessed by a front door and a rear service door. Late this morning, when Hanifah took Ahmed out for a stroll and some shopping, we slipped in the back door and put a—" She looked at Gabriel. "What was the device called that we put on their phone?"

"It's called a glass," said Gabriel. "It provides room coverage along with coverage of any conversations conducted over the telephone."

"Christ," Carter said softly. "Please tell me you didn't involve my officer in a B-and-E job in broad daylight in Copenhagen."

"She's well trained, Adrian. You would have been proud of her."

"We also put a transmitter on the phone at the Islamic Affairs Council of Denmark," Sarah said. "The junction box is located behind the offices in an alley. That one was easy."

"You have them under visual surveillance, too, I take it."

Gabriel frowned at Carter, as though he found the question mildly offensive. Carter looked down at the images of mayhem on the television screen.

"I was sent here to fire you and now I find myself volunteering for a suicide mission." He shut off the television and looked at

Gabriel. "All right, you win. We actually gave NSA the telephone number last night. Assuming that Ishaq is calling from a cell phone, NSA says it will take roughly one hour to pin down the approximate location. At that point we'll notify the relevant local authorities and start looking."

"Just make sure those relevant local authorities know that they'll kill her if anyone tries to rescue her."

"We've already made it clear to our friends here in Europe that if there's any rescuing to be done, we intend to do it. In fact, we've already moved four Delta Force teams into various European capitals for just this scenario. They're on hot standby. If we come up with hard intelligence on Elizabeth Halton's whereabouts, those Delta Forces will go in and get her, and we'll worry about assuaging hurt Euro-feelings later."

"We have an entire division that deals with that sort of thing, Adrian. If you need any advice, just let us know."

"You have enough to worry about." Carter frowned and looked at his watch. "You and your team are now responsible for physical surveillance of the wife and son here in Copenhagen. I'm going to London to explain why I disobeyed a direct order to terminate your involvement in his operation. The fate of Elizabeth Halton is in your hands, Gabriel, along with my career. Please do your best not to drop us."

30

TORAH PRISON, EGYPT:
4:19 P.M., TUESDAY

T he Scorpion: Hell on earth, thought Wazir al-
Zayyat. One hundred squalid cells containing
the most dangerous Islamic radicals and jihadists in Egypt, a dozen
interrogation chambers where even the most hardened of Allah's
holy warriors vomited their secrets after just a few hours of "questioning" at the hands of Egypt's secret police. Few who entered the
Scorpion emerged with their souls or their body intact. Those who
encountered Wazir al-Zayyat face-to-face rarely lived to talk about it.

The Scorpion was more crowded that afternoon than it had been
in many years. Al-Zayyat did not find this particularly remarkable,
since he was the man most responsible for the sudden surge of new
arrivals. The prisoner now under interrogation in Room 4 was
among the most promising: Hussein Mandali, a middle school
teacher from the Sword of Allah stronghold of Imbaba. He had been
captured twelve hours earlier on suspicion of distributing a recorded
sermon by Sheikh Tayyib Abdul Razzaq. That in itself was hardly a
novel offense—the sheikh's scorching sermons were the hip-hop of
Egypt's downtrodden masses—but the content of the sermon found
on Mandali was highly significant. In it the sheikh had made refer-

ence to the abduction of the American woman in London and had called for a popular uprising against the regime, a set of circumstances that suggested the sermon had been recorded very recently. Al-Zayyat knew that tapes did not appear by magic or by the divine will of Allah. He was convinced that Hussein Mandali was the break he had been looking for.

Al-Zayyat pushed open the door and went inside. Three interrogators were leaning against the gray walls, sleeves rolled up, faces glistening with sweat. Hussein Mandali was seated at the metal table, his face bloodied and swollen, his body covered with welts and burns. A good start, thought al-Zayyat, but not enough to break a boy from the slums of Imbaba.

Al-Zayyat sat down opposite Mandali and pressed the PLAY button on the tape recorder resting in the center of the table. A moment later, the thin, reedy voice of Sheikh Tayyib was reverberating off the walls of the interrogation room. Al-Zayyat allowed the sermon to go on for several minutes before finally reaching down and jabbing the STOP button with his thick forefinger.

"Where did you get this tape?" he asked calmly.

"It was given to me by a man in a coffeehouse in Imbaba."

Al-Zayyat sighed heavily and glanced at the three interrogators. The beating they administered was twenty minutes in duration and, even by Egyptian standards, savage in its intensity. Mandali, when he was returned to his seat at the interrogation table, was barely conscious and weeping like a child. Al-Zayyat pressed the PLAY button for a second time.

"Where did you get this tape?"

"From a man in—"

Al-Zayyat quickly cut in. "Yes, I remember, Hussein—you got it from a man in a coffeehouse in Imbaba. But what was this man's name?"

"He didn't . . . tell me."

"Which coffeehouse?"

"I can't . . . remember."

"You're sure, Hussein?"

"I'm . . . sure."

Al-Zayyat stood without another word and nodded to the interrogators. As he stepped into the corridor he could hear Mandali begging for mercy. *"Do not fear the henchmen of Pharaoh,"* the sheikh was telling him. *"Place your faith in Allah, and Allah will protect you."*

31

C OPENHAGEN :
5 : 3 4 P . M . , T UESDAY

There had been no time for Housekeeping to
acquire proper safe lodging for Gabriel's
team in Copenhagen, and so they had settled instead at the Hotel
d'Angleterre, a vast white luxury liner of a building looming over the
sprawling King's New Square. Gabriel and Sarah arrived shortly
after 5:30 and made their way to a room on the fourth floor. Mordecai was seated at the writing desk in stocking feet, headphones over
his ears, eyes fixed on a pair of receivers like a doctor reading a brain
scan for signs of life. Gabriel slipped on the spare set, then looked at
Mordecai and grimaced.

"It sounds as though there's a pile driver in the room."

"There is," Mordecai said. "And his name is Ahmed. He's bang-
ing a toy against the floor a few inches from the phone."

"How long has it been going on?"

"An hour."

"Why doesn't she ask him to stop?"

"Maybe she's deaf. God knows I will be soon if he doesn't stop."

"Any activity on the line yet?"

"Just one outgoing call," Mordecai said. "She called Ibrahim in

Amsterdam to complain about Ishaq's prolonged absence. Unless it was an elaborate ruse, she doesn't know anything."

, Gabriel looked at his wristwatch. It was 5:37. A spy's life, he thought. Mind-numbing boredom broken by brief interludes of sheer terror. He slipped on the headset and waited for Hanifah's telephone to ring.

· · ·

They adopted the uncomfortable silence of strangers at a wake and together endured an evening of frightening banality. Ahmed ramming his toy against the kitchen floor. Ahmed pretending to be a jet airplane. Ahmed kicking a ball against the wall of the sitting room. At 8:15, there was an ear-shattering crash. Though they were never able to accurately identify the object lost, it was of sufficient value to launch Hanifah into a hysterical tirade. A remorseful Ahmed responded by asking whether his father was going to telephone that night. Gabriel, who was pacing the floor as though looking for lost valuables, froze and awaited the answer. He'll call if he can, Hanifah said. He always does. Ibrahim, it seemed, had been telling the truth after all.

At 8:20, Ahmed was ordered into a bath. Hanifah cleaned up the disaster in the sitting room, then switched on the television. Her choice of channels was illuminative, for it soon became clear she was watching al-Manar, the official television network of Hezbollah. For the next twenty minutes, while Ahmed splashed about in his tub, they were forced to sit through a sermon by a Lebanese cleric who extolled the bravery of the Sword of Allah and called for more acts of terror against the infidel Americans and their Zionist allies.

At 8:43, the sermon was interrupted by the shrill scream of the telephone. Hanifah answered it quickly and, in Arabic, said, "Ishaq, is that you?" It was not Ishaq but a very confused Danish man looking for someone named Knud. Hearing the voice of an Arabic-speaking woman—and, no doubt, the clerical rant in the background—he apologized profusely and hastily rang off. Hanifah

returned the receiver to the cradle and shouted at Ahmed to get out
of the bath. The Hezbollah preacher shouted back that the time had
come for the Muslims of the world to finish the job Hitler had started.

Mordecai looked at Gabriel in exasperation. "Both of us don't
have to sit through this shit," he said. "Why don't you get out of here
for a few minutes?"

"I don't want to miss his call."

"That's what the recorders are for." Mordecai handed Gabriel his
coat and gave him a little shove toward the door. "Go get something
to eat. And take Sarah with you. You two make a nice couple."

• • •

A string quartet was sawing away indifferently at a Bach minuet
downstairs in the parlor. Gabriel and Sarah slipped past them without a glance and struck out across the square toward the cafés along
the New Harbor. It had turned much colder; Sarah wore a beret, and
her coat collar was turned up dramatically. When Gabriel teased her
about looking too much like a spy, she seized his arm playfully and
pressed her body against his shoulder. They sat outside along the
quay and drank freezing Carlsberg beneath a hissing gas heater.
Gabriel picked at a plate of fried cod and potatoes while Sarah stared
at the colorful floodlit façades of the canal houses on the opposite embankment.

"Better than Langley, I suppose."

"Anything is better than Langley," he said.

She looked up at the hard black sky. "I suppose your fate is now
in the hands of NSA and its satellites."

"Yours, too," Gabriel said. "You would have been wise to go to
London with Adrian."

"And miss this?" She lowered her gaze toward the canal houses.
"If he calls tonight, do you think we'll be able to find her?"

"It depends on how well NSA is able to pinpoint Ishaq's location.
Even if NSA does manage to locate Elizabeth, Washington is going
to have another problem—how to get her out alive. Ishaq and his col-

leagues are more than willing to die, which means that any attempt to storm the hideout will no doubt end violently. But I'm sure *expert opinion* will come up with a plan."

"Don't play the wounded martyr, Gabriel. It doesn't suit you."

"I didn't appreciate some of the things that were said about me in Washington today."

"Washington is a town without pity."

"So is Jerusalem."

"Then you're going to need a thicker skin when you become the chief of the Office." She gave him a mischievous sideways glance over the top of her collar. "Adrian says it's just a rumor, but, judging from your reaction, it's true." She raised her glass. *"Mazel tov."*

"Condolences would be more appropriate."

"You don't want the job?"

"Some men have greatness thrust upon them."

"You're in a fine mood tonight."

"Forgive me, Sarah. Talk of genocide and extermination tends to spoil the evening for me."

"Oh, that." She sipped her beer and fought off a shiver. "You know, this restaurant does have an indoor section."

"Yes, but it's harder for me to tell whether we're being watched."

"Are we?"

"You're trained in countersurveillance. You tell me."

"There was a man drinking in the bar when we left the hotel," she said. "He's now standing on the other side of the canal with a woman who's at least fifteen years older than he is."

"Is he Danish security?"

"He was speaking German in the bar."

"So."

She shook her head. "No, I don't think he's Danish security. What do you think?"

"I think he's a German gigolo who's going to take that poor woman for every penny she has."

"Should we warn her?"

"I'm afraid we have enough to worry about tonight."

"Are you always such a charming date?"

"I didn't realize this was a date."

"It's the closest thing to a date I've had in a long time."

Gabriel gave her a disbelieving look and popped a piece of fish into his mouth. "Do you really expect me to believe you have difficulty attracting men?"

"Perhaps you've forgotten, but at the moment I'm living under an assumed identity because of my role in the al-Bakari operation. It makes it rather difficult to meet men. Even my coworkers in the CTC don't know my real name or anything about my past. I suppose it's for the best. Anyone I met now wouldn't stand a chance anyway. I'm afraid my heart has been taken hostage by someone else." She peered at him over her glass. "Now is the time you're supposed to bashfully ask me the name of the man who's kidnapped my heart."

"Some questions are better left unasked, Sarah."

"You're such a stoic, aren't you, Gabriel?" She took a drink of her beer and resumed her appraisal of the canal houses. "But your heart is spoken for, too, isn't it?"

"Trust me, Sarah—you can do far better than a fifty-something misanthrope from the Valley of Jezreel."

"I've always been attracted to misanthropic men, especially gifted ones. But I'm afraid my timing has always been lousy. It's why I studied art instead of music." She gave him a bittersweet smile. "It's Chiara, isn't it?"

Gabriel nodded his head slowly.

"I could always tell," Sarah said. "She's a very lucky girl."

"I'm the lucky one."

"She's far too young for you, you know."

"She's older than *you*, but thanks for the reminder anyway."

"If she ever throws you over for a younger man . . ." Her voice trailed off. "Well, you know where to find me. I'll be the lonely former museum curator working the graveyard shift on the Saudi Arabia desk of the Counterterrorism Center."

Gabriel reached out and touched her face. The cold had added a dab of crimson to her alabaster cheeks.

"I'm sorry," he said.

"For what?"

"We should have never used you. We should have found someone else."

"There is no one else like me," she said. "But I guess you already know that."

. . .

A band of Chinese tourists, Europe's newest packaged invaders, were posing for pictures in the center of the King's New Square. Gabriel took Sarah by the arm and led her the long way round, while privately he waxed poetic on the splendid irony of a people on the march vacationing in the shrines of a civilization in twilight. They entered the lobby of the d'Angleterre under the admiring gaze of the concierge and climbed the stairs to the strains of Pachelbel's Canon. Mordecai was pacing nervously as they slipped quietly into the room. He pressed a pair of headphones into Gabriel's hand and led him over to the recorders. "He called," he whispered. "He actually called. We've got him, Gabriel. You've done it."

CAIRO: 10:19 P.M., TUESDAY

The truth had come out in Interrogation Room 4 of the Scorpion, but then it always did. Just as Wazir al-Zayyat had suspected, Hussein Mandali was no ordinary middle school teacher. He was a senior operative of the Sword of Allah and commander of an important cell based in Imbaba. He had also confessed to being present when Sheikh Tayyib recorded his sermon calling for an uprising against the regime, a recording session that had taken place Sunday morning in Apartment 2408 of the Ramses Towers, a luxury block north of the Gezira Sporting Club filled with foreigners, film stars, and newly rich friends of the regime. A quick check of the files had revealed that the apartment in question was owned by a company called Nejad Holdings, and a second check had confirmed that Nejad Holdings was controlled by one Prince Rashid bin Sultan al-Saud.

It was not the first time the prince's name had arisen in connection with Islamic terrorism in Egypt. He'd funneled millions of dollars into the pockets of the Egyptian jihadists over the years, including fronts and entities controlled by the Sword of Allah. But because the prince was a Saudi—and because impoverished Egypt was beholden to Saudi economic aid—al-Zayyat had had no choice but to turn a blind eye to his charitable endeavors. *This is different,* he thought now. Giving money to Islamist causes was one thing; providing aid and shelter to a terrorist bent on the destruction of the Mubarak regime was quite another. If the SSI managed to find Sheikh Tayyib hiding in a Saudi-owned property, it might very well give al-Zayyat the ammunition he needed to end Saudi meddling in Egypt's internal affairs once and for all.

Al-Zayyat arrived at the Ramses Towers shortly after 10:30 and found the building surrounded by several hundred raw police recruits. He knew that many of the young officers secretly supported the goals of the Sword—and that many of them, if given the opportunity, would gladly duplicate the actions of Lieutenant Khaled Islambouli and put a bullet through Pharaoh's chest. He directed his driver to a spot across the street and lowered his window. A man from his directorate, spotting the official Mercedes, came over at a trot.

"We went in about two minutes ago," the officer said. "The place was empty, but it was clear someone had been there recently and that whoever it was had left in a hurry. There was food on the table and pans in the kitchen. Everything was still warm."

Al-Zayyat swore softly. Was it bad luck, or did he have a traitor in his midst—someone inside the SSI who had alerted the sheikh that Mandali had been captured and was talking?

"Close the Zamalek bridges," he said. "No one gets off the island without a thorough search. Then start knocking on doors inside the Ramses. I don't care if you have to ruffle the feathers of the rich and famous. I want to make sure the sheikh isn't still hiding somewhere inside."

The officer turned and ran back toward the entrance of the building. Al-Zayyat drew his mobile phone from his pocket and dialed a number inside the Scorpion.

"We hit a dry well," he told the man who answered.

"Shall we have another go at Mandali?"

"No, he's dry, too."

"What do you want us to do with him?"

"We never had him," al-Zayyat said. "We've never heard of him. He's nothing. He's no one."

33

G abriel sat before the recorder, slipped on a pair of headphones, and pressed PLAY.

"I was afraid you were never going to call tonight. Do you know what time it is?"

"I've been busy. You've seen the news?"

"The bombings? It's all anyone's talking about."

"What are they saying?"

"The Danes are shocked, of course. They're wondering when it's going to happen in Copenhagen. Here in Nørrebro, they say Europe is getting what it deserves for supporting the Americans. They want the Americans to release the sheikh."

"Be careful what you say on the telephone, Hanifah. You never know who's listening."

"Who would bother to listen to me? I'm no one."

"You're married to a man who works for the Islamic Affairs Council of Denmark."

"A man who thinks nothing of leaving his wife and child to roam the Middle East conducting research on the state of the Islamic world. Where are you tonight anyway?"

"*Istanbul. How's Ahmed?*"

Gabriel pressed STOP, then REWIND, then PLAY.

"*Where are you tonight anyway?*"

"*Istanbul. How's Ahmed?*"

"*He misses his father.*"

"*I want to talk to him.*"

"*It's too late, Ishaq. He's been asleep for almost an hour.*"

"*Wake him.*"

"*No.*"

"*It's important I speak to him tonight.*"

"*Then you should have called earlier. Where are you, Ishaq? What's that noise in the background?*"

"*It's just traffic outside my hotel room.*"

"*It sounds like you're on a highway.*"

"*It's loud here in Istanbul. It's not like Copenhagen. Did you speak to my father today?*"

STOP. REWIND. PLAY.

"*Where are you, Ishaq? What's that noise in the background?*"

"*It's just traffic outside my hotel room.*"

"*It sounds like you're on a highway.*"

"*It's loud here in Istanbul. It's not like Copenhagen. Did you speak to my father today?*"

"*This afternoon.*"

"*He's well?*"

"*He seemed so.*"

"*How's the weather in Copenhagen?*"

"*Cold, Ishaq. What do you think?*"

"*Any strangers around the apartment? Any unfamiliar faces in the streets?*"

"*A few more police than usual, but it's calm here.*"

"*You're sure?*"

"*I'm sure. Why are you so nervous?*"

"*Because the Muslim communities across Europe are under siege at the* moment. *Because we are being rounded up and brought in for questioning simply because we happen to speak Arabic or pray toward Mecca.*"

"*No one's being rounded up in Copenhagen.*"

"*Not yet.*"

"*When does this conference of yours end, Ishaq? When are you coming home?*"

"*Actually, you're coming here. Not Istanbul. Some place better.*"

"*What are you talking about?*"

"*Go to the bottom drawer of my dresser. I left an envelope for you there.*"

"*I don't feel like playing games, Ishaq. I'm tired.*"

"*Just do as I tell you, Hanifah. You won't be disappointed. I promise.*"

Hanifah gave an exasperated sigh and slammed the receiver down next to the telephone so hard that the sound caused Gabriel's eardrums to vibrate like a snare drum. The next sounds he heard were distant: the patter of slippered feet, a drawer being yanked open, the rustle of crisp paper. Then, a few seconds later, Hanifah's startled voice.

"*Where did you get this money?*"

"*Never mind where I got it. Do you have the tickets?*"

"*Beirut? Why are we going to Beirut?*"

"*For a holiday.*"

"*The plane leaves Friday morning. How am I supposed to be ready that soon?*"

"*Just throw a few things in a bag. I'll have someone from the Council take you to the airport. A colleague of mine from Beirut will meet you at the airport and take you and Ahmed to an apartment that we've been given use of. I'll come from Istanbul in a couple of days.*"

"*This is crazy, Ishaq. Why didn't you tell me until now?*"

"*Just do as I say, Hanifah. I have to go now.*"

"*When am I going to hear from you again?*"

"*I'm not sure.*"

"*What do you mean you're not sure? You tell me to get on a plane to Beirut and that's it?*"

"Yes, that's it. You're my wife. You do as I say."

"No, Ishaq. Tell me when I'm going to hear from you again or I'm not getting on that plane."

"I'll call tomorrow night."

"When?"

"When it's convenient."

"No, not when it's convenient. I want to know when you're going to call."

"Nine-thirty."

"Whose time, yours or mine?"

"Nine-thirty Copenhagen time."

"At nine thirty-one, I stop answering the phone. Do you understand me, Ishaq?"

"I have to go now, Hanifah."

"Ishaq, wait."

"I love you, Hanifah."

"Ishaq—"

Click.

"What have you done, Ishaq? My God, what have you done?"

STOP. REWIND. PLAY.

"I want to know when you're going to call."

"Nine-thirty."

"Who's time, yours or mine?"

"Nine-thirty Copenhagen time."

"At nine thirty-one, I stop answering the phone. Do you understand me, Ishaq?"

STOP.

Gabriel looked at Mordecai. "I'm going to listen to the spot where Ishaq asks Hanifah to go get the tickets and money. Can you turn down the room coverage so I can hear only Ishaq?"

Mordecai nodded and did as Gabriel asked. The interlude was twenty-three seconds. Gabriel listened to it three times, then removed his headphones and looked at Sarah.

"Tell Adrian not to wait for NSA," he said. "Tell him that Ishaq is calling from a highway rest stop in Germany—the northwest, judging by the accents of the people I can hear in the background. Tell him he's traveling with at least one other man. They're moving her around in a cargo truck or a transit van. He won't be stopping again for several hours. He just filled the tank with gas."

34

ABOVE COLORADO:
3:28 P.M., TUESDAY

The Falcon 2000 executive jet began to pitch as it sank into the storm clouds above the plains of eastern Colorado. Lawrence Strauss removed his reading glasses and pinched the bridge of his nose between his thumb and forefinger. One of Washington's most powerful lawyers, he was a nervous flier by nature and avoided planes whenever he could—especially private planes, which he regarded as little more than death traps with wings. Given the nature of his current case, Strauss's client had mandated he fly from Washington, D.C., to Colorado on a borrowed jet under conditions of extreme secrecy. Usually Lawrence Strauss didn't permit clients to dictate his personal schedule or method of travel, but in this case he had made an exception. The client was a personal friend who also happened to be the president of the United States—and the mission he had given Strauss was so sensitive that only the president and his attorney general knew it existed.

The Falcon came out of the clouds and settled into a stratum of smoother air. Strauss slipped his glasses back on and looked down at the file open on the worktable in front of him: *The United States v. Sheikh Abdullah Abdul-Razzaq.* It had been given to him late the previous evening inside the White House by the president himself. Strauss had learned much by reading the government's case against the Egyptian cleric, mainly that it had been a house of cards. In the hands of a good defense lawyer, it could have been toppled with the flick of a well-presented motion to dismiss. But the sheikh hadn't had a good defense lawyer; instead he had enlisted the services of a grandstanding civil rights warrior from Manhattan who had walked straight into the prosecutor's trap. If Lawrence Strauss had been the sheikh's lawyer, the case would never have gone to trial. Abdullah would have pleaded down to a much less serious offense or, in all likelihood, walked out of the courtroom a free man.

But Lawrence Strauss didn't take cases like Sheikh Abdullah's. In fact, he rarely took cases at all. In Washington he was known as the lawyer no one knew but everyone wanted. He never spoke to the press, stayed clear of Washington cocktail parties, and the only time he had been inside a courtroom in the last twenty years was to testify against a man who assaulted him during an early-morning run through northwest Washington's Battery Kemble Park. Strauss had never won a major trial, and no groundbreaking appeal bore his name. He operated in Washington's shadows, where political connections and personal friendships counted for more than legal brilliance, and, unlike most of his brethren in the Washington legal community, he possessed the ability to cross political lines. His politics were the politics of pragmatism, his opinion so highly valued that he usually spent several weekends a year at Camp David, no matter which party was in power. Lawrence Strauss was a cutter of deals and a smoother of ruffled feathers, a conciliator and a crafter of compromises. He made problems and prosecutors go away. He believed trials were a roll of the dice, and Lawrence Strauss didn't play games of chance—except for his Thursday-night poker game, which included the chief justice of the United States Supreme Court, two former attorneys general, and the chairman of the Senate Judiciary Committee. Last week he'd won big. He usually did.

A burst of static came over the plane's intercom system, followed

by the voice of the pilot, informing Strauss that they would be landing in ten minutes. Strauss slipped the file into his briefcase and
watched the snow-covered plains rising slowly to receive him. He
feared he had been sent on a fool's errand. He had been dealt a lousy
hand, but then so had his opponent. He'd have to bluff. He didn't
like to bluff. Bluffing was for losers. And the only thing Lawrence
Strauss hated worse than flying was losing.

.   .   .

The United States Penitentiary Administrative Maximum Facility,
also known as the Supermax, and the Alcatraz of the Rockies, stands
two miles south of Florence, Colorado, hidden from public view by
the rolling brown hills of Colorado's high desert. Four hundred of
the country's most hardened and dangerous prisoners are incarcer-
ated there, including Theodore Kaczynski, Terry Nichols, Eric
Rudolph, Matthew Hale, David Lane, and Anthony "Gaspipe"
Casso, underboss of the Lucchese crime family. Also residing within
the walls of the Supermax is a large contingent of Islamic terrorists,
including Zacarias Moussaoui, Richard Reid, and Ramzi Yousef,
mastermind of the first World Trade Center attack in 1993. Despite
the high-profile inmate population, recent investigations had revealed that the prison was dangerously understaffed and far from
secure. Prosecutors in California had learned that Mexican mafia
leader Ruben Castro was running his Los Angeles criminal enterprises from his cell in the Supermax, while authorities in Spain discovered that World Trade Center conspirator Mohammed Salameh
had been in written communication with terror cells linked to the
Madrid subway bombings. Lawrence Strauss, as he passed through
the outer gate in the back of an FBI Suburban, hoped the belea-
guered guards managed to keep a lid on the place until he was airborne again.

The warden was waiting for Strauss in the reception area. He extended his hand solemnly as Strauss came inside and offered a murmured greeting, then turned and led him wordlessly into the bowels

of the complex. They passed through a series of barred doors, each of which closed behind them with an irrefutable finality. Strauss had taken a ride with the president once on a nuclear submarine, an experience he had vowed never to repeat. He felt the same way now—confined, claustrophobic, and sweating despite the sharp chill.

The warden led him into a secure interview room. It was divided into two chambers separated by a Plexiglas wall—visitors on one side, prisoner on the other, a telephone line between them. A sign warned that all conversations were subject to electronic monitoring. Strauss looked at the warden and said, "I'm afraid this won't do."

"The recording devices and surveillance cameras will be turned off."

"Under no circumstances is this conversation going to be conducted electronically."

"It's good enough for the CIA and the FBI when they come here."

"I don't work for the CIA or the FBI."

"I'm afraid it's regulations, Mr. Strauss."

Strauss reached into his coat pocket and pulled out his cell phone. "One phone call—that's all it will take. One phone call and I get what I want. But let's not waste valuable time. Let's find some reasonable compromise."

"What do you have in mind?"

Strauss told him.

"He hasn't been out of his cell in weeks."

"Then the fresh air will do him good."

"Do you know how cold it is outside?"

"Get him a coat," Strauss said.

. . .

It was beginning to get dark by the time Strauss was shown through a secure doorway leading to the west exercise yard. A folding table and two folding chairs had been placed in the precise center and arc lamps were burning along the top of the electrified fence. Four guards stood like statuary along the perimeter; two more were perched along the parapet of the watchtower with weapons trained downward. Strauss nodded in approval to the warden, then headed into the yard alone and took his seat.

Sheikh Abdullah Abdul-Razzaq emerged from the cellblock five minutes later in shackles, sandwiched between a pair of hulking guards. He was shorter than Strauss anticipated, five-six perhaps, and thin as a pauper. He wore an orange prison jumpsuit and a tan parka was draped over his boney shoulders. His beard was un-kempt, and what little Strauss could see of his face was gray and slack with illness. It was the face of a dying man, he thought, a face that had not seen sunlight in many years. His eyes, however, still shone with a condescending intelligence. Lawrence Strauss was a man who earned his living making instantaneous judgments about people. His first opinion of Sheikh Abdullah was that he was a coura-geous and committed man—hardly the raving zealot that had been portrayed by the media and the prosecution at the time of his trial. He would be more than a worthy opponent.

As the sheikh lowered himself into the chair, Strauss looked at one of the guards. "Remove his shackles, please."

The guard shook his head. "It's against the rules."

"I'll take full responsibility."

"Sorry," the guard said, "but it's a rule we never bend at the Max. Prisoners are never unshackled when they're outside the cell. Right, Sheikh Abdullah?"

The guards gave the sheikh a pat on the back and started back to the cellblock. The Egyptian made no response other than to fix his dark eyes directly on those of Lawrence Strauss.

"Who are you?" he asked in heavily accented English.

"My name is Arthur Hamilton," said Strauss.

"You work for the American government, Mr. Hamilton?"

Strauss shook his head. "I want to make clear from the outset that I am a private citizen. I have no connection to the government of the United States whatsoever."

"But surely you didn't come to this place on your own volition. Surely you have been sent here by others."

"That is correct."

"Who sent you here?"

Strauss looked up at the guards in the tower, then gazed directly at Sheikh Abdullah. "I am an emissary of the president of the United States."

The sheikh accepted this piece of information with an air of detachment. "I've been expecting you," he said calmly. "What can I do for you, Mr. Hamilton?"

"I assume you are aware of the fact that your group has kidnapped the daughter of the American ambassador in London and is threatening to murder her if the United States does not release you and return you to Egypt."

"Choose your words carefully, Mr. Hamilton. Elizabeth Halton is a legitimate target in our eyes. Her death, should it come to pass, would not be murder, but a justifiable killing."

"So then you *are* aware of what has transpired on your behalf?"

"I am fully aware, Mr. Hamilton."

"Are you in any way connected to the attack?"

"Are you asking me if I ordered it or helped plan it?"

"That is precisely what I'm asking."

He shook his head slowly. "I have had no contact with the Sword of Allah since my incarceration in this facility. What has been done on my behalf was set in motion without my approval or knowledge."

"By your brother?"

"I wouldn't know." The sheikh gave a fleeting smile. "You are very good at asking questions, Mr. Hamilton. Am I to assume that you are a lawyer?"

"Guilty as charged, Sheikh Abdullah."

"I appreciate your candor. May I now ask *you* a question?"

Strauss nodded.

"Will you convert to Islam, Mr. Hamilton?"

"I beg your pardon?"

"As a devout Muslim, I am obligated to do many things, including bringing the gift of Islam to the unbelievers."

"I'm afraid my allegiances are already spoken for, Sheikh Abdullah."

"You are a person of the Book?"

"I believe in the law, Sheikh Abdullah."

"The only law that matters is God's law."

"And what would God say about the atrocities that have been committed in Europe on your behalf? What would God say about the murder and kidnapping of innocents?"

"The number of dead pale in comparison to the number who have been tortured and killed by your friend Hosni Mubarak. They are but a pittance compared to the number of innocent Muslims who have died because of the American and British adventure in Iraq." The sheikh fell silent for a moment. "Do you know what happened in my country after Osama's airplanes hit your Twin Towers? Your government gave the Mubarak regime a list of names—*hundreds* of names, Mr. Hamilton. And do you know what Mubarak and his secret police did? They arrested all those men and tortured them mercilessly, even though they had absolutely nothing to do with 9/11."

"And this justifies the kidnapping and murder of an innocent woman?"

"Without question." The sheikh turned his face to the arc lamps. The harsh light washed all color from him. "But the president didn't send you all the way here from Washington to engage in a debate, did he, Mr. Hamilton?"

"No, Sheikh Abdullah, he did not."

"What then is the purpose of your visit?"

"The president has dispatched me here to request a favor. He would like you to issue a fatwa condemning the actions of your group and calling for Elizabeth Halton's immediate release. The president feels your words would have a profound influence on the minds of her captors."

"Her captors are listening to other voices, Mr. Hamilton. Mine would be mere background noise."

"The president thinks otherwise." Strauss's next words were spoken with care. "And he would be extremely grateful for whatever help you could provide us in this matter."

"How would the president demonstrate this gratitude?"

"I'm not here to negotiate, Sheikh Abdullah."

"Of course you are, Mr. Hamilton."

"The president believes you are a reasonable man who would not want Elizabeth Halton harmed. The president believes bargaining at a time like this would be inappropriate. It would also be against the stated policy of the United States of America."

"If the president believes I am such a reasonable man, then why did he refer to me as a bloodthirsty terrorist?"

"Sometimes things are said for public consumption that don't necessarily reflect true feelings," Strauss said. "As a man of the Middle East, I'm sure you can understand this."

"More than you might think," the Egyptian said. "But the president doesn't need my cooperation in this fatwa. He can tell his clever spies in the CIA to fabricate one."

"The president feels it won't be believed by the captors unless it is spoken by you. He would like you to read your statement on camera. We would make provisions here, of course."

"Of course." The sheikh tugged thoughtfully at his beard. "Am I to understand that the president of the United States is asking me to end this crisis for him and yet he is offering me nothing in return?"

Strauss removed the file from his briefcase and placed it on the table. "It has come to my attention that the prosecutors from the U.S. Attorney's Office for the Eastern District of Virginia did not turn over to your lawyers certain exculpatory evidence that they were required by law to give them. I believe a well-crafted Section 2255 motion would receive a favorable reception in the courts."

"How favorable?"

Again Strauss proceeded with caution. "I can foresee a scenario in which your conviction is overturned, at which point the government would have to decide whether to retry you or simply release you. In the meantime, steps can be taken to make your stay here more comfortable."

"You make it sound as though I am an invited guest."

"You *were* an invited guest, Sheikh Abdullah. We granted you permission to enter our country and you repaid our hospitality by conspiring to attack some of our most important landmarks."

"But you would be willing to take my case nonetheless?"

"It's not the sort of work I do," Strauss said. "But I can think of several lawyers who would do a very fine job."

"And how long would such a process take?"

"Two years," Strauss said. "Three years at most."

"Do I look like a man who has three years to live?"

"You have no other options."

"No, Mr. Hamilton, the president is the one without options. In fact, his options are so limited he has sent you here cap in hand to plead for my help. In return you offer me false hope and expect me to be grateful. But that's what you Americans always do, isn't it, Mr. Hamilton? What you don't seem to understand is that there is more at stake now than just the fate of a single American woman. The Sword has set fire to Egypt. The days of the Mubarak regime are now numbered. And when it falls, the entire Middle East will change overnight."

Strauss put the file back into his briefcase. "I'm not an expert on the Middle East, but something tells me you have miscalculated. Issue the fatwa, Sheikh Abdullah. Save Elizabeth Halton's life. Do the decent thing. God will reward you." He hesitated, then added: "And so will the president."

"Tell your president that America doesn't negotiate with terrorists and we don't negotiate with tyrants. Tell him to comply with the

Sword's demands or he'll be standing at Andrews Air Force Base soon, watching a coffin coming off an airplane."

Strauss stood abruptly and looked down at the sheikh. "You're making a grave mistake. You're going to die in this prison."

"Perhaps," the Egyptian said, "but you'll die before me."

"I'm afraid my health is better than yours, Sheikh Abdullah."

"Yes, but you live in Washington and someday soon our brothers are going to turn it to ashes." The sheikh turned his face toward the blackening sky. "Enjoy your flight home, Mr. Hamilton. And please give my regards to the president."

35

COPENHAGEN:
1:15 P.M., WEDNESDAY

Y ou were right about the call coming from Germany," said Adrian Carter.

They were walking along a gravel footpath in the Tivoli gardens. Carter was wearing a woolen greatcoat and a fur *ushanka* hat from his days in Moscow. Gabriel wore denim and leather and was hovering dourly at Carter's shoulder like a restless conscience.

"NSA determined Ishaq was just outside Dortmund when he made his call, probably somewhere along the A1 autobahn. We are now working under the assumption that the kidnappers managed to get Elizabeth out of Britain and are moving her from hiding place to hiding place on the Continent."

"Did you tell the Germans?"

"The president was on the phone with the German chancellor two minutes after NSA pinned down the location. Within an hour every police officer in the northwest corner was involved in the search. Obviously they didn't find them. No Ishaq, no Elizabeth."

"Maybe we should consider ourselves fortunate," Gabriel said.

"If the wrong sort of policeman had stumbled upon them, we might have had a Fürstenfeldbruck on our hands."

"Why is that name familiar to me?"

"It was the German airfield outside Munich where our athletes were taken in seventy-two. The terrorists thought they were going to board an airplane and be flown out of the country. It was a trap, of course. The Germans decided to stage a rescue attempt. We asked them if we could handle it, but they refused. They wanted to do it themselves. It was amateurish, to put it mildly."

"I remember," Carter said distantly. "Within a few seconds, all your athletes were dead."

"Shamron was standing in the tower when it happened," Gabriel said. "He saw the entire thing."

They sat down at a table in an outdoor café. Gabriel ordered coffee and apple cake, then watched as Sarah drifted slowly past. The ends of her scarf were tucked into her coat, a prearranged signal that meant she had detected no signs of Danish security.

"Munich," said Carter distantly. "All roads lead back to Munich, don't they? Munich proved that terrorism could bring the civilized world to its knees. Munich proved that terrorism could work. Yasir Arafat's fingerprints were all over Munich, but two years later he was standing before the General Assembly of the United Nations." Carter made a sour face and sipped his coffee. "But Munich also proved that a ruthless, merciless, and determined campaign against the murderers could be effective. It took a while, but eventually you were able to put Black September out of business." He looked at Gabriel. "Did you see the movie?"

Gabriel shot Carter a withering look and shook his head slowly. "I see it every night in my head, Adrian. The real thing—not a fantasy version written by someone who questions the right of my country to exist."

"I didn't mean to touch a nerve." Carter stabbed at his cake without appetite. "But in a way it was easier then, wasn't it? Eliminate the leaders, and the network dies. Now we are fighting an idea and ideas don't die so easily. It's rather like fighting cancer. You have to find the right dosage of medicine. Too little and the cancer grows. Too much and you kill the patient."

"You're never going to be able to kill the cancer as long as Egypt keeps churning out terrorists," Gabriel said. "Ibrahim Fawaz was an exception. When he was tortured and humiliated by the regime, he chose to leave the extremist Islamist movement and get on with what remained of his life. But most of those who are tortured go in the opposite direction."

"Wouldn't it be wonderful if we could snap our fingers and create a vibrant and viable democracy along the banks of the Nile. But that's not going to happen any time soon, especially given our track record in Iraq. Which means we're stuck with Mubarak and his thuggish regime for the foreseeable future. He's a son of a bitch, but he's *our* son of a bitch—and yours, too, Gabriel. Or is it your wish to have an Islamic Republic of Egypt along your western flank?"

"In many respects Egypt already is an Islamic republic. The Egyptian government is unable to provide the most basic services to its people and the Islamists have filled the void. They've penetrated the elementary schools and the universities, the bureaucracy and the trade unions, the arts and the press, even the courts and the legal guilds. No book can be published, and no film can be produced, that doesn't first meet the approval of the clerics at al-Azhar. Western influences are slowly being extinguished. It's only a matter of time before the regime is extinguished, too."

"Hopefully we'll have found some other way to fuel our cars before that happens."

"You will," said Gabriel. "And we'll be left to face the beast on our own."

Gabriel tucked a few bills under his coffee cup and stood. They walked along the far edge of the park, past a row of food kiosks. Sarah was seated at a wooden table, eating a plate of chilled shrimp on black bread. She dropped it unfinished into a rubbish bin as Carter and Gabriel filed slowly past, then followed after them.

"Speaking of Egypt, we nearly caught a break there last night," Carter said. "The SSI arrested a Sword of Allah operative named Hussein Mandali. He had the misfortune of being caught while in possession of one of Sheikh Tayyib's tape-recorded sermons—a sermon that had been recorded *after* the kidnapping. It turns out that Mandali was present at the recording session, which took place at an apartment in Zamalek. The apartment was owned by a Saudi benefactor of the Sword named Prince Rashid bin Sultan. The prince has been on our radar screens for some time. It seems that giving support to Islamic terrorists is something of a hobby for him, like his falcons and his whores."

Carter fished his pipe from the pocket of his greatcoat. "The SSI searched the apartment and found the premises recently vacated. We requested permission to question Mandali ourselves and were informed that he was unavailable for comment."

"That means he's no longer presentable."

"Or worse."

"Still want to pack my Joe off to Egypt for an interrogation?"

"You've prevailed on that point, Gabriel. The question is what do we do now?"

"Maybe it's time we had a word with Ishaq."

Carter stopped walking and looked at Gabriel directly. "What exactly do you have in mind?"

Gabriel told Carter his plan as they walked through the heart of Copenhagen along a quiet cobblestone street.

"It's risky," Carter said. "We also have no guarantee he's going to call back again tonight. We asked the German police to conduct the search as quietly as possible, but it didn't go unnoticed by German media, and there's a good chance Ishaq noticed, too. If he's smart— and we have no evidence to the contrary—he's bound to suspect his phone call had something to do with it."

"He'll call, Adrian. He's trying to hold on to his family. And as for risk, no option before us is without risk."

Carter gave it another moment of thought. "We'll have to come clean with the Danes," he said finally. "And the president would have to approve it."

"So call him."

Carter handed Gabriel the phone. "He's your friend," he said. "*You* call him."

· · ·

One hour would elapse before the president gave Gabriel's gambit his blessing. The operation's first step came ten minutes after that, not in Copenhagen but in Amsterdam, where, at 12:45 P.M., Ibrahim Fawaz stepped from the al-Hijrah Mosque after midday prayers and started back toward the open-air market in the Ten Kate Straat. As he was nearing his stall at the end of the market, a man came alongside him and touched him lightly on the arm. He had pockmarks across his cheeks and spoke Arabic with the accent of a Palestinian. Five minutes later, Ibrahim was sitting next to the man in the back of a Mercedes sedan.

"No handcuffs or hood this time?"

The man with pockmarked cheeks shook his head slowly. "Tonight we're going to take a nice comfortable ride together," he said. "As long as you behave yourself, of course."

"Where are we going?"

The man answered the question truthfully.

"Copenhagen? Why Copenhagen?"

"A friend of yours is about to cross a dangerous bridge there, and he needs a good man like you to serve as his guide."

"I suppose that means he's heard from my son."

"I'm just the delivery boy. Your friend will fill in the rest of the picture for you after we arrive."

"What about my daughter-in-law and my grandson?"

The man with pockmarked cheeks said nothing. Instead he

glanced into the rearview mirror and, with a flick of his head, ordered the driver to get moving. As the car slipped away from the
curb, Ibrahim wondered if they were really going to Copenhagen or
whether their true destination was the torture chambers of Egypt. He
thought of the words Sheikh Abdullah had spoken to him in another
lifetime. *Rely on God,* the sheikh had said. *Don't be defeated.*

.   .   .

Denmark's not-so-secret police are known as the Security Intelligence Service. Those who work there refer to it only as "the Service," and among professionals like Adrian Carter it was known as
the PET, the initials of its impossible-to-pronounce Danish name.
Though its address was officially a state secret, most residents of
Copenhagen knew it was headquartered in an anonymous office
block in a quiet quarter north of the Tivoli gardens. Lars Mortensen,
PET's profoundly pro-American chief, was waiting in his office when
Carter was shown inside. He was a tall man, as Danish men invari-
ably are, with the bearing of a Viking and the blond good looks of a
film star. His sharp blue eyes betrayed no emotion other than a mild
curiosity. It was rare for an American spy of Adrian Carter's stature
to pop into Copenhagen for a visit—and rarer still that he did so with
just five minutes' warning.

"I wish you would have told us you were coming," Mortensen
said as he nodded Carter into a comfortable Danish Modern armchair. "We could have arranged for a proper reception. To what do
we owe the honor?"

"I'm afraid we have something of a situation on our hands."
Carter's careful tone was not lost on his Danish counterpart. "Our
search for Elizabeth Halton has led us onto Danish soil. Well, not us,
exactly. An intelligence service working on our behalf."

"Which service?"

Carter answered the question truthfully. The look in Mortensen's
blue eyes turned from curiosity to anger.

"How long have they been in Denmark?"

"Twenty-four hours, give or take a few hours."

"Why weren't we informed?"

"I'm afraid it fell into the category of a hot pursuit."

"Telephones work during hot pursuits," Mortensen said. "So do fax machines and computers."

"It was an oversight on our part," Carter said, his tone conciliatory. "And the blame lies with me, not the Israelis."

"What *exactly* are they doing here?" Mortensen narrowed his blue eyes. "And why are you coming to us now?"

The Danish security chief tapped a silver pen anxiously against his knee while he listened to Carter's explanation.

"Exactly how many Israelis are now in Copenhagen?"

"I'm not sure, to be honest."

"I want them on their way out of town in an hour."

"I'm afraid at least one of them is going to have to stay."

"What's his name?"

Carter told him. Mortensen's pen fell silent.

"I have to take this to the prime minister," he said.

"Is it really necessary to involve the politicians?"

"Only if I want to keep my job," Mortensen snapped. "Assuming the prime minister grants his approval—and I have no reason to think he won't, given our past cooperation with your government—I want to be present tonight when Fawaz calls."

"It's likely to be unpleasant."

"We Danes are tough people, Mr. Carter. I think I can handle it."

"Then we would be pleased to have you there."

"And tell your friend Allon to keep his Beretta in his holster. I don't want any dead bodies turning up. If anyone dies anywhere in the country tonight, he'll be our top suspect."

"I'll tell him," said Carter.

The curiosity returned to Mortensen's eyes. "What's he like?"

"Allon?"

Mortensen nodded.

"He's a rather serious chap and a bit rough around the edges."

"They all are," said Mortensen.

"Yes," said Carter. "But, then, who can blame them?"

. . .

There are few ugly buildings in central Copenhagen. The glass-and-steel structure on the Dag Hammarskjölds Allé that houses the American embassy is one of them. The CIA station there is small and somewhat cramped—Copenhagen was an intelligence backwater during the Cold War and remains so today—but its secure conference room seats twenty comfortably, and its electronics are fully up-to-date. Carter thought they needed a code name, and Gabriel, after a brief deliberation, suggested Moriah, the hill in Jerusalem where God ordered Abraham to sacrifice his only son. Carter, whose father was an Episcopal minister, thought the choice inspired, and from that point forward they were referred to in all Agency communications as the Moriah Team and nothing else.

Ibrahim Fawaz arrived from Amsterdam at six that evening, accompanied by Oded and Yaakov. Lars Mortensen appeared at 6:15 and accepted Gabriel's act of contrition for the sin of failing to obtain Danish authorization before barging onto Danish soil. Gabriel then requested permission for the rest of his team to remain in Denmark to see the operation through, and Mortensen, clearly starstruck to be in the presence of the legend, immediately agreed. Mordecai and Sarah joined them after breaking camp at the Hotel d'Angleterre, while Eli Lavon came gratefully in from the cold of Nørrebro, looking like a man who had been on near-constant surveillance duty for more than a week.

The hours of the early evening were the province of Mortensen and the Danes. At seven o'clock they disabled the phone line leading to the Nørrebro apartment and forwarded all calls to a number inside the CIA station. Fifteen minutes later two Danish agents—Mortensen wisely chose female agents to avoid a cultural confrontation—paid a quiet visit to the apartment for the expressed purpose of asking a few "routine" questions concerning the whereabouts of one Ishaq Fawaz. Mordecai's original "glass" was still active and, much to Mortensen's dismay, it was used by the Moriah Team to monitor the proceedings. They were fifteen minutes in duration and ended with the sound of Hanifah and Ahmed being taken into Danish custody for additional questioning. Hanifah was immediately relieved of her cell phone and the phone was ferried at high speed to the embassy, where Mordecai, with Carter and Mortensen looking over his shoulder, hastily mined it for any nuggets of useful intelligence.

At eight o'clock a scene commenced that Carter would later liken to a deathwatch. They crowded around the rectangular table in the conference room, Americans at one end, Gabriel's field warriors at the other, and Sarah perched uneasily between them. Mortensen placed himself directly in front of the speaker. Ibrahim sat to his right, nervously working the beads of his *tasbih*. Only Gabriel was in motion. He was pacing the length of the room like an actor on opening night, with one hand pressed firmly to his chin and his eyes boring into the telephone as though willing it to ring. Sarah tried to assure him that the call would come soon, but Gabriel seemed not to hear her. He was listening to other voices—the voice of Ishaq promising his wife that he would call at 9:30, and the voice of Hanifah warning that if he was one minute late she would refuse to answer. At 9:29, Gabriel ceased pacing and stood over the telephone. Ten seconds later it rang with the harshness of a fire alarm in a night ward. Gabriel reached for the receiver and lifted it slowly to his ear.

36

C O P E N H A G E N :
9 : 3 0 P . M . , W E D N E S D A Y

Gabriel listened for several seconds without speaking. Traffic rushing at speed along wet pavement. The distant blare of a car horn, like a warning of trouble to come.

"Good evening, Ishaq," he said calmly in Arabic. "I want you to listen very carefully, because I'm only going to say this once. Are you listening, Ishaq?"

"Who is this?"

"I'll take that as a yes. I have your father, Ishaq. I also have Hanifah and Ahmed. We're going to make a deal, Ishaq. Just you and me. You're going to give me Elizabeth Halton, I'm going to give you back your family. If you don't give me Elizabeth, I'm going to put your family on a plane to Egypt and hand them over to the SSI for questioning. And you know what happens in the interrogation chambers of the SSI, don't you, Ishaq?"

"Where's my father?"

"I'm going to give you a telephone number, Ishaq. It's a number no one else has but me. I want you to write it down, because it's important you don't forget it. Are you ready, Ishaq?"

Silence, then: "I'm ready."

Gabriel recited the number, then said, "Call me on that number in ten minutes, Ishaq. It's now nine thirty-one. At nine forty-two, I stop answering the phone. Do you understand me, Ishaq? Don't test my patience. And don't make the wrong choice."

Gabriel hung up the phone and looked at Ibrahim.

"Was it him?"

Ibrahim closed his eyes and fingered the beads of his *tasbih*.

"Yes," said Ibrahim. "That was my son."

Carter and Mortensen reached for separate telephones and quickly dialed. Mortensen called one of his men who was inside the offices of Tele Danmark, the Danish telecom company, while Carter dialed a CIA liaison officer at the Fort Meade, Maryland, headquarters of the NSA. Five minutes later they hung up simultaneously and eyed each other like poker players across the table. Mortensen laid down his hand first.

"According to Tele Danmark, the call was placed from a mobile phone in Belgium," he said. "If we contact our brethren in Brussels, we should be able to find out where he was when he made the call."

"Don't bother," Carter said. "He was east of Liège, probably on the A3. It was a different phone than the one he used last night. And it's no longer on the air."

· · ·

He called Hanifah's mobile, then dialed the apartment again. Gabriel let the phones ring unanswered. Finally, with the deadline hard approaching, he called the number Gabriel had given him. The Agency technicians had patched the line into the recorders and it was being fed live to Washington. Much to the irritation of all those listening, Gabriel allowed the phone to ring four times before answering. His tone, when finally he brought the receiver to his ear, was brisk and businesslike.

"You cut it rather close, Ishaq. I wouldn't make a habit of it."

"Where are my wife and son?"

"As of this moment they are sitting aboard a private plane on an airfield outside Copenhagen. What happens to them next depends entirely on you."

"What about my father?"

"You father is here with me."

"Where is *here*?"

"Where I am at the moment is completely unimportant, Ishaq. The only thing that matters now is Elizabeth Halton. You have her, I want her back. We're going to make it happen, just you and me. No one else needs to be involved. Not your controller. Not your mastermind. Just us."

"Who do you work for?"

"I can be whoever you want me to be: CIA, FBI, DIA, an agency so fucking secret you've never heard of it before. But just be sure of one thing. I'm not bluffing. I made your father disappear from the al-Hijrah Mosque in Amsterdam, and I made your wife and son vanish from Nørrebro. And if you don't do exactly what I tell you to do, I'll put them all on a plane to Egypt. And you know what happens there, don't you? I know what happened to your sister, Ishaq. Jihan was her name, right? Your father told me about Jihan. Your father told me everything."

"I want to talk to him."

"I'm afraid that's not possible at the moment. Your father has suffered enough because of the Egyptian secret police. Don't make him suffer again. Have you seen the scars on his arms? Have you seen the scars on his back? Don't put him through another night in the torture chambers of Egypt."

Ishaq was silent for a moment. Gabriel listened intently to the noise in the background. The truck was moving again.

"Where are you calling from, Ishaq?"

"Afghanistan."

"That's quite a feat of driving, given the fact you were just outside Dortmund when you called last night. My patience is not un-limited. Tell me where you are, or I'll hang up and you'll never hear from me again. Do you understand me?"

"And I'll push a button and the American woman will die a mar-tyr's death. Do you understand *me*?"

"We've had enough of bombs and blood, Ishaq. You've made your point. The world has taken notice of Egypt's plight. But the president isn't going to release the sheikh, no matter how many peo-ple you kill. It's not going to happen. You alone have the power to make it stop. Spare Elizabeth Halton's life. Give her back to me and I'll give you back your family."

"And what happens to me?"

"I'm not interested in you. In fact, I couldn't give a shit about you. What I want is Elizabeth Halton. Leave her somewhere safe, tell me where I can find her, then make your way to Afghanistan or Pak-istan or Wherever-the-fuck-istan you want to spend the rest of your life. Just give me the girl back. You love death, we love life. You're strong, we're weak. You've already won. Just let me have her back."

"I'm going to find you one day, you bastard. I'm going to find you and kill you."

"I guess that means you're not interested in a deal. It's been nice talking to you, Ishaq. If you happen to change your mind, you have ten minutes to call me back. Think about it carefully. Don't make the wrong decision. Otherwise, your family is as good as dead. Ten min-utes, Ishaq. Then the plane leaves for Cairo."

Gabriel hung up the phone for a second time. Carter gave him a pat on the back. It was drenched in sweat.

        . . .

Gabriel slipped from the conference room without a word and made his way to the toilets. He stood before the basin, hands braced on the edge of the cold porcelain, and gazed at his own reflection in the mir-ror. He saw himself not as he appeared now but as a boy of twenty-one, a gifted artist with the ashes of the Holocaust flowing in his veins. Shamron was standing over his shoulder, hard as an iron bar, urgent as a drumbeat. *You will terrorize the terrorists,* he was saying. *You will be Israel's avenging angel of death.*

But Shamron had neglected to warn Gabriel of the price he would one day pay for climbing into the sewer with terrorists and murderers: a son buried in a hero's grave on the Mount of Olives, a wife lost in a labyrinth of memory in an asylum on Mount Herzl. Having lost his own family to the terrorists, he had vowed to himself that he would never target the innocent in order to achieve his goals. Tonight, if only for the purposes of deception, he had broken that promise. He felt no guilt over his actions, only a profound sense of despair. The creed of the global jihadists was not just; it was a mental illness. One could not reason with those who massacred the innocent in the belief that they were doing God's will on earth. One had to kill them before they killed you. And if one had to threaten the family of a murderer to save an innocent life, then so be it.

He splashed icy water on his face and stepped out into the corridor. Carter was leaning against the wall with the calm detachment of a man waiting for a long-delayed train.

"Are you all right?" he asked.

"I will be when this is over," Gabriel said. "Did NSA get a fix on him?"

"It appears he was somewhere close to the interchange of the A3 and the A26."

"Which means he could now be heading in any direction at considerable speed," said Gabriel. "What about the phone itself?"

"It was different," Carter said.

"I suppose it's now off the air?"

Carter nodded.

"Anything else?"

"Washington is worried that you're pushing him too hard."

"What would they have me do? Ask him nicely to release her?"

"They just want you to give him a little room to maneuver."

"And what if he uses that room to kill Elizabeth Halton?"

Carter led the way back to the conference room. As they passed through the doorway, Gabriel looked up at the wall clock. Three minutes remained until the next deadline. Lars Mortensen was drumming his fingers anxiously against the tabletop.

"What are you going to do if he doesn't call?"

"He'll call," Gabriel said.

"How can you be sure?"

It was Ibrahim who answered for him. "Because of Jihan," he said, fingers still working his prayer beads. "He'll call because he doesn't want his wife and son to suffer the same fate as Jihan."

Mortensen, perplexed by the response, looked to Carter for an explanation. Carter raised his hand in a gesture that said he would explain the reference at a more appropriate time. Gabriel resumed his pacing. Two minutes later, the telephone rang again. He snatched up the receiver and brought it quickly to his ear.

"Ishaq," he said with an artificial brightness. "I'm glad you called. I assume we have a deal?"

"We do, as long as you agree to my one condition."

"You're not in much of a position to make demands, Ishaq."

"Neither are you."

"What's your condition?"

"I'll give her to my father, but no one else."

"That's not necessary, Ishaq. Just stop the car and leave Elizabeth by the side of the road—somewhere safe and dry, somewhere out of harm's way—then drive away. It doesn't need to be any more complicated than that."

"I need proof my father is still in Europe." A pause. "I need proof he's still alive."

"Your father is a founding member of the Sword of Allah, Ishaq. Your father isn't going to go anywhere near my girl."

"My father is an innocent man. And unless he's there, you don't get your girl."

Gabriel looked at Carter, who nodded his head.

"All right, Ishaq, you win. We'll do it your way. Just tell me where you want to do it."

"Are you in Denmark?"

"I told you, Ishaq—it doesn't matter where I am."

"It matters to me."

"Yes, Ishaq. I'm in Denmark. Let's just do it here, shall we? It's a small country, lots of open spaces, and the Danish police are willing to let you be on your way after you release Elizabeth."

"I need a guarantee of safe passage over the border. No checkpoints. No roadblocks. If a policeman so much as looks at me twice, the woman is dead. Do you understand?"

"I understand. We'll tell the local authorities to stand down. No one is going to bother you. Just tell me how you want to do it."

"I'll call you tomorrow and tell you what to do."

"Tomorrow? That's not good enough, Ishaq."

"If tomorrow isn't good enough, then your girl dies tonight."

Another glance at Carter. Another nod of the head.

"All right, Ishaq. What time are you going to call me tomorrow?"

"I'll call at noon Copenhagen time."

"Too long, Ishaq. I want to hear from you much sooner than that."

"It's noon or nothing. It's your choice."

"All right, noon it is. Don't disappoint me."

The line went dead. Gabriel hung up the phone and buried his face in his hands. "I gave him room to maneuver, Adrian, just like Washington wanted, and he maneuvered me right into a corner."

"We'll wait until tomorrow and listen to what he has to say."

"And what if we don't like what he has to say?"

"Then we won't accept the deal."

"No, Adrian, we'll do exactly what he tells us to do. Because if we don't, he's going to kill her."

T heir security had been exceptionally good. They never entered her cell without their faces covered, and not once since the initial seconds of her capture had they spoken a single word to her. They had permitted her no newspapers or reading material of any kind, and a request for a radio to help pass the empty hours had been met by a slow shake of Cain's head. She had lost track of how long she had been in captivity. She had no idea whether the rest of the world thought she was alive or dead. Nor did she have any clue as to her whereabouts. She might still be in the east of England, she thought, or she might be in a cave complex in Tora Bora. Of one thing, however, she was certain: her captors were moving her on a regular basis.

The proof of movement was plain for her to see. The rooms where she was being held were all variations of the first—white walls, a camp bed, a single lamp, a door with a spy hole—but each was clearly different. She would have been able to discern this even if they had forced her to wear a blindfold, because her senses of smell and hearing were now heightened to an animal acuteness. She could hear them coming long before they slid the notes beneath her door and now could distinguish Cain from Abel by scent alone. Her last cell had stunk of liquid bleach. The one where she was being held now was filled with the pleasant aroma of coffee and Middle Eastern spices. She was in a market, she thought, or perhaps the warehouse of a distributor that supplied grocers in Arab neighborhoods.

Her heightened senses had allowed her to gather one other piece of information: there was a distinct rhythm to her movements. This rhythm was not measured by hours and minutes—time, for all her attempts to capture it, remained a mystery to her—but in the number of meals she was given in each location. It was always the same: four meals of identical content, then a shot of the ketamine, then she would awaken in a new room with new smells. Thus far she had been given three meals in her current location. Her fourth would be coming soon. Elizabeth knew that, in all likelihood, it would be followed several hours later by an injection of ketamine. She would struggle, but her struggle would quickly turn to submission in the face of greater strength and numbers.

Submission . . .

That was their goal. Submission was the overall goal of the global jihadists and it was the goal of Elizabeth's captors as well. The global jihadists wanted the West to submit to the will of violent Salafist Islam. Elizabeth's captors wanted her to submit to the needle and the mind-numbing rhythm of their movements and their notes. They wanted her weak and compliant, a sheep that offers its throat willingly to the ritual knife. Elizabeth had decided that her days of submission were over. She had decided to stage a rebellion, a rebellion she hoped would provide her with information as to her whereabouts, a rebellion fought with the only two weapons available to her—her own life and her knowledge of medicine. She closed her eyes and inhaled the pleasant aroma of coffee and cinnamon. And she waited for Cain to open the door and present her with her fourth meal.

38

C O P E N H A G E N :
2 : 5 2   P . M . ,   T H U R S D A Y

S o it comes down to the two of us once again,"
Ibrahim said. "I suppose that's fitting."

Gabriel cleared the windshield of his Audi A8 sedan with a flick
of the wiper blades. The King's New Square appeared before him,
shrouded in a bridal veil of snowfall. Ibrahim was sitting silently in
the passenger seat, freshly scrubbed and dressed for his own funeral
in a borrowed gray suit and overcoat. His hands were folded primly
in his lap, good hand atop ruined hand, and his eyes were on his
shoes. Gabriel's telephone lay in the console. Its signal was being
monitored inside the CIA station at the American embassy and at
NSA headquarters.

"You're not going to give me another one of your lectures, are
you, Ibrahim?"

"I'm still a professor at heart," he said. "I can't help it."

Gabriel decided to indulge him. A lecture was better than silence.

"Why do you suppose it's fitting?"

"We have both seen the worst this life has to offer. Nothing can
frighten us, and nothing that happens today will surprise us." He

looked up from his shoes and gazed at Gabriel for a moment. "The things they wrote about you in the newspapers after London—it was all true? You were the one who killed the members of Black September?"

Ibrahim interpreted Gabriel's silence as affirmation the newspapers accounts were all true.

"I remember Munich so clearly," Ibrahim said. "We spent that day standing around our televisions and radios. It electrified the Arab world. We cheered the capture of your athletes, and when they were massacred at the airport we danced in the streets. In retrospect, our reaction was appalling, but completely understandable. We were weak and humiliated. You were strong and rich. You had beaten us many times. We had finally beaten you, in Germany of all places, land of your greatest catastrophe."

"I thought you Islamists didn't believe in the Holocaust. I thought you regarded it as a great lie, foisted upon the world by clever Jews so we could rob the Arabs of their land."

"I've never been one to dabble in self-delusion and conspiracy theory," Ibrahim said. "You Jews deserve a national home. God knows you need one. But the sooner you give the Palestinians a state in the West Bank and Gaza, the better for all of us."

"And if that means giving it to your spiritual brethren in Hamas?"

"At the rate we're going, Hamas will look like moderates soon," Ibrahim said. "And when the Palestinian issue is finally removed from the table, the Arabs will have no one else to blame for their miserable condition. We will be forced to take a hard look in the mirror and solve our problems for ourselves."

"That's just one of the reasons why there will never be peace. We're the scapegoat for Arab failings—the pressure valve for Arab unrest. The Arabs loathe us, but they cannot live without us."

Ibrahim nodded in agreement and resumed the study of his shoes. "Is it also true that you are a famous art restorer?"

This time Gabriel nodded slowly. Ibrahim pulled his lips into an incredulous frown.

"Why, if you have the ability to heal beautiful paintings, do you engage in work such as this?"

"Duty," said Gabriel. "I feel an obligation to protect my people."

"The terrorists would say the same thing."

"Perhaps, but I don't murder the innocent."

"You just threaten to send them to Egypt to be tortured." Ibrahim looked at Gabriel. "Would you have done it?"

Gabriel shook his head. "No, Ibrahim, I wouldn't have sent you back."

Ibrahim looked out his window. "The snow is beautiful," he said. "Is it a good omen or bad?"

"A friend of mine calls weather like this operational weather."

"That's good?"

Gabriel nodded. "It's good."

"You've done this kind of thing before?"

"Only once."

"How did it end?"

With the Gare de Lyon in rubble, thought Gabriel. "I got the hostage back," he said.

"This street that he wants us to walk down—do you know it?"

Gabriel lifted his hand from the wheel and pointed across the square. "It's called Strøget. It's a pedestrian mall lined with shops and restaurants, two miles long—the longest in Europe, if the hotel brochures are to be believed. It empties into a square called the Rådhuspladsen."

"We walk and they watch—is that how it works?"

"That's exactly how it works. And if they like what they see, someone will phone me when we reach the Rådhuspladsen and tell me where to go next."

"When do we start?"

"Three o'clock."

"Three o'clock," Ibrahim repeated. "The hour of death—at least that's what the Christians believe. Why do you think they chose three o'clock?"

"It gives them a few minutes of daylight to see us properly in Strøget. After that, it will be dark. That gives them the advantage. It makes it harder for me to see them."

"What about your little helpers?" Ibrahim asked. "The ones who plucked me from that street corner in Amsterdam?"

"Ishaq says if he detects surveillance, the deal is off and Elizabeth Halton dies."

"So we go alone?"

Gabriel nodded and looked at his watch. It was 2:59. "It's not too late to back out, you know. You don't have to do this."

"I made you a promise in that house two nights ago—a promise that I would help you get the American woman back. It is a promise I intend to keep." He squeezed his face into a quizzical frown. "Where were we, by the way?"

"We were in Germany."

"A Jew threatening to torture an Arab in Germany," Ibrahim replied. "How poetic."

"You're not going to give me another one of your lectures, are you, Ibrahim?"

"I'm inclined to, but I'm afraid there isn't time." He pointed to the dashboard clock. "The hour of death is upon us."

. . .

The atmosphere along Strøget was one of feverish festivity. To Gabriel it seemed like the last night before the start of a long-feared war, the night when fortunes are spent and love is made with headlong abandon. But there was no war coming, at least not for the shoppers along Copenhagen's most famous street, only the holidays. Gabriel had been so absorbed in the search for Elizabeth Halton he had forgotten it was nearly Christmas.

They drifted through this joyous streetscape like detached spirits of the dead, hands thrust into coat pockets, elbows touching, silent. Ishaq had decreed that their journey would be a straight line and would include no stops. That meant that Gabriel was unable to conduct even the most basic countersurveillance maneuvers. It had been more than thirty years since he had walked a European street without checking his tail and to do so now made him feel as though he were trapped in one of those anxiety dreams where he was naked in a world of the fully clothed. He saw enemies everywhere, old and new. He saw men who might be Sword of Allah terrorists and men who might be Danish security—and, in the shelter of a storefront, he swore he saw Eli Lavon playing Christmas carols on a violin. It wasn't Lavon, only his doppelgänger. Besides, Gabriel remembered suddenly, Lavon couldn't play the violin. Lavon, for all his gifts, had an ear of stone.

They paused for the first time at the intersection of a cross street and waited for the light to change. A Bengali man pressed a flyer into Gabriel's palm with such urgency that Gabriel nearly drew his Beretta from his coat pocket. The flyer was for a restaurant near the Tivoli gardens. Gabriel read it carefully to make sure it contained no hidden instructions, then crushed it into a ball and dropped it into a rubbish bin. The light turned to green. He hooked Ibrahim by the elbow and walked on.

It was beginning to grow dark now; the streetlamps were burning more brightly and the lights in the shopwindows glowed with a greeting-card warmth. Gabriel had given up on trying to find the watchers and instead found himself gazing in wonder at the scenes around him. At children eating ice cream despite the falling snow. At the pretty young woman kneeling over the contents of a spilled shopping bag. At carolers dressed like elves singing about the birth of God with voices of angels. He remembered the words Uzi Navot had spoken that first night, as they drove through the hills outside Jerusalem. *The Europeans condemned us for Lebanon, but what they don't understand is that Lebanon is merely a preview of coming attractions. The movie will soon be showing in theaters all across Europe.* Gabriel only hoped it wasn't coming to Copenhagen tonight.

They paused at another crosswalk, then struck out across the vast Rådhuspladsen. On the left side of the square stood City Hall, the spire of its clock tower jutting knifelike into a low cloud. In the center of the square was a brightly lit yuletide tree, fifty feet in height, and, next to the tree, a small kiosk selling sausages and hot cider. Gabriel walked over to the kiosk and joined the queue, but before he reached the service window the phone in his coat pocket rang softly. He brought it to his ear and listened without speaking. A few seconds later, he returned the phone to his pocket and took Ibrahim by the elbow.

"They want us to retrace our steps and go back to the car," Gabriel said as they walked across the square.

"Then what?"

"They didn't say."

"What are we going to do?"

"We're going to do what they tell us to do."

"Do they know what they're doing?"

Gabriel nodded. They knew exactly what they were doing.

. . .

The Audi was where he had left it and was now covered with a dusting of fresh snow. Sarah was seated alone in the window of a nearby café. She was wearing her beret and it was tilted slightly to the left, which meant that the car had not been tampered with in their absence. Even so, Gabriel dropped his keys onto the paving stones and gave the undercarriage a quick inspection before opening the door and climbing in. The telephone rang immediately after Ibrahim joined him. Gabriel listened to the instructions, then severed the connection and started the engine. He looked once more into the café window and saw that Sarah had lifted her hand into the air. He feared that she was waving good-bye to him in blatant contravention of all known tradecraft, but a few seconds later a waiter appeared and deposited a check at her elbow. Sarah placed a few bills onto the table and stood. Gabriel slipped the car into gear and eased away from the curb. *Take your time*, Ishaq had said. *We have a long night ahead of us.*

39

The note appeared beneath her door. She swung her shackled feet to the floor and shuffled slowly across her cell. It was Cain who stood on the other side awaiting her reply. She could smell him. The note said: *Do you want food?* "Yes," she replied in a low, evenly modulated voice. Then, like a model prisoner, she laid down on her cot again and waited for him to come inside.

She heard the sound of a key being shoved into a padlock, followed by the groaning of hinges. This door was louder than the door of her last cell and the sound of it opening always set her teeth on edge. Cain placed the food at the foot of her cot and quickly withdrew. Elizabeth sat up again and scrutinized the meal: a few inches of baguette, a lump of cheese of indeterminate origin, a bottle of Evian water, chocolate because she had been good.

She devoured the food and gulped the water. Then, when she was certain no one was watching through the spy hole, she shoved her fingers down her throat and vomited her fourth meal onto the floor of her cell. Cain burst in two minutes later and glared at her angrily. Her blanket was now wrapped around her shoulders and she appeared to be shivering uncontrollably. "The ketamine," she whispered. "You're killing me with the ketamine."

. . .

Abel brought a bucket of water and a rag and made her clean her own vomit. Only when her cell was cleansed of impure female excretions did Cain reappear. He stood as far from her as possible, as though he feared catching whatever was ailing her, and with a terse movement of his hand invited her to explain her affliction.

"Idiopathic paroxysmal ventricular tachycardia." She paused for a moment and drew a series of rapid heavy breaths. "It is a fancy way of saying that I suffer from sporadic arrhythmia in the lower chambers of my heart: the ventricles. This sporadic arrhythmia has been exacerbated by too many injections of ketamine. My heartbeat is now dangerously rapid and arrhythmic and my blood pressure is extremely low, which is causing the nausea and the chills. If you give me another shot of ketamine, you could very well kill me."

He stood silently for a moment, gazing at her though the eye slits of his hood, then withdrew. Several minutes later—about twenty, she guessed, but she couldn't be sure—he returned and handed her a typewritten note:

FOR REASONS WE CANNOT EXPLAIN TO YOU, IT IS NECESSARY FOR YOU TO BE MOVED THIS EVENING. IF YOU ARE CONSCIOUS DURING THIS MOVEMENT, YOU WILL BE EXTREMELY UNCOMFORTABLE. DO YOU WANT THE KETAMINE OR DO YOU WANT TO BE MOVED WHILE YOU ARE AWAKE?

"No more ketamine," she said. "I'll do it conscious."

Cain looked at her as though she had made the wrong choice, then handed her a second note.

IF YOU SCREAM OR MAKE ANY NOISE WHATSOEVER, WE WILL KILL
YOU AND LEAVE YOU BY THE SIDE OF THE ROAD.

"I understand," she said.

Cain collected the two notes and slipped out of her cell. Elizabeth
stretched out on her cot and stared into the blinding white light. Her
rebellion was only a few minutes old, but already she had managed
to gather two small pieces of information. She was to be moved by
road and at night.

.   .   .

When next they entered her cell, they did so without first alerting her
with a note. They bound her quickly in her own woolen blanket and
secured it to her body cocoonlike with heavy packing tape. Foam-
rubber plugs were inserted into her ears, a gag placed over her
mouth, and a blindfold tied tightly over her eyes. Now robbed of all
senses but touch and smell, she felt them take hold of her body, one
at each end, and carry her a short distance. The container into which
she was placed was so narrow that the sides pressed hard against her
hips and shoulders. It smelled of plywood and glue and vaguely of
old fish. A lid was placed over the top, so close that it nearly touched
the end of her nose, and several nails were hurriedly hammered into
place. She wanted to scream. She did not. She wanted to cry out for
her mother. She prayed silently instead and thought of the slender
man with gray temples who had tried to save her life in Hyde Park.
I will not submit, she thought. *I will not submit*.

40

FUNEN ISLAND, DENMARK:
8:35 P.M., THURSDAY

The lights of the Great Belt Bridge, second-longest suspension bridge in the world, lay like a double strand of pearls over the straits between the Danish islands of Zealand and Funen. Gabriel glanced at the dashboard clock as he headed up the long sweep of the eastern ramp. The trip from Copenhagen to this point should have taken no more than two hours, but the worsening storm had stretched it to nearly four. He returned his eyes to the road and put both hands firmly on the wheel. The bridge was swaying in the high winds. Ibrahim asked again if the weather was truly a good omen. Gabriel replied that he hoped Ibrahim knew how to swim.

It took them twenty minutes to make the eight-mile crossing. On the Funen side of the bridge, a small seaside rail station lay huddled against the storm. A mile beyond the station was a roadside gas station and café. Gabriel topped off the Audi's tank, then parked outside the café and led Ibrahim inside. It was brightly lit, smartly decorated, and spotlessly clean. In the first room was a well-stocked market and cafeteria-style eatery; in the next was a seating area filled with stranded travelers. There was much animated conversation and, judging from the large number of empty Carlsberg bottles scattered about the pale wooden tables, considerable drinking had taken place.

They bought egg sandwiches and hot tea in the cafeteria and sat at an empty table near the window. Ibrahim ate silently, while Gabriel sipped his tea and stared out at the car. Thirty minutes elapsed before the cell phone finally rang. Gabriel brought it to his ear, listened without speaking, then severed the connection. "Wait here," he said.

He stopped briefly in the men's toilet, where he buried his Beretta and phone in the rubbish bin, then went into the market and purchased a large-scale map of Denmark and an English-language tourist guide. When he returned to the dining room, Ibrahim was in the process of unwrapping the second egg sandwich. Ibrahim slipped it into his coat pocket and followed Gabriel outside.

. . .

"Here it is," said Ibrahim. "Lindholm Høje."

He was hunched over the guidebook, reading it by the light of the overhead lamp. Gabriel kept his eyes fastened to the road.

"What does it say?"

"It's an old Viking village and cemetery. For centuries it was buried beneath a thick layer of sand. It only was discovered in 1952. According to the book, it has more than seven hundred graves and the remains of a few Viking longhouses."

"Where is it?"

Ibrahim consulted the book again, then plotted the position of the site on the road map. "Northern Jutland," he said. "Very northern Jutland, actually."

"How do I get there?"

"Take the E20 across Funen, then head north on the E45. Lindholm is just after Aalborg. The book says it's easy to find the place. Just follow the signs."

"I can't see the road, let alone the signs."

"Is that where they're going to leave the woman?"

Gabriel shook his head. "More instructions. This time they'll be written. They say they'll be in the ruins of the longhouse, in the corner farthest from the museum entrance." He looked briefly at Ibrahim. "It wasn't Ishaq this time. It was someone else."

"Egyptian?"

"He sounded Egyptian to me, but I'm no expert."

"Please," said Ibrahim dismissively. "Why did they make you get rid of your telephone?"

"No more electronic communication."

Ibrahim looked down at the map. "It's a long way from here to Lindholm."

"Two hours in perfect weather. In this . . . four at least."

Ibrahim looked at the clock. "That means it will be Friday morning, if we're lucky."

"Yes," said Gabriel. "He's running us up against the deadline."

"Who? Ishaq?"

A very good question, thought Gabriel. Was it Ishaq? Or was it the Sphinx?

. . .

It took four and a half hours to reach Lindholm and, just as Gabriel had feared, the guidebook's assurances that the cemetery was easy to find turned out to be false. He drove in circles for twenty minutes through a neighborhood of matching brick houses before finally spotting a postcard-sized sign he had missed three times previously. It was obscured by snow, of course; Gabriel had to climb out of the Audi and brush away the flakes, only to learn that in order to reach the site he had to first scale a formidable hill. The Audi handled the conditions with only a single episode of fishtailing, and two minutes later Gabriel was easing into a car park surrounded by towering pine. He shut down the engine and sat for a moment, his ears ringing from the strain of the drive, before finally opening the door and putting a foot into the snow. Ibrahim stayed where he was.

"You're not coming?"

"I'll wait here, if you don't mind."

"Don't tell me you're afraid of cemeteries."

"No, just *Viking* cemeteries."

"They were only warlike when they took to the seas," Gabriel said. "Here at home they were largely an agrarian people. The scariest thing we're likely to run across tonight is the ghost of a vegetable farmer."

"If it's all the same to you, I'll just stay here."

"Suit yourself," Gabriel said. "If you want to sit here alone, that's fine with me."

Ibrahim made a show of thought, then climbed out. Gabriel opened the trunk and removed the flashlight and the tire iron.

"Why are you bringing that?" asked Ibrahim.

"In case we come across any Vikings." He slipped the tool down the front of his jeans and quietly closed the trunk. "They made me leave my gun back in that service station, too. A crowbar is better than nothing."

Gabriel switched on the flashlight and set out across the car park with Ibrahim at his side. The snow was six inches deep and within a few steps Gabriel's brogans were sodden and his feet freezing. Thirty seconds after leaving the car, he stopped suddenly. There were two sets of faint tracks in the snow, one set obviously larger than the other, leading from the car park into the burial ground. Gabriel left Ibrahim alone and followed the footprints back to their point of origin. Judging from the condition of the snow's surface, it appeared as though a small truck or transit van had entered the lot from a second access road several hours earlier. The larger of the two occupants had stepped into the snow from the driver's side of the vehicle, the smaller from the passenger side. Gabriel crouched in

the snow and scrutinized the smaller prints as though he were examining brushstrokes on a canvas. The prints were feminine, he decided, and whoever had left them had been wearing athletic shoes.
There was no evidence of any struggle.

Gabriel rejoined Ibrahim and led him down a footpath into the
site. The cemetery fell away before them, down the slope of the hill
toward a vast inland bay in the distance. Despite the snowfall it was
possible to discern, in the glow of Gabriel's flashlight, the outlines of
individual graves. Some were mounds of stones, some were circles,
and still others were shaped like Viking ships. It was not difficult to
find the far corner of the longhouse; all Gabriel had to do was follow
the twin sets of tracks. He crouched down and probed with his bare
hands beneath the surface of the snow. A few seconds later he found
what had been left there for him, a small plastic ziplock bag containing a portion of a detailed map. He examined it by the glow of his
flashlight. Then he stood and led Ibrahim back to the car.

· · ·

"Skagen," said Gabriel as he drove slowly down the hill. "They want
us to go to Skagen. Well, almost to Skagen. The spot they circled on
the map is a little to the south."

"You know this place?"

"I've never been there, but I know it. There was an artist colony
that formed there in the late eighteen hundreds. They were known
as the Skagen School of painters. They came there for the light. They
say it's unique—not that we'll be seeing any of it."

"Perhaps this is another good omen," said Ibrahim.

"Perhaps," said Gabriel.

"Will the ambassador's daughter be there?"

"It doesn't say. It just tells us to go to a spot along the North Sea."

"Was she in the burial ground tonight?"

"They wanted me to think she was," Gabriel said. "But I don't believe she was there."

"How can you tell?"

"Because the woman got out of the vehicle and walked into the cemetery on her own," Gabriel said. "I saw Elizabeth at the moment of her abduction. She wouldn't have walked in there on her own. She would have fought them."

"Unless they told her she was about to be released," said Ibrahim.

Gabriel gave him an admiring sideways glance. "You're not bad," he said.

"I was a professor once," he said. "And I love detective novels."

41

She did not know the duration of her journey, for she had tried to think of anything but the clock. It was but a few minutes, she told herself. It was the blink of an eye. She had told herself other lies as well. She was in a comfortable bed, not a wooden box that smelled faintly of fish. She was wearing faded blue jeans and her favorite sweater, not the same dirty tracksuit she had been wearing since the morning of her capture. She could see her favorite mountain range through her favorite window. She was listening to beautiful music. The rest were just scenes from a bad dream. She would wake soon and it would all be over.

She had been prepared for the appalling discomfort—Cain's note had made it abundantly clear what lay in store for her—but the earplugs had taken her by surprise. They had robbed her of one of her most potent weapons, the ability to hear what was taking place around her, and had reduced her world to a monotonous droning. She had been left with only one sense, the ability to feel motion. She knew that they had driven at high speeds and at moderate speeds, on good roads and bad. Once she'd had the sensation of being in a large city surrounded by people who did not realize she was only inches away. Now she felt certain they were on an unpaved track, in a place near the end of the earth.

They stopped suddenly—so suddenly that her head was pressed painfully against the end of her coffinlike container—and a moment later the droning of the engine went silent. Several minutes elapsed before they finally removed her from the vehicle, and several more passed before she finally heard the screech of the nails being removed by the claw of a hammer. Cold salty air streamed over her face as the lid came off. Hot tears spilled involuntarily into the fabric of her blindfold as she was lifted to her feet. No one spoke to her as she was led inside the new hideout. No one asked about the condition of her arrhythmic heart as she was placed on the cot in her new cell. When the door closed on her again, she removed the blindfold and the earplugs and gazed at a new set of white walls. There was a plate of food—bread, cheese, and chocolate because she had been good during the drive—and there was a yellow bucket for her toilet. She had no idea where they had moved her but was certain of one thing. She could smell the sea.

42

KANDESTEDERNE, DENMARK:
2:15 A.M., FRIDAY

The road from the Baltic port of Frederikshavn to Skagen was abandoned and barely passable. Gabriel sat hunched over the steering wheel for mile after mile as a string of silent snowbound towns flashed past. Their names were full of strange consonant combinations that even Gabriel, whose first language was German, found impenetrable. Danish is not a language, he thought resentfully as he plunged through the gloom. Danish is merely an affliction of the throat.

After leaving the town of Ålbæk, a seemingly endless moonscape of dunes opened before them. The cutoff toward the summer resort town of Kandestederne lay near the northern end of the wasteland; Gabriel, after making the turn, saw a single set of freshly made tire tracks in the snow. He suspected they had been left by the same vehicle that had been at the cemetery in Lindholm Høje.

They sledded past a few small farms, then entered another expanse of dunes—vast dunes this time, dunes the size of foothills. Here and there Gabriel glimpsed the outlines of cottages and small homes. There were no lights burning, no other cars, and no other signs of life. Time, it seemed, had stopped.

The tire tracks bent to the right, into a narrow road, and vanished behind a curtain of snowfall. Gabriel continued straight and stopped a moment later at a small car park overlooking the beach, next to a boarded-up café. He started to switch off the engine, then thought better of it. "Wait here," he said. "Lock the doors after I get out. Don't open them for anyone but me."

He took the tire tool and flashlight and walked over to the café. There were fresh footprints all around—two sets at least, perhaps more. Whoever had left them had come to this spot from the dunes. One set of tracks led down to the beach. They were identical to the ones he had seen at Lindholm. The woman's.

He glanced back toward the Audi, then turned and followed the tracks across the beach. At the water's edge, they disappeared. He looked left, then right, but could see no sign of them, so he turned around and headed back to the car. As he drew near, he could see that Ibrahim was leaning forward awkwardly and had his palms pressed to the dashboard. Then he saw a set of fresh tracks leading from the dunes to the rear passenger-side door of the Audi. Just then the window slid down halfway and a gloved hand beckoned him forward. Gabriel hesitated for a few seconds, then obeyed. Along the way he made a slight detour in order to examine the prints. Size six, he reckoned. Adidas or Nike. A woman's shoe.

· · ·

He had been wrong about the brand of the shoes. They were Pumas. The woman who was wearing them looked no older than twenty-five. She wore a navy blue peacoat and a wool hat pulled down close to her dark eyes. She was seated directly behind Ibrahim and had a Makarov pointed at his spine. Her hand was vibrating with cold.

"Why don't you point that gun at the floor before someone gets hurt?" Gabriel said.

"Shut up and put your hands on the steering wheel."

She spoke very calmly. Gabriel did as he was told.

"Where's Ishaq?"

"Ishaq who?" she asked.

"Let's not play any more games. It's been a long cold night." He looked at her in the rearview mirror. "Just tell us where we can find Elizabeth Halton and we'll be on our way."

"You are the Israeli, yes? The Zionist pig who killed our comrades in Hyde Park?"

"No, I'm an American pig."

"You speak very good Arabic for an American pig."

"My father was a diplomat. I grew up in Beirut."

"Really? Then speak English for me, American pig."

Gabriel hesitated. The girl leveled the gun at the back of Ibrahim's head.

"You've made your point," Gabriel said.

She pointed the gun at Gabriel. "I should kill you now," she said. "But you're fortunate. You won't be dying tonight. Others have already laid claim to your life."

"Lucky me."

She hit him in the back of the head with the gun, hard enough for Gabriel to see a burst of fireworks before his eyes. When he reached reflexively toward the wound, she hit him again, harder still, and commanded him to put his hands back on the wheel. A moment later he could feel something warm and sticky running along the back of his right ear.

"Feel better?" he asked.

"Yes," she said sincerely.

"Let's get this over with, shall we?"

"Turn the car around," the woman said. "Slowly."

Gabriel eased the car into gear, executed a careful three-point turn, and headed inland.

"Make the first left into the dunes," the woman said. "Then follow the tire tracks."

He did as she instructed. The road was wide enough for only a single car and led to a colony of cottages tucked within the dunes. The cottages were small and wooden and abandoned to the winter.

Some were painted Skagen yellow; others inexplicably had grass growing on the roof. Gabriel navigated only by the amber light of the parking lamps. The blood was now running freely down the side of his neck into his shirt collar.

He followed the tracks up a small humpbacked hill, then plunged down the other side and saw another knoll ahead. Fearful of becoming lodged in the snow, he kept his foot on the gas and heard a loud crunching sound when the car ran aground at the bottom of the dip. He gunned it hard up the next hill and swerved to the left, then glided down the other side into the drive of the farthest cottage. A silver LDV Maxus transit van was parked outside, lights doused. Gabriel came to a stop and looked into the rearview mirror for instructions. The woman jabbed Ibrahim in the back with the barrel of the Makarov and told him to open the door. When Gabriel reached for his own latch, she hit him in the back of the head for a third time.

"You stay here in the car!" she snapped. "We'll give the woman only to Ibrahim—not you, Zionist pig."

Ibrahim unclasped his safety belt and opened the door. The overhead light burst suddenly on. Gabriel put a hand atop Ibrahim's forearm and squeezed.

"Don't go," he said. "Stay in the car."

Ibrahim looked at him incredulously. "What are you talking about, my friend? We've come all this way."

"It was all just a game to run out the clock. She's not here. Your son has lured you here in order to kill you."

"Why would my son kill me?"

"Because you betrayed him to the Crusaders and the Jews," Gabriel said. "Because he is a *takfiri* Muslim and, in his eyes, you are now an apostate worthy only of death. You are worse than a Crusader—even worse than a Jew—because you were once a devout Islamist who has now renounced the path of jihad. The woman is taking you inside to be killed, Ibrahim. Don't go with her."

"My son would never harm me."

"He's not your son anymore."

Ibrahim smiled and removed Gabriel's hand from his arm. "You must have faith, my friend. Let me go. I'll bring the girl out to you, just as I promised."

Gabriel felt the barrel of the Makarov pressing against the base of his skull. "Listen to Ibrahim, Zionist pig. He speaks the truth. We do not kill our parents. *You* are the murderers, not us. Let him bring you the girl, so you can be on your way."

Ibrahim climbed out of the car before Gabriel could stop him and started toward the cottage. The woman waited until he was several yards away before lowering the gun from Gabriel's head and setting off after him. As they neared the entrance, a man appeared in the doorway. In the snow and darkness Gabriel could discern little of his appearance—only that his hair had been dyed platinum blond. He greeted Ibrahim formally, with kisses on both cheeks and a hand reverentially over his heart, and led him inside. Then the woman closed the door and the windshield exploded in Gabriel's face.

THE BRIDGE
OVER JAHANNAM

WINFIELD HOUSE, LONDON: 7:05 A.M., FRIDAY

It would be nearly an hour before word of the disaster in northern Denmark reached Washington, and another thirty minutes would elapse before the first news reached Winfield House, the official residence of the American ambassador to the United Kingdom. Despite the lateness of the hour—it was 3:15 A.M. in London and 10:15 P.M. in Washington—Robert Halton was seated at the desk in his private study, where he had remained throughout that long night, waiting for word from the White House Situation Room. Though he had been expecting a call for many hours, the sound of the ringing telephone caused him to recoil involuntarily, as though from a nearby gunshot. As he snatched the receiver from the cradle, he thought for an instant that he could hear the sound of Elizabeth weeping. It must have been a burst of interference on the line—or a hallucination, he would think later—for the voice he heard when he brought the phone to his ear belonged not to his daughter but to Cyrus Mansfield, the president's national security advisor.

Halton could tell from Mansfield's guarded greeting that the news from Denmark was not what he had been praying for, though nothing could have prepared him for what was relayed to him next. Gabriel Allon and his Egyptian asset had been led from Copenhagen to the tip of Denmark, said Mansfield. There had been an incident of some sort at an isolated cottage on the North Sea, the details of which were still unclear. There had been an explosion. There were at least three known deaths. Until additional resources arrived on the scene, including Danish forensic teams, it would be impossible to know whether Elizabeth was among those killed.

For the remainder of that night, Robert Halton was cast into a new kind of Hell. Cyrus Mansfield called with a maddening regularity, even when there was little new or vital to report. As is common in situations such as these, much of the information was contradictory and later proven wrong. Halton was told there were three bodies in the house, then, thirty minutes later, was informed that there were four. There was evidence Elizabeth had been in Denmark, said Mansfield. There was speculation she might still be there. There had been gunfire. Allon had been gravely wounded. Allon had been killed.

Finally, at 7:05 A.M. London time, as a gray dawn was breaking over Regent's Park, the president telephoned to say that Danish fire-and-rescue had found just three bodies in the charred ruins of the residence. According to a statement from Gabriel Allon, who was injured but very much alive, the dead consisted of two terrorists—one male and one female—and the Egyptian asset Ibrahim Fawaz. The National Security Council, the FBI, the CIA, and the State Department were all operating under the assumption that Elizabeth was still alive, and frantic efforts to secure her release would continue until the deadline and beyond. Robert Halton hung up the phone and fell to his knees in a desperate prayer of thanksgiving. Then he stumbled into his bathroom and was violently sick.

He lay for several minutes on the cold marble floor, his body seemingly paralyzed by anguish and grief. *Where are you, Robert Halton?* he thought. Where was the business maverick who had turned a small oil exploration company into a global energy conglomerate? Where was the man who, for the sake of his daughter, had stoically endured the loss of his beloved wife? Where was the man who, against all odds, had managed to put his best friend in the White House? He was gone, thought Halton. He had been kidnapped by the terrorists, just as surely as Elizabeth had been.

He rose to his feet and rinsed his mouth in the sink, then stepped from the bathroom and returned to his office. It was now Friday morning. By nightfall his daughter would be dead. Robert Carlyle Halton, billionaire and kingmaker, had watched helplessly while the combined forces of American intelligence, diplomacy, and law enforcement, along with their counterparts across Europe and the Middle East, had searched in vain for his daughter. He had stood idly by and listened to their empty assurances that eventually Elizabeth would be brought home to him alive. He was prepared to stand idly by no longer. He would now deploy the only weapon available to him, a weapon even the jihadists understood. The course of action he was about to undertake bordered on treason, for, if successful, Halton would be providing the terrorists a weapon they could later use against the United States and its allies. But if treason was necessary to save his daughter, then Robert Halton was prepared to be a traitor, if only for a few hours.

He walked calmly to his desk and sat down before the computer, imagining for a moment that he was no longer a helpless and grief-stricken father but once again a steady and assured CEO and magnate. A click of the mouse brought a letter onto the screen. It had been composed by Halton during the first week of the crisis and saved for this very moment. His eyes scanned the arid prose: *Due to present circumstances . . . unable to continue in my role as your ambassador in London . . . an honor and pleasure to serve . . . Robert Carlyle Halton . . .* He added the proper date, clicked the print icon, and watched the letter slide onto his desk. After adding his signature, he loaded the letter into his fax machine. He did not send it just yet. The CEO had a few more deals to close.

He picked up the telephone and dialed a local London number. The number was located inside Number 10 Downing Street, the official residence of the British prime minister, and was answered instantly by Oliver Gibbons, the prime minister's chief of staff. Halton and Gibbons had spoken several times during the past two weeks and there was no need for formalities. Halton said he needed to speak to the prime minister urgently; Gibbons responded by saying that the prime minister was in a breakfast meeting and would not be free for another twenty minutes. The meeting apparently ended sooner than anticipated because, twelve minutes later, the prime minister returned the call. "I'm about to try something desperate," Halton said. "And I want to know whether I can count on you and your authorities to make it happen."

The conversation that ensued next was brief—later, at the official inquest, much would be made of the fact it was just six minutes in length—and concluded with a promise by the prime minister that the police and intelligence services of Britain would do anything necessary to help Halton in his endeavor. Halton thanked the prime minister, then dialed a number in his own embassy. It was answered by Stephen Barnes, the deputy public affairs officer. His boss, Jack Hammond, had been killed in Hyde Park the morning of Elizabeth's abduction. Barnes had been given a field promotion of sorts and had served ably as the embassy's chief spokesman throughout the crisis.

"I need to make a statement to the press, Steve. I'd like to do it here at Winfield House instead of the embassy. It will be important. The networks need to know that they should carry it live and in its entirety—especially the European networks and the Arab satellite channels."

"What time?"

"Noon should be fine. Can you arrange it by then?"

"No problem," Barnes said. "Is there anything I can draft for you?"

"No, I can handle this one without a text. I do need you to prepare the ground for me, though."

"How so?"

"Do you have any contacts at al-Jazeera?"

Barnes said he did. He had taken al-Jazeera's London bureau chief to lunch a couple times in a futile effort to get the network to stop broadcasting al-Qaeda propaganda messages.

"Give your friend a call now. Let it leak that I'm about to make an offer to the kidnappers."

"What sort of offer?"

"One they can't refuse."

"Is there something else I should know, Mr. Ambassador?"

"I'm resigning my post, Steve. You can call me Bob."

"Yes, Mr. Ambassador."

Halton hung up the phone, then stood up and headed toward his bedroom to shower and change. He was no longer Ambassador Robert Halton, the desperate and broken American diplomat who had no choice but to watch his daughter die. He was once again Robert Carlyle Halton, multibillionaire and kingmaker, and he was going to get Elizabeth back, even if it took every penny he had.

44

AALBORG, DENMARK:
12:15 P.M., FRIDAY

Your chariot has arrived, Mr. Allon."
Lars Mortensen lifted his hand and pointed toward the heavy gray sky. Gabriel looked up and watched a Gulfstream V sinking slowly toward the end of the runway at Aalborg Airport. The slight movement caused his head to begin throbbing again. It had taken eighteen sutures, administered by a sleepy Skagen doctor, to close the three wounds in his scalp. His face bore a crosshatched pattern of tiny cuts, inflicted by the exploding safety glass of the windshield. Somehow he had managed to shield his eyes at the instant of detonation, though he had no memory of doing it.

He could recall the events of the rest of the evening, however, with faultless clarity. Ordered by the kidnappers to relinquish his telephone in Funen, he had been forced to drive the crippled Audi with its blasted-out windshield three miles in order to find a public phone. He had rung Carter and Mortensen from the parking lot of a small market on the outskirts of Skagen and, in language fit for an insecure line, had told them what had transpired. Then he had driven back to the dunes and watched the cottage burn slowly to the ground. Twenty more minutes would elapse before he heard the distant scream of the sirens and saw the first police and firefighters stumble bewildered onto the scene. A uniformed policeman had peppered Gabriel with questions while an ambulance attendant wiped the blood from his face. Talk to Lars Mortensen of the PET, was all Gabriel said. Mortensen will explain everything.

"You're sure about the body count in the cottage?" Gabriel asked Mortensen now.

"You've asked me that ten times."

"Answer it again."

"There were only three—the two terrorists and the old man. No Elizabeth Halton." Mortensen fell silent as the Gulfstream set down on the runway and flashed past their position with the roar of reversing engines. "Not exactly the way the story of Abraham and Isaac turned out in the Bible. I still can't quite believe he actually set up his own father to be killed."

"It's the al-Qaeda version," said Gabriel. "Murder anyone who dares to oppose you, even your own flesh and blood."

The Gulfstream had reached the end of the runway and was now taxiing back toward their position on the tarmac.

"You'll do your best to keep my role in this affair a secret?" Gabriel asked.

"There's always a chance it could leak out up here. Unfortunately, you came in contact with many people last night. But as far as my service is concerned, you and your team were never here."

Gabriel zipped his leather jacket and extended his hand. "Then it was a pleasure not meeting you."

"The pleasure was mine." Mortensen gave Gabriel's hand an admonitory squeeze. "But the next time you come to Denmark, do me the courtesy of telling me first. We'll have lunch. Who knows? Maybe we'll actually have something pleasant to talk about."

"I suppose anything's possible." Gabriel climbed out of the car, then peered at Mortensen through the open door. "I nearly forget something."

"What's that?"

He told him about the Beretta he had been forced to leave at the rest stop on Funen. Mortensen frowned and murmured something in Danish under his breath.

"I'm sorry," Gabriel said. "It slipped my mind."

"I don't suppose you removed the bullets before throwing it into that rubbish bin."

"Actually, it was quite loaded."

"If I were you, I'd get on that plane before I change my mind about covering up your hand in this mess."

Gabriel set out across the tarmac toward the Gulfstream. The airstair had been lowered; Sarah was leaning against the side of the open doorway, hands in the pockets of her jeans, legs crossed at the ankles. Carter was seated at the front of the cabin and was deep in conversation on the telephone. He nodded Gabriel into the opposite seat, then hung up and regarded him speculatively as the plane rose once more into the slate gray sky.

"Where's my team?" asked Gabriel.

"They slipped quietly out of Copenhagen early this morning. They were understandably vague about their destination. I assume they were headed toward Amsterdam."

"And us?"

"The British have granted us landing rights at London City Airport. I'm going to the embassy to wait out the deadline. You will be escorted to Heathrow, no questions asked. I assume you can find your own way home from there."

Gabriel nodded slowly.

"Consider yourself fortunate, Gabriel. You get to go home. I get to go to London and face the music for our failure here last night. You're not exactly popular in Washington at the moment. In fact, there are a good many people baying for your blood, the president included. And this time I'm in the shit with you."

"A career free of scandal is not a proper career at all, Adrian."

"Shakespeare?"

"Shamron."

Carter managed a weak smile. "The Office operates by a different set of standards than the Agency. You accept the occasional mistake if it occurs in the service of a noble cause. We don't tolerate failure. Failure is not an option."

"If that were the case, they would have turned the lights out at Langley a long time ago."

Carter squinted as a sudden burst of sunlight came slanting through the cabin window. He pulled down the shade and stared at Gabriel for a long moment in silence.

"She wasn't there, Adrian. She was *never* there. In all likelihood she's still somewhere in Britain. It was all an elaborate deception orchestrated by the Sphinx. They planted that ferry reservation number on the body of the man I wounded in Hyde Park and left him in the dunes of Norfolk for the British to find. The Sphinx instructed Ishaq to remain in touch with his wife in Copenhagen, knowing that eventually NSA, or someone else, would overhear him and make the connection. And when we *did* make the connection, the Sphinx played it out slowly, so there would be almost no time left before the deadline. He wants you frustrated and dejected and tearing yourself to shreds behind the scenes. He wants you to feel you have no choice but to release Sheikh Abdullah."

"Fuck Sheikh Abdullah," said Carter with uncharacteristic venom. He quickly regained his composure. "Do you think Ibrahim was a part of this grand illusion?"

"Ibrahim was the real thing, Adrian. Ibrahim was the answer to our prayers."

"And you got him killed."

"You're tired, Adrian. You haven't slept in a long time. I'm going to do my best to forget you ever said that."

"You're right, Gabriel. I haven't slept." Carter glanced at his watch. "Seven hours is all we have—seven hours until an extraordinary young woman is put to death. And for what?"

Carter was interrupted by the ringing of his phone. He brought it to his ear, listened in silence, then rang off.

"Robert Halton just faxed his letter of resignation to the White House Situation Room," he said. "I suppose the pressure finally got to him."

"Wrong, Adrian."

"You can think of another explanation?"

"He's going to try to save his daughter's life by negotiating directly with the kidnappers."

Carter snatched up the telephone again and quickly dialed. Gabriel reclined his seat and closed his eyes. His head began to throb. *A preview of coming attractions*, he thought.

45

PARIS: 2:17 P.M., FRIDAY

There was a small Internet café around the corner from the Islamic Affairs Institute with decent coffee and pastries and even better jazz on the house sound system. Yusuf Ramadan ordered a café crème and thirty minutes of Web time, then he sat down at a vacant computer terminal in the window overlooking the street. He typed in the address for the home page of the BBC and read about the developments in London, where Ambassador Robert Halton had just resigned his post and offered twenty million dollars in exchange for his daughter's release. While the news appeared to have come as a shock to the BBC, it was no surprise to the Egyptian terrorist known as the Sphinx. The perfectly executed operation in Denmark had no doubt broken the ambassador's will to resist. He had now decided to take matters into his own hands, just as Yusuf Ramadan had always known he would. Robert Halton was a billionaire from Colorado—and billionaires from Colorado did not allow their daughters to be sacrificed on the altar of American foreign policy.

Ramadan watched a brief clip of the ambassador's Winfield House news conference, then visited the home pages of the *Tele-*

graph, Times, and *Guardian* to read what they had to say. Finally, with ten minutes to spare on his thirty-minute chit, he typed in the address of a Karachi-based site that dealt with Islamic issues. The site was administered by an operative of the Sword of Allah, though its content was so benign it never attracted more than a passing glance from the security services of America and Europe. Ramadan entered a chat room as DESMOND826. KINKYKEMEL324 was waiting for him. Ramadan typed: "I think the Sword of Allah should take the deal. But they should definitely ask for more money. After all, the ambassador is a billionaire."

KINKYKEMEL324: How much more?

DESMOND826: Thirty million feels right.

KINKYKEMEL324: I think the Zionist oppressor should pay, too.

DESMOND826: The *ultimate* price, just as we discussed during our last conversation.

KINKYKEMEL324: Then it will be done, in the name of Allah, the beneficent, the merciful.

DESMOND826: Master of the day of judgment.

KINKYKEMEL324: Show us the straight path.

DESMOND826: Peace be upon you, KK.

KINKYKEMEL324: Ciao, Dez.

Ramadan logged out and drank his café crème. "Ruby, My Dear," by Coltrane and Monk, was now playing on the stereo. Too bad all Americans weren't so sublime, he thought. The world would be a much better place.

46

GROSVENOR SQUARE,
LONDON: 2:10 P.M., FRIDAY

The first calls arrived at the embassy switchboard before Ambassador Halton disappeared
through the doorway of Winfield House. FBI hostage negotiator John
O'Donnell, who had been given just five minutes' warning of the
pending statement, had hastily broken the staff of the ops center into
two teams: one to dispense with obvious charlatans and criminal con-
men, another to conduct additional screening of any call that sounded
remotely legitimate. It was O'Donnell himself who assigned the calls
to the appropriate teams. He did so after a brief conversation, usually
thirty seconds in length or less. His instincts told him that none of the
callers he had spoken to thus far were the real kidnappers, even the
callers he had passed along to the second team for additional vetting.
He did not share this belief with any of the exhausted men and women
gathered around him in the embassy basement.

Two hours after Robert Halton's appearance before the cameras,
O'Donnell picked up a separate line and dialed the switchboard.
"How many do you have on hold?"

"Thirty-eight," the operator said. "Wait . . . make that forty-
two . . . forty-four . . . forty-seven. You see my point."

"Keep them coming."

O'Donnell hung up and quickly worked his way through ten more calls. He assigned seven to team number one, the team that dealt with obvious cranks, and three to the second team, though he knew that none of the callers represented the real captors of Elizabeth Halton. He was about pick up another call when his private line rang. He answered that line instead and heard the voice of the switchboard operator.

"I think I've got the call you're looking for."

"Voice modifier?"

"Yep."

"Send him down on this line after I hang up."

"Got it."

O'Donnell hung up the phone. When it rang ten seconds later, he brought the receiver swiftly to his ear.

"This is John O'Donnell of the Federal Bureau of Investigation. How can I help you?"

"I've been trying to get through to you for a half hour," said the electronically modified voice.

"We're doing the best we can, but when twenty million is on the table, the nutcases tend to come out of the woodwork."

"I'm not a nutcase. I'm the one you want to talk to."

"Prove it to me. Tell me where you left the DVD of Elizabeth Halton."

"We left it under the rowboat on the beach at Beacon Point."

O'Donnell covered the mouthpiece of the receiver and pleaded for quiet. Then he looked at Kevin Barnett of the CIA and motioned for him to pick up the extension.

"I take it you're interested in taking the deal," O'Donnell said to the caller.

"I wouldn't be calling otherwise."

"You have our girl?"

"We have her."

"I'm going to need proof."

"There isn't time."

"So we'll have to make some time. Just answer one question for me. It will just take a minute."

Silence, then: "Give me the question."

"When Elizabeth was a little girl, she had a favorite stuffed animal. I need you to tell me what kind of animal it was and what she called it. I'm going to give you a separate number. You call me back when you've got the answer. Then we'll discuss how to make the exchange."

"Make sure you pick up the phone. Otherwise, your girl dies."

The line went dead. O'Donnell hung up the phone and looked at Barnett.

"I'm almost certain that was our boy."

"Thank God," said Barnett. "Let's just hope he has our girl."

. . .

She woke with the knock, startled and damp with sweat, and stared at the blinding white lamp over her cot. She had been dreaming, the same dream she always had whenever she managed to sleep. Men in black hoods. A video camera. A knife. She raised her cuffed hands to her throat and found that the tissue of her neck was still intact. Then she looked at the cement floor and saw the note. An eye was glaring at her through the spy hole as if willing her to move. It was dark and brutal: the eye of Cain.

She sat up and swung her shackled feet to the floor, then stood and shuffled stiffly toward the door. The note lay faceup and was composed in a font large enough for her to read without bending down to pick it up. It was a question, as all their communications were, but different from any other they had put to her. She answered it in a low, evenly modulated voice, then returned to her coat and wept uncontrollably. *Don't hope*, she told herself. *Don't you dare hope.*

. . .

John O'Connell's private number in the ops center rang at 3:09. This time he didn't bother identifying himself.

"Do you have the information I need?"

"The animal was a stuffed whale."

"What did she call it?"

"Fish," the man said. "She called it Fish and nothing else."

O'Donnell closed his eyes and pumped his fist once.

"Right answer," he said. "Let's put a deal together. Let's bring my girl home in time for Christmas."

The man with the modified voice listed his demands, then said: "I'm going to call back at five fifty-nine London time. I want a one-word answer: yes or no. That's it: yes or no. Do you understand me?"

"I understand perfectly."

The line went dead again. O'Donnell looked at Kevin Barnett.

"They've got her," he said. "And we are completely fucked."

.   .   .

A Jaguar limousine was waiting at the edge of the tarmac as Adrian Carter's Gulfstream V touched down at London City Airport. As Gabriel, Carter, and Sarah came down the airstair, a long, boney hand poked from the Jaguar's rear passenger-side window and beckoned them over.

"Graham Seymour," said Gabriel theatrically. "Don't tell me they sent you all the way out here to give me a lift to Heathrow."

"They sent me out here to give you a lift," Seymour said, "but we're not going to Heathrow."

"Where are we going?"

Seymour left the question momentarily unanswered and instead gazed quizzically at Gabriel's face. "What in God's name happened to you?"

"It's a long story."

"It usually is," he said. "Get in. We don't have much time."

47

10 DOWNING STREET:
4:15 P.M., FRIDAY

Graham Seymour's limousine turned into Whitehall and stopped a few seconds later at the security gates of Downing Street. He lowered his window and flashed his identification to the uniformed Metropolitan Police officer standing watch outside the fence. The officer examined it quickly, then signaled to his colleagues to open the gate. The Jaguar eased forward approximately fifty yards and stopped again, this time before the world's most famous door.

Gabriel emerged from the limousine last and followed the others into the entrance hall. To their right was a small fireplace and next to the fireplace an odd-looking Chippendale hooded leather chair once used by porters and security men. To their left was a wooden traveling chest, believed to have been taken by the Duke of Wellington into battle at Waterloo in 1815, and a grandfather clock by Benson of Whitehaven that so annoyed Churchill he ordered its chimes silenced. And standing in the center of the hall, in an immaculately tailored suit, was a handsome man with pale skin and black hair shot with gray at the temples. He advanced on Gabriel and cautiously extended his hand. It was cold to the touch.

"Welcome to Downing Street," said the British prime minister. "Thank you for coming on such short notice."

"Please forgive my appearance, Prime Minister. It's been a long few days."

"We heard about your misadventure in Denmark. It appears you were deceived. We all were."

"Yes, Prime Minister."

"We treated you shabbily after the attack in Hyde Park, but the fact that your name and face appeared in the newspapers has provided us with an opportunity to save Elizabeth Halton's life. I'm afraid we need your rather serious help, Mr. Allon. Are you prepared to listen to what we have to say?"

"Of course, Prime Minister."

The prime minister smiled. It was a replica of a smile, thought Gabriel, and about as warm as the December afternoon.

.   .   .

They hiked up the long Grand Staircase, beneath portraits of British prime ministers past.

"Our logs contain no evidence of any previous visits by you to Downing Street, Mr. Allon. Is that the case, or have you slipped in here before?"

"This is my first time, Prime Minister."

"I suppose it must seem rather different from your own prime minister's office."

"That's putting it mildly, sir. Our staterooms are decorated in early kibbutz chic."

"We'll meet in the White Room," the prime minister said. "Henry Campbell-Bannerman died there in 1908, but, as far as I know, no one has died there today."

They passed through a set of tall double doors and went inside. The heavy rose-colored curtains were drawn, and the Waterford glass chandelier glowed softly overhead. Robert Halton was seated on a striped couch, next to Dame Eleanor McKenzie, the director general of MI5. Her counterpart from M16 was pacing, and the commissioner of the Metropolitan Police was off in one corner, speaking quietly into a mobile phone. After a set of hasty introductions, Gabriel was directed to the end of the second couch, where he sat beneath the mournful gaze of a Florence Nightingale statuette. A log fire was burning brightly in the hearth. A steward brought tea that no one drank.

The prime minister lowered himself into the wing chair opposite the fireplace and brought the proceedings to order. He spoke calmly, as though he were explaining a bit of dull but important economic policy. At noon London time, he said, Ambassador Halton submitted his resignation to the White House and made an offer of twenty million dollars' ransom to the terrorists in exchange for his daughter's freedom. Shortly after two o'clock London time, the terrorists made contact with FBI negotiators in the American embassy and, after providing proof that they were indeed holding Elizabeth captive, made a counteroffer. They wanted thirty million dollars instead of twenty. If the money was delivered as instructed—and if there were no traps or arrests—Elizabeth would be released twenty-four hours later.

"So why am I here?" asked Gabriel, though he already knew the answer.

"You are an intelligent man, Mr. Allon. You tell me."

"I'm here because they want *me* to the deliver the money."

"I'm afraid that is correct," said the prime minister. "At five fifty-nine London time, they are going to call the FBI negotiator at the embassy. They want a one-word answer: yes or no. If the answer is no, Elizabeth Halton will be executed immediately. If it is yes—meaning that you have agreed to *all* their demands—she will be released forty-eight hours from now, give or take a few hours."

A heavy silence fell over the room. It was broken by Adrian Carter, who objected on Gabriel's behalf. "The answer is no," he said. "It is an obvious trap. I can think of three possible outcomes, none of them pleasant."

"We all know the pitfalls, Mr. Carter," said the director-general of MI6. "There's no need to review them now."

"Humor me," said Carter. "I'm just a dull-witted American. Scenario number one, Gabriel will be killed immediately after delivering the money. Scenario number two, he will be taken captive, tortured savagely for some period of time, and then killed. The third scenario, however, is probably the most likely outcome."

"And what's that?" asked the prime minister.

"Gabriel will take Elizabeth Halton's place as a hostage. The Sword of Allah and al-Qaeda will then make demands on the Israeli government instead of ours, and we'll all be right back at square one."

"With one important difference," added Graham Seymour. "Much of the world will be rooting for the Sword to kill him. He is an Israeli and a Jew, an occupier and an oppressor, and therefore in the eyes of many in Europe and the Islamic world he is worthy of death. His murder would be a major propaganda victory for the terrorists."

"But his cooperation will buy us something we have in exceedingly short supply at the moment," said Eleanor McKenzie. "If we say yes tonight, we will be granted at least twenty-four additional hours to look for Miss Halton."

"We've been looking for her for two weeks," said Carter. "Unless someone has made some serious inroads that I'm not aware of, twenty-four additional hours aren't going to make much of a difference."

Gabriel looked at Robert Halton. It had been more than a week since Gabriel had seen him last, and in those days the ambassador's face appeared to have aged many years. The prime minister would have been wise to conduct this conversation without Halton present, because to say no at this moment would be an act of almost unspeakable cruelty. Or perhaps that was exactly the reason the prime minister had invited him here. He had left Gabriel no option but to agree to the scheme.

"They're going to make additional demands," Gabriel said. "They'll demand that I come alone. They'll warn that if I'm followed, the deal is off and Elizabeth dies. We're going to abide by those rules." He looked at Seymour and Carter. "No surveillance, British or American."

"You can't go into this thing with no one watching your back," said the chief of the Metropolitan Police.

"I don't intend to," said Gabriel. "MI5 and the Anti-Terrorist Branch of Scotland Yard will give us all the intelligence and support we require, but this will be an Israeli operation from start to finish. I will bring whomever and whatever I need into the country to conduct it. Afterward, there will be no scrutiny and no inquiries. If anyone is killed or wounded during the recovery of Elizabeth, no one from my team will be questioned or prosecuted."

"Out of the question," said Eleanor McKenzie.

"Done," said the prime minister.

"How long will it take you to assemble the cash?"

"Every major bank in the City is already involved," the prime minister said. "The task should be complete by late tomorrow afternoon. Obviously it's a large consignment and therefore it will be somewhat unwieldy. They think it will fit into two large rolling duffel bags."

Gabriel glanced from face to face. "Don't even think about putting any tracking devices in the cash or the bags."

"Understood," said the prime minister. "It occurs to me that tomorrow is Christmas Eve. Clearly it is not a coincidence."

"No, Prime Minister, I suspect they've been preparing for this for a long time." Gabriel looked at his wristwatch. "Can someone give me a lift to the American embassy? There's a telephone call coming there in a few minutes that I'd like to take."

"Graham will take you," the prime minister said. "We'll give you a police escort. The traffic in central London this time of day is really quite dreadful."

. . .

On the wall above John O'Donnell's workstation was a large digital clock with red numerals set against a black background. Gabriel, however, had eyes only for the telephone. It was a modern device, with access to twenty lines, including extension 7512, which was available nowhere else in the building. Extension 7512 was O'Donnell's private reserve. Now it belonged to Gabriel, along with O'Donnell's warm chair and O'Donnell's wrinkled legal pad.

The clock rolled over to 17:59 and the seconds began their methodical march from :00 to :59. Gabriel kept his eyes on the phone— on the green light in the box marked 7512, and on the small crack in the receiver, inflicted by O'Donnell during a blind rage early in the crisis. A minute later, when the clock rolled over to 18:00:00, there was an audible gasp in the room. Then, at 18:01:25, Gabriel heard one of O'Donnell's team members begin to weep. He did not share the pessimism of his audience. He knew the terrorists were cruel bastards who were just using the opportunity of the deadline to have a spot of fun at the expense of their American and Israeli opponents.

At 18:02:17, the telephone finally rang. Gabriel, unwilling to cause his audience any additional stress, answered before it could ring a second time. He spoke in English, with his heavy Hebrew accent, so there would be no misunderstanding about who was on the line.

"The answer is yes," he said.

"Be ready at ten o'clock tomorrow night. We'll give you the instructions then."

Under normal circumstances, a professional negotiator like O'Donnell would have begun the delay tactics: trouble assembling the money, trouble getting the permission of local authorities for the handover, anything to keep the hostage alive and the kidnappers talking. But this was not a normal situation—the terrorists wanted Gabriel—and there was no point delaying the inevitable. The sooner it started, the sooner it would be over.

"You'll call on this number?" he asked.

"Yes."

"I look forward to hearing from you."

Click.

.   .   .

Gabriel stood, pulled on his leather jacket, and started toward the stairs.

"Where do you think you're going?" asked Carter.

"I'm leaving."

"You can't just *leave.*"

"I can't stay here, Adrian. I have work to do."

"Let us give you a lift. We can't have you wandering around London unprotected."

"I think I can look after myself, Adrian."

"At least let me rustle you up a gun."

"What are you boys carrying these days?"

"Browning Hi-Power," said Carter. "It doesn't have the grace and beauty of your Berettas, but it's quite lethal. Would you like one magazine or two?"

Gabriel frowned.

"I'll bring you two," said Carter. "And an extra box of ammo for laughs."

.   .   .

Five minutes later, with Carter's loaded Browning pressing against the base of his spine, Gabriel slipped past the Marine guard at the North Gate and turned into Upper Brook Street. The sidewalk along the embassy fence was closed to pedestrian traffic and lined with Metropolitan Police officers in lime green jackets. Gabriel crossed to the opposite side of the street and headed toward Hyde Park. He spotted the motorcyclist two minutes later as he rounded the corner into Park Lane. The bike was a powerful BMW and the figure seated atop it was long-legged and helmeted. Gabriel noticed the bulge beneath the leather jacket—the left side, for the right-handed cross draw. He continued north to Marble Arch, then headed west along the Bayswater Road. As he was approaching Albion Gate he heard the roar of the BMW bike at his back. It came alongside him and braked to an abrupt stop. Gabriel swung his leg over the back and wrapped his arms around the rider's waist. As the bike shot forward he heard the sound of a woman singing. Chiara always sang when she was at the controls of a motorcycle.

48

K E N S I N G T O N , L O N D O N :
6 : 2 8 P . M . , F R I D A Y

She drove for fifteen minutes through the streets of Belgravia and Brompton to make certain they were not being followed, then made her way to the Israeli embassy, located in Old Court Place just off Kensington High Street. Shamron was waiting for them in the office of the station chief, a foul-smelling Turkish cigarette in one hand and a handsome olive-wood cane in the other. He was angrier than Gabriel had seen him in many years.

"Hello, Ari."

"What do you think you're playing at?"

"How did you get here so quickly?"

"I left Ben-Gurion this morning after learning about your exploits in Denmark. It was my intention to ease your way through Heathrow and bring you home again. But when I placed a call to the station to let them know I had arrived, I was told you had just left Downing Street."

"I tried to steal some matches for you, but I was never alone."

"You should have consulted with us before agreeing to this!"

"There wasn't time."

"There was abundant time! You see, Gabriel, it would have been a very short consultation. You would have asked for clearance to undertake this mission and I would have told you no. End of consultation." He crushed out his cigarette and looked at Gabriel malevolently for a long moment without speaking. "But to back out of this arrangement *now* is not an option. Can you imagine the headlines? Vaunted Israeli intelligence service, afraid to rescue the American girl. You've left us no choice but to proceed. But that's exactly what you intended, isn't it? You are a manipulative little bastard."

"I learned from the master."

Shamron stuck another cigarette between his lips, cocked the lid of his old Zippo lighter, and fired. "I held my tongue when you decided to return to Amsterdam to kidnap and interrogate this man Ibrahim Fawaz. I held my tongue again when you went to Copenhagen and tried to negotiate with his son. If I had obeyed my first instinct, which was to bring you home, it wouldn't have come to this. You had no right to agree to this assignment without first obtaining the permission of your director and your prime minister. If it were anyone but you, I would bring you up on charges and throw you into the Judean Wilderness to atone for your sins."

"You can do that when I get home."

"You're liable to come home in a *box*. You don't need to commit suicide in order to get out of being the next chief, Gabriel. If you don't want the job, just say so."

"I don't want the job."

"I know you don't really mean that."

"God, but you're sounding more and more like a Jewish mother every day."

"And you are providing me ample proof that you are not up to the job. By way of deception, thou shalt do war—this is our creed. We are not *shaheed*s, Gabriel. We leave the suicide missions to Hamas and all the other Islamic psychopaths who wish to destroy us. We move like shadows, strike like lightning, and then we vanish into thin air. We do not volunteer to serve as delivery boys for rich Americans, and we certainly don't sacrifice ourselves for no good reason. You are one of the elite. You are a prince of a very small tribe."

"And what do we do about Elizabeth Halton? Let her die?"

"If it is the only way to end this madness, then the answer is yes."

"And if it were your daughter, Ari? If it were Ronit?"

"Then I would shake hands with the Devil himself in order to get her back again. But I wouldn't ask the Americans to do it for me. Blue and white, Gabriel. Blue and white. We do things for ourselves, and we do not help others with problems of their own making. The Americans threw in their lot with the secular dictatorships of the Middle East a long time ago, and now the oppressed are rising up and taking their revenge on symbols of American power. On September eleventh it was the World Trade Center and the Pentagon. Now it is the innocent daughter of the American ambassador to London."

"And next it will be *us*."

"And we will fight them—*alone*." Shamron managed a faint smile of reminiscence. "I remember a boy who came home from Europe in 1975, a boy who looked twenty years older than he really was. A boy who wanted nothing more do to with this life in the shadows, nothing more to do with fighting and killing. What happened to this boy?"

"He became a man, Ari. And he is sick to death of this shit. And he will not let this woman be murdered because the Americans refuse to release a dying sheikh from prison."

"And is this man prepared to die on behalf of this cause?" He looked at Chiara. "Is he prepared to give up his life with this beautiful woman in order to save one he does not know?"

"Trust me, Ari, I'm not a martyr, and the only people who are going to die are the terrorists. When we lost Ibrahim, we lost our only way into the conspiracy. Now, by demanding that I deliver the money, they've opened the door to us again. And we're all going to walk through it, together."

"You're telling me that I should think of you as nothing more than an agent of penetration?"

Gabriel nodded. "Taking possession of money will be a major operational undertaking for them. It will expose their operatives and their means of communication. And if they *do* seize me, it will expose some of their hideouts and safe properties, which will give us additional names and telephone numbers. The British and the Americans have agreed to stay away and leave it to us. We're going to fight them, Ari, right here on British soil, just the way we've always fought them. We're going to kill them, and we're going to bring that girl home to her father alive." Gabriel paused, then added: "And then maybe they will stop blaming us for all their problems."

"I don't care what they say about us. You are like a son to me, Gabriel, and I cannot afford to lose you. Not now."

"You won't."

Shamron appeared suddenly fatigued by the confrontation. Gabriel used his silence as an opportunity to close the door on the debate and press forward.

"Where's the rest of my team?"

"They returned to Amsterdam after the debacle in Denmark," Shamron said. "They can all be here by morning."

"I'm going to need Mikhail and his gun."

Shamron smiled. "Gabriel and Michael: the angel of death and the angel of destruction. If you two can't bring the woman out alive, then I don't suppose anyone can."

"So you'll give me your blessing?"

"Only my prayers," he said. "Get some sleep, my son. You're going to need it. We'll assemble here at nine in the morning and start planning. Let us hope we are not planning a funeral."

.   .   .

The apartment on the Bayswater Road was precisely as he had left it the morning of the attack. His half-drunk cup of coffee stood on the desk by the window, next to the *London A–Z* atlas, which was still

THE SECRET SERVANT 297

open to map number 82. In the bedroom his clothes lay scattered about, evidence of the haste with which he had dressed in the moments before disaster had struck. Samir al-Masri's notebook, with his mountaintops and sand dunes and spider web of intersecting lines, lay on the unmade bed next to the woman with riotous auburn hair. A Beretta pistol protruded from the front of her faded blue jeans. Gabriel removed the weapon and placed his hand softly against her abdomen.

"Why are you doing this?" she asked.

"An insatiable desire to touch something beautiful."

"You know what I'm asking you, Gabriel. Why did you agree to the demands of the kidnappers?"

Gabriel, silent, deftly unsnapped Chiara's jeans. Chiara pushed his hand away, then reached up to his face. He recoiled from her touch. His skin was throbbing again.

"It's because of Dani, isn't it? You know what it's like to lose a child to the terrorists. You know how it makes you hate, how it can destroy your life." She ran her fingers through the ash-colored hair at his temples. "Everyone always thought it was Leah who made you burn. They seemed to forget that you lost a son. It's Dani who drives you. And it's Dani who's telling you to take this insane assignment."

"There's nothing insane about it."

"Am I the only person to at least consider the possibility that these terrorists have no intention of releasing Elizabeth Halton— that they will take Ambassador Halton's money and *then* kill her?"

"No," said Gabriel. "That is exactly what they're going to do."

"Then why are we engaging in this folly of a ransom payment?"

"Because it is the only way to save her. They're not going to kill her in some cellar where no one can see it. They kidnapped her in a terrorist spectacular and they'll kill her in one." He paused, then added: "And me with her."

"We are not *shaheed*s," she said, parroting the words of Shamron. "We leave the suicide missions to Hamas and all the other Islamic psychopaths who wish to destroy us."

Gabriel tugged at the zipper of her jeans. Once again she pushed his hand away.

"Did you enjoy working with Sarah again?"

"She performed better than I expected."

"You trained her, Gabriel. Of course she performed well."

Chiara lapsed into silence.

"Is there something you want to know?" Gabriel asked.

"Whose idea was it for her to work with you on this operation?"

"It was Carter's. And it wasn't an idea. It was a demand. They wanted an American component to our team."

"He could have picked someone else." She paused. "Someone who didn't happen to be in love with you."

"What are you talking about, Chiara?"

"She's in love you, Gabriel. Everyone could see it during the al-Bakari operation—everyone but *you*, that is. You're rather thick when it comes to matters of the heart." She looked at him in the darkness. "Or maybe you're not so thick after all. Maybe you're secretly in love with her, too. Maybe you want Sarah watching your back tomorrow instead of me."

His third attempt to remove her jeans met no resistance. The cashmere sweater was a joint operation. Chiara dealt with the brassiere alone and guided his hands to her breasts.

"Fraternization between employees in Office safe houses is strictly forbidden," she said through his kisses.

"Yes, I know."

"You're going to be a terrible chief."

He was about to take issue with her statement when the blue light on the telephone flashed. When Gabriel reached for it, Chiara seized his hand.

"What if it's the *Memuneh*?" he asked.

She rolled on top of him. "Now I'm the *Memuneh*."

She pressed her mouth against his. The blue light flashed unanswered.

"Marry me," she said.

"I'll marry you."

"Now, Gabriel. Marry me now."

"I do," he said.

"Don't die on me tomorrow night."

"I won't die."

"Promise me."

"I promise you."

49

BAYSWATER, LONDON:
7:15 A.M., SATURDAY

Gabriel woke suddenly and with the sensation of having slept an eternity. He glanced at the alarm clock, then looked at Chiara. She lay tangled in the blankets next to him like a Greek statue toppled from its plinth. He slipped out of bed quietly and listened to the news on the radio while he made coffee. According to the BBC there had been no response to Ambassador Halton's offer of ransom, and the fate of his missing daughter was still unknown. Londoners had been warned to expect heavy security along the city's main shopping streets and in the Underground and rail stations. Gabriel took comfort in the weather forecast: light rain with intervals of brightness.

He drank his first cup of coffee, then spent an inordinate amount of time standing beneath the shower. The cuts on his face made shaving impossible. Besides, there was something he liked about the look of several days' growth on his cheeks. Chiara stirred as he entered the bedroom. She drew him into the bed and made drowsy love to him one last time.

They left the apartment together at ten minutes to nine and climbed aboard Chiara's BMW bike. The forecasted rain had not yet started, nor was there evidence of the expected rush of Christmas Eve shoppers. They sped down Bayswater Road to Notting Hill, then followed Kensington Church Street to Old Court Place. A small knot of protesters was gathered in the street outside the embassy; they waved Israeli flags emblazoned with swastikas and shouted something about Jews and Nazis as Gabriel and Chiara slipped through the open gate and disappeared inside.

The rest of the team had already arrived and was gathered in the largest of the embassy's meeting rooms, looking like a band of refugees from a natural disaster. All of Gabriel's original team was there, along with the entire staff of the London Station and several other European stations as well. Uzi Navot had made the trip overnight from King Saul Boulevard and had brought with him another half-dozen field operatives. It occurred to Gabriel that this would be the largest and most important Office operation ever conducted on European soil—and yet they had no idea how it would unfold.

He sat down at the conference table next to Shamron, who was dressed in khaki trousers and his leather bomber jacket. They looked at one another in silence for a long moment; then Shamron rose slowly to his feet and called the room to order.

"At ten o'clock this evening, Gabriel is going to walk into Hell," he said. "It is our job to make sure he comes out the other end alive. I want ideas. No idea, no matter how *meshuganah*, is beyond consideration."

Shamron sat down again and opened the floor to debate. Everyone in the room started talking at once. Gabriel threw his head back and laughed out loud. It was good to be home again.

. . .

They worked through the morning, broke for a working lunch, then worked throughout the afternoon. At 5:30, Gabriel drew Chiara into an empty office and kissed her one final time. Then, wishing to avoid an awkward scene with Shamron, he slipped out of the embassy alone and headed through the streets of Kensington toward Mayfair. As he crossed Hyde Park, he paused briefly at the place where on the morning of the attack he had come upon the body of Chris Petty, the American Diplomatic Security agent. A few yards beyond lay a pile of wilted memorial flowers and a crude cardboard placard of tribute to the fallen Americans. Then, on the spot where Samir al-Masri had died in Gabriel's grasp, there was a second memorial to the "Hyde Park Martyrs," as the terrorists had become known to their supporters in London. Here was the coming clash of civilizations, thought Gabriel, played out on a few square yards of a London park.

He crossed the open lawns at the eastern edge of the park and entered Upper Brook Street. Adrian Carter was standing next to the Marine guard at the North Gate, puffing nervously on his pipe. He greeted Gabriel as though mildly surprised to see him, then took him by the arm and led him inside.

· · ·

The duffel bags of money were waiting in Ambassador Halton's top-floor office, surrounded by a detachment of DS agents. Gabriel inspected them, then looked at Carter.

"No beacons, right, Adrian?"

"No beacons, Gabriel."

"What kind of car did you get me?"

"A Vauxhall Vectra, dark gray and unassuming."

"Where is it now?"

"Upper Brook Street."

"The bags fit in the truck?"

"We checked it out. They fit."

"Put the money inside now."

Carter frowned. "I don't know about you, Gabriel, but I never leave my wallet in the car, let alone thirty million in cash."

"At this moment the embassy is surrounded by a hundred Metropolitan Police officers," Gabriel said. "No one is going to break into the car."

Carter nodded at the DS agents, and a moment later the bags were gone.

"You, too, Adrian. I'd like to have a word with the ambassador alone."

Carter opened his mouth as though he were about to object, then thought better of it. "I'll be down in the ops center," he said. "Don't be late, Gabriel. The show can't start without you."

.   .   .

Precisely what was said between Gabriel Allon and Ambassador Robert Halton never became known and was not included in any record of the affair, overt or secret. Their conversation was brief, no more than a minute in duration, and the DS agent standing guard outside the ambassador's office later described Gabriel as looking damp-eyed but determined as he emerged and made his way toward the ops center. This time the kidnappers did not make him wait. The call, according to the clock above John O'Donnell's workstation, came at 20:00:14. Gabriel reached for it instantly, though he remembered thinking as he did so that he would be happy never to speak into a telephone again for as long as he lived. His greeting was calm and somewhat vague; his demeanor, as he listened to the instructions, was that of a traffic officer recording the details of a minor accident. He posed no questions, and his face registered no emotion other than profound irritation. At 20:00:57, he was heard to murmur: "I'll be there." Then he stood and pulled on his coat. This time Carter made no attempt to stop him as he started toward the stairs.

He paused for a moment in the ground-floor atrium to slip on his miniature earpiece and throat microphone, then nodded silently to the Marine guard as he exited the embassy grounds through the North Gate. Carter's Vauxhall sedan was parked in a flagrantly illegal space on the corner of North Audley Street. The keys resided in Gabriel's coat pocket, along with a GPS beacon the size of a five-pence coin. He opened the trunk and quickly inspected the cargo before adhering the beacon near the driver's-side taillight. Then he

climbed behind the wheel and started the engine. A moment later he
was turning into Oxford Street and marveling at the crush of last-
minute shoppers. Carter's watchers followed him as far as Albany
Street, where they photographed him making a left turn and heading north. That would be their last contact with him. As far as the
Americans and British were concerned, Gabriel had now disappeared from radar.

That was not the case, however, at the Israeli embassy in South
Kensington, where, in one of the more bizarre coincidences of the entire affair, a group of well-meaning Christians had chosen that night
to conduct a candlelight vigil calling for peace in the Holy Land. Inside the building, Ari Shamron and Uzi Navot were holding a vigil
of their own. Their thoughts were not of peace or the holidays or
even of home. They were huddled round a smoky table in the
makeshift operations room, moving their forces into place, and
watching a winking green light heading along the eastern fringe of
Regent's Park toward Hampstead.

50

He parked where they told him to park, in the Constantine Road at the southern tip of Hampstead Heath. There was no other traffic moving in the street, and Gabriel, as he had made his final approach, detected no signs of surveillance, opposition or friendly. He shut off the engine and pressed the interior trunk release, then opened the center console hatch and dropped the keys inside. A gentle rain had started to fall. As he stepped outside, he cursed himself for failing to bring a hat.

He walked to the back of the car and removed the first duffel. As he was reaching for the second, he heard noises at his back and wheeled around to find a pack of young carolers advancing festively toward him. For a mad instant he wondered whether they might be the Sphinx's watchers but quickly dismissed that notion as they bade him a Happy Christmas and paraded obliviously by. He placed the second bag in the street and closed the trunk. The carolers were now singing "O Come, All Ye Faithful" outside a small brick cottage strung with holiday lights. A sign in the window read: GIVE US PEACE IN OUR TIME.

Gabriel towed the duffel bags a few yards along the street, then crossed a footbridge over a set of sunken railroad tracks and entered the heath. To his right was a darkened running track. In the cement esplanade outside the padlocked gate, four immigrant men in their twenties were kicking a football about beneath the amber glow of a sodium lamp. They appeared to pay Gabriel no heed as he labored past and started up the slope of Parliament Hill, toward the bench where they had told him to wait for their next contact. He arrived to find it occupied by a small man with a frayed coat and matted beard. His accent, when he spoke to Gabriel, was East London and leaden with drink.

"Happy Christmas, mate. What can I do for you?"

"You can get off the bench."

"It's my bench tonight."

"Not anymore," said Gabriel. "Move."

"Piss off."

Gabriel drew Adrian Carter's Browning Hi-Power and leveled it at the man's head. "Get the fuck out of here and forget you ever saw me. Do you understand?"

"Loud and fucking clear."

The man got quickly to his feet and melted into the darkness of the Heath. Gabriel ran his hand along the back and underside of the bench and found a mobile phone taped to the bottom of the seat on the left side. He quickly removed the battery and searched the phone for any concealed explosive charges. Then he reconnected the battery and pressed the POWER button. When the telephone was back on-line, he spoke quietly into his throat microphone.

"Nokia E50."

"Number?" asked Uzi Navot.

Gabriel recited it.

"Any recent activity."

"It's clean."

"Text activity?"

"Nothing."

Gabriel stared down at the lights of London and waited for the phone to ring. Fifteen minutes later, he heard a thin, tinny version of the *Adhan*, the Muslim call to prayer. He silenced it with a press of a button and raised the phone to his ear. It took them only thirty seconds to deliver the next set of instructions. Gabriel dropped the phone into the rubbish bin next to the bench, then took hold of the duffel bags and started walking.

. . .

At the makeshift command center inside the Israeli embassy, Uzi Navot laid down the handset of his secure radio and snatched up the receiver of his telephone. He quickly dialed a number for Thames House, the riverfront headquarters of MI5, and ten seconds later heard the voice of Graham Seymour.

"Where is he now?" Seymour asked.

"Heading across Hampstead Heath toward Highgate. They just told him that if he has a radio or a weapon on him at the next stop, Elizabeth Halton will be executed immediately. In a few seconds he's going to be off the air."

"What can we do for you?"

"Trace a telephone."

"Give me everything you have on it."

Navot gave Seymour the model and telephone number.

"I don't suppose they were foolish enough to leave any information in the calling history."

"The phone was clean, Graham."

"We'll run it and see if we come up with anything. But I wouldn't hold out much hope. Unfortunately, there is no shortage of jihadists in our local telecommunications industry. They're damned clever when it comes to covering their tracks with phones."

"Just give us anything you come up with."

Navot slammed down the phone and picked up the radio handset again. He grunted a few words in terse Hebrew, then looked at Shamron. He was pacing the room slowly, leaning heavily on his cane.

"You're wasting your time chasing that phone, Uzi. You should be chasing the watchers instead."

"I know, boss. But where are the watchers?"

Shamron stopped in front of a computer monitor and peered at a grainy night-vision image of four young men playing football outside the padlocked Hampstead Heath running track.

"At least one of them is right there in front of you, Uzi."

"We've had them under watch since before Gabriel arrived. No phone calls. No text messaging. Only football."

"Then you should assume that's what the Sphinx told him to do," Shamron said. "That's the way I would have done it—an old-school, physical signal. If Gabriel is clean, keep playing football. If Gabriel is being followed, have an argument of some sort. If Gabriel has a radio, take a cigarette break." Shamron poked at the screen. "Like that boy is doing right there."

"You think one of them is a spotter?"

"I'd bet my life on it, Uzi."

"That means that there's someone else in the heath who can see him—someone with a cell phone or a two-way pager."

"Exactly," said Shamron. "But you're never going to find him. He's already gone by now. Your only option is to follow the spotter."

Navot looked at the screen. "I don't have the resources to follow four men."

"You don't have to follow four. You only have to follow one. Just make sure you pick the right one."

"Which one is that?"

"Eli has good instincts about these things," Shamron said. "Let Eli decide. And whatever you do, make sure you get another beacon on Gabriel before he leaves Highgate. If we lose him now, we might never find him again."

Navot reached for his radio. Shamron started pacing again.

· · ·

Gabriel jettisoned the Browning and the radio in a stand of trees at the center of the heath, then crossed the levee between the Highgate Ponds and made his way to Millfield Lane. Taped to the nearest lamppost was a snapshot of a dark blue BMW station wagon. The car itself was fifty yards farther along the lane, outside a large freestanding brick house with a string of smiling reindeer on the lawn. Gabriel opened the rear hatch and peered inside. The keys lay in plain sight, in the center of the cargo area. He removed them, placed the bags inside, then subjected the vehicle to a thorough inspection before climbing behind the wheel and tentatively turning the key.

The engine started right away. Gabriel opened the glove box and saw a single sheet of paper, which he examined by the ambient light of the dashboard. Listed on the page was a detailed set of driving instructions—a journey that would take him from Highgate to a headland for the distant reaches of Essex appropriately named Foulness Point. On the passenger seat was a well-thumbed *Bartholomew Road Atlas*. It was dated 1995 and opened to map number 25. The drop site was was marked with an X. The surrounding waters were labeled in red: DANGER ZONE.

Gabriel slipped the car into gear and eased away from the curb under the watchful gaze of the smiling reindeer. He turned right into Merton Lane, just as they instructed him to do, and headed east along the edge of the Highgate Cemetery. In Hornsey Lane, a male pedestrian in a shoddy mackintosh raincoat stepped in his path. Gabriel put his foot hard on the brake, too late to avoid a minor collision that sent the pedestrian tumbling to the asphalt. The man bounced quickly to his feet and pounded his fist on the hood in a rage; then, after reaching briefly beneath the passenger-side wheel well, he stormed off. Gabriel watched him go, then made his way to the Archway Road. He turned left and headed for the M25.

· · ·

At that same moment in Hampstead Heath, the vagrant returned to his encampment atop Parliament Hill. He spent a few seconds picking through the rubbish bin, as if looking for a morsel of something edible, then settled himself once more on his bench overlooking the cityscape of London. His thoughts were focused not on food or even drink but on the four young men now filing over the footbridge to the Constantine Road. *We think one of them is the spotter*, Uzi Navot had said. *The Memuneh wants you to decide.* He already had. It was the one in the denim jacket, black high-top Converse sneakers, and Bob Marley knit cap. He was good for so young a man, but Lavon was better. Lavon was the best there ever was. He waited until the four men were out of sight, then he removed his false beard and tattered overcoat and started after them.

· · ·

For the first ninety minutes of Gabriel's journey, the weather had held to a persistent drizzle, but as he crossed the drawbridge leading to Foulness Island, God in His infinite wisdom unleashed a torrential downpour that turned the road into a river. There were no headlamps in his rearview mirror and none coming toward him from the opposite direction. Gabriel, as he sped past dormant farms and grassy tidal creeks, allowed himself to wonder if this would be his last earthly vision—not the Jezreel Valley of his birth, not Jerusalem or the narrow streets of his beloved Venice, but this windswept headland at the edge of the North Sea.

Five miles beyond the drawbridge, Gabriel glimpsed a sign amidst the deluge, warning that soon the road would end. For reasons known only to himself, he took careful note of the time, which was 12:35. A quarter-mile later he turned into an abandoned car park at Foulness Point and, as instructed, switched off the engine. *Leave the keys in the ignition,* the voice had said to him in Hampstead Heath. *Take the bags out to the point and place them on the beach.* For a few desperate seconds he considered hurling the money into the car park and driving at the speed of light back to London. Instead he extracted the bags slowly, then dragged them through an opening in the earthen seawall and down a sandy path to the narrow beach.

As he was nearing the water's edge he heard a noise that sounded like the wind in the dune grass. Then, from the corner of his eye, he noticed the movement of something black which, on a clear night, he might have mistaken for a passing moon shadow. He never saw the one who delivered a sledgehammer blow to the side of his head, nor did he ever see the needle that was rammed into the side of his neck. Chiara appeared, dressed in a white gown stained with blood, and pleaded with him not to die. Then she receded into flashing blue light and was gone.

.   .   .

Shamron and Navot stood side by side in the command post, staring wordlessly at the flashing green light. It had not moved for ten minutes. Shamron knew it never would.

"You'd better send someone out there to have a look," he said, "just to make sure."

Navot raised the handset of his radio to his lips.

.   .   .

Yossi had followed Gabriel's beacon as far as Southend-on-Sea and was sheltering in an all-night café overlooking the Thames Estuary when he received Navot's urgent call. Thirty seconds later, he was behind the wheel of his Renault sedan and driving at a thoroughly unsafe speed toward Foulness Point. When he turned into the car park, he saw the BMW station wagon standing alone with its rear hatch open and the keys still in the ignition. He drew a flashlight from the glove box and followed a set of fresh footprints down to the beach. There were more footprints there of varying sizes, along with a set of parallel grooves that led from the center of the beach to the water's edge. The grooves had been left by the toes of a man, Yossi thought—a man who was unconscious or worse. He brought his radio to his lips and raised Navot at the command post. "He's gone," Yossi said. "And it looks like they took him away by boat."

.   .   .

Navot lowered his handset and looked at Shamron.

"I doubt these lads took him into the North Sea on a night like this, Uzi."

"I agree, boss. But where *did* they take him?"

Shamron walked over to the map. "Here," he said, poking at a spot on the other side of the river Crouch. "It's lined with marinas and other places to land small craft. And the only way to get across it at this time of night is by boat, which means we're going to have to take the long way around."

Navot returned to the radio and ordered his teams to give chase. Then he picked up the phone and broke the news to Graham Seymour at MI5 Headquarters.

51

He was lost in a gallery of memory hung with portraits of the dead. They spoke to him as he drifted slowly past—Zwaiter and Hamidi; the brothers al-Hourani; Sabri and Khaled al-Khalifa, father and son of terror. They welcomed him to the land of martyrs and celebrated his death with sweets and song. At the end of the gallery, a bloodless boy with bullet holes in his face guided Gabriel through the doors of a church in Venice. The nave was hung with a cycle of paintings depicting scenes from his life and above the main altar was an unfinished canvas, clearly painted by the hand of Bellini, portraying Gabriel's death. The master himself was standing in the sanctuary. He took Gabriel by the hand and led him into a garden in Jerusalem, where a woman scarred by fire sat in the shade of an olive tree with a cherubic boy on her lap. *Look at the snow,* the woman was saying to the child. *The snow absolves Vienna of its sins. The snow falls on Vienna while the missiles rain on Tel Aviv.* He heard someone calling his name. He went into the church but found it empty. When he returned to the garden, the woman and the boy were gone.

. . .

When finally he woke, it was with the sensation that he had drunk himself sick. His headache was catastrophic, his mouth felt as though it were filled with a wad of cotton wool, and he feared he might throw up, even though it had been many hours since he had taken food. He opened his eyes slowly and, without moving a muscle, took stock of his situation. He lay on his back atop a narrow camp bed, in a small chamber with walls as white as porcelain. His hands were cuffed and the cuffs were attached to an iron loop in the wall behind his head so that his arms were stretched painfully backward. His clothing and wristwatch had been removed; his mouth had been taped closed. A searing white light shone fiercely into his face.

He closed his eyes, fought off a wave of nausea, and shivered violently from the cold. A good hiding place, this. Surely much planning and enterprise had gone into creating it. Despite the al-most clinical cleanliness of the chamber, there were foul smells on the air, the smell of feces and body odor, the odor of a woman held for a long time in captivity. Elizabeth Halton had been here be-fore him—he was certain of it. Was she still close by, he wondered, or had they moved her to another location to make way for the new tenant?

There were noises beyond the door. Gabriel turned his head a few degrees and saw an eye glaring at him through the peephole. Next he heard the sound of a padlock opening, followed by the groan of the cold hinges. A single man entered his cell. He was no more than thirty, slightly built and dressed in a collared shirt with a burgundy V-necked pullover. He gazed at Gabriel quizzically for a long moment through a pair of horn-rimmed spectacles, as if he had been looking for a library or bookshop and had stumbled onto this scene instead. Gabriel found something familiar in the arrangement of the man's features. Only when he tore the tape from Gabriel's face and in Arabic wished him a pleasant evening did he under-stand why. The voice belonged to a young man from the Oud West in Amsterdam—a young man who was half Egyptian and half Palestinian, a volatile mix.

It belonged to Ishaq Fawaz.

. . .

He vanished as quickly as he had appeared. A few minutes later, four men entered his cell. They hit him several times in the abdomen before uncuffing his hands, then, after lifting him to his feet, hit him some more. The chamber was too small for a proper beating and so, after a brief conference, they dragged him naked up a flight of stairs and into a darkened warehouse space. Gabriel struck first, a move that seemed to catch them off guard. He managed to incapacitate one of them temporarily before the other three jumped onto his back and drove him onto the cold cement floor. There they throttled, kicked, and pounded on him for several minutes until, from somewhere in the warehouse, came an order to cease and desist. They let him lay there for some time, vomiting his own blood, before finally returning him to his cell and securing his hands to the wall again. He fought to remain conscious but could not. The door of the church in Venice was still ajar. He slipped inside and saw Bellini standing atop his work platform high above the main altar, putting the finishing touches on the canvas depicting Gabriel's death. Gabriel climbed slowly upward and, with Bellini at his side, began to paint.

52

WALTHAMSTOW, LONDON:
2:15 A.M., CHRISTMAS DAY

The spotter was good. Cairo good. Baghdad good.

The route he had taken from Hampstead Heath had been long and needlessly complicated: four different buses, two long hikes, and a final tube ride on the Victoria Line from King's Cross to Walthamstow Central. Now he was walking up the Lea Bridge Road with a mobile phone pressed to his ear and Eli Lavon trailing a hundred yards behind him. He turned into Northumberland Road and thirty seconds later entered a small terraced house with a pebble dash exterior. There were lights burning in the windows on the second floor, evidence of other operatives inside.

Lavon circled around the block and made his way back to Lea Bridge Road. On the opposite side of the road was an empty bus shelter with an adequate view of the target house. As he lowered himself wearily onto the bench, he could hear Uzi Navot relaying the address to Graham Seymour at MI5 Headquarters. Lavon waited until Navot was finished, then murmured into his throat mic: "I can't stay here for long, Uzi."

"You won't have to. The cavalry is on the way."

"Just tell them to come quietly," Lavon said. "But hurry. I'm about to freeze to death."

. . .

It took MI5 and the Anti-Terrorist Branch of Scotland Yard just ten minutes to produce a list of the four men now using 23 Northumberland Road as a legal address and just twenty minutes to acquire the records of every telephone call placed from the residence for the previous two years. Calls placed to numbers that appeared on government watch lists, or to phones located in areas known for the extremism of their Islam, were automatically flagged for additional scrutiny. The records of calls placed from *those* numbers during the past two years were pulled as well. As a result, within an hour of Lavon's first contact, MI5 and Scotland Yard had constructed a matrix of several thousand numbers and more than five hundred corresponding names.

Shortly after three A.M., a copy of the matrix was placed before the special MI5 task force that had been working around the clock since Elizabeth Halton's disappearance. Five minutes later Graham Seymour personally delivered a second copy of the document to the fourth-floor conference room, which was occupied at that moment by three rather young women. One was an attractive American in her early thirties with shoulder-length blond hair and skin the color of alabaster. The other two were both Israelis, a curt Rubenesque woman with the bearing of a soldier and a small dark-haired girl who walked with a slight limp. Though all three had entered the United Kingdom on false passports, Seymour had agreed to let them into Thames House on the condition they did so under their real names. The Rubenesque Israeli was Major Rimona Stern of AMAN, the Israeli military intelligence service. The quiet girl was an analyst for the Israeli foreign intelligence service named Dina Sarid. The American's credentials identified her as Irene Moore, a CIA desk officer attached to the Counterterrorism Center at Langley..

They accepted the document gratefully, then divided it among themselves. The American and the Rubenesque Israeli took the telephone numbers. The girl with the slight limp handled the names. She was good with names—Graham Seymour could see that. But there was something else: the intense seriousness of purpose, the stain of early widowhood in her dark eyes. She had been touched by terror, he thought. She was both victim and survivor. And she had a mind like a mainframe computer. Graham Seymour was convinced the matrix of names and numbers contained a valuable clue. And he had no doubt who would find it first.

He slipped out of the conference room and returned to the ops center. Waiting on his desk when he arrived was a dispatch from the Essex Police Headquarters in Chelmsford. A shallow-bottomed craft had been discovered abandoned along the northern banks of the river Crouch near Holliwell Point. Based on the condition of the outboard engine, it appeared that the boat had been used that evening. Graham Seymour picked up the phone and dialed Uzi Navot's line at the Israeli command post in Kensington.

.   .   .

Thirty seconds later, Navot hung up the phone and relayed the news to Shamron.

"It looks like you were right about them taking him over the river."

"You doubted me, Uzi?"

"No, boss."

"He's alive," Shamron said, "but he won't be for long. We need a break. One name. One telephone number. Something."

"The girls are looking for it."

"Let's hope they find it, Uzi. *Soon.*"

53

The next time Gabriel awakened, his body was being washed. For an instant he feared they had killed him and that he was witnessing the ritual cleansing of his own corpse. Then, as he passed through another layer of consciousness, he realized it was only his captors trying to clean up the mess they had made of him.

When they were finished, they unchained his hands long enough to clothe him in a tracksuit and a pair of slip-on sandals, then withdrew without further violence. Some time later, a half hour perhaps, Ishaq returned. He regarded Gabriel with a perverted calmness for several moments before posing his first question.

"Where are my wife and son?"

"Why are you still here? I would have thought you would have been long gone by now."

"To Pakistan? Or Afghanistan? Or Wherever-the-fuck-istan?"

"Yes," said Gabriel. "Back to the House of Islam, refuge of murderers."

"I was planning to go there," Ishaq said with a smile, "but I asked to come back here to deal with you, and my request was granted."

"Lucky you."

"Now, tell me where my wife and son are."

"What time is it?"

"Five minutes till midnight," said Ishaq, proud of his wit. Then he gave his watch an exaggerated glance. "*Four* minutes, actually. Your time is running out. Now, answer my question."

"I suspect they're in the Negev by now. We have a secret prison there for the worst of the worst. It is the equivalent of a galactic black hole. Those who enter are never heard from again. Hanifah and Ahmed will be well taken care of."

"You're lying."

"You're probably right, Ishaq."

"When we were negotiating over the phone, you told me you were an American. You told me that my family was going to Egypt to be tortured. Now you tell me they are in Israel. You see my point?"

"Have you attempted to make one?"

"You are not to be trusted—that is my point. But, then, that is not surprising. You are, after all, a Jew."

"The patricide lectures me about the immorality of deceit."

"No, Allon, it was *you* who murdered my father. I saved him."

"I know my brain is a little fuzzy at the moment, Ishaq, but you're going to have to explain that one to me."

"My father was once a member of the Sword of Allah, but he turned his back on jihad and lived the life of an apostate in the land of strangers. Then he compounded his offenses by throwing in his lot with you, the Jewish murderer of Palestinian mujahideen. Under the laws of Islam my father was condemned to Hell for his actions. I gave him a martyr's death. My father is now a *shaheed* and therefore he is guaranteed a place in Paradise."

The words had been spoken with such a profound seriousness that Gabriel knew further debate was pointless. It would be like arguing with a man who believed the earth was flat or that American astronauts had never landed on the moon. He felt suddenly like Winston Smith in Room 101 of the Ministry of Love. Freedom is slavery. Two and two make five. Murder of one's father is divine duty.

"You were good in Denmark," Gabriel said. "Very professional. You must have been planning that for a long time. I don't suppose killing your own father was part of the original plan, but you improvised extraordinarily well."

"Thank you," Ishaq said earnestly.

"Why weren't you there for the finale? And why wasn't I killed along with him?"

Ishaq smiled calmly but made no response. Gabriel answered his own question.

"You and the Sphinx had other plans for me, didn't you—plans that were laid the moment my picture appeared in the London papers after the kidnapping?"

"Who is this person you refer to as the Sphinx?"

Gabriel ignored him and pushed on. "The Sphinx knew that if the Americans didn't release Elizabeth, eventually her father would take matters into his own hands. He knew that Robert Halton would offer the only thing he had: money. He also knew that someone would have to deliver the money. He waited for Halton to make the offer, then he seized the opportunity to take his revenge."

"And yet you came anyway." Ishaq was unable to prevent a note of astonishment from creeping into his voice. "Surely you knew this would be your fate. Why would you do such a thing? Why would you be willing to trade your life for another—for the spoiled daughter of an American billionaire?"

"Where is she, Ishaq?"

"Do you really think I would tell you, even if I knew where she was?"

"You know exactly where she is. She's an innocent, Ishaq. Even under your perverted notion of *takfir*, you have no right to kill her."

"She is the daughter of the American ambassador, the goddaughter of the American president, and spoke out in favor of the war in Iraq. She is a legitimate target, under our laws or anyone else's."

"Only a terrorist would consider Elizabeth Halton a legitimate target. We had a deal. Thirty million dollars for Elizabeth's life. I expect you to live up to that deal."

"You are in no position to make demands, Allon. Besides, our laws permit us to lie to infidels when necessary and to take the infidels' money when it suits our needs. Thirty million dollars will go a very long way toward funding our global jihad. Who knows? Perhaps we'll even be able to use it to buy a nuclear weapon—a weapon we can use to wipe your country off the map."

"Keep the money. Buy your fucking weapon. But let her go."

Ishaq pulled a frown, as if bored by the topic. "Let us return to my original question," he said. "Where are Hanifah and Ahmed?"

"They were in custody in Copenhagen. When you demanded that I deliver the money, we went to the Danes and asked for your wife and son as collateral. The Danes, of course, granted our request without hesitation. If I don't come back alive from this—and if Elizabeth Halton is not freed—your family will disappear from the face of the earth."

He appeared shaken but put on a defiant face. "You're lying."

"Whatever you say, Ishaq. But trust me, if anything happens to me, you'll never see them again."

"Even if it is true that you have taken them to Israel as *collateral*, once the world learns they are being held, great pressure will be brought to bear in order to secure their release. Your government will have no recourse but to bend." He stood abruptly and looked at his watch. "It is now two minutes to midnight. We have something we need from you before your execution. Give it to us without a struggle and your death will be relatively painless. If you insist on fighting us again, the boys will have their way with you. And this time, I won't call them off."

He opened the door and took a step outside, then turned and looked at Gabriel once more. "It occurs to me that soon you will be a *shaheed,* too. If you convert to Islam before your death, your place in Paradise will be assured. I can help, if you wish. The procedure is really quite simple."

Ishaq, receiving no answer, closed the door and secured it with a padlock. Gabriel closed his eyes. *Two and two make four,* he thought. *Two and two make four.*

54

I think I may have found something."

Graham Seymour looked up. It was the Israeli girl with dark hair and a limp: Dina Sarid. He gestured toward the empty chair next to his desk in the operations room. The girl remained standing.

"According to British Telecom records, twenty-seven calls have been placed from the telephone in the Northumberland Road residence to a phone located at Number Fourteen Reginald Street in Luton during the past eighteen months. Five of these calls were placed *after* the disappearance of Elizabeth Halton."

Seymour frowned. Luton, a heavily Muslim suburb north of London, was one of MI5's worst problems.

"Go on," he said.

"According to your matrix, the telephone in Luton is located in the home of a man named Nabil Elbadry. Mr. Elbadry runs an import-export business and several other enterprises. He does not appear on any of your lists of known terrorist sympathizers or jihadi activists."

"So what's the problem?" Seymour asked.

"When I saw the name a few minutes ago, I knew I'd seen it somewhere before."

"Where?"

"In a cache of Sword of Allah files we obtained from the Egyptian SSI."

Seymour felt his stomach begin to burn. "Keep going, Miss Sarid."

"Five years ago, the Egyptians arrested a man named Kemel Elbadry in Cairo. Under interrogation at the Torah Prison complex, he admitted to taking part in several Sword of Allah operations inside Egypt."

"What does this have to do with Nabil Elbadry from Luton?"

"According to Kemel's file, he had a brother named Nabil who immigrated to England in 1987. That corresponds exactly with the details on Nabil Elbadry's immigration records."

"Is Kemel still in custody?"

"He's dead."

"Executed?"

"Unclear."

Graham Seymour stood up and called for quiet in the operations room.

"Nabil Elbadry," he shouted. "Number Fourteen Reginald Street, Luton. I want to know everything there is to know about this man and his business interests and I want to know it in five minutes or less."

He looked at the girl. She nodded her head once and limped slowly back to the conference room.

· · ·

The boys in black came for him ten minutes after Ishaq left the cell. As they led him up the narrow stairs, Gabriel prepared himself for another beating. Instead, upon his arrival in the warehouse, he was lowered rather cordially into a folding aluminum chair.

He looked straight ahead and saw the lens of a video camera.

Ishaq, now playing the role of director and cinematographer, ordered the four men in black to stand at Gabriel's back. Three held Heckler & Koch compact submachine guns. One held a knife ominously. Gabriel knew his time had not yet come. His hands were cuffed in front. Infidels about to suffer the profound indignity of beheading always had their hands bound in back.

Ishaq made a few minor changes to the arrangement of his props, then stepped from behind his camera and handed Gabriel his script. Gabriel looked down. Then, like an actor unhappy with his lines, he tried to hand it back.

"Read it!" Ishaq demanded.

"No," replied Gabriel calmly.

"Read it or I'll kill you now."

Gabriel let the script fall from his hands.

.   .   .

It took Graham Seymour's task force only ten minutes to assemble a detailed inventory of all business interests and properties registered to Nabil Elbadry of Reginald Street, Luton. His eyes stopped halfway down the list. A company in which Elbadry was a minority partner owned a warehouse in West Dock Street in Harwich, not far from the ferry port. Seymour stood and went quickly to the map. Harwich was approximately forty miles from the spot where the Essex police had discovered the abandoned boat. He walked back to his desk and dialed the Israeli command post in Kensington.

.   .   .

Ishaq snatched up the fallen pages, then, after composing himself, read the statement on Gabriel's behalf. Gabriel had committed many crimes against Palestinians and Muslims, Ishaq declared, and for these crimes he would soon face the justice of the sword. Gabriel did not listen to the entire recitation of his sins. Instead he looked down at the floor of the warehouse and wondered why Ishaq had not bothered to obscure his face before stepping in front of the camera. He knew the answer, of course: Ishaq was a martyr in the making and they were going to die together. When Ishaq was finished reading Gabriel's death sentence, he walked over to the camera and checked to make certain it had recorded properly. Satisfied, he signaled the boys in black to commence their next beating. It seemed to last an eternity. The stab of the needle was an act of mercy. Gabriel's eyes fell shut and he felt himself drowning in black water.

. . .

"How long will it take you to get your teams in place, Uzi?"

"I moved everyone that way after the Essex police found the boat. I can have three teams in Harwich in twenty minutes or less. The question is, what do we do when we get there?"

"First we determine whether he's really there and, if so, whether he is still alive. Then we wait."

"*Wait?* For what, boss?"

"We came here to get the American girl, Uzi. And we're not leaving without her."

HARWICH, ENGLAND:
5:30 A.M., CHRISTMAS DAY

H arwich, ancient port of fifteen thousand souls at the confluence of the rivers Stour and Orwell, lay darkened and slumbering beneath a steady onslaught of rain. The waters of Ramsey Creek were empty of commercial craft, and only a handful of cars had gathered at the ferry terminal for the morning's first passage to the Continent. The medieval town center was tightly shuttered and abandoned to the gulls.

It was into this setting that six field operatives from the foreign intelligence service of the State of Israel arrived at precisely 4:45 A.M. on Christmas morning. By five o'clock they had confirmed that the warehouse in West Dock Road was indeed occupied, and by 5:15 they had managed to place a small wireless camera in the corner of a broken window at the back. They were now carefully dispersed among the surrounding streets. Yaakov had taken up a post hundred yards from the warehouse in the Station Road. Yossi was encamped in the Refinery Road. Oded and Mordecai had hastily concealed the surveillance van beneath an overpass of the A120. Mikhail and Chiara, who had spent that night atop the BMW bike, were sheltering in the back of the van, staring at the screen of the video receiver. The image there was poorly framed and prone to static. Even so, they could see clearly what was taking place inside the warehouse. Four men dressed in black were loading large drums of liquid into the back of a Vauxhall panel van, under the supervision of a slender Egyptian-looking man in a burgundy V-necked sweater.

At 5:40, the five men slipped out of camera range. Then, ten minutes later, they returned with the final component of their weapon of mass murder—a man in a blue-and-white tracksuit, bound and trussed in packing tape, his face bloodied and swollen.

"Please tell me he's alive, Mikhail."

"He's alive, Chiara."

"How can you tell?"

"They wouldn't be putting him in with the bomb if he was dead."

But the best evidence he was alive, Mikhail thought darkly, was his head. If Gabriel were dead, it wouldn't still be attached to his shoulders. He didn't share this observation with Chiara. She'd been through enough that night already.

At 5:55, the four men in black stripped down to their street clothes. Three climbed into a Mercedes cargo truck and departed. The fourth climbed behind the wheel of the Vauxhall panel van, while the Egyptian-looking man with the burgundy sweater joined Gabriel in the back. At precisely six A.M., the van turned into West Dock Street and made its way toward the entrance of the A120. Four vehicles followed carefully after it. Yaakov took the first shift at the point, while Chiara and Mikhail brought up the rear on the BMW bike. Mikhail sat on the back. The gunner's seat.

. . .

Gabriel opened one eye, then, slowly, the other. He tried to move his limbs but could not. The crown of his head was pressing against something metallic. He was able to twist his neck just enough to see that the object was a steel drum. There were other drums, five more in fact, linked by a network of wires leading to a detonator switch on the console next to the driver. Ishaq was seated opposite Gabriel. His legs were crossed and a gun lay in his lap. He was smiling, as though proud of the clever way in which he had unveiled the method of Gabriel's pending execution.

"Where are we going?" Gabriel asked.

"Paradise."

"Does your driver know the way, or is he just following his nose?"

"He knows," said Ishaq. "He's been preparing for this ride for a very long time."

Gabriel twisted his head around and looked at him. He was several years younger than Ishaq, clean shaven, and had both hands on the wheel like a novice out for his first drive alone.

"I want to sit up," Gabriel said.

"It's probably better if you stay down. If you sit up, it's going to hurt."

"I don't care," Gabriel said.

"Suit yourself."

He took hold of Gabriel's shoulders and propped him carelessly against the passenger-side wall of the cargo hold. Ishaq was right. It *did* hurt to sit up. In fact, it hurt so damned much he nearly fainted. But at least now he could see out through a portion of the windshield. It was still dark out, but one side of the sky was gradually turning a deep, luminous blue—the first light, Gabriel reckoned, of Christmas morning. Judging from the modest speed they were making, and the absence of any other traffic noise, they were traveling on a B-road. He glimpsed a road sign as it flashed past: SHRUB END 3. *Shrub End?* Where in God's name was Shrub End?

He closed his eyes from the pain and heard an engine note not their own. It was high and tight, the sound of a high-performance motorcycle approaching from behind at considerable speed. He opened his eyes and watched as it flashed past in a cyclone of road spray. Then he looked at Ishaq again and for a second time asked where they were going. This time Ishaq only smiled. It was a martyr's smile. Gabriel closed his eyes and thought of the motorcycle. *Go for the kill shot*, he thought. But then Mikhail knew no other kind.

. . .

Uzi Navot lowered the handset of the radio and looked at Shamron.

"Mikhail says they're still in the same position that they were when they left the warehouse. One driving, one in the back with Gabriel. He says he can get the driver cleanly, but there's no way he can get them both."

"You have to make them stop, Uzi—someplace where an explosion won't take innocent life."

"And if they won't stop?"

"Have a backup plan ready."

. . .

Gabriel tried not to think about them. He tried not to wonder how they had tracked him down, how long they had been watching and following, or how they planned to extract him. As far as Gabriel was concerned, they did not exist. They were nonpersons. Ghosts. Lies. He thought of anything else. The pain of his broken ribs. The burning numbness of his limbs. Shamron, leaning on his olive-wood cane. *We move like shadows, strike like lightning, and then we vanish into thin air.* Strike soon, Gabriel thought, because he feared he couldn't keep his balance atop the bridge over Jahannam much longer.

He made a clock in his head and watched the second hand go round. He listened for other vehicles and read the road signs as they flashed past: HECKFORDBRIDGE . . . BIRCH . . . SMYTH'S GREEN . . . TIPTREE . . . GREAT BRAXTED . . . Even Gabriel, Office-trained expert in European geography, could not place their whereabouts. Finally, he saw a sign for Chelmsford and realized they were heading toward London from the northeast, along the route of the ancient Roman road. As they were approaching a village called Langford, the driver slowed suddenly. Ishaq seized hold of his pistol and brought it up near his chest in a defensive position. Then he looked quickly at the driver.

"What's wrong?" he murmured in Arabic.

"There's an accident ahead. They're waving for me to stop."

"Police?"

"No, just the drivers."

"Don't stop."

"It's blocking the road."

"Go around," snapped Ishaq.

The driver turned the wheel hard to the left. The van heeled a few degrees to port as it tipped onto the shoulder and the machine-gun thumping of the tires over the rumble strips sent shock waves of pain through Gabriel's body. As they shot past the wreck, he saw a tall balding man in his forties waving his arms plaintively and pleading for the van to stop. A man with pockmarked cheeks was standing next to him, gazing at his smashed headlight as though trying to concoct a suitable story for his wife. Gabriel looked at Ishaq as the van lurched back onto the road and sped on toward London.

"It's Christmas, Ishaq. What kind of person leaves two motorists stranded on the road on Christmas morning?"

Ishaq responded by shoving Gabriel hard to the floor. Gabriel's view was now limited to the soles of Ishaq's shoes—and the base of the six barrels filled with explosives—and the wiring leading to the detonator switch on the console. Ishaq, in his rush to reach London on schedule, had inadvertently thwarted the first rescue attempt. The second, Gabriel knew, would involve no subterfuge. He closed his eyes and listened for the sound of the motorcycle.

. . .

Navot ordered Yossi and Yaakov back into the smashed cars and looked one final time at Shamron for guidance. "I'm afraid this has gone on long enough," Shamron said. "Put them down in a field where no one else gets hurt. And get him out in one piece."

. . .

Ishaq was reading quietly from a copy of the Quran when Gabriel heard the drone of the approaching bike. He focused his gaze on the gun, which lay in Ishaq's lap, and coiled his bound legs for a single strike. The engine note rose steadily in volume for several more seconds, then went suddenly silent. Ishaq looked up from his Quran and peered out the windshield. When the bike didn't appear, he looked at Gabriel in alarm, as though he had a premonition of what would come next. As he grabbed for the gun, there was an explosion of glass and blood in the front seat. The driver, hit several times in the head, slumped to the left and with a spasm of his lifeless hand took the wheel with him. Ishaq tried to level the gun at Gabriel as the van hurtled from the roadway, but Gabriel lifted his bound legs and kicked the weapon from Ishaq's grasp. Ishaq made one last desperate lunge for it. And then the van began to roll.

56

He came to rest in wet earth, blinded with pain, struggling for breath. A woman was shouting into his face and pulling at the packing tape that bound him. Her voice was muffled by the helmet and her face invisible behind the dark visor. "Are you all right, Gabriel?" she was saying. "Can you hear me? Answer me, Gabriel! Can you *hear* me? Damn you, Gabriel! You promised me you wouldn't die! *Don't die!*"

57

RUNSELL GREEN, ENGLAND:
6:42 A.M., CHRISTMAS DAY

There had been a fine old hedgerow along the side of the road. They had burst through it, like the tip of a pencil through tissue paper, and plunged into a farmer's field. The van had come to rest on its roof and its contents were now strewn over the muddy ground like children's toys on the floor of a nursery. Not fifty yards away from the van's final resting spot, a gathering of fat pheasant were pulling at the earth as though nothing out of the ordinary had happened. At the edge of the field, lights were coming on in a limestone cottage, the first moments of a Christmas morning the occupants would not soon forget.

"Where's Ishaq?" asked Gabriel as Chiara cut away the last of the packing tape.

"Inside the van."

"Is he alive?"

"Yes."

"Is he conscious?"

"Barely," she said. "You were thrown from the van early. He wasn't so lucky."

"Put me on my feet."

"Just stay down, Gabriel. You're hurt badly."

"Do what I say, Chiara. Put me on my feet."

Gabriel groaned in pain as she lifted him upright. He took a step forward and staggered. Chiara seized hold of his arm and kept him from falling.

"Lie down, Gabriel. Wait for the ambulance."

"No ambulances. Help me walk."

Mikhail came over at an awkward trot, gun still in his hand, and together with Chiara helped Gabriel slowly toward the van. The driver hung upside down from his seat belt, blood flowing freely from his burst skull. Ishaq lay in the back, bleeding from his nose and mouth, left leg snapped above the knee like a broken matchstick. Gabriel looked at Mikhail.

"Pull him out by the leg," he said in Hebrew. "The *broken* leg."

"Don't do this," Chiara said.

"Walk away." Gabriel looked at Mikhail. "Do what I tell you or I'll do it myself."

Mikhail ducked into the van through the open cargo doors and seized hold of the shattered leg. A moment later Ishaq lay writhing on the ground at Gabriel's feet. Chiara, unable to bear the sight, walked away across the field. Gabriel looked down at Ishaq and asked, "Where's my girl?"

"She's already dead," Ishaq spat through the blood.

Gabriel held out his hand to Mikhail. "Give me your gun."

Mikhail handed it over. Gabriel pointed it toward the broken leg and fired once. Ishaq's screams echoed over the flat landscape and his fingers clawed at the sodden earth. The pheasants took flight and circled above Gabriel's head.

"Where's my girl?" Gabriel repeated calmly.

"She's dead!"

Another shot. Another scream of agony.

"Where's my girl, Ishaq?"

"She's already—"

Pop.

"Where's my girl, Ishaq?"

"Allahu Akbar!"

Pop.

"Where's Elizabeth?"

"Allahu Akbar!"

Pop. Pop.

"Tell me where she is, Ishaq."

He leveled the gun and prepared to fire again. This time a hand went up, and Ishaq, between cries of pain, began hurling information at Gabriel like stones. Number 17 Ambler Road. Two martyrs. Westminster Abbey. Ten o'clock. God is Great.

58

FINSBURY PARK, LONDON:
7:30 A.M., SUNDAY

They barged into her cell with a demeanor she had never seen before. Cain spoke to her for the first time in more than two weeks. "You're going to be released," he blurted. "You have twenty minutes to prepare yourself. If you are not ready in twenty minutes, you will be killed." And then he was gone.

Abel appeared next, bearing a plastic bucket of warm water, a bar of soap, a washcloth and towel, a parcel of clean clothing, and a blond wig. He placed the bucket on the floor and the rest of the things on her cot, then removed her handcuffs and shackles. "Wash carefully and take your time dressing," he explained calmly. "We brought you something nice to wear. We don't want the world to think we mistreated you."

He went out and closed the door. She wanted to scream for joy. She wanted to weep with relief. Instead, model prisoner to the end, she did exactly what they told her to do. She used only fifteen minutes of her allotted time and was seated on the edge of her cot, knees together and trembling, when they entered her cell again.

"You are ready?" Cain asked.

"Yes," she replied in a low, evenly modulated voice.

"Come, then," he said.

She stood and followed them slowly up a flight of darkened stairs.

.   .   .

Word of Gabriel's successful extraction arrived at the Israeli embassy in Old Court Place at 7:48 A.M. It was transmitted via ordinary cell phone by Chiara, who was at that moment seated next to Gabriel in the back of a Volkswagen Passat with a smashed headlamp and crumpled fender. The call was taken by Shamron, who, upon hearing the news, covered his face with his hands and wept. So deep was Shamron's emotion that for several seconds those gathered around were uncertain whether Gabriel was alive or dead. When it became clear that he was indeed alive and back in their hands, a great roar went up in the room. The brief celebration that followed was intercepted and recorded by the British eavesdroppers at GCHQ—which had monitored all Israeli communications that night—as were Shamron's pleas for quiet as he listened to the next part of Chiara's report. Shamron immediately placed two calls, the first to Adrian Carter in the American ops center beneath Grosvenor Square and the second to Graham Seymour, who was with the prime minister and the COBRA committee at Downing Street. Seymour quickly arranged for a police escort to bring Gabriel and the remnants of his team safely into London; then he rushed to the American embassy, as did Shamron. The two men were standing next to Adrian Carter as the battered Passat and its police escorts screeched to a stop at the North Gate.

The car was immediately surrounded by two dozen of the uniformed Met officers standing guard outside the embassy grounds. Shamron's view was momentarily blocked; then the sea of lime green parted and he glimpsed Gabriel for the first time. He had one arm draped over Yossi's shoulder and the other over Oded's. His face was contorted with pain and swelling, and his blue-and-white tracksuit was covered in blood and mud. They brought him through the gate and propped him upright for a moment before the three senior spymasters. Shamron kissed his cheek gently and murmured something in Hebrew that the others could not understand. Gabriel lifted his head slightly and looked at Graham Seymour.

"If you tell me not to complain about a nasty bump on the head, I just may lose my temper."

"You're a damned fool—and damned brave." Seymour looked at Adrian Carter. "Let's get him inside, shall we?"

. . .

Ambassador Robert Halton was waiting in the embassy's ground-floor atrium, along with FBI hostage negotiator John O'Donnell and several other members of the American team. As Gabriel came inside, still clinging to Yossi and Oded for support, they broke into restrained applause, as though they feared too much noise might inflict additional damage to him. Robert Halton walked over to Gabriel and put his hands carefully on his shoulders. "My God, what have they done to you?" He looked at Adrian Carter. "Let's take him up to my office. The doctors can have a look at him there."

They shepherded him into a waiting elevator and whisked him up to the ninth floor. Yossi and Oded lowered him onto the couch in the ambassador's office, but when the doctors tried to enter the room, Graham Seymour held them back and quickly closed the door.

"Twenty minutes ago, a team of Met special operatives raided the house in the Ambler Road where Ishaq claimed Elizabeth was being held. She wasn't there, but they found plenty of evidence that she had been recently. The Sphinx led us on a wild-goose chase across western Europe, and all the while she's been here in England, right under our noses. The question is, where is she now?"

"The information Ishaq gave Gabriel about Elizabeth's location was correct," said Adrian Carter. "So it stands to reason that the information about what they intend to do with her is also correct."

"It is," said Gabriel. "They're going to execute her outside Westminster Abbey before the start of Christmas services. She's to be murdered by a pair of suicide bombers, who will take many innocent lives along with their own. I was supposed to be part of the second act, a massive car bombing that would have killed hundreds of your first responders."

"A bloodbath in front of our most important national symbol on the morning of our Savior's birth," said Graham Seymour. "One that is intended to spark an armed uprising in Egypt and bring this country to its knees." He hesitated, then said: "And one that we cannot allow to happen. As of this moment there are several hundred people congregated outside the north entrance of the Abbey, waiting to be admitted for a service of carols and readings that begins at ten-thirty. Our only option is to seal off Westminster and quickly evacuate everyone from the area."

"A move that will automatically condemn Elizabeth to death," said Gabriel. "If the *shaheed*s arrive in Westminster to find the Abbey evacuated and under siege, they'll resort to their backup plan, which is to kill her instantly, no matter where they are."

"Forgive my bluntness," said Seymour, "but that is a vastly better outcome than their primary plan."

"I didn't go through Hell to give up on her now," Gabriel said. "There *is* another way."

"Which is?"

"Ishaq told us that Elizabeth would be accompanied by two men," Gabriel said. "He told us—"

Graham Seymour held up his hand. "Don't go any further, Gabriel. It's madness."

"We wait for the *shaheed*s to arrive, Graham. And then we kill them before they can kill Elizabeth."

"*We?*"

"What do you think you're going to do? Shoot them like snipers from a long way off? Shoot them like gentlemen from twenty paces? You have to let them get close. And then you have to kill them before they can hit their detonator switches. That means headshots at close range. It's not pleasant, Graham. And if the gunmen hesitate for an instant, it will end in disaster."

"The Met has a unit called SO19: the Blue Berets. They're special firearms officers, trained for this very sort of thing. If memory serves, we sent them to Israel for training."

"You did," said Shamron. "And they're very good. But they've never been placed in a live situation like this. You need gunmen who've done something like this before—gunmen who aren't going to fold under the pressure." Shamron paused, then added: "You need gunmen like Gabriel and Mikhail."

"Gabriel can barely stand up," Seymour said.

"Gabriel will be fine," Shannon said without bothering to consult him. "Let us finish what we started."

"How are you going to be sure it's really her?"

Gabriel looked at Robert Halton. "If anyone can tell, it's her own father. Put him in the yard on the north side of the Abbey with a miniature radio. He'll be able to see anyone approaching from Whitehall or Victoria. When he sees Elizabeth, send the signal to us. Mikhail and I will take care of the rest."

"There's one thing I don't understand," Seymour said. "How are they going to get Elizabeth to walk to her own execution?"

Gabriel thought of what Ibrahim had said the night of his death in Denmark. "They'll tell her she's about to be released," he said. "That way she'll go willingly and do exactly what they tell her."

"Bastards," Seymour said softly. He glanced at his watch. "I take it you have all the firearms and ammunition you need?"

Gabriel nodded slowly.

"What about communications?"

"They can borrow radios from our embassy security staff," Carter said. "Our DS agents work routinely with the Met on protective details. We can all tie in on the same secure frequency."

Seymour looked at Gabriel. "What do we do about *him*? He can't go to Westminster looking like that?"

"I'm sure we can find something for him to wear here," Carter said. "We have two hundred people down in the basement who came to London from Washington with suitcases filled with clothing."

"What about his face? He looks bloody awful."

"Fixing his face, I'm afraid, would require a Christmas miracle."

Graham Seymour frowned, walked over to the ambassador's desk, and dialed the phone.

"I need to speak to the prime minister," he said. *"Now."*

59

WESTMINSTER ABBEY:
9:45 A.M., CHRISTMAS DAY

The Gothic towers of Westminster Abbey—
England's national house of worship, setting
for royal coronations since William the Conqueror, and burial
ground for British monarchs, statesmen, and poets—sparkled in the
crisp winter sunlight. The bright interval promised by the forecast-
ers the previous morning had finally materialized.

Gabriel did not wonder if it was a good omen or bad. He was only
pleased to have the radiant warmth of the sun against his swollen
cheek. He was seated on a bench in Parliament Square, dressed in
borrowed clothes and borrowed wraparound sunglasses over his
battered eyes. The doctors at the embassy had given him enough
codeine to temporarily dull the pain of his injuries. Even so, he was
leaning slightly against Mikhail for support. The younger man's
leather jacket was still damp from a night pursuing Gabriel across
Essex by motorcycle. His right hand was tapping a nervous rhythm
against his faded blue jeans.

"Stop," said Gabriel. "You're giving me a fucking headache."

Mikhail stopped for a moment, then started up again. Gabriel
stared toward the triangular-shaped lawn on the north side of the

Abbey. Adrian Carter was standing beneath a bare-limbed tree along Victoria Street, wearing the *ushanka* hat he had worn the afternoon they had walked together in the Tivoli gardens of Copenhagen. Standing next to him, with a fedora on his head, dark glasses over his eyes, and a wire in his ear, was Ambassador Robert Halton. And next to Halton was Sarah Bancroft, formerly of the Phillips Collection museum in Washington, D.C., lately of the Central Intelligence Agency, and now a fully indoctrinated citizen of the night. Of all those present, only Sarah truly had a sense of the atrocity that was about to occur. Would she watch? Gabriel wondered. Or this time would she take the opportunity to look the other way?

He glanced around the sunlit streets of Westminster. Eli Lavon and Dina Sarid were loitering in Great George Street, Yaakov and Yossi were flirting with Major Rimona Stern outside the Houses of Parliament, and Mordecai was standing in the shadow of Big Ben with a tourist guidebook open in his hands. Graham Seymour was in an unmarked command vehicle on the other side of Victoria Street in Storey's Gate, along with the commissioner of the Metropolitan Police and the chief of SO19, the special operations division. Twenty of SO19's best gunmen had been summoned at short notice and were now scattered around the Abbey and the surrounding streets of Westminster. Gabriel could hear their clipped communications in his ear, but thus far he had only been able to pick out a half dozen of them. It didn't matter if he knew their identities. It only mattered that they knew his.

"Was it bad?" Mikhail asked. "The beatings, I mean."

"They were just having a bit of fun," said Gabriel dismissively. He was in no mood to relive the previous night. "It was nothing compared to what Ibrahim endured at the hands of the Egyptian secret police."

"Did it feel good to shoot him like that?"

"Ishaq?"

The younger man nodded.

"No, Mikhail, it didn't feel good. But then, it didn't feel bad either." Gabriel lifted his hand and pointed toward the north entrance of the Abbey. "Look at all those people over there. Many of them would soon be dead if I hadn't acted the way I did."

"If we don't hit our targets, they still may die." Mikhail looked at Gabriel. "You sound as if you're trying to convince yourself that you were morally justified in torturing him."

"I suppose I am. I crossed a line. But then we've all crossed a line. The Americans crossed a line after 9/11, and now they're trying to find their way back to the other side. Unfortunately, the goals of the terrorists haven't changed—and the generation soon to emerge from the killing fields of Iraq is going to be much more violent and volatile than the ones who came out of Afghanistan."

"We dare to fight back, and the terrorists accuse us of being the real terrorists."

"It's their secret weapon, Mikhail. Get used to it."

Gabriel heard a crackle in his earpiece. He looked toward the north entrance of the Abbey and saw the vast doors swing slowly open. Graham Seymour had arranged for the Abbey's staff to admit the Christmas worshippers earlier than was customary, a simple maneuver that would drastically reduce the number of potential targets. Gabriel only hoped the *shaheed*s didn't deduce from the change that they were walking into a trap.

"Where was I?" Gabriel asked.

"You were talking about secret weapons."

"Last night, Mikhail. Where was I last night?"

"Harwich."

"I've always wanted to visit Harwich," Gabriel said. "How much did Chiara see?"

"Only the end, when they were loading you into the van." Mikhail put a hand on Gabriel's shoulder. "I wish you would have let me shoot that bastard for you."

"Relax, Mikhail. It's Christmas."

"Not for us," Mikhail said. "I only hope Ishaq wasn't lying."

"He wasn't," said Gabriel.

"What if they bring her somewhere else?"

"They won't. You have your cigarettes?"

Mikhail tapped the left-hand pocket of his jacket.

"And your lighter?" asked Gabriel.

"I have everything. We just need Elizabeth."

"She's coming," said Gabriel. "It will be over soon."

. . .

The car was a Ford Fiesta, pale gray and well worn. Abel, the one with green eyes, handled the driving, while Cain sat next to her in the backseat. Absent their balaclava masks, she saw their faces for the first time and was shocked by their youth. They wore heavy coats, were carefully shaven, and smelled of sandalwood cologne. Cain was squeezing her arm with his left hand and holding a gun in his right. Elizabeth tried not to look at the weapon or to even think about it. Instead she stared silently out her window. It had been more than two weeks since she had been outside; two weeks since she had seen another human other than Cain and Abel and their masked accomplices; two weeks since she had seen the sun or had possessed even the most basic sense of time. The window was her portal on reality. Cain and Abel were from the world of the damned, she thought. On the other side of the glass was the land of the living.

For a few minutes her surroundings were unfamiliar. Then the entrance of the Camden Town Underground station flashed past, and from there she was able to track their route south across London. Despite the pleasant weather, the streets were oddly quiet. In the Tottenham Court Road she saw holiday wreaths and realized it was probably Christmas morning.

They crossed Oxford Street and headed down Charing Cross to Trafalgar Square, then made their way along Whitehall to Westminster. As they turned into Victoria Street, Elizabeth saw a crowd milling about beneath the North Tower of the Abbey. Standing beneath a leafless tree, next to a tired-looking man in an *ushanka* hat, was a tall, distinguished-looking figure in a fedora who bore a sharp resemblance to her father. It wasn't her father, of course. Her Colorado-born father would never be caught dead in a hat like that.

A moment later they turned into Abbey Orchard Street. Abel pulled into an illegal spot and shut down the engine. Cain slipped the gun into his coat pocket and squeezed her arm tightly.

"We're going to take a very short walk," he said. "At the end of it, you will be released. Get out of the car slowly and put both your hands in the pockets of your raincoat. We will lead you where we want you to go. Keep your eyes on the ground and don't say a word. If you don't do exactly what we tell you, I'll shoot you in the heart. Do you understand me?"

"Yes," she said calmly.

Cain reached across Elizabeth Halton's lap and opened her door. She swung her legs out of the car and stepped into the street, her first step toward freedom.

. . .

The hands of Big Ben lay at 9:57 when Gabriel's earpiece crackled. The voice he heard was Adrian Carter's.

"Victoria Street," said Carter calmly. "She's about to cross Storey's Gate into the Sanctuary. She's wearing a blond wig and a tan raincoat."

"*Shaheeds*?"

"One on each arm."

"Halton has just condemned two men to death, Adrian. Is he sure?"

"He's sure."

"Get him out of there. *Now*."

Carter took Robert Halton by the elbow and led him toward Great George Street, with Sarah trailing two paces behind. Gabriel and Mikhail stood in unison and started walking. Sarah was watching them. *Look away*, he thought. *Keep walking and look away.*

. . .

They paused for a few seconds on the corner of Parliament Square to allow a London bus to rattle past, then quickly crossed the street and entered the grounds of the Abbey. Mikhail walked on Gabriel's left, his breath shallow and fast, the footfalls sharp and crisp, like an echo of Gabriel's own. Gabriel's Beretta was on his left hip and the butt was pressing painfully against a broken rib. A split second is all he would have. A split second to get his weapon off his hip and into firing position. When he was a boy, like Mikhail, he could do it in the time it took most men to clap their hands. *And now?* He walked on.

They passed through the thin shadows beneath the trees where Carter and Halton had been standing a few seconds earlier. When they emerged again into the sunlight, they saw Elizabeth and her escorts for the first time, moving deliberately along the sidewalk close to the northern façade of the Abbey. Her eyes were concealed behind a large pair of movie-starlet sunglasses, and her hands were in her coat pockets. A *shaheed* was holding each arm. Their free hands were shoved into the outward-facing pockets of their heavy jackets.

"They've got their fingers on the detonator switches, Mikhail. You see it?"

"I see it."

"Do you see the people behind them? When we start shooting, you can't miss."

"I won't miss."

"You have your cigarettes?"

"I'm ready."

"Keep walking."

Two hundred worshippers were still standing outside the North Tower, waiting patiently to be admitted. Gabriel put a hand on Mikhail's elbow and nudged him along the fringes of the crowd, onto the intersecting walkway. Elizabeth and the terrorists were directly in front of them, forty yards away and closing fast. *One second,* thought Gabriel. One second.

. . .

Cain's fingers were digging into her upper arm and his hand was shaking with fear. She wondered why they had decided to release her in a crowded public place like Westminster Abbey. Then Cain murmured something to Abel in Arabic that made her feel as though a stone had been laid over her heart and Elizabeth realized that she had been brought to this place not to be freed but to be executed.

She glanced from one terrorist to the other. The heavy coats, the look of death in their eyes, the trembling hands . . . They were going to die here, too, she thought. They were *shaheed*s wrapped in suicide belts. And in a few seconds she would be a *shaheed,* too.

She looked toward the crowd of people gathered outside the Abbey's North Tower. They were the real targets. Elizabeth had been kidnapped in a bloodbath and it appeared they planned to execute her in one as well. She couldn't allow more innocent blood to be shed because of her. She had to do something to save as many lives as she could.

"Look down," Cain snapped.

No, Elizabeth thought. *I will not look down. I will not submit.*

And then she saw him . . .

The angular man of medium height with wraparound sunglasses and ash-colored temples. The man walking along the edge of the crowd with a younger pale man at his side. It was the same man who had tried to save her in Hyde Park—she was sure of it. And he was going to try to save her again now.

But how could he possibly do it?

Cain and Abel had their hands in their pockets. It would only take them an instant to hit their detonators. It was an instant Elizabeth had to take from the terrorists and give to the two men advancing toward her—the two men who had just stopped walking and were in the process of lighting cigarettes. *I will not submit,* she thought. Then she drove the toe of her left foot into her right heel and felt herself falling to the pavement.

.   .   .

Cain caught her, a single reflexive act of kindness that would cost him his life. When she was upright again, she saw the two men draw their guns like twin flashes of lightning and start shooting. Cain's face disappeared behind a blossom of blood and brain tissue, while Abel's green eyes simultaneously exploded inside their sockets. The gunmen streaked past her in a blur, guns in their outstretched hands, as if they were chasing after their own bullets. Cain fell to the ground first, and the man with gray temples leaped onto his chest and fired several more rounds into his head, as though he were trying to shoot him into the ground. Then he tore Cain's hand from his coat pocket and yelled at Elizabeth to run away. Model prisoner to the end, she sprinted across the lawn of the Abbey toward Victoria Street, where the distinguished-looking man with the fedora hat was suddenly standing with his arms open to receive her. She hurled herself against his chest and wept uncontrollably. "It's all right, Elizabeth," said Robert Halton. "I've got you now. You're safe, my love."

A WEDDING

BY THE LAKE

60

JERUSALEM

Two homecomings of note occurred the day after Christmas. The first had for its backdrop Andrews Air Force Base outside Washington and was broadcast live around the world. A president was in attendance, as was his entire national security team and most of the Congress. A Marine band played; a country-music star sang a patriotic song. Speeches were made about American determination and resolve. Praise was heaped upon the men and women of American and British intelligence who had made this day possible. No mention was made of ransom or negotiation and the name Israel was not uttered. Elizabeth Halton, still traumatized by her captivity and the circumstances of her rescue, attempted to address the crowd, but managed only a few words before breaking down. She was immediately placed aboard a waiting helicopter and flown under heavy guard to a secret location to begin her recovery.

The second homecoming took place at Ben-Gurion Airport and, by coincidence, occurred at precisely the same moment. There were no politicians in attendance and no television cameras present to record the event for posterity. No patriotic music was performed, no speeches were made; indeed, there was no official reception of any kind. As far as the State of Israel was concerned, the twenty-six men and women aboard the arriving charter from London did not exist. They were nonpersons. Ghosts. Lies. They disembarked in darkness and, despite the lateness of the hour, were shuttled immediately to an anonymous office block in Tel Aviv's King Saul Boulevard, where they endured the first of what would be many debriefings. There was nothing pro forma about these sessions; they knew that once the celebrations had ended the questions would begin. A storm was coming. Shelters would have to be hastily constructed. Provisions set aside. Cover stories made straight.

For the first seventy-two hours after Elizabeth Halton's dramatic rescue, the official British version of events went unchallenged. Her recovery, according to this version, had been the result of tireless efforts by the intelligence and police services of the United Kingdom, working in concert with their friends in America. While ransom had been offered by Ambassador Halton in desperation, it had not been paid. The two gunmen who had killed the would-be suicide bombers at Westminster Abbey were members of the Met's SO19 division. For obvious reasons of security, the two men could not be identified publicly or made available to the media for comment—now or at any point in the future, said the Met commissioner emphatically.

The first cracks in the story appeared four days after Christmas, not in the United Kingdom but in Denmark, where a local newspaper carried an intriguing report about a mysterious explosion at a summer cottage along the North Sea. The Danish police had originally said the cottage was unoccupied, but a local paramedic, speaking on condition of anonymity, disputed that claim, saying he had personally seen three bodies removed from the charred rubble. The paramedic also claimed to have treated a German-speaking man for superficial facial wounds. Lars Mortensen, chief of the Danish Security Intelligence Service, appeared before a hastily convened news conference in Copenhagen and confirmed that, yes, there were indeed three people killed in the incident and, yes, it was linked to the search for Elizabeth Halton. Mortensen then declared he would have nothing else to say about the matter until a formal investigation had been carried out.

The next crack in the official version of events came two days later in Amsterdam, where an Egyptian woman of late middle age appeared at a press conference and confirmed that one of the people killed in northern Denmark had been her husband, Ibrahim Fawaz. Speaking in Arabic through an interpreter, Mrs. Fawaz said that she had been informed by American officials that her husband had been working on their behalf and had perished during a failed attempt to rescue Miss Halton. She also said that all attempts to reach her son, daughter-in-law, and grandson in Copenhagen had been unsuccessful. Her left-leaning lawyers speculated that Ibrahim Fawaz had been kidnapped by American agents and co-erced into working on the CIA's behalf. They called on the Dutch justice minister to order an investigation of the matter and the minister did so at four that afternoon, promising that it would be full and unflinching.

The next morning in London, a Home Office spokesman confirmed that the son of Ibrahim Fawaz had been one of two terrorists found dead in a bomb-laden transit van that crashed into a field in Essex shortly after dawn on Christmas morning. The spokesman also confirmed that Fawaz the younger had been shot several times in the leg and that the driver of the van, as yet still unidentified, had been fatally shot in the head. Who had inflicted the wounds, and precisely what had transpired in Essex, was not yet known, though British investigators were operating under the assumption that a second attack had been planned for Christmas morning and that it had somehow gone awry.

On New Year's Day the *Telegraph* called into question the government's version of the events at Westminster Abbey. According to the authoritative newspaper, several witnesses said the gunman who shouted at Elizabeth to run away did so in an accent that was not British. Another witness, who walked past the two gunmen seconds before the shootings, heard them speaking to one another in a language other than English. After listening to recordings of twenty different languages, the witness identified Hebrew as the one he had heard.

The dam broke the following day when the *Times*, in an explosive exposé headlined THE JERUSALEM CONNECTION, laid out a compelling case of Israeli involvement in the rescue of Elizabeth Halton. Contained in the coverage was a photograph, snapped by a man waiting to enter the Abbey, that showed two gunmen fleeing Westminster seconds after the rescue. Facial-recognition experts hired by the *Times* stated conclusively that one of the men was none other than Gabriel Allon, the legendary Israeli agent who had killed three of the terrorists in Hyde Park the morning of Elizabeth's abduction.

By that evening there were full-throated demands in Parliament for Her Majesty's Government and secret services to come clean about the events that had led to Miss Halton's recovery. Those demands were echoed across the capitals of western Europe, and in Washington, where reporters and members of Congress called on the White House to explain what the president knew of Allon's connection to the affair. It was becoming increasingly clear, said the president's detractors, that American intelligence officers and their Israeli allies had run roughshod over Europe in their frantic quest to find Miss Halton before the deadline and secure her release. What, precisely, had transpired? Had laws been bent or broken? If so, by whom?

The government of Israel, besieged by press inquiries at home and abroad, broke its official silence on the affair the following morning. A spokeswoman for the Prime Minister's Office conceded that the secret intelligence service of Israel had indeed granted assistance to American investigators. Then she made clear that the nature of the assistance given would never be divulged. As for suggestions that Gabriel Allon travel to London and Washington to assist in the official inquiries into the affair, her response was vague at best. Gabriel Allon was on an extended leave of absence for personal reasons, she explained, and as far as the government of Israel was concerned his whereabouts were unknown.

.   .   .

Had they made any serious attempt to locate him, which they most certainly had not, they would have found him resting quietly at his tidy little apartment in Narkiss Street. He had weathered storms like this before and knew that the best course of action was to place boards over the doors and windows and say nothing at all.

His injuries were such that he had little energy for anything else. Between the beatings he had suffered at the hands of his captors and the crash that occurred during his rescue, he had suffered numerous broken and cracked bones, dozens of facial and other lacerations, and deep bruises to every limb of his body. His abdomen ached so badly he could not take food, and two days after his return to Jerusalem he found that he could not turn his head. A doctor affiliated with the Office came round to see him and discovered he had suffered a previously undiagnosed injury to his neck that made it necessary for him to wear a stiff brace for several weeks.

For two weeks he did not move from his bed. Though used to the process of healing and recovery, his naturally restless nature made him a poor patient. To help pass the long empty hours, he diligently followed his own case in the newspapers and on television. As evidence of Israeli involvement in the affair mounted, so did expressions of outrage from Europe's restive Islamic communities and their quisling supporters on the European left. The horror of the London bombings and Elizabeth Halton's abduction seemed quickly forgotten, and in its place rose a Continent-wide indignation over the tactics that had been used to find and rescue her. Shamron's carefully brokered agreements with the justice ministries and security services of Europe soon lay in tatters. Gabriel was once more a wanted man—wanted for questioning in the Netherlands and Denmark over the death of Ibrahim Fawaz, wanted for questioning in the United Kingdom over his role in Elizabeth Halton's rescue.

There was another storm raging, one that went largely unnoticed by the global media and a human rights community seemingly obsessed with the alleged misdeeds of Gabriel and his team. On the other side of Israel's western border, in Egypt, the regime of Hosni Mubarak was dealing with a Sword of Allah–inspired insurrection the way it had dealt with every Islamic challenge in the past—with overwhelming force and ruthless brutality. The Office had picked up reports of street battles between the army and Islamists from the Nile Delta to Upper Egypt. There were also reports of massacres, summary executions, widespread use of torture, and a concentration camp in the Western Desert where thousands of radicals were being held without charge. A hastily prepared Office estimate had concluded that Mubarak would likely survive the challenge and that, for the moment at least, Israel would not be confronted with an Islamic republic on its western flank. But at what cost? Repression breeds radicals, said the estimate, and radicals commit acts of terror.

By the middle of January, Gabriel was strong enough to leave his bed. The doctor came round again and, after poking and prodding at his neck, decided it had healed sufficiently to remove the brace. Eager to shut out the unpleasant events swirling around him, he focused solely on plans for the wedding. He sat for hours with Chiara in the living room, leafing through glossy bridal magazines and engaged in deep and meaningful discussions about matters such as food and flowers. They chose a date in mid-May and prepared a provisional guest list, which included seven hundred names. After two hours of hard bargaining, they managed to pare only twenty of them. A week later, when the bruising in his face finally dissipated to an acceptable level, they ventured out into Jerusalem together to inspect hotel ballrooms and other potential sites for the ceremony and reception. The special events coordinator at the King David Hotel, after inquiring about the size of the guest list, jokingly insisted they consider holding the wedding at Teddy Kollek Stadium instead, a suggestion Chiara did not find at all amusing. She sulked during the short drive back to Narkiss Street.

"Maybe this is a mistake," said Gabriel carefully.

"Here we go again," she replied.

"Not the wedding—only the *size* of the wedding. Maybe we should have something small and private. Family and friends. *Real* friends."

She exhaled heavily. "Nothing would make me happier."

By early February he felt a strong desire to work. He left Narkiss Street at ten o'clock one morning and drove up to the Israel Museum to see if there was anything lying about that might occupy his time. After a brief meeting with the head of the European paintings division, he left with a lovely panel by Rembrandt, appropriately called *St. Peter in Prison*. The panel was structurally sound and required only a clean coat of varnish and a bit of inpainting. He set up shop in the spare bedroom of the apartment, but Chiara complained about the stench of his solvents and pleaded with him to move his operations to a proper studio. He found one, in the artists' colony overlooking the Valley of Hinnom, and began working there the following week.

With the arrival of the Rembrandt, his days finally acquired something of a routine. He would arrive at the studio early and work until midday; then, after taking a break for a leisurely lunch with Chiara, he would return to the studio and work until the light was no good. Once or twice a week, he would cut his afternoon session short and drive across Jerusalem to the Mount Herzl Psychiatric Hospital to spend time with Leah. It had been many months since he had seen her last, and the first three times he appeared she did not recognize him. On his fourth visit she greeted him by name and lifted her cheek to him to be kissed. He wheeled her into the garden and together they sat beneath an olive tree—the same olive tree he had seen in his dreams while in the hands of the Sword of Allah. She placed her hand against his face. Her skin was scarred by fire and cold to the touch.

"You've been fighting again," she said.

He nodded his head slowly.

"Black September?" she asked.

"That was a long time ago, Leah. They don't exist anymore."

She looked at his hands. They were smudged with pigment.

"You're painting again?"

"Restoring."

"Can you work on me when you're finished?"

A tear spilled onto his cheek. She brushed it away and looked again at his hands.

"Why aren't you wearing a wedding ring?"

"We're not married yet."

"Second thoughts?"

"No, Leah—no second thoughts."

"Then what are you waiting for?" She looked away suddenly and the light went out of her eyes. "Look at the snow, Gabriel. Isn't it beautiful?"

He stood and wheeled her back into the hospital.

61

JERUSALEM

He drove back to Narkiss Street through a cloudburst and entered his apartment to find the table set for four and the air scented with roasted chicken and Gilah Shamron's famous eggplant with Moroccan spice. A small, thin woman with sad eyes and unruly gray hair, she was seated on the couch next to Chiara looking at photographs of wedding dresses. When Gabriel kissed her cheek it smelled of lilac and was smooth as silk.

"Where's Ari?" he asked.

She pointed to the balcony. "Tell him not to smoke so much, Gabriel. You're the only one he listens to."

"You must have me confused with someone else, Gilah. Your husband has a well-honed ability to hear only what he wants to hear, and the last person he listens to is me."

"That's not what Ari says. He told me about your terrible quarrel in London. He said he didn't even try to talk you out of delivering the money because he knew you had your mind made up."

"I would have been wise to take his advice."

"But then the American girl would be dead." She shook her head.

"No, Gabriel, you did the right thing, no matter what they're saying about you now in London and Amsterdam. When the storm is over, they'll come to their senses and thank you."

"I'm sure you're right, Gilah."

"Go sit with him. I think he's a little depressed. It's not easy to grow old."

"Tell me about it."

He poured himself a glass of red wine and carried it out onto the balcony. Shamron was seated in a wrought-iron chair beneath the stripped awning, watching rainwater dripping from the leaves of the eucalyptus tree. Gabriel plucked the cigarette from his fingertips and tossed it over the balustrade onto the wet sidewalk.

"It's against the law in this country to litter," Shamron said. "Where have you been?"

"You tell me."

"Are you suggesting that I'm having you followed?"

"I'm not *suggesting* anything. I know you're having me followed. Therefore it is merely a statement of fact."

"Just because you're home doesn't mean you're safe. You have far too many enemies to wander around without bodyguards—and far too many enemies to be working in plain view in an artist's studio overlooking the walls of the Old City."

"Chiara wouldn't let me work in the apartment." Gabriel sat down in the chair next to Shamron. "Are you angry because I'm working in a studio near the Old City, or are you angry because I'm working and it's not for you?"

Shamron pointedly lit another cigarette but said nothing.

"The restoration helps, Ari. It always helps. It makes me forget."

"Forget what?"

"Killing three men in Hyde Park. Killing a man on the lawn of Westminster. Killing Ishaq in a field in Essex. Shall I go on?"

"That won't be necessary," said Shamron. "And when this Rembrandt is finished? What then?"

"I'm lucky to be alive, Ari. I hurt everywhere. Let me heal. Let me enjoy life for a few days before you begin hounding me about coming back to the Office."

Shamron smoked his cigarette and watched the rain in silence. Devoutly secular, he marked the passage of time not by the Jewish festivals but by the rhythms of the land—the day the rains came, the day the wildflowers exploded in the Galilee, the day in early autumn when the cool winds returned. To Gabriel, he seemed to be wondering how many more such cycles he would be witnessing.

"Our ambassador in London received a rather humorous letter from the British Home Office this morning," he said.

"Let me guess," said Gabriel. "They would like me to testify before the commission of inquiry into the kidnapping and recovery of Elizabeth Halton."

Shamron nodded. "We've made it very clear to the British that they will have to conduct their formal inquiry without our cooperation. There will be no replays of your testimony before Congress after the affair at the Vatican. The only way you're going to set foot in England is to collect your knighthood." Shamron smiled to himself. "Can you imagine?"

"East London would burn," said Gabriel. "But what about our relationships with MI5 and MI6? Won't they go into the deep freeze if I refuse to cooperate in the inquiry?"

"Quite the opposite, actually. We've been in contact with the heads of both services in recent days, and they've made it clear that the last thing they want is for you to testify. Graham Seymour sends his best, by the way."

"There's another good reason for me to stay away from London," Gabriel said. "If I agree to testify, the inquiry will naturally focus on us and the sins of the Israelis. If I stay away, it might just force them to confront the real problem."

"Which is?"

"Londonistan," said Gabriel. "They have allowed their capital to become a breeding ground, a spiritual mecca, and a safe haven for Islamic terrorists of every stripe. And it's a threat to us all."

Shamron nodded his head in agreement, then looked at Gabriel. "So what else have you been doing besides cleaning this Rembrandt and spending time on Mount Herzl with Leah?"

"I see your little surveillance men give you detailed watch reports."

"As they were instructed to do," said Shamron. "How is she?"

"She's lucid at times," Gabriel said. "*Very* lucid. Sometimes she sees things more clearly than I do. She always did."

"Please tell me you're not planning to get cold feet again."

"Quite the opposite. Didn't your watchers tell you about my search for a site for the ceremony?"

"They did, actually. I took the liberty of asking Shabak to draw up a contingency security plan for a public wedding of such proportions. I'm afraid the requirements will be such that it will not seem much like a wedding at all." He crushed out his cigarette slowly. "Will you take some advice from an old man?"

"I'd like nothing more."

"Perhaps you and Chiara should consider something smaller and more intimate."

"We already have."

"Do you have a date in mind?"

Gabriel told him.

"May? Why are you waiting until May? Did you learn nothing from this affair? Life is precious, Gabriel, and terribly short. I may not even be alive in May."

"I'm afraid you'll just have to hang in there, Ari. Chiara needs time to plan the reception. We can't do it any sooner."

"Plan? What plan? You and I could do it in an afternoon."

"Weddings aren't operations, Ari."

"Whoever said that?"

"Chiara."

"Of course weddings are operations." He brought his fist down on the arm of the chair. "Chiara has had to put up with considerable dithering and nonsense on your part. If I were you, I'd plan the wedding myself and surprise her."

"She's an Italian Jew, Ari. She has something of a temper and doesn't like surprises."

"All women like surprises, you dolt."

Gabriel had to admit he liked the idea. "I'll need help," he said.

"So we'll get you some help."

"Where?"

Shamron smiled. "Silly boy."

.   .   .

They were the dark side of a dark service, the ones who did the jobs no one else wanted, or dared, to do. But never before in the storied history of Special Ops had they ever planned a wedding, at least not a real one.

They gathered the following morning in Room 456C, Gabriel's subterranean lair at King Saul Boulevard: Yaakov and Yossi, Dina and Rimona, Mordecai and Oded, Mikhail and Eli Lavon. Gabriel walked to the front of the room and tacked a photograph of Chiara to his bulletin board. "Ten days from now, I am going to marry this woman," he said. "The wedding must be everything she wants and she must not know or suspect a thing. We must work quickly and we will make no mistakes."

Like all good operations it started with intelligence gathering. They scoured her bridal magazines for telltale markings and interrogated Gabriel carefully about everything she had ever said to him. Alarmed by the poor quality of his answers, Dina and Rimona scheduled a crash luncheon meeting with Chiara the following afternoon at a trendy Tel Aviv restaurant. They returned to King Saul Boulevard slightly drunk but armed with all the information they needed to proceed.

The following morning Gabriel and Chiara were awakened at Narkiss Street by an officer from Personnel who informed Chiara that she was alarmingly overdue for a complete physical. There was an opening that morning, said the man from Personnel. Could she come to King Saul Boulevard immediately? Having nothing better to do that day, she complied with the request and by ten o'clock was being subjected to rather close scrutiny by two Office-affiliated physicians—one of whom was not a physician at all but a tailor from Identity. He was less interested in matters such as blood pressure and heart rate and more concerned with the length of her arms and legs and the size of her waist and bust. Later that afternoon he slipped down to Room 456C to ask Gabriel whether he was to leave room in the garment for a weapon. Gabriel said that would not be necessary.

With three days remaining, everything was in place with one notable exception: Chiara herself. For this phase of the operation Gabriel drafted none other than Gilah Shamron, who telephoned Chiara later that evening and asked whether they could come to Tiberias for a surprise birthday party for Shamron that Saturday. She agreed to Gilah's request without even bothering to check with Gabriel and told him about their plans for the weekend that night over dinner.

"How old is he going to be?" she asked.

"It's a carefully guarded state secret, but rumor has it he fought in the rebellion against Roman rule."

"Did you know his birthday was in March?"

"Oh, yes, of course," he said hastily.

It was in late August, actually, and the last person who had tried to throw Shamron a surprise party still walked with a limp. But Chiara didn't know that. Chiara didn't know anything.

. . .

It had rained steadily all week, a contingency for which they had not planned, but by midmorning Saturday the sun was shining brightly and the newly washed air was scented with stone pine and jasmine and eucalyptus. They slept late and ate a leisurely breakfast on the balcony, then packed a few things into an overnight bag and set out for the Galilee.

Gabriel drove down the Bab al-Wad to the Coastal Plain, then north to the Valley of Jezreel. They stopped there for a few minutes to collect Eli Lavon from the dig atop Tel Megiddo, then continued on to Tiberias. Shamron's honey-colored villa was just a few miles north of the city, on a ledge overlooking the Sea of Galilee. Two dozen cars lined the steep drive, and in the forecourt was a large American Suburban with diplomatic license plates. Adrian Carter and Sarah Bancroft were standing at the balustrade of Shamron's terrace, chatting with Uzi Navot and Bella.

"Gilah never told me Carter was coming," Chiara said.

"She must have forgotten to mention it."

"How do you forget to mention that the deputy director of the CIA is coming all the way from Washington? And what is Sarah doing here?"

"Gilah's old, Chiara. Give her a break."

Gabriel climbed out before she could pose another question, then retrieved the overnight bag from the trunk and led her up the steps. Gilah was standing in the entrance hall as they came inside. The large rooms had been emptied of their furniture and several round tables put in their place. Chiara stared at the place settings and the flower arrangements, then walked past Gilah and stepped on the terrace, where a hundred white chairs stood in neat rows around a chuppah hung with flowers. She spun round, mouth open, and looked at Gabriel.

"What's going on here?"

Gabriel held up the overnight bag and said, "I'm going to take this up to our room."

"Gabriel Allon, come back here."

She followed quickly after him and chased him down the corridor to their room. As she stepped inside, she saw the dress laid out on the bed.

"My God, Gabriel, what have you done?"

"Made amends for all my mistakes, I hope."

She threw her arms around him and kissed him, then ran a hand through her hair.

"It's a mess. What am I going to do?"

"We brought a hair stylist from Tel Aviv. A very good one."

"What about my family?"

He looked at his watch. "We flew them out of Venice aboard a charter. They landed at Ben-Gurion twenty minutes ago. We're bringing them up here by helicopter."

"And the rings?"

He pulled a small jewelry box from his coat pocket and opened it.

"They're beautiful," she said. "You thought of everything."

"Weddings are operations."

"No, they're not, you dolt." She slapped his arm playfully. "What time is the ceremony?"

"Whenever you want it to be."

"What time is sundown?"

"Five-oh-eight."

"We'll start at five-oh-nine." She kissed him again. "And don't be late."

62

JERUSALEM

Y ou and your team ran a very nice operation,"
said Adrian Carter.

"Which one?"

"The wedding, of course. Too bad London didn't go as smoothly."

"If it had gone smoothly, we wouldn't have gotten Elizabeth back."

"This is true."

A waiter approached their table and freshened Carter's coffee. Gabriel turned and looked toward the walls of the Old City, which were glowing softly in the gentle sunlight. It was Monday morning. Carter had rung Gabriel's apartment at seven on the off chance he was free for breakfast. Gabriel had agreed to meet him here, the terrace restaurant of the King David Hotel, knowing full well that Adrian Carter never did anything on the off chance.

"Why are you still in Jerusalem, Adrian?"

"Officially, I am here to conduct meetings with our generously staffed CIA station. Unofficially, I stayed in order to see you."

"Is Sarah still here?"

"She left yesterday. Poor thing had to fly commercial." Carter raised his coffee cup to his lips and stared at Gabriel for a moment without drinking. "Did anything ever happen between you two that I should know about?"

"No, Adrian, nothing happened between us, during this operation or the last one." Gabriel made swirls in his Israeli yogurt. "Is that why you stayed in Jerusalem? To ask me whether I slept with one of your officers?"

"Of course not."

"Then why are you here, Adrian?"

He reached into the breast pocket of his Brooks Brothers blazer, withdrew an envelope, and handed it to Gabriel. The front bore no markings, but when he turned it over he saw THE WHITE HOUSE printed on the flap in simple lettering.

"What's this? An invitation to a White House barbecue?"

"It's a note," said Carter, then he added somewhat pedantically: "From the president of the United States."

"Yes, I can see that, Adrian. What's the topic of the letter?"

"I'm not in the habit of reading other people's mail."

"You should be."

"I assume the president wrote to you in order to thank you for what you did in London."

"It might have been helpful if he had said something publicly a month ago, while I was twisting in the wind."

"Trust me, Gabriel. If he had spoken out on your behalf, you would have been in more trouble than you are now. These things have a way of blowing themselves out, and sometimes the best course of action is to take no action at all."

A cloud passed in front of the sun, and for a moment it seemed several degrees colder. Gabriel opened the note, read it quickly, and slipped it into his coat pocket.

"What does it say?"

"It is private, Adrian, and it will remain so."

"Good man," said Carter.

"Did you get one, too?"

"A note from the president?" Carter shook his head. "I'm afraid that my position is somewhat tenuous at the moment. Isn't it amazing? We got Elizabeth back and now we are under siege."

"This, too, shall pass, Adrian."

"I know," he said. "But it doesn't make it any more pleasant to go through. There are a band of Young Turks at Langley who think I've been running the DO for too long. They say I've lost a step. They say I should have never agreed to turn over so much of the operation to you."

"Do you have any intention of ceding power?"

"None," said Carter forcefully. "The world is too dangerous a place to be left to Young Turks. I intend to stay until this war against terrorism is won."

"I hope longevity runs in your family."

"My grandfather lived to be a hundred and four."

"What about Sarah? Has she been hurt by this in any way?"

"None whatsoever," Carter replied. "Only a handful of people even knew she was a part of it."

The sun emerged from behind the clouds again. Gabriel slipped on his wraparound glasses while Carter pulled a second envelope from the pocket of his blazer. "This is from Robert Halton," he said. "I'm afraid I know what's inside that one."

Gabriel withdrew the contents: a brief handwritten note and a check made out in Gabriel's name for the sum of ten million dollars. Gabriel kept the letter and handed the check back to Carter.

"Are you sure you don't want to think about that for a minute?" Carter asked.

"I don't want his money, Adrian."

"You're entitled to it. You risked your life to save his daughter's— not once but *twice*."

"It's what we do," Gabriel said. "Tell him thanks but no thanks."

Carter left the check on the table.

"You have anything else in your pocket for me, Adrian?"

Carter turned his gaze toward the Old City walls. "I have a name," he said.

"The Sphinx?"

Carter nodded. The Sphinx.

.   .   .

His voice, already underpowered, fell to an almost inaudible level. It seemed that Carter, before coming to Israel for Gabriel's wedding, had made a brief stopover in the South of France, not for the purposes of recreation—Carter hadn't taken a proper holiday since 9/11—but for an operation. The target of this operation was none other than Prince Rashid bin Sultan, who had come to the French Riviera himself for a spot of gambling in the casinos of Monaco. The prince had played poorly and lost mightily, a fact the puritanical Carter seemed to find most offensive, and upon returning to the airport at Nice early the next morning in a highly inebriated state had found Carter and a team of CIA paramilitary officers relaxing in the luxurious confines of his private 747. Carter had presented the prince, now irate, with a CIA dossier detailing his many sins—sins that included financial support for al-Qaeda, the foreign fighters and Sunni insurgents in Iraq, and a militant Egyptian group called the Sword of Allah, which had just carried out the abduction of the goddaughter of the president of the United States. Carter had then given the prince a choice of destinations: Riyadh or Guantánamo Bay, Cuba.

"That sounds like something we would do," Gabriel said.

"Yes, it did have a very Office-like quality to it."

"I take it the prince chose Riyadh as his destination."

"It was the only wise bet he made all night."

"How much did the ride home cost him?"

"A name," Carter said. "The question now is, what do we do with this name? Option one, we work with our Egyptian brethren and bring this fellow to trial in United States. Justice will be served if we follow this course but at a considerable price. A trial will expose the underside of our relationship with the Egyptian security services. It will also leave us saddled with another Sword of Allah prisoner whom they will almost certainly attempt to get back, thus placing American lives at risk."

"And we can't have that."

"No, we can't," agreed Carter. "Which brings us to option number two: dealing with the matter quietly."

"Our preferred method."

"Indeed."

Gabriel held out his hand. Carter delved into his pocket again and came out with a slip of paper. Gabriel read what was written there and smiled.

"Can you make him go away?" asked Carter.

"It shouldn't be a problem," Gabriel said. "But I'm afraid we'll have to spread a little money around Cairo to make it happen."

Carter held up Robert Halton's check. "Will this be enough to get the job done?"

"More than enough. But what should I do with the change?"

"Keep it."

"Can I kill the prince, too?"

"Maybe next time," said Carter. "More coffee?"

63

CYPRUS

He left Jerusalem for Cyprus three days later. Chiara pleaded with him to take her along but he refused. He had lost one wife to his enemies and had no intention of losing another.

He entered the country on an Israeli passport bearing the name Gideon Argov and told the Cypriot customs officers that the purpose of his visit was vacation. After collecting his rental car, a C-Class Mercedes that he subjected to a thorough inspection, he set out along the south coast toward the whitewashed villa by the sea. Wazir al-Zayyat had been vague about when he might appear, so Gabriel stopped briefly in a small village market and bought enough food to last him three days.

The March weather was unseasonably mild and he spent the first day relaxing on the terrace overlooking the Mediterranean, guilt-ridden for having abandoned Chiara to Jerusalem. By the second day he was restless with boredom, so he searched the Internet for a decent art-supply shop and found one a few miles up the coast. He spent the remainder of the afternoon producing sketches of the villa, and, late in the afternoon of the third day, he was working on a decent watercolor seascape when he spotted al-Zayyat's car coming up the road from Larnaca.

Their encounter was conducted at a leisurely pace and in the cool sunshine on the terrace. Al-Zayyat worked his way slowly through the bottle of single malt while Gabriel sipped mineral water with wedges of lemon and lime. For a long time they talked in generalities about the situation inside Egypt, but as the sun was sinking slowly into the sea Gabriel brought the topic of conversation around to the real reason why he had asked al-Zayyat to come to Cyprus: the name he had been given in Jerusalem earlier that week by Adrian Carter. Upon hearing it, al-Zayyat smiled and nipped at his whisky.

"We've had our suspicions about the professor for some time," he said.

"He was in Paris for the last year working on a book at something called the Institute for Islamic Studies. It's a well-known front for jihadist activities, funded in part by Prince Rashid. He left Paris the day after Christmas and came back to Cairo, where he resumed his teaching duties at the American University."

"I take it you'd like to grant the good professor a sabbatical?"

"A permanent one."

"It's going to cost you."

"Trust me, Wazir—money is no obstacle."

"When would you like to do it?"

"Late spring," he said. "Before the weather gets too hot."

"Just make sure it's a clean job. I don't want you making a mess in my town."

One hour later al-Zayyat left the villa with a briefcase containing half a million dollars. The next morning Gabriel burned his sketches and the watercolor and flew home to Chiara.

64

CAIRO

The name on the reservation list sent a chill down the neck of Mr. Katubi, the chief concierge of Cairo's InterContinental Hotel. Surely there was a glitch in the computer reservation system, he thought as he stared at it in disbelief. Surely it had to be a different Herr Johannes Klemp. Surely he hadn't decided to come back for a return engagement. Surely it was all some sort of terrible misunderstanding. He picked up his house phone and dialed Reservations to see if the guest had made any special requests. The list was so long and detailed it took three minutes for the girl to recite them all.

"How long is he planning to be with us?"

"A week."

"I see."

He hung up the phone, then spent the remainder of the morning giving serious thought to taking the week off. In the end he decided that such a course of action would be cowardly and would inflict undue hardship on his colleagues. And so at 3:30 that afternoon he was planted firmly at the center of the glossy lobby, hands behind his back and chin raised like a defiant soldier before a firing squad, as Herr Klemp came whirling through the revolving doors, dressed head to toe in Euro black, sunglasses shoved into his head of silver hair. "Katubi!" he called brightly as he advanced on the steadfast little concierge with his hand extended like a bayonet. "I was hoping you would still be here."

"There are things about Cairo that never change, Herr Klemp."

"That's what I love about the place. It does get under your skin, doesn't it?"

"Just like the dust," said Mr. Katubi. "If there's anything I can do to make your stay more enjoyable, don't hesitate to ask."

"I won't."

"I know."

Mr. Katubi braced himself and his staff for a sandstorm of complaints, tirades, and lectures about Egyptian incompetence. But within forty-eight hours of Herr Klemp's arrival, it had become clear to Mr. Katubi that the German was a changed man. His accommodations—an ordinary single room high on the north side of the building overlooking Tahrir Square and the campus of the American University—he declared to be Paradise on earth. The food, he announced, was ambrosia. The service, he raved, was second to none. He did his sightseeing in the morning, while it was still cool, and spent his afternoons relaxing by the pool. By dusk each day, he was resting quietly in his room. Mr. Katubi found himself longing for a flash of the old Herr Klemp, the one who berated the maids for making his bed improperly or lashed out at the valet staff for ruining his clothing. Instead, there was only the silence of a contented customer.

At 6:30 on the penultimate day of his scheduled stay, Herr Klemp appeared in the lobby, dressed for dinner. He asked Mr. Katubi to book a table for him at a French bistro on Zamalek for eight o'clock, then darted through the revolving doors and disappeared into the Cairo dusk. Mr. Katubi watched him go, then reached for the telephone, not knowing then that he would never see Herr Klemp again.

· · ·

The silver Mercedes sedan was parked in Muhammad Street, within sight of the staff parking lot at the American University. Mordecai was seated calmly behind the wheel. Mikhail sat next to him in the front passenger seat, drumming his fingers nervously against his thigh. Gabriel climbed into the backseat and quietly closed the door. Mikhail drummed on, even after Gabriel told him to stop.

Five minutes later, Mikhail said, "There's your boy."

Gabriel watched as a tall, thin Egyptian in Western clothing handed a few piastres to the Nubian attendant and climbed behind the wheel of a Fiat sedan. Thirty seconds later he sped past their position and headed toward Tahrir Square. The traffic light on the edge of the square turned red. The Fiat came to a stop. The Sphinx was a careful man.

"Do it now," Gabriel said.

Mikhail offered Gabriel the detonator switch. "You sure you don't want him?"

"Just do it, Mikhail—before the light changes."

Mikhail pressed the switch. An instant later the small, focused charge of explosives concealed inside the headrest exploded in a brilliant white flash. Mikhail started drumming his fingers again. Mordecai slipped the car into gear and headed for Sinai.

Author's Note

The *Secret Servant* is a work of fiction. The names, characters, places, and incidents portrayed in this novel are the product of the author's imagination or have been used fictitiously. Any resemblance to actual persons, living or dead, businesses, companies, events, or locales is entirely coincidental. The al-Hijrah Mosque does not exist, though no visit to Amsterdam would be complete without a walk through the lively outdoor market on the Ten Kate Straat. To the best of my knowledge there is no Institute for Islamic Studies in Paris and no Islamic Affairs Council in Copenhagen. Visitors to Parliament Square in London will search in vain for a bench upon which to sit, for no such bench exists. Christmas services at Westminster Abbey are usually held in the afternoon, not the morning. Foulness Island, though inhabited by two hundred rugged souls, is actually a restricted military zone and thus hardly an ideal place to leave thirty million dollars' ransom. Those wishing to visit Foulness can do so by obtaining a pass from the Ministry of Defence or by booking a table for lunch at the George & Dragon pub in Church End. Deepest apologies to the management of the Europa and d'Angleterre hotels for running intelligence operations from their fine establishments without obtaining prior consent.

The Sword of Allah is entirely fictitious, though its background, creed, and operations are consistent with actual Egyptian terrorist groups such as al-Gama'a al-Islamiyya and al-Jihad. Anwar Sadat did indeed provide material and other support to Egyptian Islamists shortly after assuming power in an ill-considered gambit designed to bolster his base of popular support. The descriptions of torture as practiced by the Egyptian security services are based on accounts provided by victims who have lived to tell about it. The CIA program known as "extraordinary rendition," the practice of clandestinely transferring suspected terrorists from one country to another for the purposes of incarceration or interrogation, has been well documented. It was put into place not by President George W. Bush but by his predecessor, Bill Clinton.

The statistics used to illustrate the terrorist threat now confronting the United Kingdom are based on reports by the British police and intelligence services, as is the contention that Great Britain has supplanted the United States as al-Qaeda's top target. The rise of militant Islam across Europe and the Continent's rapidly changing demographics are, of course, factual. Professor Bernard Lewis of Princeton has estimated that Europe will have a Muslim majority by the end of the century, and Zachary Shore, in his thoughtful study of Europe's future titled *Breeding Bin Ladens,* stated that "America may not recognize Europe in a few short decades." Whether Europe will remain a strategic ally of the United States or become a staging ground for future attacks on American soil is not yet known. What is clear, however, are the intentions of al-Qaeda and the global jihadists. Mohammed Bouyeri, the unemployed Dutch-Moroccan immigrant from Amsterdam who murdered the filmmaker Theo van Gogh, stated them unambiguously in the manifesto he adhered to his victim's body with the point of a knife: "I surely know that you, O America, will be destroyed. I surely know that you, O Europe, will be destroyed. I surely know that you, O Holland, will be destroyed."

ACKNOWLEDGMENTS

This novel, like the previous books in the Gabriel Allon series, could not have been written without the assistance of David Bull, who truly is among the finest art restorers in the world. I spoke to many intelligence officers, diplomats, ambassadors, and Bureau of Diplomatic Security agents while preparing this manuscript—men and women who, for obvious reasons, I cannot thank by name. Suffice it to say that because of them I know far more about embassy security procedures—and the way in which the United States would respond to an attack like the one portrayed in the novel—than I would ever put in a work of entertainment during a time of war. I would be remiss, however, if I did not extend a warm thanks to Margaret Tutwiler, the former undersecretary of state who was serving as the American ambassador to Morocco on September 11, 2001. Her descriptions of that day, some terrifying, others uproariously funny, provided me with a unique perspective of what it is like to be inside an American embassy in a time of crisis. I am honored to call her a friend, and grateful for her service.

The remarkable Bob Woodward generously shared with me his

knowledge of the cooperation between the CIA and Egyptian security services. The eminent Washington orthopedist Dr. Benjamin Schaeffer taught me how to crudely treat a bullet wound in the field, while Dr. Andrew Pate, the renowned anesthesiologist of Charleston, South Carolina, explained the side effects of repeated ketamine injections and the symptoms of idiopathic paroxysmal ventricular tachycardia. Martha Rogers, a former federal prosecutor and now a much-in-demand Washington defense attorney, reviewed the case against the fictitious Sheikh Abdullah. Alex Clarke, my British editor, accompanied me on a fascinating journey through Finsbury Park and Walthamstow in the days after last summer's London airline bomb plot, while Marie Louise Valeur Jaques and Lars Schmidt Møller gave me a tour of Copenhagen that I will never forget. A special thanks to the housepainter who verbally assaulted my wife and children on the Groenburgwal in Amsterdam. He unwittingly provided the inspiration for an opening chapter.

I interviewed many Islamists while serving as a correspondent for United Press International in Cairo in the late 1980s, but *Journey of the Jihadist* by Fawaz A. Gerges gave me additional insights into the minds of Egypt's religious radicals, as did *A Portrait of Egypt* by Mary Anne Weaver. *While Europe Slept* by Bruce Bawer and *Menace in Europe* by Claire Berlinski helped sharpen my thoughts on the dilemma facing Europe today, especially the Netherlands, while *Londonistan* by Melanie Phillips gave me a deeper understanding of the crisis now confronting Great Britain. *Ghost Plane* by Stephen Grey contained many compelling personal accounts of those who have become ensnared, in some cases innocently, in the CIA program of "extraordinary rendition." *Over Here,* Raymond Seitz's memoir of his tenure as American ambassador to the Court of St. James's, helped me create the world of Robert Halton.

I was spared much embarrassment by the sure and careful hand of my copy editor, Tony Davis, whose great-uncle John W. Davis served as American ambassador to the Court of St. James's from 1918 to 1921. Had he defeated Calvin Coolidge for president in 1924, the post of American ambassador to London would have produced *six* presidents instead of just five. Louis Toscano, my personal editor and longtime friend, made countless improvements to the manuscript, as did my literary agent, Esther Newberg of ICM in New York. A special thanks to Chris Donovan, who ably shouldered some of the research burden, and to a friend in the FBI who helped me get my terminology straight. It goes without saying that none of this would have been possible without the support of the remarkable team of professionals at Putnam—Ivan Held, Marilyn Ducksworth, and especially my editor, Neil Nyren—but I shall say it in any case.

Last, I wish to extend the deepest gratitude and love to my children, Lily and Nicholas, who spent their August vacation roaming Europe's extremist hot spots, and to my wife, the brilliant NBC News *Today* correspondent Jamie Gangel. She listened patiently while I worked out the plot and themes of the novel, skillfully edited each draft, and helped drag me across the finish line with minutes to spare on my deadline. Orwell once described writing a book as "a horrible, exhausting struggle, like a long bout of some painful illness." He neglected to mention that the only people who suffer more than the writer himself are the loved ones forced to live with him.